SEA OF CRISES

MARTY STEERE

PENFIELD PUBLICATIONS
2533 Eastwind Way
Signal Hill, California 90755

Cover art by Ben Lizardi
Layout and typesetting by Guido Henkel
Published by Penfield Publications

ISBN: 978-0-9854014-0-5

Printed in U.S.A.

For Martha

PART ONE

1

Nate Cartwright paused in the quiet hallway outside his condominium and listened intently. No sound came from the other side of the door. But that was misleading. He knew with an overwhelming certainty the moment he stepped inside he'd be under attack. With as much stealth as he could muster, he inserted his key in the door handle and slowly rotated it. He stood frozen for an instant. Then, in one quick motion, he swung the door open, took two steps in and braced.

There was nothing but silence.

Then he heard it.

From the deep shadows in the kitchen at the far end of the hallway came a sound he knew all too well. Suddenly, Buster flashed across the width of the corridor, his tiny paws skittering on the hardwood floor as he worked frantically to alter direction. Just before banging into the bedroom doorway, he managed to get himself turned, somehow staying upright on short splayed limbs. As he caromed off the door frame, he pumped his legs furiously, finally found purchase, and came hurtling down the hallway.

Nate had just enough time to set down his briefcase before Buster was on him, his front paws scrambling at the fabric of Nate's slacks and his stub of a tail convulsing wildly. At his full extension, Buster barely reached Nate's knees, but his relative lack of height did nothing to discourage his enthusiasm. Nate reached down with both hands and gave the dog an affectionate scratch behind the ears.

"Good to see you too, buddy."

Then he gently lowered the dog, closed the front door and retrieved his briefcase. He strode down the hall to the den, Buster padding after him, panting happily, his paws making little tapping sounds on the floor.

The small den, which doubled as Nate's home office, was dominated by a large floor-to-ceiling window. In the morning, the inky blackness beyond would dissolve to reveal an unobstructed view of the Santa Monica Bay. Now, however, the window merely framed a reflection of Nate standing in the pool of light from the desk lamp, his visage staring back at him intently from beneath heavy dark eyebrows - a perpetual look of solemnity that, try as he might, never seemed to leave him.

What had Anna called it? His "brooding omnipresence?" They'd both laughed at it back then. But it had always made Nate feel a little self-conscious. In the end, he wondered, had his seriousness driven her away? Not that it mattered. The two of them would never have lasted beyond law school. He knew that. And, anyway, it was so many years ago. No point in dwelling on it.

The man in the reflection looked as tired as he felt.

Nate set his briefcase on the desk and was removing his jacket when the phone rang. He glanced reflexively at the clock on the wall. Almost two in the morning. Who the hell would be calling at this hour?

He lifted the handset out of its cradle as the phone rang again and saw his brother's number in the illuminated display. He stabbed at the talk button and put the device up to his head.

"Peter?"

There was no immediate reply. In the background, Nate heard metallic voices echoing through a large space - the arrival of a flight being announced. United Airlines. Peter must be in an airport terminal.

"Peter?" he repeated.

"Nate, it's me."

Anxiety strained his brother's voice.

"Peter, what's wrong?"

"I think I'm in trouble."

That got Nate's full attention.

"What do you mean? Where are you?"

"LAX. And I'm pretty sure they're here."

"Who's 'they'?"

"I don't know."

Nate took a deep breath and let it out slowly. "What do *they* look like?"

"I don't know that either. Nate, I'm serious. Someone's following me, more than one person. I can feel it. They followed me here from Minneapolis."

Nate rubbed a hand over his face. This made no sense, and it was completely unlike his brother. "Why would someone be following you, Peter?"

Through the phone came another announcement over the public address system drowning out most of Peter's next words. The only thing Nate could make out was: "…my project."

"Peter, I didn't get all of…"

"Can you pick me up?" Peter interrupted. "I know it's late."

"Of course," Nate replied, already sliding back into his jacket. "I can be there in twenty minutes."

"Ok." Nate heard relief in his brother's voice. "Hurry, please. I'll be out in front of baggage claim, Terminal 6."

At the front door, Nate stopped and looked back down at Buster. Eyes bright with excitement, the dog stared up at him. His tongue, actually longer than his tail, lolled out one side of his mouth.

Buster was, without question, the ugliest dog on the planet. He was the product of an insane mixture of breeds, predominated, as near as Nate could tell, by Dachshund and Rottweiler, though Nate suspected there was probably some Chihuahua thrown in for good measure. Buster stood on tiny legs that barely kept his hairless, low-slung torso off the ground. His head, in comparison to the rest of his body, was massive. Nate liked to tell people it was because Buster had such a large brain. In reality, Buster was not one of the brightest stars in the canine galaxy. He did, however, have a stout heart and a sweet personality. Nate had rescued him years before from the pound, and the little dog had repaid him with a fierce loyalty.

"Sorry, buddy," Nate said, "got to do this solo. But I won't be long, and I'll be bringing back Uncle Peter. You stay here," Nate waved a hand, "and guard the domicile. Ok?"

Buster emitted a short bark that came out more like a "hmmph." Incongruously, in that crazy concoction of genes, Buster had apparently inherited some hound dog.

As Nate wheeled his car out of the subterranean garage and turned up Ocean Avenue, he replayed Peter's call in his mind.

It wasn't like his younger brother to become rattled. Though Nate still thought of Peter as a kid, the man was forty-six years old. For the past twenty years, Peter had worked as a reporter for the San Francisco *Chronicle*, winning a number of awards for investigative journalism. He'd also written a pair of best-selling books, one on the international drug trade, another dealing with nuclear weapons left over from the Soviet era. He'd traveled from the jungles of Nicaragua to the frozen Siberian tundra. Along the way, he'd been jailed more than once, including a two-week stay in a rat-infested Burmese prison. And he'd managed to bear it all with an unwavering sense of humor.

No, this evening's call was not like his brother.

Despite what he'd heard, or thought he'd heard, over the phone, Nate didn't think Peter's state of mind could have anything to do with his current project.

For the past couple of months, Peter had thrown himself into something he'd talked about doing for a long time. Something he'd only recently been able to get himself in the right frame of mind to tackle. The topic was close to both of them, and, though it came with heavy emotional baggage, Nate didn't see how it could possibly cause Peter to start imagining he was being followed.

The subject was Apollo 18, the last of NASA's manned lunar missions, and a catastrophe that ranked up there with the Apollo 1 fire and the Challenger and Columbia space shuttle disasters. What made it particularly personal for Nate and Peter was the fact that the Apollo 18 commander, and one of the three astronauts who died in the tragedy, had been their father, Bob Cartwright.

It had happened on September 28, 1976. Three days before Peter's tenth birthday, and a month before Nate's twelfth.

Nate and the twins, along with their grandmother, had gathered in front of the television in the living room at their old home in Houston. Outside, reporters congregated on the sidewalk in front of the house, but Gamma refused to let any of them near the front door. She'd made it clear they were to stay off the property and leave the boys alone.

Nate had been old enough to understand the situation. The twins, maybe not so much, though Peter had always been sensitive and uncommonly attuned to things happening around him, so he might have had some appreciation for the perilous state of affairs. For Matt, it was just another exciting chapter in the saga of his father, the astronaut and sudden celebrity. And, of course, an opportunity to stay home on a school day.

A week earlier, the spacecraft bearing their father and his two crewmates had completed a successful transit to the moon and entered lunar orbit. On September 22, the module carrying Bob Cartwright and Mason Gale touched down on the lunar surface, and the two of them became the thirteenth and fourteenth men to walk on the moon.

As extraordinary an accomplishment as it was, it initially garnered little public attention. While the first moonwalk by the astronauts from Apollo 11 seven years earlier had captivated the world, subsequent missions to the moon had attracted an ever-decreasing audience. Odd, considering the incredible effort required to put men on the moon, the whole thing seemed like yesterday's news, and the activities of Cartwright and Gale were conducted, for the most part, without media fanfare. That was, of course, until their last transmission.

The astronauts had been in the process of their first moonwalk, technically referred to as an EVA, or extra-vehicular activity. They'd retrieved the lunar rover from its storage position along the side of the module and were in the process of working their way across the ancient sea of the moon known as the *Mare Crisium*, or Sea of Crises, when Bob Cartwright uttered the words that, to this day, remained shrouded in mystery.

Cartwright had kept up a running commentary as the rover bounced along the uneven surface. He'd stopped briefly to allow Gale to retrieve a rock sample, and had just started the rover up again. There were a few seconds of silence before Cartwright, clear as day, said in a startled voice, "That shouldn't be here."

Then the video stream from the camera mounted on the front of the rover went to black, and the audio fell silent.

At the time, the command service module, manned by the third member of the Apollo 18 crew, Steve Dayton, was on the far side of the moon, outside radio contact and not scheduled to be within range of Earth for another twenty minutes. During that time, Mission Control tried unsuccessfully to raise the two astronauts on the lunar surface. When the module bearing Dayton emerged from behind the moon, attempts were made to contact him, also to no avail. All transmissions from the spacecraft had ceased, almost as if someone had pulled a plug.

Suddenly, Apollo 18 had captured the world's attention. With no way of knowing what was happening on and around the moon, speculation abounded. Was it simply a failure of the communications equipment, or was loss of contact indicative of a larger problem? And what had Cartwright been referring to when he'd uttered those last mysterious words? Were the men still alive? Could they return to earth?

NASA scrambled, hasty plans drawn up for a rescue mission. But putting another team on the moon could take weeks... months.

To everyone's relief, three days later, precisely at the scheduled time, astronomers on Earth confirmed a burn of the service propulsion system and, still in eerie silence, the command service module began its return transit.

On September 28, the world had been transfixed, awaiting first sight of the spacecraft. And, almost exactly when expected, in the clear blue skies over the South Pacific, only a few miles north of the anticipated entry point, a distant speck appeared, slowly morphing into the welcome sight of the Apollo 18 capsule dangling beneath the canopy of a trio of parachutes.

On the television, the steady voice of Walter Cronkite provided commentary as the vessel bearing their father majestically descended and splashed down in the calm waters north of the waiting navy armada. Images captured by cameras on one of the helicopters deployed from the U.S.S. *Coral Sea* showed navy divers jumping into the water near the capsule, inflating a large raft to accommodate the returning astronauts.

The first indication of a problem came just after the hatch was sprung. One of the divers perched on the inflated rubber collar encircling the capsule took a quick look inside and immediately pulled back, turning his head away with a grimace that was caught on camera. After a few seconds, he waved off the helicopter bearing the television crew. It turned back toward the carrier, leaving the newscasters fumbling for explanations.

As young Nate had watched that day, a feeling of dread had washed over him. He knew the news was bad long before any kind of announcement was made. The minutes, even the days after, were a blur. But Nate never forgot that gut-wrenching moment when he watched the diver look away. To this day, Nate could close his eyes and see it happening all over again.

Years later, Nate heard that the sailor who'd been the first to peer into the capsule had subsequently struggled with serious psychological issues. It had to have been difficult for him. He'd unwittingly opened the door to a smoldering coffin. The official finding was that the heat shield had failed on re-entry. The three men inside had been baked to a crisp, their bodies barely recognizable as having once been human. Everything within the capsule had been charred or melted, or both. The stench that assaulted the young petty officer had to have been overwhelming.

As bad as it had been for the diver, however, it could not have been anything compared to the final agonizing seconds of Bob Cartwright, Mason Gale and Steve Dayton. Their skin peeling off of their skeletons. Their bodies cooking in their own juices. Death a blessing.

Given the condition of the capsule's contents, there had never been a resolution of the mystery surrounding the loss of contact with Apollo 18. What had those last few cryptic words uttered by Bob Cartwright meant? What had happened to the astronauts during those few days of radio silence? Of course, human nature being what it was, countless theories had been advanced, ranging from the pedestrian to the bizarre.

A small, but stubborn percentage of the population believed that the men must have encountered extra terrestrials. Others speculated that Cartwright had, at that moment, noticed something left on the rover when it had been packed into position on the side of the lunar module prior to launch, something that wasn't supposed to have made the journey into space. Perhaps, it was suggested, whatever it was somehow interfered with the communications system when either Cartwright or Gale reached down to pick it up.

The most common and widely accepted theory was that Cartwright had simply seen some man-made debris. Both the United States and the Soviet Union had deposited a fair amount of junk on the lunar surface during the 1960s and 70s. The United States had successfully landed a number of unmanned probes on the moon. On each of six prior Apollo missions, the lunar module had been ejected and allowed to crash back on to the surface of the moon after returning its astronauts to the command module. The Soviets had, in turn, launched their own series of unmanned probes, and, though many of them had not made it to the moon, a number had. There was no record of any of those prior missions having resulted in the deposit of space junk in the Sea of Crises, but it was still possible. And it would have explained Cartwright's surprise.

Of course, that didn't account for the sudden loss of radio contact. With nothing else to explain that unusual event, the pundits had chalked it up to simple equipment failure.

One thing was certain. Unless and until man again ventured to the moon, something that did not seem likely to occur any time in the near future, this was one mystery that would remain unsolved.

No, Nate reflected, there was nothing about that bit of old history that could possibly explain why his brother was so spooked. It had to be something else.

At this late hour, with few vehicles on the road between Santa Monica and LAX, the drive didn't take long. Nate quickly circumnavigated the airport, pulling up in front of Terminal 6 no more than twenty minutes after he'd hung up the phone.

Peter stood out front, his already slight figure further diminished by a canvas suitcase slung over one shoulder and a computer bag over the other. To Nate, his brother's anxiety was obvious. In place of his normal impish look, Peter's jaw was clenched, lips tightly pursed, eyes darting about. As Nate eased the car to the curb, Peter opened the back door and tossed in his suitcase, then he slid into the front passenger seat.

"Thanks. Sorry about the late hour."

Though it was a cool October evening, a sheen of sweat coated Peter's broad forehead below his receding blond hairline. As Nate pulled back out into the light traffic, his brother craned his neck, scanning the sidewalk and roadway.

"Want to tell me what's going on?" Nate asked.

Still looking about, Peter replied, "Let's get out of here, first."

"Ok."

Nate took the ramp down to Sepulveda Boulevard and merged onto the wide thoroughfare, heading north. In the rear view mirror, he saw no other vehicles, either entering from the airport or on the street itself. They drove into Westchester, as near as Nate could tell, the only car on the road. The stores on either side were shut down, the sidewalks deserted.

"Peter, unless they're invisible, I don't think anyone is following us."

For the first time since he'd gotten into the car, Peter turned to face forward and sat back in his seat. After a moment, he let out a deep breath and gave a rueful laugh. "You must think I'm nuts."

"You did have me going there." Nate shrugged. "Now, do you want to tell me what's up? Let's start with why you were in Minneapolis."

"I flew out there to see Mason Gale's sister and mother."

"For your research?"

Peter nodded.

"Gale's mother is still alive? She must be ancient."

"She's ninety-three, but she still gets around. Her daughter lives with her and helps take care of her."

"So, did you see them?"

"I did," Peter said. "But only for a couple of minutes."

"You flew all the way out there, and you only saw them for a couple of minutes? That seems a little silly."

"Yeah, well, I've been trying to talk to them for a few weeks now, and they've been giving me the cold shoulder. I figured, if I show up in person, what are they going to do? Tell me to get lost?"

"So, what did they do?"

"They told me to get lost."

"Seriously?"

"In so many words, yes." Peter turned to face him. "Nate, they're afraid of something. They were afraid to talk to me." Slowly, he said, "I have never in my entire life seen anyone as terrified as those two women. They couldn't get me off their property fast enough. I thought they were going to come after me with brooms."

Nate thought about that. Finally, he asked, "Do you have any idea why?"

"Not exactly," Peter said. He slid his computer out of the case and turned it on. "But let me show you something. Maybe it has nothing to do with their reaction. Then again, maybe it does. I'll let you be the judge. You need to see this anyway," he added.

Nate slowed the car and pulled into the deserted parking lot of a low-rise office complex. He parked and turned off the engine.

"When I decided to write about Apollo 18," Peter began, "the first thing I did was submit a Freedom of Information request. It took a while, but I got quite a bit of documentation, including a few things that were previously classified. There were some photos."

"Photos," Nate repeated, an ominous chill creeping up his spine.

"Yeah," Peter said. "I've got to warn you, this is a little tough to take."

In the glow of the laptop monitor, Nate saw that Peter's expression was grim. His brother rotated the computer so Nate could view the screen. At the moment it was a solid blue. Peter touched one of the keys, and the display immediately changed. It took Nate a second to realize what he was looking at. When he did, his stomach constricted.

The picture had been taken from just outside the capsule. It showed clearly the three bodies within. It was almost as if someone had staged the scene to generate the greatest amount of revulsion. The physical remains of the three astronauts were still seated on the wide bench, ostensibly strapped in, though the straps, if present, had melted into what was left of the bodies -

17

grotesque caricatures of human forms, black, with bits of white bone and teeth here and there.

Nate knew that the body seated in the left hand commander's position was what had once been Bob Cartwright. He closed his eyes. This was not how he wanted to remember his father.

"Damnit Peter. Shut it off."

"Wait," said Peter. "You haven't seen it yet."

Reluctantly, Nate opened his eyes as Peter set his cursor at a spot in the picture near the bottom of the hatch opening. Then he drew that spot out into a rectangular box about an inch high. He tapped the keypad, and, for a moment, the display was a blur. Then it came into focus, and the screen was filled with the portion of the original picture that had been inside the small box.

"I had this photo digitally enhanced," Peter said. "If you look closely at the lip where the hatch door seats when it's closed, you'll see initials and three numbers."

Nate leaned closer. He saw the notation "CSM-116" stamped into the metal.

"Each command service module was assigned a serial number," Peter explained. "On the Apollo 17 mission, CSM-114 was used. The module for Apollo 18 was CSM-115, not 116. The module designated CSM-116 was supposed to be used on the Apollo 19 mission, which, as you know, was cancelled."

Nate was still processing what his brother had just told him when Peter gave him a direct look and said, quietly, "Nate, that capsule was not our father's capsule. And that body we buried thirty-six years ago was not our father."

2

Raen and his men moved with a practiced grace, making no unnecessary noise. They'd long ago mastered the art of invisibility, whether they were in a noisy crowd or, as now, in a quiet, deserted setting. They knew and could anticipate each other's movements. They were well-trained. And they were the best at what they did.

At the door to the condominium unit Raen halted. His two colleagues quietly assumed positions against the wall to either side, statuary to a casual observer.

From a pocket, Raen retrieved a narrow metallic device and slid it into the deadbolt slot above the door handle. With a paucity of motion, he manipulated the tumblers and shot back the bolt. The door handle itself had a lock. He again deployed the picking device. Identical to the mechanism above, this lock took but a second to spring.

Displaying an agility that would have impressed the most sophisticated of magicians performing up-close sleight-of-hand, Raen produced a pistol in place of the pick. The weapon was small, its size dominated by the silencer screwed into the barrel. In his hands, though, it was as deadly as a .357 magnum.

He crouched, and Dacoff silently swung the spotlight, mounted on a telescoping rod, into position above him. They'd already doused the lights in the corridor.

Anyone waiting inside when Raen opened the door would see only a blinding glare. Gunfire would likely be directed at the light. Of course, Raen couldn't completely discount the possibility that another professional waited on the other side of the door, in which case he'd be exposed and probably killed. But that, he knew, was the nature of their business, and one of the reasons he was paid so well.

He did not hesitate. He swung the door open quickly, extending his gun hand and sweeping the interior with his eyes.

Ten feet inside the door, brightly illuminated by the spotlight, stood a squat dog with a big head. His mouth was open, and a long tongue extended nearly to the floor. As Raen performed his visual reconnaissance, the dog licked his own snout and swallowed. Then he again dropped his jaw, allowing his tongue to flop back out, and he stood panting, his rear end gyrating back and forth. There was no other movement inside the dwelling.

Raen entered, still crouched, ignoring the dog, which he knew was no threat. Ozaki came after him, a silenced machine pistol at the ready. When they'd cleared the doorway, Dacoff followed, examining the doorframe as he did for signs of an entry detection device.

Once he and Ozaki had confirmed that the other rooms were empty, Raen returned to the kitchen. Dacoff, holding a small electronic transceiver, was methodically sweeping the dwelling for listening devices. He signaled silently that he'd completed his inspection for motion sensors. With a dog roaming free, they hadn't expected to find any, but, as with everything else, they took no chances. Raen collected the bag Dacoff had dropped by the front door and, from a side pocket, began removing a series of sharp implements, placing them on the kitchen counter. Ozaki picked up the dog and gave Raen an inquiring look. Raen nodded solemnly.

#

When the elevator doors opened, Nate was surprised to find the hallway in complete darkness.

"Someone forget to pay the electric bill?" Peter asked.

Nate shrugged. "Maybe there's a circuit out," he said, stepping into the gloom.

The elevator doors slid shut behind them, and they were plunged into a Stygian blackness. Perhaps it was because of their earlier conversation, but Nate was suddenly struck with a deep sense of unease.

He reached out and cautiously stepped forward, feeling for the far wall. When his fingers made contact, he set down Peter's computer bag and ran his hand up the surface, searching for the light fixture he remembered was affixed at a point immediately across from the elevators. His fingertips brushed against the metal base, and he reached up with his other hand, cupping the glass sconce and feeling for the light bulb. He touched it, and it jiggled slightly. Gripping the bulb between thumb and middle finger, he gave it a slight clockwise turn.

The light came on.

He looked back at Peter. The expression he'd seen on his brother's face earlier had returned.

Nate gave a quick dismissive wave of his hand. "Just kids," he said. "They think they're being funny."

A woman with two teenage boys had recently moved in one floor below. Nate had seen the boys a few days earlier, riding their skateboards in the breezeway between his building and the one next door, just beneath the sign that read "No skateboarding." It had annoyed him, until he realized he'd have done the same thing at their age.

"Really, Peter, it's just kids being kids."

After a moment, Peter nodded. Adjusting the shoulder strap on his suitcase, he said, "Let's get inside."

As they made their way down the hall, Nate paused at two other light fixtures and tightened the bulbs. He did likewise with the lamp just outside the door to his condo. He made a mental note to say something to the building manager. It was one thing for the kids to engage in activities where *they* could be hurt. It was another to create dangerous conditions for the rest of the residents.

He unlocked the door, pushed it open, and was again met with darkness. That's odd, he thought. He was sure he'd left the light on in the den. He stepped inside, and his senses prickled.

A strange odor permeated the air. A musky scent, with a metallic tinge to it. He felt for the switch beside the door, found it, and clicked on the hall light.

He saw immediately that the left half of the floor at the end of the hallway was covered with something dark. Light from the overhead fixture shimmered off its surface. Slowly, Nate lowered the computer bag and took a couple of cautious steps forward. Around the corner to his left, the small kitchen island that contained the sink and dishwasher came into view. Above the island was a rack from which normally hung a collection of pots and pans. Instead of the usual kitchenware, however, there dangled a single large object. It was in shadow, and Nate again reached for a switch.

A series of lights came on, brightly illuminating the kitchen. The sight that greeted Nate caused him to gag, and he stepped back involuntarily, his shoulder striking the frame of the bedroom door.

"Oh my God," Peter said from behind. His eyes were wide, and he'd put a hand up to his mouth.

Nate's eyes darted from his brother back to the horrible tableau.

Suspended above the kitchen island was the mutilated body of a small animal, impaled on a metal hook, the point of which had been driven into the lower abdomen between the hind legs, its sharp tip poking out near the stubby tail. Drenched in dark crimson, strips of flesh dangled off the body in grotesque random patterns. The poor creature appeared to have been decapitated. Blood in copious amounts had poured out, collecting on the counter below, the overflow running down the front of the dishwasher and pooling on the floor in a mass of congealed maroon, almost black.

In the puddle on the counter below the hideous thing lay a dog collar. A green tag with the name "Buster" in florid script lay half-submerged in the coagulating mess.

Lightheaded, knees weak, Nate's heart pounded in his chest; his stomach heaved. He shook his head, slowly at first, but then with vehemence as anger welled up through the revulsion. Breathing heavily, he looked back up at the gruesome remains, opening his mouth to vent his rage.

Then he stopped. He frowned, studying the corpse. Something about it was wrong.

He looked at Peter. There were tears in his brother's eyes. Peter pulled away the hand that had been covering his mouth and said in a choked voice, "Buster."

"No," Nate said.

His brother started to say something else, but Nate held up a hand, cocking his head and listening intently. From behind came a faint scratching sound. Barely audible.

Nate whirled and stepped quickly into the bedroom. At the far side, the door to the master bathroom was closed. In rapid strides, Nate covered the distance, gripped the handle and pushed the door open. He stared for a moment at the floor tile. Then, to his immense relief, Buster poked his head around the door. His tail end jerking back and forth with excitement, the little dog emerged and did a quick figure eight through Nate's legs before Nate was able to reach down and pick him up. Hugging him with relief, Nate carried Buster back to the front hallway, the dog wriggling in his arms and licking his face with unabashed gusto.

When Peter saw them, he blurted, "Thank God."

The phone rang.

Peter froze and stared at Nate.

The phone rang a second time, sound reverberating throughout the otherwise quiet condominium from multiple extensions.

23

Nate looked at the nearest one, which was mounted on the kitchen wall near the hallway. Unlike the hands-free devices in the den and bedroom, this was an older unit, the handset attached to its base by a long cord that dangled almost to the floor. There was no digital readout to indicate the source of the call. Not that it really mattered. Nate knew with a cold certainty that the person on the other end of the line had been in his home earlier, and he knew there would be nothing to learn from any such readout.

He handed the squirming Buster to Peter and stepped forward, lifting the handset and cutting short a third ring. He held the phone up to his ear, but said nothing.

There was silence on the other end. Nate waited. After a long moment, a man's voice, deep and gravely, said, "Did we get your attention?"

Nate bit back a retort.

"That's ok," the man said. He spoke in a flat tone, with no accent and almost no inflection. "I'll do the talking. You do the listening."

"You didn't need to do that," Nate said quietly.

"Sure I did. You wouldn't have taken me seriously otherwise. You see," the man continued, and his voice took on a hard edge, "you need to know what kind of person you're dealing with."

Forcing a calm on himself that he didn't feel, Nate reached his free hand up to the bottom of the handset, pinched the tab on the jack and slid the end of the cord out, severing the connection to the base of the phone. Holding it an inch away from the handset, he said, "Who are you?" and then he immediately slid the jack back in place.

"Who I am is not important." The man seemed to hesitate halfway through the last word. There was a long silence. When his voice came again, it had, if possible, an even harder edge to it. It also, Nate realized, had a very distinct southern accent. "Don't get cute with me, Cartwright."

There was another pause. Then, returning to the same flat intonation, the man said, "Believe me, if it were my call, you wouldn't even get this one warning. If I were you, I'd heed it. Because, if you don't, I'll be back. And this time it'll really be your dog. And then it'll be you and your brother. You'll be last. I'll make you watch the first two.

"Now," he continued, "here's your warning: Forget about Apollo 18. No more questions. No more investigation. It's over. Done. Follow that advice, and you'll live a nice, long life. Don't, and I'll be coming for you."

The line went dead.

#

They took down the carcass, hook and all, and put it in a trash bag, which they then placed into yet another bag. The blood they mopped up with several towels, and those went into a separate trash bag. They wiped down the counter and cabinets, using copious amounts of disinfectant.

They worked in grim silence. After Nate had hung up the phone, he'd looked at Peter, tapped his ear and swung a finger around, indicating that there were listening devices. It was the only way the man on the phone could have heard him after he'd disconnected the phone jack. Peter had nodded his acknowledgement.

Through his shock, Nate had realized belatedly that the body hanging in his kitchen wasn't a dog, but a pig. The person who set up the macabre scene had mutilated the ends of the legs, but the vestiges of hoofed toes were still visible. Nate hoped the animal was one that had been acquired from a butcher and not one killed in his home. There was no sign of the head, and he didn't think the noise a squealing pig would have made could possibly have gone undetected by the rest of the building, so he felt reasonably certain it had to have already been dead before being brought in. He also doubted that the amount of blood deposited in his kitchen could have come from just the one animal, so he assumed whoever had staged the scene had brought the blood in a separate container.

Nate carried the two large bags to the trash chute in the small room next to the elevator. Then he packed an overnight bag. He'd carefully cleaned the collar, put it back on Buster and attached the leash they used for their walks. The little dog was delighted with the attention, his animation a stark contrast with the gloomy mood of the two brothers.

When they left the condo, Peter took a step toward the elevator, but Nate reached out, lightly touched his brother's shoulder, and nodded his head in the other direction. He led Peter to the stairway, picked up Buster, and they wordlessly descended.

When they were three flights down, Nate stopped and whispered, "I don't trust the elevator. For that matter, I don't trust any place we'd be expected to go."

Peter nodded. "What now?"

"I'm working on it. Better not talk in the car though."

"What about the police?"

Nate had considered that. "I don't think whoever did that is worried about the police, do you?"

Peter grimaced, then shook his head.

They continued down another five flights and stepped out into the garage below the building. As they approached Nate's car, he studied it suspiciously. Nothing appeared out of the ordinary. However, if a listening or tracking device, or both, had been installed, Nate knew it would take him longer to find than they could afford.

Fortunately, he had a backup.

When they pulled out of the garage, the sky was just beginning to lighten. It was early enough that traffic on the Santa Monica Freeway was moving well. At Overland, Nate exited and made his way north to Century City. His office was in one of the twin towers. He did not, however, intend to go to the office.

Considering he had a staff of one - and he was the one - he knew he wouldn't be missed.

Nate had started out years before on a career track much different from his current one. An honors graduate from Northwestern, he'd had his pick of law schools, and he elected to go to the University of Chicago, staying close to the family home in nearby Indiana. When he took his law degree, he again had plenty of options, including offers from a number of top law firms throughout the country. He settled on a blue chip Wall Street firm and quickly established himself as one of the top young litigators in New York.

Shortly after Nate became a partner, the youngest in the history of the firm, the partnership decided to expand to the West Coast, and Nate was tapped to head up a new office in Los Angeles. At the time it seemed a good opportunity, and Nate agreed to make the move, swapping the small midtown apartment in which he'd spent little time over the previous few years for a beautiful new ocean front condominium, in which, it turned out, he wound up spending even less time.

Nate had always worked insane hours, routinely staying at the office late into the evening and working through the weekends. If anything, the move to Los Angeles intensified the demand on his time. He made good money, but it came at a heavy personal price.

He took no vacations, rarely socialized. Though he dated sporadically, he never was able to sustain a meaningful relationship. None of the women he'd gone out with had been able to understand, much less tolerate, the hours his schedule demanded. And, truth be told, he'd considered none of them worth making the effort to try to change.

At least that's what he kept telling himself.

Then, when he had turned forty, it was as if he'd hit a wall.

His birthday was on a Monday. He arrived in court for an early morning hearing on a discovery dispute, one of those mundane battles that took place constantly in the give and take between attorneys. This one was over whether or not opposing counsel should have provided answers to interrogatories posed weeks before. There was no reason why the other side hadn't responded. In the scheme of things, the questions hadn't even been that controversial. The refusal to answer was just part of a game litigants played on a regular basis, forcing their opponents to incur fees, needlessly wasting the court's time, and ultimately costing taxpayers money.

Suddenly, the thought of standing before the judge and participating in the charade had been too much for Nate. He asked the bailiff to pass a note to the clerk informing her that he'd become ill, and, just like that, he walked out. In the seven years since, Nate had yet to set foot again in a courthouse.

He'd managed to burn himself out, and he knew it.

Employing the same rigorous scrutiny he'd given to his cases, Nate re-evaluated his life. Fortunately, one of the things at which he had excelled as an attorney was making sense out of chaos. His talent at analysis had contributed to his always being in demand. Even though he'd carried his own heavy slate of cases and borne management responsibility for the office, he stepped in regularly to consult on his colleagues' matters, particularly the complex ones with voluminous documentation and massive amounts of testimony. Nate, it turned out, had an uncanny ability to ferret out and connect sometimes wildly disparate facts, bringing into focus things that no one else could see. Lawyers at other firms clamored for an opportunity to engage Nate as co-counsel, even at the eye-popping hourly rate his law firm charged for his services.

What if, Nate had asked himself, he were to strike out on his own? He wouldn't even have to practice law, a priority in his then-state of mind. As he'd mulled it over, a plan took shape.

He gave his resignation to the firm a week after his birthday. A month later, he opened the doors on a new venture, *Cartwright Consultants*. Since he was the only consultant, he worried that maybe the name was a tad presumptuous. No one seemed to mind, though, and he'd had plenty of business from day one.

Old habits being hard to break, Nate still worked like a dog. Of late, however, he'd found himself in unfamiliar territory, the rock-solid foundation on which he'd built his life shifting beneath his feet at weird and unexpected times. The latest upheaval had come a week before.

He'd returned to the office after a long day in El Segundo culling through records at one of the large defense contractors, his arms weighed down by the banker's box full of documents he'd copied and was planning to review that evening. To his surprise, waiting for him in the small lobby of the executive suite he shared with a group of accountants was the woman he'd been seeing on and off for the past few months. She was dressed in a long blue silk gown, her honey blond hair done up in a way she'd never worn it before.

"Tell me," she said when they made eye contact, Nate halfway across the threshold, awkwardly propping the door open with his back as he eased his heavy load through, "that your tuxedo is hanging in your office." There was an almost pleading look on her face.

It took Nate a moment to make the connection. And, when it came, it was with a sour wave of recrimination.

"The charity thing," he said softly.

He could see the hope in her eyes transition to something cold.

"The charity *thing*? Really Nate?"

He remembered her telling him that the star-studded gala - it was to be at one of the studios, but he couldn't for the life of him remember which one - would be the social event of the year. And, yes, he *had* said he'd go. If work permitted. He hadn't expected that it would though. And, of course, it hadn't. But, then, he'd never told her that, had he? He'd just never... focused on it, which, he now realized with acute embarrassment was a mistake.

One, he reflected with a sudden rueful clarity, he'd made too many times in the past with the women he'd dated.

They stood there for a long moment, neither saying anything. Finally, knowing it was lame, Nate offered, "I'm sorry, Jan."

She looked away quickly. Then she turned, gathering from the sofa behind her a small purse and a long black wrap, the latter of which she threw across her neck. As she spun to face him again, she hurled one end of the wrap over a shoulder.

Her lips were pursed, and there was a new look to her eyes.

After a beat, she said, "It's *Jen.*"

Nate felt as if he'd been slapped.

"Do you mind?" she asked, now looking at the door, which Nate was effectively blocking with his body and the large box.

Not knowing what else to do or say, Nate stepped back, pushing the door open further, and she breezed past him, a wave of perfume there, then gone. He watched as she stalked to the elevator controls and punched the down button several times. One of the doors opened, and she stepped half in before turning and giving him a fierce look.

"Get a life, Nate Cartwright," she said. Then she was gone.

Turning off Century Park East, Nate entered the massive garage beneath the iconic twin office towers that dominated the Century City skyline. He drove down to the lowest level, at this early hour mostly vacant, and parked next to a black Ford Taurus. He shut off the engine and got out. Peter followed with Buster. Nate retrieved his bag from the back seat of his car, unlocked the trunk of the Taurus and placed the bag inside. With arched eyebrows, Peter did the same with his suitcase.

Without a word, Nate closed the door to his car, locked it, and made his way around to the driver's side of the Taurus. He climbed in and started the engine. Peter slid into the passenger seat, Buster in his arms. After closing the door, he gave Nate an inquiring look. "This is yours, I hope?"

Nate nodded as he backed the Taurus out of the parking space. "It is, though you wouldn't know it checking the registration. The official owner is a Nevada limited liability company. That company is owned by a corporation in Anguilla, a small island in the Caribbean that happens to have some nice corporate privacy laws."

"And you own the corporation?"

Again, Nate nodded.

"Why go to all that trouble?"

"Occasionally, clients ask me to do a little research. It's not exactly cloak-and-dagger stuff," Nate added, with a self deprecating wave of his hand, "but sometimes it's better to be anonymous. There's a lot of money at stake in some of the cases I work."

Nate steered the car up toward the exit onto Constellation Boulevard. "In any event," he continued, "it's coming in handy now."

He pulled out of the garage, made a left turn, then turned again onto the Avenue of the Stars, headed back toward the Santa Monica Freeway. "We need to talk."

Nate told Peter about the warning given by the man on the phone.

"So this *is* about Apollo 18," Peter said finally. "What the hell?"

Nate shook his head. "I don't know. But I damn sure intend to find out."

"What are we going to do?"

"We're going to do exactly what they told us not to."

"Aren't you afraid?"

Nate glanced over at his brother. "Yeah, I'm afraid. But I'll be damned if I'll live my life that way. Someone's hiding something. Something so important they'll go to pretty much any length to keep it covered up. Something," he added grimly, "that apparently involved our father."

When they reached the freeway, Nate took the entry ramp and merged the Taurus into the eastbound traffic.

After a moment, Peter observed, "You seem to have a destination in mind."

"I do."

"So, where are we going?"

"Minneapolis. But first, we're stopping in Idaho."

Peter was silent for a long moment. Finally, he asked, "Do we have to?"

"Yes," Nate said quietly. "Yes, we do."

3

Raen turned the rental car off the highway and steered it through the opening in the rusted chain link fence. The gate, a dilapidated affair, was propped open as usual. He drove down the center aisle separating the small businesses to either side, passing a handful of auto repair shops and a furniture refinisher. He parked in front of the building at the end, a squat structure with a weather-beaten sign above the door that read "Zeke's Auto Body."

When he stepped inside, a bored looking young man seated behind a wooden counter peered up at him over the top of a newspaper. The place had a pervasive shabbiness. It looked as though the next time anyone took a broom to the floor or a dust rag to the counter would be the first. The front windows had been pasted over with a series of posters advertising various exotic automobiles, models whose owners wouldn't be caught dead within miles of the establishment.

Hanging on the wall behind the young man was a calendar advertising a parts manufacturer, featuring a well-endowed woman leaning against the hood of a pickup truck, wearing only a tool belt. A large sign pasted on the wall announced, "In God we trust. All others pay cash."

Once the door closed, the young man, his eyes now much more alert, tilted his head slightly to his left. Raen nodded, lifted the hinged section of the countertop, and walked through.

In the wall behind the counter was a small, narrow door. Raen opened it and entered what was, by all appearances, a closet.

Shelves lined the back wall, filled, somewhat incongruously, with a collection of cleaning supplies. A mop and a broom hung from hooks to one side.

Raen allowed the door to close behind him. In the ceiling above, a dingy, dust-covered twenty-five watt bulb in an open fixture provided just enough light for him to see what he was doing. On one of the back shelves, at about chest level, sat an old metal pail. He pushed it to one side, revealing a cracked mirror bolted to the wall. He reached in and placed his right palm against the mirror. There was a slight buzz, followed by an audible click.

In a smooth motion, the rear wall, shelves and all, swung open on well-oiled hinges, revealing a brightly illuminated staircase with concrete steps leading down at a sharp angle. Raen stepped through and began descending. At a narrow landing, he turned and started down in the opposite direction. As he did, the rear wall of the closet above him swung shut, making almost no sound.

At the bottom of the stairway, he entered a tiny, bright chamber, the floor and ceiling of which each appeared to be one large square of light. The walls to either side were smoked glass, behind which Raen knew a series of cameras, conventional and infrared, was in the process of scanning him. In the wall straight ahead was a door. It had no handle. Instead, a small glass panel was inset at about chest height. Against this panel Raen again placed his right palm. As before, there was a buzz and a click, then the door swung open, revealing a broad corridor, carpeted and lit in a much more muted fashion.

A young man in a business suit stood on the other side. "This way sir," the man said. "The director is waiting for you."

Raen nodded and followed him down the corridor. He allowed no expression on his face. Nothing in his body language would have revealed to an observer that he was agitated.

A man of action, Raen hated being at headquarters, hated being around anyone that he had to treat as his ostensible superior. It was all the more aggravating being summoned back in the middle of an operation. The whole thing carried with it the suggestion of being called to the principal's office, a stigma from a time past, a time long before Raen had become what he was: One of the top operatives in the most clandestine of the United States' intelligence services.

It was known simply as The Organization. Few people outside of the Joint Chiefs of Staff were even aware of its existence. Its members were carefully culled from various branches of the military. They were all of a certain type: Loners, outsiders, most importantly, individuals who did not possess, for lack of a better term, the moral constraints that would prevent normal people from even considering, much less carrying out, the activities tasked to The Organization.

Raen knew The Organization was considered a necessary evil, looked upon by many of the few who were privy to its existence as a true abhorrence. He didn't care. He loved what he did, what it allowed him to do. They could gnash their teeth, thump their self-righteous chests, rue the circumstances that required maintaining such a loathsome weapon. At the end of the day, however, there was no way they were going to give it up, to lose the flexibility it offered. And that was just fine with Raen.

In the outer room of the director's suite, he paused while the young man escorting him knocked softly on the door to the private office and stuck his head in. A secretary sitting at a desk just outside alternately scanned a stack of notes lying next to her computer monitor and made strokes on the keypad. Raen didn't acknowledge the elderly woman, but he knew who she was. Rumor had it Ruth Branson had been with The Organization since its founding, working for the succession of men who had served as its director. Though she also didn't acknowledge his presence, Raen knew she was very much aware of *his* identity. And that was what was important.

"The director will see you now," the young man said.

Again, Raen nodded. He stepped into the office.

The director sat behind a large oak desk, the top of which was empty, save for a laptop computer and a short stack of papers sitting immediately in front him. He had one of the pages from the stack in his hand and was reading from it when Raen entered. He continued reading for several seconds, ignoring Raen.

Doing a slow burn, Raen stood quietly in front of the desk and studied the man. He was in his sixties, with thinning gray hair. With the exception of his eyes, which were dark and penetrating, there was nothing about him that would draw attention - precisely the characteristic routinely cultivated in all of the men who served The Organization.

It was hard to be invisible when standing out in a crowd.

The director was known as Krantz. Each of the men in The Organization went only by a single sobriquet. As with his other colleagues, Raen had no idea what the man's real name was, or, for that matter, anything about his life before joining The Organization. None of that was important.

Krantz, Raen knew, had been one of The Organization's top field men for almost three decades, a long time in their line of business. Most of the operatives, or, more to the point, most of the ones who weren't killed, retired after twenty or so years. By then, they'd made plenty of money and could afford to live out their days in relative luxury. Krantz, however, had evidenced no particular desire to leave the fold. When age had finally begun to slow his physical reflexes, he'd opted to stay in an administrative role, eventually inheriting the top position when the prior director had dropped dead of a heart attack a few years earlier.

Though he might have lost a step or two physically, Krantz' mind was still as sharp as ever. Raen knew from experience that he had to be on his toes around him.

Finally, Krantz looked up at him and fixed him with those dark eyes. "Any update?"

Raen had filed his last report shortly after landing at Dulles. That had been about a half hour earlier. "No change."

Krantz considered him for a moment. "How did the Cartwrights get away?"

"We still don't know. We tracked them to the garage in the building where the older one works. But he never showed at the office. That means they left on foot or in another vehicle. There's no record of either of them owning or having access to such a vehicle. We're checking security tapes, but nothing yet. They're not very high quality. We're also monitoring banking and credit card activity. So far, again, nothing."

Krantz nodded. Raen had not said anything that wasn't in the prior reports he'd filed.

"Odd that they knew they were under surveillance," Krantz observed.

Raen kept his face impassive. He had not mentioned in his reports that the elder Cartwright had disconnected the phone jack while they were talking, tricking him into revealing the presence of the listening devices they'd planted in the condominium.

"They both have much higher than average intelligence," said Raen.

"Then you will not underestimate them again." Krantz said it lightly, but it was a stinging rebuke. Raen nodded. Inside, he smoldered.

Krantz dropped his eyes to the paper in front of him for a moment, then looked back up at Raen. "There's been a development."

Raen was curious, but he waited patiently.

"It appears," Krantz said, "that we have to deal with a third brother."

"What third brother?"

"Peter Cartwright's twin, Matthew Cartwright."

That made no sense and had the unusual effect of catching Raen up short. He thought for a moment. He had personally gone through the dossiers on Nathaniel and Peter Cartwright. There was nothing in either file that suggested a third brother. He was certain of it.

He shook his head. "No," he said with confidence, "there is no twin. He doesn't exist."

"That's right," Krantz said. "He doesn't exist. The same way you don't exist."

It took a moment for the significance of that statement to sink in. When it did, Raen took in a sharp breath. "Shit."

Krantz nodded grimly.

"Shit," Raen said again. "How the hell was that not communicated to me?"

Krantz shrugged. "You know how it works. Once you're invisible, you're invisible. If you become visible, you become dead. We didn't put it together until about," he consulted his watch, "thirty-nine minutes ago."

Raen was thinking fast, running cold calculations. "Where is he?"

"He's been living in Idaho, near Pocatello."

"Do we have assets on the ground?"

Krantz nodded. "Landing as we speak. A full action team. Led by Parker."

Good, thought Raen. He was working through the logistics of getting himself and his men to Idaho when an important thought occurred to him. "Who is he?"

Krantz didn't respond immediately. Finally, he said, "His operational name was Marek."

"Shit," said Raen for a third time. This time he *really* meant it.

#

Near Idaho Falls, Nate exited the interstate and pointed the car east. Though, on the long drive from Los Angeles, Peter had been his typically voluble self, as they began wending their way through the mountains of southeast Idaho he fell silent, staring out the side window. Nate didn't need to ask why.

It had been over twenty-five years since Peter had last seen his twin brother, more years, Nate realized with a start, than they'd actually spent together. That, alone, was extraordinary, but it didn't even begin to tell the story - a story that, to this day, Nate still could not reconcile.

Matt and Peter were identical twins. Almost impossible to tell apart. And, from the day they were born, they'd been inseparable. They possessed very different personalities - Peter, the happy-go-lucky jokester, quick witted, always the center of a crowd, and Matt the quiet one, a terrific athlete and dare-devil, equally as popular, though completely comfortable in his own space. In a strange, almost mystical way, however, they had always complemented each other.

Then, when the twins were in their senior year of high school, everything changed. Peter revealed that he was gay. Though Nate had suspected it for some time, it came as a complete shock to Matt. And he didn't handle it well. At a time when Peter needed his closest friend, Matt turned his back on him. It was almost as if, overnight, Matt became a different person.

Matt started getting into fights at school, more than one of them, Nate knew, triggered by boorish comments from classmates questioning Matt's sexuality. Always an excellent student, Matt's grades plummeted during his final semester, and he almost didn't graduate. Months before, he and Peter had both been accepted by Stanford on full scholarships. On the day after graduation, however, Matt enlisted in the army. He told no one what he was doing, and he didn't bother to say goodbye, leaving only a short note on the kitchen counter. Years would pass before Nate again heard from him.

"Look," Nate ventured, "I know it's a little awkward."

"No," Peter said quickly, turning back from the window, "it's a lot awkward. I understand why you think we need to involve Matt in this. But I don't have to like it. And I don't." He turned again and, looking out the window, added, "I'm sorry to say this, but I wish he'd just stayed wherever the hell it was he went."

Nate winced. He didn't blame Peter, and he wasn't surprised at his brother's reaction. He knew deep down that Peter didn't really mean it this way, but, effectively, Peter was saying he wished Matt was dead.

Or, put more accurately, still dead.

Nate had been in his senior year at Northwestern when he'd returned from a late class one spring afternoon to find a pair of officers in Army uniforms waiting in a car parked outside his apartment building. They'd brought with them the tragic news that his younger brother had been killed in a training accident. The helicopter in which he'd been riding, they explained, had gone down in the Gulf of Mexico. All on board had perished. They hadn't even been able to recover the bodies.

Nineteen years later, Nate had almost had a heart attack when he climbed into his car late one evening after making an ATM deposit, and Matt was sitting in the back seat. Matt explained to Nate only that it had been necessary to stage his death for security reasons. He gave Nate a scrap of paper with a phone number on it and asked him to come to Idaho when he had a couple of days. Then, as quickly as he'd appeared, Matt slipped out of the car and vanished into the night.

A week later, Nate flew to Pocatello. Matt met him outside the airport and they drove to a cabin Matt had constructed in the mountains. Nate was full of questions, but Matt made it clear that he couldn't talk about what he'd been doing for the previous twenty-one years. He also impressed on Nate the fact that no one else should know that he was alive. When Nate explained that he'd already informed Peter, Matt insisted that he pass along to Peter the admonishment that he was to tell no one else. And, he told Nate in no uncertain terms, he wanted no contact with his twin brother.

They spent a couple of days dancing around subjects they apparently couldn't discuss. Nate revealed - or at least thought he was revealing - that Gamma, their paternal grandmother and the woman who'd raised them after their father's death, had passed away in 1992. Matt, however, surprised Nate by telling him that, not only was Matt aware of her passing, he'd been at the funeral. Nate remembered the relatively small affair. There was no way, he knew, that Matt could have been present without his being aware of it. Nate chose, however, not to dispute it.

Nate tried to get Matt to explain what had happened to him after leaving home, but Matt refused to go into it. Any of it. It was as if Matt had withdrawn from the world. Something, Nate knew, had occurred. Something that had taken away a big chunk of his brother's soul. He didn't think it had anything to do with Matt's falling out with Peter. In fact, the only times over the weekend Matt showed any emotion occurred when Nate endeavored, unsuccessfully, to get Matt to open up on that subject, and, even then, Matt's reactions were extraordinarily vague. Anyone who didn't know Matt the way Nate knew him would have missed the tinge of melancholy.

No, Nate reflected sadly, there were things about Matt that he still didn't understand. As he steered the car through the narrow mountain passes, Nate hoped that, maybe, the silver lining in this new dark cloud would be an opportunity to finally bring some sense to all of the mystery. And, in any event, as Peter had acknowledged, there was no way they could avoid involving Matt in this.

Though Nate had been here the one time before, it had been in full daylight, and he'd not been driving. Now, with the sun low on the horizon, it was difficult making out landmarks, and he almost missed his turn, a narrow track leading off the two-lane highway at a point just beyond a bridge that crossed a small stream. After passing the spot, Nate braked, backed the car up, and turned it down the gravel path.

The lane led straight into a densely wooded area for a quarter of a mile before angling upward and beginning a series of sharp, hairpin turns that took them up the side of a mountain. They finally crested a ridge and, before them, constructed of stone and logs and surrounded by large evergreen trees, sat the comfortable-looking dwelling Nate remembered from his previous visit. He saw that a new covered porch spanning the entire front of the structure had been added. In the gloaming, Nate could make out wisps of smoke escaping from the top of the chimney. But no lights were visible in the house, and there was no other indication that anyone was home.

He parked the car in the large open area in front of the building, noting the absence of any other vehicles. As he stepped out, he realized that the temperature had dropped about twenty degrees from the time they'd last been outside, filling up at a service station north of Salt Lake City. He retrieved his jacket and started for the front door. Peter, with Buster on his leash, hung back.

When Nate gave him a look, Peter said, "We'll wait here for now."

Nate nodded and climbed the steps to the porch. He knocked on the front door. After several seconds and no response, he knocked again. A full minute passed. He looked back at Peter standing by the car. Peter shook his head. He was about to knock again, when a quiet voice came from the far corner.

"It's good to see you, Nate."

Startled, Nate turned. He'd heard nothing, yet there at the end of the porch, where there was no obvious point of access, stood his brother Matt. Nate paused a moment to regain his wits.

"That's a neat trick," he said, finally.

Matt shrugged. "Mountain magic."

Matt had the fair hair and light skin he'd inherited from their mother. Though the twins barely remembered her, Nate saw her clearly when he looked at each of them, particularly in their open expressions, eyes sharp and penetrating. Nate, in contrast, had the dark, serious countenance of their father. And, at six-three, as their father had been, he was several inches taller than his brothers. People meeting the boys for the first time had wondered how they could possibly be related. But it was a question that never occurred to Nate. Quite simply, the twins were no less a part of him than his own limbs.

Matt stepped forward, and Nate did the same. Matt opened his arms, and they embraced. Then Matt stepped back and gave Nate a thorough appraisal. "You look good."

Nate smiled, though he knew it was a weak effort. "I wish I felt good."

Matt continued looking at him for a long time. Then he said, "Yeah, I figured there was a problem." He paused, then made a vague gesture toward the car. "Otherwise, you wouldn't have brought him."

"Oh, that's nice," Peter called out. "I see you haven't let your age interfere with your immaturity."

Matt was about to respond when there was a sudden beeping sound. He stopped and reached into a pocket of the nylon vest he was wearing. He pulled out a small electronic device and studied it for a moment. Then he looked at Nate with arched eyebrows.

"Is anyone else with you?"

Nate shook his head.

Matt walked quickly to the front door, opened it and entered. After a moment, Nate followed.

Just inside was a small reading desk on which sat a computer monitor. Matt had his hands on the back of the wooden chair still pushed in under the desk. He was leaning forward, peering intently at the display on the monitor. Without taking his eyes off the screen, he said, "Damn, these guys know what they're doing."

He straightened and gave Nate a serious look. "We've got to go. Now."

Nate's heart jumped. The tension that had been with him over much of the past twenty-four hours returned.

Matt took a step toward the rear of the house, then paused and turned, an enigmatic expression on his face. He tilted his head toward the door. "Get him."

Nate leaned out the door and gestured urgently for Peter. With a sudden look of alarm, his brother pushed himself off the side of the car on which he'd been leaning and took several steps toward the house. "What's going on?"

"Someone's coming. We've got to go."

Peter glanced around as he reached down to pick up Buster. Then he turned and walked quickly back to the car, opened the passenger door and retrieved his computer bag. Slinging the bag over a shoulder, he ran to the porch and took the steps two at a time.

When Peter got to the door, Nate reached out, grabbed the computer bag and lifted it off his brother's shoulder, throwing the strap over his own head. He turned and looked toward the back of the house. Matt was waiting for them near the end of the hall-way, standing half in a doorway on the left hand side. It was a door, Nate recalled, that had always been locked during his previous visit. When they made eye contact, Matt nodded, stepped in and disappeared.

"Go," Nate said to Peter, and his brother started toward the back of the house. Nate closed the front door, threw a curious glance at the computer screen Matt had been studying, then followed.

Through the doorway at the end of the hall was a set of stairs angling down to the right, headed toward and apparently extending below the rear of the house. Peter, Nate saw, had reached the bottom of the steps. And then he was gone. Pulling the door shut behind him, Nate began to descend.

The steps led down to a narrow passageway, lined on each side with cinder block walls. The floor and ceiling were concrete. Lights placed about twenty feet apart provided illumination. It had the appearance of a service tunnel and seemed to extend forever. Peter, Nate could see, was already a good thirty yards away, moving rapidly. He picked up his pace.

Nate wasn't sure how far he'd traveled, but, after a couple of minutes, the floor angled downward. At the end of another long stretch, it again leveled out and, a short distance away, he could see an opening. As he got closer, he realized that it was similar to a hatchway on a naval warship. A heavy metal door on oversized hinges had been swung inward.

In the corridor just before the entryway was a small alcove occupied by a desk on which sat another computer monitor. Nate paused and studied it. On the screen was what looked to be a map, with a series of small illuminated dots scattered about. As he watched, the dots moved slightly.

Finally, taking care to duck his head so as not to strike the top of the low entrance, Nate stepped gingerly over the threshold, passed through the hatchway, and, straightening, was surprised to find himself standing in a large wooden structure with a high open-beamed ceiling. Weak late afternoon light filtered through gaps in the walls below the ceiling. Beneath his feet, a thin layer of hay covered a hard packed dirt floor. The air was ripe with the sickly sweet smell of manure.

Peter, still holding Buster, was looking about. "Yep," he said, after a moment, "I always figured Matt probably lived in a barn."

They were standing in what seemed to be a stall, the door to which was hanging open. Matt suddenly appeared in the doorway. "Horseshit," he said, looking at Peter.

"No," Peter said, immediately, "I really did always figure that."

"Horseshit," Matt said again, but this time he pointed at Peter's feet. "You're standing in a pile of horseshit."

Peter looked down and immediately threw his head back in disgust. "Oh, for crying out loud."

"Come on," Matt said, "we don't have much time."

Nate followed Matt out of the stall. Behind him, he could hear muttering and what sounded like a shoe being scraped against one of the slats lining the stall. A few feet away, Matt stood near a large open door, holding the reins of three horses, each of which had been saddled.

"Matt, let me tell you…"

Matt shook his head quickly. "No time now. We'll talk later." He handed Nate one of the leather straps. "Hop on."

Nate hesitated briefly. He hadn't been on a horse since he was what? Five years old, visiting Gamma in Indiana. Awkwardly, he set his foot in the left stirrup, and, with some difficulty, pulled himself up, throwing his right leg over the animal's large rear end, and settling into the saddle.

"You're kidding, right?" said Peter, as he came up behind them.

"No, I'm not," replied Matt, giving Peter a serious look. "Don't tell me you're too much of a sissy to ride a horse."

"Too much of a what?"

"You heard me."

Peter affected a dour expression. Then he put a hand out.

Silently, Matt tossed him the reins to one of the horses, a big black stallion. Peter held out Buster, and Matt took the dog, who immediately began licking Matt's face. Peter stepped closer to the horse, lifted a foot and slid it into the stirrup. In one easy motion, he swung himself up onto the back of the large animal. He reached down, nodding toward the dog. Matt handed Buster up, and Peter easily cradled him in one arm. With his free hand, he confidently backed the stallion up a couple steps and turned him toward the open barn door.

"All right, Tonto," he said. "Now what?"

With what appeared to be a barely suppressed grin, Matt slung himself into the saddle on the remaining horse. "Now, we ride."

With Matt in the lead, they exited the barn and crossed a short meadow at a canter, entering the trees at the far end. The path they were on appeared to be well worn, and there was plenty of clearance above them and to the sides.

Bouncing uncomfortably on the hard, leather saddle, Nate didn't so much ride the horse, as hang on to it. Fortunately, the animal seemed content to tag along after the one ridden by Matt.

For fear of falling, Nate didn't dare turn to look behind him, but he could hear the hoof beats of Peter's horse following.

They kept a steady pace, not fast, but not slow either. The trail seemed to carry them slightly downhill. After several minutes, they came to a dirt road. Matt turned onto it and pushed his horse to a gallop. Despite the increased speed, Nate found the motion easier on his sore tailbone. They rode for what Nate estimated was about two miles before Matt suddenly reined in his mount, turned and guided it down a narrow lane.

Twenty yards in from the road was a windowless structure with a gated pen to one side. Matt jumped off, opened the gate, and led his horse inside. Nate gratefully climbed down and followed. Working quickly, Matt unbuckled the straps on his horse, lifted the saddle off and threw it onto a wooden platform. He slid the bridle off the horse's head and hung it from a hook on the side wall of the structure. He then did the same with Nate's horse. Peter in the meantime had unsaddled the black stallion.

"This way," Matt said. Closing the gate as soon as they were through, he led them to a door at the side of the small building, which he unlocked with a key, then stepped aside for them to enter. Buster took the lead, pulling on his leash.

The building was a garage. There were two vehicles inside, one an old pickup truck with dented fenders and spots of rust peeking through the worn paint, the other a much newer SUV, black, with tinted windows.

Matt took a seat on a stool in front of a counter that ran along the rear of the garage. A peg board panel with a collection of hand tools hanging from it slid to one side, revealing a series of electronic screens. Matt reached forward and pulled toward himself a tray on which sat a computer keyboard.

With a couple of strokes, the map Nate had seen on the monitor just inside the entryway to the barn appeared on one of the screens. The same bright dots shifted slowly, seeming now to converge on a single spot. Two of the other screens came on, showing the front of Matt's home from different angles. On a third, an interior view materialized. Nate assumed it was a room in the house.

Suddenly, a dark figure appeared on one of the screens, moving quickly along the base of the front porch. The display showing the interior flashed brightly and went dark.

Matt typed some commands, and the rest of the monitors shut off. He pushed in the tray holding the keyboard, and the wall containing the hand tools slowly slid back into place. He sat motionless, staring off into the distance.

Nate looked at Peter. He knew Peter was thinking the same thing he was. Somehow, the people who had paid a visit to Nate's condominium the night before had followed them to Idaho. Nate wasn't sure how they'd managed to do it. He and Peter hadn't used their credit cards. They hadn't made any calls. There was no way the car could have been traced to him, was there?

Finally, Matt stood. He nodded toward the SUV. "We should get going. It'll take them a while, but they'll eventually find this place."

Nate reached a hand out and touched Matt's sleeve. "Matt," he said solemnly, "these are not good people."

Matt gave him an odd look. "No," he said after a moment. "No, they're not."

4

"Ok," Matt said, "let's have it from the beginning."

Nate glanced back at Peter, sitting behind him in the rear seat of the SUV, Buster on his lap. Peter made a face and shrugged as if to say, You tell it. Nate returned his attention to the road ahead of them, illuminated now by the headlights of their vehicle. They had pulled out of the garage in twilight, Matt at the wheel, and turned onto the dirt path they'd followed earlier on horseback. Almost immediately, they'd come to a paved highway. "East or west?" Matt had asked.

"East," Nate had replied. "We're going to Minneapolis."

Matt had simply nodded and pulled out onto the highway. They'd driven in silence for a few minutes, each apparently lost in his own thoughts.

Nate paused now, thinking how best to tell a still-confusing story. He started with the late call from Peter at the airport, describing Peter's trip to Minneapolis, his encounter with the Gale women and the certainty that he was being followed. Matt listened intently, his eyes focused on the road. When Nate got to the bombshell about the Apollo 18 capsule, Matt looked over for just an instant. The warning that the man on the phone had given them drew another quick glance.

Nate was struck by the otherwise calm manner in which Matt absorbed the story. There were no exclamations of surprise, and, though Matt asked a few follow up questions, they were each on point. It wasn't so much that his brother didn't care or wasn't interested. It was, Nate thought, for lack of a better term, that he was being professional.

The only time Matt displayed any animation during the telling was when Nate explained how they slipped away using a car registered to an off-shore corporation.

"Oh, yeah," Matt asked, "what country?"

When Nate told him Anguilla, Matt shrugged. "Eh," he said. "There's better."

On the horizon ahead of them, a glow appeared. A sign announced that they were approaching Interstate 80, and, as they rounded a slight bend, a collection of fast food joints and gas stations came into view, their bright neon lights a sharp contrast to the darkness through which they'd been traveling. Just before they reached the oasis of light, Matt pulled the SUV into the poorly lit parking lot of a run-down motel and backed into a space in a dark corner of the lot, well away from the office.

"Can I see that photo?" he asked.

Peter retrieved his lap top, worked the keyboard for a minute, then handed the computer up to Nate. On the screen was the enlarged section of the picture showing the capsule's serial number.

"If you want to zoom out," Peter said, "just hit backspace."

Nate passed the device to Matt, who studied the display intently. After a moment, Matt raised a finger and put it on the backspace button. He glanced at Nate. Nate nodded, then looked away. A couple seconds later, he heard Matt grunt softly.

After a long moment, Matt said, "All right." As Nate turned back, Matt handed the computer to him. The display had been minimized. Nate returned the computer to Peter as Matt put the SUV in gear and guided the vehicle back onto the road.

When they'd merged onto the interstate, Peter, who'd been awake for over forty-eight hours, lay down on the rear seat and almost immediately fell into a deep slumber. Nate was also bone-tired, but he was too keyed up to sleep.

Neither Nate nor Matt spoke for several minutes. Finally, Nate broke the silence.

"Do you want to tell me about all that stuff back there?"

"Not really."

Nate considered that, then said, "Sorry, that's not going to work."

Matt took a deep breath, held it for a moment, then let it out slowly. "I know. I just didn't want to have go there."

Nate nodded. "Yeah, well, I think I've let that whole twenty-year disappearing act slide for too long now. Somehow, I get the impression what I saw back there has something to do with it. It's long past time you explained yourself, don't you think?"

He added, "If it's any consolation, I'm sorry we led those guys to your place. I have no idea how the hell they followed us."

Matt surprised Nate by saying, "They probably didn't. I'll bet they didn't even know you were in Idaho."

Nate mulled that over. If the people who had broken into his condominium had gone to all that trouble to warn off Nate and Peter, why not Matt?

"So you think they came to give you a message too?"

"A message?" Matt repeated. In the dim light reflected off the dashboard, Nate wasn't sure how to read his brother's expression, but it looked almost bemused. "No," he said, and his expression became serious again, "those guys weren't there to deliver a message. They came to kill me."

That, Nate realized, should have shocked him, but, after all the mind-numbing things he'd encountered over the past twenty-four hours, it didn't. Nothing in his previous experience had prepared him for this, and it was uncharacteristically disorienting. Focus, he told himself. For a long moment, he studied Matt, so familiar, yet so different. What, he asked himself, not for the first time, had happened to his brother?

Finally, he said, "You know who these people are."

Matt didn't answer immediately. Then, with a barely perceptible motion, he nodded.

Nate said nothing, waiting. Matt looked at him and tilted his head slightly toward the back of the vehicle. Nate turned. Peter was still stretched out on the rear seat, snoring softly, Buster curled up next to him, also dead to the world. He looked back at Matt. "Sound asleep."

Again, Matt nodded. Nate continued to wait patiently. They had time. A light rain began to fall, and Matt turned on the windshield wipers.

"Right after basic training," Matt said without taking his eyes off the road, "the army tapped me for Special Forces Assessment. I was near the end of that training when they pulled me out and told me they had an even more elite group they thought I'd qualify for. Something very special, they said, but also very dangerous. It sounded good to me. My head was in kind of a strange place back then." He said it in a matter-of-fact way, but Nate could detect just the slightest tinge of regret. Anyone else would have missed it.

"I was sent to a training facility in Arkansas," Matt continued, "though at the time I had no idea where I was. I only know now because I went back a couple years later to do some instructing. You won't find it on a map. It's deep in the Ozarks, part of a large military reservation. There are no roads in. Access is by helicopter only."

Matt glanced over at Nate. "By the way, what I'm telling you would get me killed if they found out. But," he added, "that ship seems to have sailed."

Unsure what to say, Nate just nodded.

"The training was intense. By the time I was done..." Matt paused. After a moment, he said, "Let's just say I was different. They taught me how to do things you wouldn't expect a man to be able to do."

He glanced again at Nate briefly and shrugged awkwardly. "I'm not saying this out of vanity. Though, I'll admit, for a time, I was pretty proud of myself."

"So, who were these people," Nate asked, "the CIA?"

"No." Matt shook his head. "This organization," he said, hesitating briefly, "this organization is a lot smaller and a lot less, I don't know, conventional. I guarantee you've never heard of it. I'm not even sure what the official name is. Something like 'Tactical Security Coordination' or some other nonsense. You'd never guess what it really is. It's buried so deep, I'll bet the President doesn't even know about it."

Maybe it was just a defensive mechanism. Nate wasn't sure. But, after the accumulation of all that Matt had said, this last statement struck him as particularly ludicrous, and, for some reason, it irritated him.

"Oh, come on Matt," Nate scoffed. "That kind of stuff only happens in the movies. This is for real."

"I know," Matt said softly. "Believe me, I know."

That was sobering, and it helped quell the irritation. Nate stared out the front window, watching small droplets slowly accumulate on the windshield, only to be brushed away after a few seconds by the wipers. Finally, he said, "What exactly does this organization do?"

When Matt responded, there was a new reluctance in his voice. "I'll tell you what *I* did. And I'll tell you the whole thing, because," he looked over, "you're probably the only person I *can* tell. And," he added, "you deserve to know."

Suddenly Nate wasn't sure he really wanted to hear whatever it was Matt was going to tell him.

"My first few years I was deployed in Eastern Europe," Matt said. "It was an extraordinary time. The Soviet Union was breaking up, and there was a lot of jockeying for power in the former republics. The U.S. had major stakes in the outcomes. But there was only so much we could do officially."

He made a vague gesture with one of his hands. "Unofficially," he said, "it was a different story.

"We needed certain people to step aside. In many cases, they could be convinced to do so on their own. I helped do a lot of that convincing. If that didn't work, well, there were other ways to get the job done."

The way Matt said it was very matter-of-fact. Nate was certain there was a whole lot more to it.

"I was like the tip of a spear being wielded behind the scenes. Some of the things I did were a little extreme, but," he hesitated, and it appeared to Nate as though he might have grimaced, "the people I did them to deserved it. Or at least I was able to convince myself that they did."

He gave Nate a quick, intense look. "I honestly believed I was doing the right thing. That I was being a patriot."

"What kind of things were you doing?" Nate asked.

"We'll get to that," Matt replied.

Nate resisted his initial impulse to fire back, realizing that Matt needed to tell this in his own way. Instead, he chose silence. Matt seemed to nod in appreciation.

"In the late '90s, I started splitting my time between Europe and the States. Terrorism was the new threat, and, to be honest, it was lot easier to target those kinds of people, especially after 9-11. It wasn't until..." His voice trailed off, and he was silent for a long time.

They were rounding a bend in the highway, and headlights from vehicles passing in the westbound lanes briefly illuminated his brother's face. Matt had set his jaw. There was a distance in his eyes.

Finally, Matt blinked and took a deep breath. "In September of 2004, I was sent to Miami. We had intelligence that indicated a group of Middle Eastern terrorists was planning an attack. The Dolphins were opening their season at home, and, because of a hurricane, it looked like the game would be pushed up a day. September 11. The plan, we were told, was to detonate a bomb in the parking lot of Pro Player Stadium. There were suggestions it might even be a dirty nuke. My assignment was to take out the leader."

"Take out," Nate repeated. He was pretty sure he knew what Matt meant, but he was hoping he was wrong.

"Eliminate, remove," Matt said. Then he gave Nate a direct look. "Kill."

Nate said nothing.

"It was a quick in and out," Matt continued, his eyes back on the road. "I'd done it more times than I could count."

He puffed some air through his nose, a mirthless laugh. "I guess I'd been doing it too long. I knew it wasn't my place to question the operation. But the whole thing didn't make sense. Why just go after the one guy? And why not go after the bomb? What if it really was a nuke?

"The target was a Palestinian-American who'd been in this country for almost thirty years. His dossier made him look legit. He was employed by a trucking company and was the union rep. Supposedly, though, he was a plant, a sleeper agent controlled by Hezbollah.

"Too many red flags there, but I didn't see them."

The back of Nate's neck was tingling, and there was a heaviness in his chest. For a moment, he considered telling Matt to stop, but he knew he had to hear it.

"He and his wife lived alone in a small house in the suburbs. I was supposed to make it look like a heart attack. We had a particularly nasty gas for that. I'd have released it in his car, and he'd have been dead before he got out of the driveway. Even if there'd been an autopsy, and, for something like that, there wouldn't have been, detection would have been unlikely.

"But I had a better plan. I slipped into the house early in the morning. Tied them both up. Told the man I'd start removing his wife's fingers one at a time until he told me where the bomb was. He claimed he didn't know what I was talking about. Said it had to be a mistake. Pleaded with me to let them go. 'Course, they all did that. But there was something in the way he said it."

He paused for a moment. "I don't know. Maybe that's what threw me off. But, then again, I'd already blown it. I didn't know the kid was there. I should have." He shook his head. "I should have," he repeated.

"When she came through the door, I just reacted. Head shot. Close range. The wife lunged at me, and I took her down the same way. At that point, I had no choice. I stood the man up. He was blubbering incoherently. I put the barrel in his mouth, wrapped his hands around the gun and fired. Then I tidied up and left."

Nate stared at his brother, trying hard to shake the feeling that he was looking at a stranger.

"I should have been disciplined for deviating from the plan," Matt said. "But I wasn't. Turns out the police bought the whole murder-suicide thing, and, apparently, my superiors were even happier with that than they would have been with the heart attack.

"It didn't sit well, though, and it gnawed at me. For months. Finally, I realized I had to do something about it. I'd accumulated a lot of time off, so I took it. Pulled in some favors. Started doing my own investigation. All indications were that the guy *was* legit. I discovered he'd been active in local politics. He'd been running for the state legislature and was considered a shoe-in. But he'd also started playing a role in some of the national races. One of the Florida senate seats was open, and the election was going to be tight. And Florida was shaping up to be a battleground in the upcoming presidential election. From what I could tell, the elimination of my guy had an impact on both races.

"Could have been coincidence, but, in my business, one of the first casualties is coincidence. What I couldn't find was anything supporting the notion that the guy was involved in planning a terrorist attack. Nobody else had any intel on it. There weren't any other unexplained deaths that week. And, needless to say, there was no bomb at the stadium on opening day, unless you count the Dolphins, who really stunk it up that year.

"I took my findings back to my boss. He wasn't happy. We had words. To this day, though, I don't know if he knew anything more than I did. And I'll never know. He died of a heart attack a few weeks later.

"But I was finished. I couldn't do it any more. I'd been in the business for twenty years, and it was time. I quietly retired and moved to Idaho. Where, by the way," he added, with a new sharpness in his voice, "I would have been willing to let sleeping dogs lie."

Afraid of what he might say, Nate turned and looked out the side window, idly watching vague dark shapes passing in the distance. Try as he might, he couldn't reconcile the Matt he remembered with the one sitting next to him. He wasn't sure he wanted to.

He closed his eyes and for a moment was no longer in the quiet, darkened SUV. Instead, he was standing under intense lights, a wave of noise assaulting him.

"*De*-fense. *De*-fense."

The chant had been started by the Evansville East cheerleaders and had been quickly picked up by the fans packing the stands surrounding them. The Barons, from the state's third largest city, had brought a huge following. While the Mackey Arena on the campus of Purdue University in Lafayette wasn't completely filled, it still contained more people than Nate had ever seen in one place. And the vast majority were there to support, at the top of their lungs, the defending state high school basketball champions.

The relatively small contingent that had accompanied the Jackson Generals did its best to counter, but it was badly outnumbered.

As the team broke the huddle on the sidelines, Nate glanced up to the spot where Peter and Gamma sat amid the Jackson crowd. At the moment, Peter had his back turned to the court and was flapping his arms wildly, exhorting the fans behind him to raise a cheer. Gamma was looking directly at Nate and clapping, her mouth open, yelling something he couldn't possibly hear over the cacophony.

The mere fact that the boys from the tiny town of Jackson in rural Winamac County had managed to make it to the 1982 Indiana Regional Championship was a huge accomplishment. And, against the odds, Nate and his teammates had managed to make a close game of it. Everyone, especially the Evansville supporters, had expected a blow out. After all, the Barons had the two best players in the state, a pair of six foot ten behemoths with the nicknames "Everest" and "K-2" - earning them the inevitable joint moniker of the "Himalayas." Jackson had only two players who stood over six feet: Nate at six three, and Skip Anderson, a gangly six foot seven junior whose only real basketball skill was his height. Still, Skip had played some inspired defense, and Nate had managed to score twenty points against the towering Himalayas, many on uncontested jump shots from outside while Everest and K-2 packed the lane down low.

K-2 had now just fouled out, and, in the process, had turned the ball over to Jackson. With fifteen seconds left in the game, and down by only one point, Jackson would have a chance at the last shot and an improbable upset victory. The prospect had the crowd in a frenzy.

Nate took up position near the foul line, where he could set a pick. Everest, who'd been covering him all night, stood just behind, leaning in, his long arms reaching around to each side, his hot breath ruffling the hair on the top of Nate's head. Nate had hoped Everest might have been switched to cover Skip after K-2 fouled out, but the Evansville coach had obviously decided he wanted his best player to stay on Nate.

One of the officials blew his whistle. The ball was brought in under the opposing basket, and Matt, the Jackson point guard, began dribbling upcourt, an Evansville player hounding him, but not too closely, showing respect for Matt's already demonstrated ability to shed defenders. Understandably, Evansville appeared to be anticipating that Jackson would let the clock wind down before putting the ball up for a last second shot. As Matt crossed the midcourt line, working to his right, Nate felt Everest shift position and reach his left arm further out to deny Nate a pass.

Nate and Matt made eye contact, and, to Nate's surprise, Matt winked his left eye, one of their special signals. Nate didn't hesitate. Pushing off with his left foot, he quickly pivoted to the right, spinning around Everest and past him before the boy had a chance to react. Nate took two long strides toward the basket, launching himself upwards. He reached his hands out and looked back over his shoulder. The pass from Matt was right on the money. Nate had just a split second to grab the ball out of the air and redirect it toward the goal.

It caromed off the backboard and dropped softly through the hoop.

Jackson had the lead.

Impossibly, the noise from the crowd intensified.

Nate came down in a slight crouch and immediately pushed off, sprinting up court. Neither team had any time outs remaining. The clock behind the basket at the far end read nine seconds.

Evansville obviously got the ball in quickly, because it came sailing over Nate's head and was snagged by the player who'd been covering Matt. He and Matt were now the only players in the front court. With Matt backpedaling furiously, the Evansville guard took two quick dribbles. Then he feinted right and dove to his left, launching the ball in an awkward motion toward the basket as Matt reached out to contest.

The ball struck high on the backboard, dropping back down at an angle that Nate, with a sinking feeling, thought would put it straight through. Instead, however, it hit the front of the rim and bounced back up. Heart in his mouth, Nate watched as the thing seemed to hang suspended over the basket. Then it dropped, struck the side of the rim, and this time bounced away. Nate, who, in the intervening time, had managed to cover the length of the court, leapt and, at full extension, wrapped his hands around the ball, gathering in the rebound. He glanced up and saw Everest bearing down. In the brief moment available to him, he registered two facts: That the clock at the far end of the court showed three seconds remaining, and that, if he held the ball, Everest would surely foul him to send him to the line, where he'd have to make free throws to seal the win. Nate stepped back with his right foot and tossed the ball in a lazy arc toward the Jackson basket. It struck the floor near the midcourt line, and, with no players nearby, bounced slowly toward the far end as time on the clock ticked down to zero.

Pandemonium erupted in the arena. Nate turned just in time to catch Matt as he flung himself into Nate's arms, letting out a roar of exultation that Nate could barely hear over his own. Fans began to descend from the stands, a few rushing onto the court. The other Jackson players were jumping about ecstatically. Nate noticed, however, that some of the Evansville players were waving their arms and pointing toward the end line. The referees were also waving their arms and blowing their whistles. The Evansville coach appeared, planting himself in front of one of the officials. The man was red in the face and gesticulating wildly.

Ushers and police officers began urging back the people who had come onto the court, and the roar began to subside. Nate saw the referee who was with the Evansville coach signal to the Jackson coach, Billy Hamilton, that he should join them. As Coach Hamilton approached, one of the officials said something, and Coach Hamilton began shaking his head vehemently. Nate couldn't hear what was being said, but he knew it couldn't be good.

Nate let go of Matt and took a step toward them. One of the referees, the older of the two, noticed him and gestured.

"Yes, I want the captains over here," he said.

Nate's counterpart, the Evansville captain, was the guard who'd taken the final shot. The boy was talking in an animated fashion to the other referee. He tapped his left forearm with his right hand and pointed at Matt. Nate glanced back at his brother. Matt had an odd look on his face.

"Gentlemen," said the older of the two referees, "Evansville is claiming there was a foul on the final shot. I'm afraid I was screened out on the play and didn't see it clearly." He looked at the other official. "Gene, did you see a foul?"

The other man shook his head. "There was definitely contact," he said, "but I thought it was incidental."

"No," the Evansville captain exclaimed, "he hit me on the arm." And he again pointed at Matt.

"Sorry, son," the older official said, "I'm afraid…"

"Ask him," the Evansville player interjected.

The official shook his head. "That's not the way it works."

"To hell with that," the Evansville coach said. "Why not just ask him? He can speak for himself." He looked at Matt. "Did you foul?"

"Now hold on a second," Coach Hamilton said. But everyone had turned to look at Matt.

Nate looked back again at his brother as the senior official said, "Son, you're not obligated to respond to that."

Matt had set his jaw.

Oh, no, Nate said to himself. No. He opened his mouth to speak, but Matt beat him to it.

"Yes, sir," he said. "I think I did."

"There you go," the Evansville coach said immediately, throwing his arms in the air once again. Looking at the head referee, he added, "You've got to call it now."

The official looked at his colleague, who simply shrugged.

Coach Hamilton said, "I've never heard of anything like this." But it wasn't very compelling, and he seemed to know it.

The senior official took a deep breath. "Ok," he said, and he turned toward the scorer's table, blowing his whistle. "We have a foul on Jackson. Number five. Number one for Evansville is at the line shooting two."

After a moment, he added, "Put three seconds back on the clock."

It took a couple of minutes to clear the court. The public address announcer tried his best to explain the situation. As it dawned on the Evansville fans that their team still had a chance to win the game they'd just lost, a great cheer went up. The reaction from the Jackson supporters was much different. Nate could hear the boos and catcalls through the general euphoria of the Evansville crowd.

Peter had brought with him a series of hand-painted signs that he'd been flashing throughout the game to the delight of the Jackson faithful, his theme apparently somewhat loosely inspired by the mythical snow creature of the Himalayas. Nate had seen a couple during the game. "Sas-squash Evansville." "It ain't over Yet-i."

Now, as the head official blew his whistle and handed the ball to the Evansville captain at the free throw line, Peter stood defiantly, holding over his head a sign Nate hadn't yet seen.

"Abominable"

Nate had taken up position along the side of the lane, hoping for a miss and an opportunity to snag the rebound. He felt a tap on his hip and turned to see Matt, an intense expression on his face.

"Get me the ball, Nate."

All Nate could think to do was nod. Then Matt turned and jogged up the court.

The Evansville captain bounced the ball a couple of times. Then he flexed his knees, lifted the ball up in front of his face and flicked his right wrist, sending the ball upward in a pretty arc. Nate knew it was good from the moment it left the boy's hands. It passed through the rim without drawing iron and barely ruffled the nylon of the net hanging below. The game was now tied.

"One shot," the referee reminded them all, then he again tossed the ball to the Evansville player. As before, the boy bounced the ball a couple of times before lifting it up, taking aim and giving the same flick of the wrist. This time the flight of the ball carried it further, and, when it came down, it struck the base of the rim, bouncing up high. Nate had stepped into the lane with the motion of the shot and peered upward, willing the ball to miss. Behind him, Everest pushed, trying to get position for a rebound, but Nate braced himself and held his ground.

The ball struck the front of the rim at an angle that sent it ricocheting toward the backboard. Nate tensed, ready to leap. But, to his chagrin, the ball bounced straight back and through the hoop.

Again, the arena erupted.

Nate wasted no time. As the ball cleared the net, he grabbed it and flipped it to one of the officials while stepping over the end line and preparing to inbound. The man immediately blew his whistle and tossed the ball back. Everest stepped in front of Nate and began hopping up and down, his long arms extended and waving, seeking to deny Nate the ability to make a clean pass. To Everest's surprise, however, Nate suddenly dashed to his right along the baseline, an unusual, but legal, move after a made basket. Everest was caught in mid-jump, and was left behind.

Looking down court, Nate saw that Matt, who'd started out under the far basket, was now sprinting in his direction. His defender - the other Evansville guard who had not been previously matched up against Matt and who had apparently not anticipated Matt's quickness - had been left flat-footed. Nate planted himself near the end of the base line and, with one hand, heaved the ball in Matt's direction as if it were a baseball. At a spot about thirty-five feet from the basket, Matt and the ball arrived at the same moment, Matt jumping up slightly and grabbing it out of the air. He came down and immediately pivoted on one foot, squaring himself with the basket. The Evansville guard was closing, but not quickly enough.

Matt bent his knees, and, in one graceful motion, pushed himself upward and let the basketball fly.

For Nate, time seemed to slow to a crawl. As the ball rose in a high arc, rotating slightly backwards, the clock at the far end of the court ticked down to zero, and the red light behind the backboard illuminated. The crowd's roar morphed into a collective scream as the orb passed through its zenith and began its downward track. Nate thought it might strike the front of the rim. But instead it passed unscathed through the iron with a satisfying swish of the net.

Jackson had won.

This time there was no stopping the crowd from charging the court, and, for the next few minutes, it was a sea of happy bedlam. Several people slapped a somewhat dazed Nate on the back. A few grabbed him in exuberant embraces. Peter had helped Gamma down from the stands, and, when she reached him, she gave him a mighty hug.

"I'm so happy for you Nate."

As the players eventually made their way to the locker room beneath the stands, Nate found himself walking next to Matt. His brother wore an expression of pure joy, and he gave Nate a friendly punch on the arm.

"Nice pass."

Nate nodded in appreciation. But, as they turned into the long corridor leading to the visitor's locker room, he gave Matt a serious look. "Why did you admit it?"

Matt's own face turned serious, and, for several seconds, the two brothers said nothing, the hoots and hollers from their teammates echoing off the concrete walls around them. When they reached the door to the locker room, Matt stepped to the side, and Nate did likewise, allowing the others to pass. Neither said anything. Finally, Matt shrugged. "If I hadn't, it wouldn't have been right. Would it?"

Nate wasn't sure what to say. He couldn't help wondering whether, had he found himself in the same situation, he'd have been able to do the same thing.

Then Matt's grin returned. "And anyway, it's better like this, right?"

Nate considered his brother for a long moment. Finally, he nodded, turned and put an arm over Matt's shoulder, and together they walked into the boisterous locker room.

The echoes faded as Nate opened his eyes, and he was back in the quiet SUV, the silence broken only by the intermittent swish of the windshield wipers and the sound of tires on the wet pavement. Minutes passed.

Matt finally broke the spell. "So this guy on the phone, you said he had a southern accent at one point?"

Nate nodded.

"There are lots of southern accents," Matt said. "Can you be more specific? Was it a drawl, did it have a twang to it?"

"Neither," Nate replied. He re-played the conversation in his mind. "I don't know if it means anything, but the first thought that came to mind was Hampton Roads."

As youngsters, the boys had moved around quite a bit. Their father, who was a naval aviator before joining the space program, had been stationed at different posts across the country. Nate spent part of the first grade attending a school in Norfolk, Virginia, where his father was assigned to a squadron at the nearby Naval Air Station. The soft southern accent of the man on the phone had conjured memories of the accents he'd heard during his time in Virginia.

At the mention of Hampton Roads, Matt turned and looked at him quickly before returning his attention to the highway. Nate could see that he was working his jaw.

"That mean something to you?" Nate asked.

"Maybe."

Matt was again quiet for a long moment. He adjusted his hands on the wheel. It seemed to Nate as though he might be tightening his grip. Then he said, "If it's who I think it is, we're dealing with someone very dangerous. Not that the others aren't. But this guy?" He paused. "He takes it to a whole new level."

"Who is he?"

"His name is Raen. And there's something wrong with him. Seriously wrong."

Nate had thought he couldn't be more scared. But Matt's words, and the way he said them, induced a terrifying chill. It took him a minute to find his voice.

"Matt, what are we going to do?"

"We're going to follow through on your first instinct. Your gut told you we needed to go to Minneapolis, to see the Gale women?"

Nate nodded, though it was more to himself.

"It was a good instinct," Matt said. "If those women have been told to keep their mouths shut, they obviously have something to say, something that we need to hear.

"And now we need to get to them before they do. Before *he* does."

#

Raen held out his palm and allowed the black stallion to sniff it. Then he reached back and patted the animal's neck at the point where it met the withers. Sliding his hand up, he scratched along the neck. Nickering softly, the big animal lifted his head and stretched as if to offer encouragement.

As a boy growing up on a farm in southwest Virginia, Raen had spent a great deal of time around horses. Of course, those had all been work animals, plugs for the most part. Nothing like this magnificent specimen.

In the garage, Raen had found a bag of carrots. He pulled one now from his pocket and held it out with his other hand. The stallion took the treat gently, biting into it only after pulling his muzzle back safely from Raen's fingers, the sign of a well-mannered, well-trained animal. Raen reached around with his other hand and scratched the far side of the neck. The horse lay his head softly on Raen's shoulder, gratefully accepting the ministrations.

Raen watched as Parker's men carried equipment from the garage and loaded it into one of the Suburbans that had been driven around to the site. They had dismantled the computer setup concealed behind the garage workbench, as well as the one in the house and in the escape tunnel near the barn. It would all be taken to the nearest lab in Denver, where it would be analyzed in an attempt to glean information that would assist them in tracking down Marek. It was a waste of time, Raen knew. Marek would not have left them anything of value.

He didn't envy Parker. He and his men had spent a long night deconstructing the site. And this was not going to be an easy after-action report to write. Failure was not something The Organization frequently experienced, or readily tolerated. Parker was a competent operative, but he'd more than met his match with Marek. Raen wondered idly whether, had he been the one leading the assault, he'd have anticipated the back door that Marek had installed. Then he dismissed the thought. No value to it.

Dacoff appeared. He held out a small device for Raen to see. "He had the whole mountain covered with these," the man said. "Top-of-the-line equipment, and well concealed. Hell, even when I knew where each one was supposed to be, they were hard to find."

Raen nodded but said nothing. He certainly wasn't surprised. Marek hadn't become Marek without being extremely thorough and prepared. Parker simply hadn't realized what he was up against. It suddenly occurred to Raen that maybe Parker hadn't known *who* he was up against. Was it possible they hadn't told him his target was Marek?

Marek. There were a few operatives who had achieved legendary status within The Organization, men who had proven themselves to be truly extraordinary among an already extraordinary elite. And then there was Marek.

He'd started out ordinarily enough. There were, Raen knew, even still a handful of men in The Organization who had served in the field with him. But they were a dwindling lot. After only a couple of years, Marek had completely dissolved into the shadows. He did have a tactical team, one that he'd held together for almost two decades. Hell, even those two guys were revered. But he also worked a lot on his own. Jobs to which an entire action team might have otherwise been assigned were routinely given to him. And some of the successes he'd had were, to this day, considered highlights in The Organization's history.

Raen had never met the man, at least not to his knowledge. Couldn't have picked him out of a police line-up. If there ever were photos of him, they'd long ago been purged.

All of the men in The Organization strove to be invisible. Marek was the only one who'd actually achieved it.

Raen glanced over at the two other horses, then took in the three saddles perched on the nearby wooden platform and the three bridles hanging from hooks attached to the exterior of the garage. Had the other two Cartwright brothers made it here first? Probably. Which meant they were now together. Fine, he thought. He wouldn't have to spend a lot of time rounding them up. He could kill them all at once.

The other two horses, he noticed, were also fine animals, but not as superb as the stallion. This, he knew, had to be the one Marek had ridden. It was too spectacular to have been offered to anyone else.

"Is Ozaki ready?"

Dacoff nodded in the direction of the road. "He's waiting for us in the car."

Raen patted the stallion's neck on both sides, and the horse lifted his head off Raen's shoulder. With his right hand, Raen reached under and softly scratched the area of the neck just behind the throat latch. With his left hand, he reached inside his jacket and withdrew a .45 caliber pistol. He placed the muzzle of the handgun against the animal's forehead, withdrew his right hand and pulled the trigger.

The boom of the weapon shattered the relative silence and was followed immediately by multiple echoes as the report bounced back off nearby mountains. The lifeless body of the stallion dropped onto the hard dust-covered surface of the pen with a massive thud.

Raen calmly re-holstered the pistol.

"Fuck you, Marek."

5

According to Peter, Eunice Gale lived in a home that she and her now-deceased husband, Alvin, had purchased shortly after World War II. They had raised two children there. The oldest, Patricia, was now 71. She'd never married, and, as near as Peter had been able to determine, had never even moved away from home. The other child, Mason, had died in the Apollo 18 tragedy in 1976 at the age of 34.

The house was a modest, single-story structure that sat in the middle of a residential block in the northwest corner of Minneapolis. Matt did not slow the SUV as they drove past, so Nate was able to catch only a quick view of the place. The lawn, he saw, needed tending, and the exterior was a few years overdue for a paint job. It was, however, essentially indistinguishable from the other homes on the street. A white compact car sat in the driveway.

At the end of the block, Matt turned right. Parked on the corner was a service van marked with the logo of a plumbing company. As they passed it, Matt glanced at Nate, arched an eyebrow and slightly tilted his head in the direction of the van. It had obviously been there for a while, as the blacktop beneath the vehicle was dry, in contrast to the rest of the roadway that shimmered from the drizzle that had been falling all morning.

Matt circled the two adjacent blocks. "Looks like that's the only one," he said eventually. Taking a circuitous route, so as not to pass the plumbing van again, he guided the SUV to a spot on the same street as the Gale house, but a block away and on the opposite side, so that it was not visible from the van. He shut off the engine.

"Now what?" asked Nate.

"Now we wait," Matt said. Then, as if realizing he was being a bit cryptic, he explained, "We don't want to try to approach the house in daylight. In fact, if we can do this without going into the house, so much the better. My guess is they've probably got listening devices in there. But," he added, "if the women stay put today, we'll have to go in tonight."

"So, we're just going to sit here all day?" Peter asked from the back seat.

Matt nodded, a sardonic smile playing on his face. "Welcome to my world."

Nate glanced back, and Peter gave him an inquiring look. Nate shook his head. "It's kind of a long story."

It turned out they didn't have to wait at all. A couple minutes after they'd parked, the front door to the house opened, and a woman stepped out. She locked the door behind herself and walked briskly to the car sitting in the driveway. She backed the car out, turned it up the street in their direction, and, at the intersection just before she reached them, she made a right and headed off down the side street. Matt started the engine, pulled out and turned up the street after her.

He kept a good distance between them and the white compact, glancing frequently in the rear and side view mirrors. She led them onto a busy commercial thoroughfare and eventually turned into a large shopping center. She parked the compact in front of a Bed Bath & Beyond store. By the front door, she retrieved a shopping cart and entered the building.

Matt parked the SUV a few spaces away. He looked at Nate. "We'll be about two minutes behind you." He pointed to the small device he'd previously given to Nate. "If it vibrates, we've got company. Find the storage room, go to the back door and wait for us behind the building."

Nate glanced briefly at Peter, who looked a little dazed. Even Buster, sitting on the seat next to his brother, seemed unusually subdued. Nate nodded, opened the passenger door and stepped out. He walked quickly to the store entrance, hoping he wasn't attracting attention, but feeling as if he were being followed by a spotlight.

He saw the woman as soon as he entered the store. She had made her way up one of the aisles to the right and paused to examine a floor display filled with coffee makers and prepackaged coffees. Tall and thin, with closely cropped grey hair, she moved with a vitality that belied her age. A pair of reading glasses hung from a chain around her neck, and, as Nate watched, she lifted the glasses and slipped them on to read one of the coffee packages. There was a quiet elegance to her.

Nate picked up a hand basket from the rack near the door, and, walking as casually as he could, he made his way up the aisle, passed the woman, and stopped a few feet beyond, pretending to look at a collection of mixing bowls. He was acutely aware of the small device in his left pocket, afraid at any moment it would start vibrating.

The woman selected a package of coffee and placed it in her cart. She then wheeled past Nate, turned and made for the escalator, where she slid the cart into the mechanism that would pull it up to the second floor and stepped onto the moving stairway. He followed slowly, making a show of looking at various items on display, and he entered the escalator only as she was reaching the top. Fortunately, there was no vibration from the device in his pocket.

As he exited the escalator, he saw that the woman had turned into a section of the store containing pillows and comforters. He didn't see anyone else in the vicinity.

He walked up the narrow aisle in which the woman stood, examining a pillow, and said quietly, "Ms. Gale?"

"Hmm?" she said, turning to look at him. "Do I know you?"

"No," he said. "But we need to talk."

73

Her face took on a startled expression that quickly morphed into one of fear. Her eyes darted behind him, and then around the area in which the two of them stood. She tensed. Nate wasn't sure whether she was ready to run or scream. Or both.

Nate raised his hands, palms forward. "I'm not here to hurt you. I want to help you."

Eyes still darting, she said, "I don't need any help."

"Yes, you do," Nate said, with as much calm as he could muster. He was about to say something else when her eyes went wide and the color seemed to drain from her face. Glancing back, Nate saw Matt step off the escalator. He returned his attention to the woman. She had a desperate look.

"I didn't talk to him," she said in a hoarse whisper. "I swear. Please. You have to believe me." Then she suddenly gasped. Nate didn't need to turn to know that she'd seen Peter as well.

"I'm with them," Nate said. "I'm not with the others."

The woman was shaking her head. There was still a pleading note to her voice. "You don't know," she said. "You don't know what they can do."

"Actually, we do," said Matt, who had made his way up the adjacent aisle. Speaking in a low, but firm voice, he said, "And we're just as afraid as you are. But what you don't know is that the situation has changed. They're coming to kill us."

To hear Matt say it so bluntly made Nate's knees weak.

"It won't make a difference to them what you do or don't say to us now," Matt added. "It's only a matter of time before they come to kill you."

The woman seemed to sag. She looked down, but her eyes were unfocused. She opened her mouth to speak, but the only thing that came out was a weak, "Oh."

Hoping that his voice was more composed than he felt, Nate said, "We want to help you. But we need your cooperation. You know something they don't want anyone else to know. We can't begin to help you unless you tell us what it is."

There were tears in her eyes, and she was shaking. "I'm so tired," she said, her voice barely audible. "I'm so tired of being afraid."

"Please," Nate said. "Let us help you."

"Do you need some assistance?" came a sharp voice from behind them. Nate turned quickly to see a young man in a blue vest emblazoned with the store logo. Brows knit, he was looking suspiciously at the slumped figure of Patricia Gale.

"No," Matt said, immediately. "Thank you. It's just that there's been a sudden death in our family."

The store clerk's expression softened. "Oh, I'm sorry to hear that."

"Yes," Matt continued. He'd come around to the aisle in which Nate and Patricia Gale stood, and he now linked an arm protectively under one of the woman's. "We need to take our mother home. Is it ok if we leave the cart here?"

"Of course," the young man said, suspicion now replaced by solicitation.

Matt began guiding the woman, and Nate took her other arm. She did not resist.

Two doors down from the store was a pizzeria. At 10:30 in the morning, they were the only customers. Peter ordered four cups of coffee, and they took a table well away from the only employee in the place, a young woman who was ostensibly manning the cash register, but who was clearly more intent on carrying out a spirited conversation on her cell phone.

Patricia Gale seemed to have regained much of her composure. She considered each of the three of them, then said, more as a statement than a question, "You're Bob Cartwright's boys."

Nate nodded. "Yes, I'm Nate. These are my brothers Peter and Matt."

"I met your father once," she said. "About a month before the launch. It was after..." Her voice trailed off. She took a sip of coffee. Then she said, as much to herself as to the three of them, "God, I am so tired of being afraid."

Matt said quietly, "Why don't you tell us what you're afraid of."

She looked at Matt for a long moment. Finally, she said, "Him. Or them, I suppose. He's probably gone now. But I know there are others like him. Still, when I think about it, it's always him."

"What can you tell us about him?" Matt asked.

#

On the television, the 1976 Democratic National Convention in New York City was winding down. Jimmy Carter and his new running mate, Walter Mondale, had just taken the stage amid raucous cheers when the knock came at the front door. Patricia glanced over at her mother, who was stretched out in the big leather recliner, the one that her father had so loved. Her mother had nodded off.

Not wanting to disturb her, Patricia set aside the needlepoint she'd been working on and quietly got up from the sofa. She reached down and turned off the television. At the door, she switched on the porch light and peered out through the side window. A man in his early thirties, with short cropped hair, stood on the stoop. When he saw her, he gave her a broad smile and called out, "Miss Gale? My name is Arthur Spelling. I served in the Marines with your brother. Here's a picture of the two of us." He held out a black-and-white snapshot.

Patricia put her face near the glass and studied the photo. It did, indeed, show Mason. He was dressed in a pair of camouflaged pants and a t-shirt and was standing next to another man who appeared to be a younger version of the man outside her door. The two were in front of a structure lined with sandbags piled almost to the roof. They each looked to be holding a can of beer. Mason had a cigarette dangling from the side of his mouth. Funny, she thought, she never knew he'd taken up smoking.

But, then again, she'd never had much of a chance to get to know about Mason's life after he'd shipped out to Vietnam in early 1967. Not that there had been much to know. He'd been sent home three months later in a sealed casket, his body apparently so badly ruined that it couldn't be viewed.

She reached up and undid the latch, then opened the door.

The man gave her a friendly nod and said, "It's very nice to finally meet you. Mason has told me so much about you. May I come in for a moment?"

He didn't wait for her to answer, stepping across the threshold and into the small living room. Taken aback, she began to close the door, but something stopped it, and then it was pushed open from the outside. Two other men entered the room, the second finally closing the door behind them and locking it.

"These men are with me," said the man who had called himself Arthur Spelling. "They also know Mason well."

Patricia shook her head. The suddenness of the appearance of these strangers, coupled with the odd turns of phrase, had her confused. "What..." she began to say, but her mother's voice interrupted her.

"Patricia, who are these men?"

Before she could respond, the man named Spelling had crossed the room and put out a hand. "Mrs. Gale," he said, "I bring you greetings from your son, Mason."

Her mother instinctively took the man's hand, but there was puzzlement on her face. "Mason," she said slowly, "Mason is dead."

"No," said the man named Spelling, "that's where you're wrong." Then he suddenly slapped his side. "Oh, where are my manners. Patricia. Is it ok if I call you Patricia? Please come and take a seat on the sofa."

Though the words were polite, there was no mistaking the tone. It was a command, not a request. Patricia looked at the other two men. One remained by the front door. The other had walked over to stand by the door next to the dining area, the one that led back to the rest of the house. They both had their arms folded. She walked to the sofa, and, as calmly as she could, she sat down.

"That's great," the man said, walking over to the dining room table. He pulled out one of the straight back chairs, carried it to the living room and set it down in front of the gap between the sofa and the recliner, facing her and her mother. He took a seat and regarded them with what Patricia now realized were a pair of extraordinarily dark eyes. With much more familiarity than he had a right to display, the man reached out with both hands and patted Patricia and her mother on their respective knees. Looking back over his shoulder at the man standing near the hallway door, he said, "Mr. Johnson, why don't you get us all something to drink."

The other man nodded, turned and walked out of the room.

"Now," he said, returning his attention to Patricia and her mother, "let me explain why I'm here. First, I need to correct a horrible mistake that was made by the Marines. And, being a former Marine, I'm a little embarrassed about this. It seems you may have received some terribly misleading news about Mason. But, I can assure you Mason is alive and well and doing just wonderfully."

Her mother, Patricia saw, was still struggling with the sudden appearance of these men, not that Patricia was having much greater success. "What kind of cruel hoax is this?" Patricia asked. "We buried Mason nine years ago."

"No." The man shook his head. "No, you didn't. That's what I'm trying to tell you. There was a tragic mix-up in Khe Sanh. Things were pretty hectic back then. The body that was shipped to you was one of the other men in our platoon. And, believe me, the visit to that young man's family is not one I'm looking forward to making."

He again reached out and patted her knee and her mother's knee. She wanted to slap him. "But this message is a happy one. Your son," he said, looking at her mother, "and your brother," he said, turning his attention to her, "is alive."

Patricia's mother had found her voice. "Mason?" she asked, hopefully. "Mason is alive?"

"No he's not, mother. These men are lying."

The man's dark eyes flashed momentarily. Then his easy smile returned. He snapped his fingers, and the man standing by the front door stepped forward and handed him a manila envelope. He opened it and extracted what appeared to be a color photograph. He looked at it briefly before turning it around and showing it to the two women.

Patricia experienced a moment of light-headedness. The photograph was a professional portrait. It depicted a man who appeared to be in his mid-thirties, seated on a stool in front of a neutral background. He was wearing a flight suit of some kind, with a large helmet sitting on his knee. The man was smiling casually, his eyes looking directly at the camera. The hair was thinner, and there were crags and creases that had never been there before. But there was no mistaking who it was.

"Mason!" her mother cried out.

The man called Johnson re-appeared. He had not brought anything from the kitchen for them to drink. Folding his arms, he again took up his stance.

"Can I see that picture again?" Patricia asked. The man named Spelling began to hand her the color portrait. "No," she said, "the one with you and Mason."

Surprised, the man hesitated for a moment. Then he shrugged, reached into his shirt pocket and extracted the black-and-white snapshot. He handed it to her, and she studied it. It was definitely Mason. She looked between the man sitting in front of her and the man standing next to her brother in the picture. "This really is you."

He smiled. "Yes it is. I was a little younger then, of course."

"May I keep this?"

Again, there was a hesitation. Then the man grinned, and there was something a little frightening about the expression. "By all means. Now," he continued, his expression becoming serious, "I need to explain something very important to the two of you." He leaned toward them. "It's essential that our government not be embarrassed by the little mistake I just told you about. Mason has been given a very important assignment, one that is going to make him well known and draw a lot of attention. And it wouldn't be appropriate for either of you to mention anything about Mason supposedly dying in Vietnam. Instead, your government expects you," he paused and fixed them with his dark eyes, "*I* expect you, to go along with the story that I'm about to lay out for you."

He reached his right hand up behind his neck, paused, then slowly drew the hand up and over his head. A long, gleaming metallic object followed, and, as he brought his hand down in front of him, Patricia realized that it was a knife. Light from the lamp in the corner glinted off the tip. He held the thing out in front of him, casually, paying it no attention. Patricia could not take her eyes off of it.

"So that we're clear," the man said slowly, "I want to impress upon you the utmost gravity with which I deliver this message."

To Patricia's horror, he reached out and brought the knife up to within a couple inches of her face, holding it there. Heart pounding in her chest, she stared at the thing. It was immense. Unlike any knife she'd ever seen before, both edges of the blade were sharp. Wickedly sharp. With a slow, deliberate motion, the man rotated the thing in front of her. She suddenly found it difficult to breath, the air catching in her chest as it shook uncontrollably.

"Now," the man said, his voice low and ominous, "I don't want you to have any misunderstandings about how serious I am."

And, with that, he brought the tip of the knife to within an inch of Patricia's nose, then casually rotated the blade and lay one of the flat sides across her right cheek. When it touched her skin, it was as if she'd been jolted by electricity. Though her entire body was now quaking, she fought to keep her head as still as possible.

The man leaned forward and peered, unblinking, into her eyes. "Do you understand how serious I am?"

"Yes," she said, immediately, the rattling of her chest causing the word to come out in multiple syllables.

The man turned to her mother. "Mrs. Gale?"

There was no response. With the knife still laying against her cheek, Patricia did not dare move her head. She turned her eyes sideways, straining. She couldn't see her mother's face, only her left hand on the arm of the recliner, fingers digging into the worn surface.

"Mother," Patricia pleaded.

"I... I," came a faint reply, "I understand."

"Good," the man said finally, and, to Patricia's relief, he pulled the knife away from her face. "Now, here's the story, and you will repeat this to anyone who asks. This, and nothing else. Got it?"

Patricia nodded quickly. The man turned his attention to her mother. "Mrs. Gale?"

Patricia again looked at her mother. The woman's ashen face could have been chiseled from marble, it was so still. But, after a second, her head bobbed in a jerky fashion.

"Mason distinguished himself in Vietnam," the man said, calmly. "When he returned from his tour of duty, he went back to school at the University of Minnesota, where he earned his masters degree and, eventually, a doctorate in geology. He's been working for the last few years in California. You haven't seen him much, because he travels a lot and tends to immerse himself in his work. But he's a fine man, and you know he'll make a wonderful astronaut."

He was silent for several seconds, considering them. No one spoke. The room was still, the only movement the slow rotation of the knife in the man's hands.

Finally, he said, in a quiet voice, "Do you understand?"

"Yes," Patricia said, her eyes on the blade, gleaming as it caught and reflected the lights in the room. "Yes," her mother repeated weakly.

The man nodded. "Good, because if you deviate from that story or volunteer any information about Mason that does not square completely with what I've just told you, then I will come back here," he raised the knife, "and I will start cutting pieces off of your bodies."

With one last flourish, the man nonchalantly reached his hand up behind his head and returned the knife to wherever he normally kept it. Patricia slumped on the couch, as if all of the strength had been sucked out of her. The man slapped his thighs, raised his head and took a deep breath. He glanced over at the man named Johnson. "Have we done everything we came here to do?" The other nodded. He looked at the man by the front door, who also nodded.

"Ok," he said, and he made as if to stand. But then he stopped and raised a hand, one finger extended. "You know," he said, adopting a pensive look, "it might be a good idea if we really hammered this one home." He looked back at the man named Johnson. "Don't you think?" The other affected an exaggerated look of thoughtfulness and nodded his head.

"I think so too," the man said. He again reached up behind his head and drew out the knife. Gripping it lightly, he casually flipped it in the air in front of him, catching the handle as it came around, this time with thumb and forefinger near the back, and, all in the same motion, he violently slammed the point of the blade down into the arm of the recliner, right at the spot where her mother gripped the leather.

Patricia screamed. Shaking, she stared in horror at the hideous thing, buried to the hilt in her mother's hand, knowing the blood would follow. But, to her surprise, there was none. Through tears, she peered closer. The knife, she suddenly realized, had not gone through the hand. Somehow, the man had managed to drive the blade between her mother's second and third fingers, missing flesh by millimeters. Relief battled with terror. She looked up at her mother. The woman had fainted.

With a grim smile, the man yanked the knife out of the chair. He lowered his chin and gave her one last look through dark eyes. "I'll be watching you."

#

Patricia Gale shuddered and sharply drew a quick breath. She fell silent and there was a sad distance to her eyes.

Nate looked at Matt and Peter. Neither of them seemed anxious to speak. He dropped his eyes to the table and studied his hands, which were wrapped around the coffee cup. After a long moment, he said, softly, "I'm sorry."

It seemed to rouse her. She gave him a quick look and a slight nod.

"Did you hear from Mason after that?" Matt asked.

She snorted. "He never tried to contact us. We did see him though. I mean, other than on the television. Once. It was the same time I met your father. They invited us to the space center in Florida. It was a big to do. Lots of people were there. Including," she said, with another shudder, "the man named Arthur Spelling. He was standing off to the side. There was no mistaking why he was there.

"It was the strangest thing," she continued. "Mason acted like there was absolutely nothing out of the ordinary going on. I've never known what to make of that. I'd like to believe they were forcing him to do things he didn't want to do. That he was as much a victim as we were. But it sure didn't seem like it.

"And the way he went on, as if he really was a doctor? Come on. He was always smart, but not doctor smart. He was the kind of guy who was just smart enough to get out of doing things. You know what I mean?"

She shook her head. "I loved my brother, sort of. But I've never been able to accept any of it." She opened her mouth to say more, but then, apparently changing her mind, she remained silent.

After a moment, she laughed, but it was a bitter laugh. "How does that happen, anyway? One day, he's dead. The next day he's alive?"

Peter looked at Matt. "Yeah, how does that happen?"

Matt turned to Patricia. "Did you ever tell anyone this story before?"

She shook her head adamantly. "Never. We were so afraid." She looked down at the table. "After the, you know, tragedy, we got a package in the mail. It was supposed to be perishable items. 'Open immediately,' it said. So we did."

She paused, a bleak expression on her face. "Inside was a human finger. It was disgusting. And it was so frightening. We," she hesitated, "we threw it away." She looked embarrassed.

"So, no, we kept our mouths shut. The press tried to get us to talk, but we wouldn't. They called us 'very private.' And, after a while, they just left us alone.

"I thought it was all over, and then," she paused, looking between Matt and Peter. "And then you called," she said to Peter. "Or you," she said, looking at Matt.

Matt held up a finger, then pointed it at Peter.

Peter looked suddenly embarrassed. "I'm sorry," he said. "I had no idea."

There was an awkward silence. Matt asked, "Do you still have that picture?"

For the first time since they'd met, Nate saw the fleeting hint of a smile on Patricia Gale's face, though it did not reach her eyes. She nodded. "I do. Something told me I should hang on to it. Just in case. And I did. For all these years."

"I wouldn't mind seeing that," Matt said.

With the vestige of a humorless smile still playing on her face, Patricia reached around and pulled her handbag from the back of her chair, where she'd hung it when they sat down. She opened it, reached in and unsnapped an interior pocket. She pulled from the pocket an envelope that appeared to have at one time been white, but had yellowed with age.

"I haven't looked at this in at least thirty years," she said. "But, for reasons I don't think I can explain, I've always had it with me."

She handed the envelope to Matt. He lifted back the flap, slid out the small snapshot and scrutinized it carefully. After a moment, he said quietly, "I'll be damned." He looked up at Nate. "I know this guy."

6

Ozaki pulled the car up in front of the Gale house, and Raen and Dacoff, wearing suits and carrying briefcases, emerged and walked to the front door. To anyone observing them, they would have appeared to be lawyers or accountants, likely visiting the Gale women to review their wills or estate plans.

They knew from the surveillance team that the older of the two women was home alone. Patricia Gale had taken the car and left an hour earlier.

At the front door, Raen set down his briefcase and made a show of knocking with his right hand. His left hand, shielded by his body from the view of anyone who might be watching, slipped the duplicate key into the lock. He pushed the door open and went through a pantomime of speaking to someone just inside, introducing his colleague. Then, looking to all the world as though the two had been asked to enter, Raen picked up his briefcase and walked in, followed by Dacoff. They closed the door and locked it behind them.

The old woman, Raen knew, was in her bedroom. She hadn't left it for the past two days. He walked quietly down the hallway, slipping on a pair of silk gloves as he did. When he entered the room, he found the woman sitting in bed, propped up by a pair of pillows. It took her a moment to register the fact that he was there. Then her eyes, rheumy and heavily lidded, flew open.

He walked over to the bed and casually took a seat next to her. She began to shake. He reached his left hand across his body and placed it over her hands, which were folded in her lap on top of the blanket. In a soothing voice, he said, "Excuse me, but there's something that I need to do."

To his amusement, the woman actually relaxed.

He reached his right hand up, placed the palm over her mouth, and, with his thumb and forefinger, squeezed her nostrils shut, cutting off her air. Impossibly, her eyes opened even wider, and she began to thrash weakly. He roughly shoved her head back against the tall headboard pinning it in place, and he held her hands in her lap.

A long minute passed.

Two minutes.

As she twitched, he leaned in closer, studying her. The pain and the terror that mingled in her eyes were delicious. He felt himself becoming aroused. This was the best part, when the victim knew, with no uncertainty, that death was coming. And it would be capped by that perfect moment, the microsecond just before life ended, when the woman would effectively be dead, but still just alive enough to know it.

He waited patiently as her struggles began to wane, staring into her eyes without blinking, not wanting to miss the precise instant. She spasmed one last time, then her pupils dilated and her corneas glassed over. He continued staring well after the moment, looking for something he knew had to be there, some eternal truth that could only be gleaned in this glorious passage from life to death.

Finally, he took a deep breath and released his grip. She was now just a corpse. He'd wrung out as much as possible. And it had been good. But, still, he longed for more.

He knew it would be coming through the front door shortly.

He left the body slumped in the bed and rejoined Dacoff, who had retrieved the listening devices and the tap on the phone. There was a comfortable recliner in the living room, the well-worn leather marred only by a patch on the left arm that didn't quite match the rest of the chair. Raen took a seat, crossed his legs and settled in for the wait.

It didn't take long. His cell phone buzzed softly. It was Ozaki. He put the device up to his ear and heard the one word message.

"Jericho."

He was out of the chair in an instant, repeating the word for Dacoff, who also reacted immediately. They cleared the back door in less than four seconds and scaled the fence at the rear of the yard in under seven. The property behind the Gale house had an overgrown backyard and appeared vacant. A simple latch on a chain link gate to one side afforded them access to the street beyond, and they hit the curb just as Ozaki pulled up. They threw in their briefcases, their bodies followed. They were still closing the car doors behind themselves as Ozaki sped away.

#

From their spot a block and a half down the street, Nate, Peter and Matt watched quietly as police officers and other official looking people came and went. Their worst suspicions had been confirmed when the coroner's vehicle had arrived. At that point, Patricia Gale had curled into a fetal position in a corner of the back seat. She remained there now. She had not spoken.

"We should go," Matt said. "We risk drawing attention. And," he added with some obvious discomfort, "there's nothing we can do here now."

Knowing that the house was under surveillance and concerned that whoever was after them might have already arrived, Matt had placed an anonymous call to the police department from a pay phone at the shopping center before they had started back. He'd reported hearing some disturbing sounds, including a scream, coming from the Gale house. The intent had been to flush out anyone who might have been lying in wait. Their hope had been that Eunice Gale would have simply been surprised to find a patrol officer at her doorstep and told him that all was fine.

And that would have been that.

They would have retrieved the white compact Nate had driven back from the shopping center and parked a block away. Patricia Gale would have driven home, picked up her mother and taken her back to the shopping center, where Matt had devised a plan to lose anyone who might be tailing them.

But the police officers who'd responded to the call had not gotten anyone to come to the door. One of them had finally gone around to the back of the house, where he obviously gained entry, because a minute later he appeared at the front door. And then it became apparent that they were too late to save Patricia's mother.

From the back seat, Peter asked, "Tell me again why we don't just talk to the police? Let them know what's going on?"

Matt shook his head. "The people we're dealing with are too sophisticated for the police. And too connected. We'd actually be putting ourselves in jeopardy."

"And you think we're better able to deal with them? On our own?"

"Well," Matt said slowly, "in a word, yes."

Peter turned to Nate. "What does he think he is, some kind of super secret agent?"

Nate shrugged. "Something like that."

Peter looked from Nate to Matt, a dubious expression on his face. Finally, he sat back. "Ok, Batman, where to now?"

Matt smiled grimly as he started the engine. "That," he said, "is a good question." He glanced at Nate. "You got any ideas?"

#

In a driving rain, they crossed over a narrow causeway onto Mount Desert Island and followed the signs directing them to the town of Bar Harbor. Nate, Matt and Peter had each taken turns at the wheel, and they'd made the drive from Minneapolis in just under thirty hours.

Nate had found driving the SUV an interesting experience. It had plenty of power and was reasonably nimble. But it felt heavy as a tank. When Nate queried Matt about it, Matt simply shrugged and said, "I made a few modifications."

Peter never mentioned anything about it.

North of Chicago, they took a short detour and visited a bank less than a mile from O'Hare Airport, where Matt maintained one of what he called his "safe drops." Matt spent twenty minutes in the bank and emerged with a small satchel containing, he explained, "a few things that might come in handy." Apparently, one of those "things" was a substantial amount of cash, which they'd used to the exclusion of credit cards on their cross-country journey.

They stopped for a few hours at a motel outside Syracuse, New York. Before resuming the drive in the morning, Peter and Nate walked to a nearby copy store, where Peter was able to print out from his laptop the research he'd accumulated for his Apollo 18 project, including the voluminous documentation he'd obtained in response to the Freedom of Information request.

When he wasn't taking his turn at the wheel, Nate had begun a review of Peter's research. By the time they reached the craggy coast of Maine, he'd made a substantial dent in the paperwork, but he'd yet to find anything he considered particularly noteworthy.

When they'd left Minneapolis, they'd been unsure of their next step, knowing only that they needed time to digest what they'd learned and to formulate a plan of action. It was Peter who suggested they pay a visit to the home of the third member of the Apollo 18 crew, Steve Dayton. Neither Nate nor Matt thought there was much likelihood they'd learn anything of value there, but they liked the idea of getting away to a relatively remote place, and they decided that, in any event, Dayton's survivors had a right to know what they'd discovered.

Dayton's widow, Peter explained, had passed away six years earlier, a victim of breast cancer. His only child, a daughter named Margaret, who'd been an infant when Dayton died, had returned to care for her mother when the cancer spread so much that she couldn't care for herself. Margaret now lived in the home that had apparently been in the Dayton family for generations.

Though Margaret Dayton would have been too young to have any memory of her father or the events surrounding the Apollo 18 tragedy, Peter informed them that he had nevertheless intended to contact her at some point to talk to her about her mother and the years following the loss of her father. He just hadn't yet gotten to that point.

Out of an abundance of caution, they'd made no attempt to warn the young woman they were coming.

Patricia Gale had seemed to shrink into herself. She said very little during the trip and did not have much of an appetite the few times they stopped to get a bite to eat. At one point she offered to drive, but it was a half-hearted effort, and Nate and his brothers immediately declined, suggesting that she take it easy. She'd not put up a fight.

When they reached Bar Harbor, Matt spent several minutes casually steering the car up and down the water-logged streets of the small seaside town as the rain pelted them. He drove at a leisurely pace, his eyes nevertheless watchful. Nate found himself staring suspiciously at every parked vehicle. Finally, Matt said quietly, "I don't see anything that jumps out at me."

Not realizing he'd been holding it, Nate released a lungful of air and took another steadying breath. "Ok, let's do it."

They drove back up Main, the wipers working overtime, and Matt turned down one of the small side streets they'd been on a few minutes earlier, pulling up in front of a tiny wooden building with a weather-beaten sign on the side advertising "Dixon's Wharf." It was the only address they had for Margaret Dayton.

Matt turned the car around and parked it across the street from the building, facing back in the direction from which they'd come. Nate didn't need to ask why. Matt gave him a sober look and nodded. Nate zipped up his jacket and glanced back at Peter, who also nodded. Next to him, Patricia Gale seemed to have rallied. She was sitting up and alert. In her lap, Buster panted softly, his tongue lolling out to one side.

Nate slipped out of the SUV, and, lowering his head against the downpour, crossed the street and made his way around to the opposite side of the building, facing the ocean. He opened the front door and entered.

The small vestibule just inside the door was separated from the rest of the space by a narrow counter, behind which an older man sat on a tall stool, a lit pipe clenched in his teeth. In one hand he held a dog-eared paperback book. With the other, he was in the process of turning a page. He appeared to be the only person in the place.

The man glanced up as Nate entered, appraising him with a look of mild curiosity. Then he slowly folded over a corner of the page he'd just turned, set the book down on the counter, and pulled the pipe from his mouth, expelling a cloud of smoke. "Can I help you?" he asked with a thick Maine accent.

"I'm looking for someone."

"Ayeah?" the man said, making a show of peering around. "If he's here, he sure is quiet."

"It's not a he. I'm looking for Margaret Dayton."

"Ah, then you'll be waitin' on the *Sarah Lynne*. Should be in soon. You a buyer?"

"I beg your pardon?"

The man studied Nate for a moment. Then he said, "You're not here for lobster, are you?"

"No," Nate said. "Just looking for Ms. Dayton."

The man took another puff from the pipe, then said casually, "Well, you're in luck." He tilted his head toward the window. "Here she comes."

Nate turned and peered back out the window in the indicated direction. Beyond the wooden jetty that jutted out into the harbor, all he could see was flat gray water and slanting rain. Then, as he watched, a boat materialized out of the mist, headed for a spot near the end of the pier.

"If you're of a mind," the man said from behind him, "you might want to go out and help tie her up. That is, of course," he added, "if you don't mind getting a little wet."

There seemed to be an almost playful challenge in the statement. Nate looked back at the man. He'd set the stem of the pipe back between his teeth and sat casually regarding Nate, crinkles at the corners of his eyes.

Despite the tension he was feeling, Nate found himself chuckling. "All right," he said, pulling the zipper of his jacket up the last inch and turning up the collar. "I will."

If anything, the rain was coming down harder as Nate walked out the short pier. He reached the end just as the boat did, her captain easing her up against a series of fenders wrapped in rope and mounted on the side of the dock. Though Nate knew next to nothing about boats, he realized that this one was a fishing vessel of some kind. Probably lobster, he thought, remembering the man's comment. To the side of the bow, just below the gunwale, was the name "Sarah Lynne." About a third of the way down the length of the boat, a wheelhouse spanned the width of the vessel. In it, Nate saw a solitary figure standing behind water-streaked glass. Aft of the wheelhouse, the deck was open.

"Here," he heard a woman's voice call out over the sound of the rain. The captain had stepped out of the wheelhouse and was holding a length of rope. She tossed the rope to him, and he caught it instinctively. "Tie us off up there," she shouted, pointing to a short vertical post sticking up from the surface of the pier. "I'll get the one back here," and, with a nimble motion, she jumped from the boat onto the slick dock, holding the end of a second line.

Uncertain exactly what he should do, Nate looped the end of the rope around the post a couple times and tied what he hoped was an acceptable knot. Then he straightened and watched as the woman tied off the rear line, turned and walked toward him in the downpour.

On her head, she wore a hat with a wide brim that caught the rain and directed it off her shoulders and back. A faded yellow rain slicker topped baggy overalls. A pair of black boots completed the ensemble.

Her hair was a vivid scarlet that stood out against the yellow of her rain gear. Pulled back and tied behind her with a piece of blue cloth, it fell in a long wavy pony tail midway down her back. When she reached him, he saw that a light sprinkling of freckles dotted her nose and the tops of two prominent check bones. She sported an easy smile, her teeth impossibly white. But, for Nate, what really stood out were her eyes. They were an extraordinary emerald green, and the contrast with her red hair was mesmerizing. She planted herself in front of him, oblivious to the rain, and considered him.

Nate was suddenly at a loss for words.

After a moment, she looked behind him at the mess of a knot he'd managed to tie on the bollard and laughed. He felt his face flush, and it drew another chuckle. Laughter, he noticed, seemed to come easy to her.

"Oh, don't take it the wrong way," she said. "I think it's cute."

She stepped around him, leaned down, took a firm grip on the mooring line and pulled it toward herself, creating slack. Undoing the knot, she re-tied it in a practiced motion, then turned and gave him a frank look. "So, now that we've established you have no nautical background, maybe you can tell me who you are and what you're doing here. You don't look like a tourist."

Despite his embarrassment, he smiled. The rain was soaking through his clothes, but he no longer cared. "You don't know me. We've never met. But our fathers knew each other."

"Really. How?"

He swallowed, then took a deep breath. "They served together. On the Apollo 18 mission."

She looked startled. Then she studied him more carefully. After a long moment, she asked, "Are you Nate?"

Surprised, he nodded.

She smiled, but it came with a touch of melancholy. "My mother thought the world of your father. Apparently, so did my dad." She paused, and there was a momentary distance to her eyes. "She told me once, Honey, if you're ever in a real pickle, track down Bob Cartwright's boys. Start with Nate."

That also surprised him. And it pleased him. A lot. He wasn't sure what to say in response, though, and there was an awkward silence. Finally, he ventured, "So, you never found yourself in a real pickle?"

She laughed at that. "Oh, I've had my share." She shrugged. "I guess maybe I wanted to hang onto that ace."

That pleased him as well, and he realized that something about this woman made him feel like he'd never felt before. He also realized with a start that he'd forgotten about the beeper in his pocket. Fortunately, it had not gone off.

"You seem a bit distracted."

He hesitated. "There's something going on that you should know about."

She looked at his eyes, alternating from one to the other. Nate had the odd feeling that she was trying to read his mind. After several seconds she said, "Looks like *you* might be the one in a pickle, huh?"

Again, he nodded. "It's kind of a long story."

She smiled. "I've got time. And you look like you could stand to dry off."

#

Krantz passed through the metal detector at the main entrance to the Russell Senate Office Building, retrieved his folio from the adjacent conveyor belt, and stepped into the rotunda. It was an impressive space, encircled by Corinthian columns and topped by a coffered dome. A glazed oculus in the center of the dome flooded the area with a natural light. On the far side, a small group of tourists congregated around the statue of Richard B. Russell, Jr., the building's namesake, while listening to a uniformed tour guide give a brief history. The space teemed with men and women in business attire coming and going.

Old habits dying hard, it required him only a couple of seconds to take it all in and register that there were no apparent threats. He turned and made his way to the elevators. Though he was running a couple of minutes late, he did not rush. He was in no hurry to meet with the man he'd come to see. And the man, he knew, would wait. There were very few people in the world the man *would* wait for. But Krantz was one of them.

His appointment today was with Harrison Burton, the senior senator from North Dakota and one of the most powerful men in the world.

Burton had first been elected to Congress in 1958, at the astonishingly young age of 28. He'd been re-elected five times and had been serving as Minority Whip when he was appointed Secretary of Defense by President Nixon, becoming the youngest man ever to hold such position. Then, when the junior senator from North Dakota died in a plane crash three years later, Burton had been appointed by the governor to complete the senator's term. He'd distinguished himself immediately, securing a position on the powerful Senate Armed Services Committee and chairmanship of the key Subcommittee on Strategic Forces. He'd eventually become the ranking member of the entire Committee. He had now been in the senate for almost four decades.

At times referred to as the "Rasputin of the Senate," he was respected - and feared - by almost everyone in Washington. It was said that Burton could make or break the political career of any man or woman. Because no one knew for certain how true that was, people, as a consequence, tended to walk on eggshells around him. Krantz was one of a handful of people who knew, without question, that the concerns were very well-founded.

In his position as chairman of the Subcommittee on Strategic Forces, Burton had stepped into the role of primary political overseer of The Organization. When he'd assumed chairmanship of the entire Armed Services Committee, he'd retained that oversight role. In those subsequent years when the Republicans were not in the majority, he'd shared it with the ranking Democratic Senator. When they were, however, he'd kept it for himself. He was no one to be trifled with, and The Organization was one of the most powerful weapons in his quiver.

At the large suite of rooms occupied by Burton's staff on the fourth floor, Krantz was escorted to the Senator's private office, a space dominated by windows that looked out across Constitution Avenue to the grounds separating the Capitol Building and the Supreme Court. It was, particularly by the standards applicable to government offices, an immense space. Krantz recalled being told that the room was several square feet larger than the oval office, a source of considerable pride for Burton.

The place practically oozed red, white and blue. Oversized American and North Dakota flags flanked the Senator's desk. The walls and most horizontal surfaces were festooned with military memorabilia. They included photographs, paintings and models of warships, aircraft and other combat hardware. Though he'd always kept it to himself, it was a continual source of amusement for Krantz the way Burton carried on about the armed forces. The Senator, Krantz knew, hadn't spent a single day in uniform, and he doubted whether the man would know the difference between a canteen and a claymore.

Burton gave Krantz a cursory handshake when the latter was shown into the office. There was no bonhomie in the Senator's makeup. He wore a perpetual scowl, and, even though Krantz had spent a lifetime exploring some of the darker sides of humanity, when he was in Burton's presence, he felt as if he'd stepped into a chilly version of hell on earth. To his knowledge, the Senator had no friends. He knew that, somewhat inconceivably, the man had been married for several decades. Though Krantz had never met the late Mrs. Burton, he suspected that, when she'd passed away a few years earlier, it had probably been a huge relief for both husband and wife.

Burton waved Krantz to a chair near one of the windows and took a seat nearby. There was no small talk and no preamble.

"I understand one of your former field operatives has taken a shit in the punchbowl."

Working hard to keep the irritation out of his voice, Krantz said, "Yes. We did such a good job wiping the man's former life clean we didn't realize he was one of Bob Cartwright's sons until we were in the middle of the operation."

"Somebody dropped the ball letting him in The Organization in the first place," the Senator observed.

That was true enough. Krantz was thankful he'd been in the field when that little screw-up had happened. Still, as the director, he'd now catch the heat. He nodded, but said nothing.

The Senator's scowl deepened. "This is the same guy who opened up that can of worms after the Miami hit. I was told that had been taken care of."

"It was," Krantz replied, evenly. "We had no reason to believe he'd do anything other than spend a quiet retirement. And, as I said, we hadn't made the connection with the Apollo thing."

"Well that was a pretty significant omission, don't you think?"

That was also true. And, though he wasn't about to admit it to Burton, Krantz held himself responsible. He'd assigned men to deal with the Cartwrights, but he'd never personally consulted the file on Peter Cartwright. If he had, he'd have immediately noticed the resemblance to Marek. Krantz, after all, was one of the few who had served with the man and knew what he looked like. It wasn't until they were well into the mission - and had already lost the trail - that he'd stumbled onto it. He was still kicking himself for that. However, since there was nothing to be gained by raising any of it now, Krantz again just nodded and kept quiet.

The Senator looked away for a moment, clearly annoyed. Still studying something on the other side of the room, he asked, "What are we doing about it?"

"We've refocused the mission," Krantz said. "It's no longer a containment. We're eliminating the players."

Burton gave him a hard look. "Are any of them veterans? You know how I feel about our veterans. And you know everything that entails."

Krantz understood completely. "Well, technically, our guy," he replied. "But that can't be helped. He's the dangerous one."

"I agree with that," said Burton. "The rest are civilians. Expendable. Ok." He stood, signaling that their meeting was at an end.

As Krantz stood, the Senator gave him one more piercing look. "Sooner rather than later," he said, his eyes narrowing. "Otherwise, you know what has to be done. And I would just personally hate to see that. Do you follow me?"

One last time, Krantz nodded. He did.

7

When Nate came downstairs in the morning, he found Patricia Gale already up, standing at the stove when he entered the kitchen.

"Morning," he said.

She turned her head slightly and, with more animation than she'd displayed in the short time he'd known her, she replied, "Good morning, Nate."

Nate wasn't sure whether it was the sleep he'd gotten, Patricia's good nature or the delightful smells that engulfed him, but he suddenly felt more alive than he had in days.

"How do you take your coffee?" Patricia had turned and was holding out a mug. He could see steam rising from the top.

Surprised, he replied, "Black."

She set the mug down on the table in the center of the room. "Why don't you take a seat? I'm making breakfast."

Shaking his head, Nate dutifully sat and took a sip of the coffee. It tasted wonderful.

They were in the Dayton home, a large, rambling two-story structure that sat alone at the end of a narrow spit of land jutting out into Frenchman Bay, a few miles outside of town. The previous afternoon, they'd made the drive to the house in the rain, Margaret Dayton leading the way in her pickup truck. Margaret, who, it turned out, went by Maggie, had refused to let Nate even begin to explain why he had suddenly shown up in Maine with his brothers and Mason Gale's sister in tow until he'd had a chance to get into some dry clothes. When they arrived at the house, she showed him to one of several rooms on the second floor and returned shortly with a change of clothes that fit remarkably well.

As the gray, dreary day settled into night, they'd all gathered in the great room on the first floor in front of a fire that Maggie had lit in the large fireplace. Nate then told how he, Peter and Buster had come to make the three-day journey across country from Los Angeles to Bar Harbor, picking up Matt and Patricia along the way. Maggie and her great uncle Tim, the man Nate had met briefly that afternoon at Dixon's Wharf, had listened in rapt attention. Maggie was visibly distraught when she heard about the horrific scene in Nate's condo and the story Patricia told them about her encounter with the dark-eyed man. When she heard about Eunice Gale's death, Maggie quietly got up from the sofa, crossed the room and embraced Patricia.

After he finished, the six of them sat in silence for a long time, the crackling of the logs in the fireplace the only sound. Finally, Maggie announced, "I think you've all been through a lot, and you could stand a good night's sleep. Tim and I have to be up before dawn tomorrow, so we need to turn in. Please make yourselves at home, and we'll be back in the afternoon."

And, with that, they'd all retired to separate rooms, and Nate *had* finally gotten a good night's sleep.

As Nate was sipping his coffee, Peter walked into the kitchen and paused, apparently as taken with the marvelous smells as Nate had been. Patricia turned with another mug of coffee in her hand, but she stood and appraised him without speaking. Peter looked from Nate to Patricia and back. Finally, he cocked his eyebrows.

"Peter," said Patricia. "Good morning."

Nate chuckled. It had been a long time since he'd watched people struggle with the difficult task of telling Peter and Matt apart. Nate had never had any problem with it, but, aside from Gamma and their father, nobody else had ever been able to distinguish one from the other with any consistency.

Patricia handed the coffee to Peter and waved him to a seat at the table across from Nate. As Peter pulled back the chair and sat, he gave Nate an inquiring look. Nate shrugged.

"It's nice of you to make breakfast," Nate ventured.

"Oh, it's nothing," Patricia said. "I found the ingredients and figured I ought to do something to contribute." She set the spatula she'd been using aside, lifted a pair of plates and laid them down in front of Nate and Peter. Each contained a stack of pancakes, golden brown and fluffy. From a carafe on the table, Nate poured some maple syrup over them and, when he took a bite, discovered they tasted as good as they looked. He and Peter dug into the meal as if it were their first in days.

As they were finishing, Patricia took a seat at the end of the table and folded her hands in front of her. Quietly, she asked, "So, what are we going to do?"

It was a question Nate had been struggling with himself. And he'd yet to find a satisfactory answer. After a moment he said, "I think we need to talk about that when Matt gets up."

"I'm up."

Nate glanced reflexively toward the doorway and was startled to see Matt standing just inside. He'd made no sound entering.

"How do you do that?" Nate asked.

Matt simply shrugged. Then he took a seat at the end of the table opposite Patricia, folded his own hands and gave Nate a level look. "I'm open to suggestions."

Nate noticed Patricia looking from Matt to Peter with undisguised curiosity. It was certainly understandable. When they weren't speaking or gesturing, each appeared to be the mirror image of the other. But, Nate saw, there was more than just curiosity in Patricia's gaze. Something about them clearly troubled her.

He turned his attention to his brothers. Though they were sitting only a few feet apart, neither acted as if the other were present. He asked himself whether that had been the case since they'd gotten together in Idaho a couple days before, and he knew the answer even as he posed the question. Not at every moment, perhaps, but for the most part it had. It was just that they'd all been under so much stress, he hadn't focused on it.

He felt a stab of guilt. He would have to address it, he told himself. He wasn't sure how, but he knew that he would. First, however, they had the problem of dealing with people who were trying to kill them.

He glanced at Patricia. "I need to finish reviewing Peter's research. Maybe there's nothing there, but I won't know until I do. For that, I'll need a few hours of quiet time. Then," he said, refocusing on Matt and returning his look with a level one of his own, "we need a plan to deal with your former..." and he paused, searching for the right word. Finally, he settled on "acquaintances."

Matt nodded. "I'm working on that."

"Well," Peter said, sliding his chair back and standing. "I'll go get the documents. Thank you, Patricia," he added, giving her a tight smile. He nodded briefly to Nate, then left the room without a glance at Matt.

After he was gone, the three of them sat quietly for a minute. Finally, Patricia cleared her throat. "How did you know that man in the picture?" She was looking at Matt. This time, Nate could not decipher her expression.

Matt, it appeared to Nate, seemed almost to wince. He studied his folded hands for several seconds. Then he raised his eyes, met Patricia's gaze, and said, simply, "We worked for the same company."

Patricia blinked a couple of times, then looked away. Without turning back, she asked, "Doing the same kinds of things?"

Matt didn't answer right away. Patricia returned her attention to him, and they stared at each other. Then Matt nodded and said in a quiet voice, "And worse."

She nodded slowly, her expression not changing. "At some point you stopped."

"I did."

She continued nodding. They sat in awkward silence, Nate searching for something to say that would lighten the mood. Finally, Patricia rose and stepped over to the stove. A moment later, she returned with a cup of coffee and a plate of pancakes. Without a word, she placed both in front of Matt. Then she turned and walked out of the kitchen.

Matt looked at Nate. His face was stoic, but Nate could see a profound sadness in his brother's eyes.

#

Raen was frustrated.

Five days had passed since they'd lost contact with the Cartwrights. It was as if the three of them had dropped off the face of the planet. Worse, they had apparently hooked up with the other Gale woman. Her car had been found a block away from her home, but there was no sign of her. Raen wasn't sure what that portended, but he knew it couldn't be good, given the fact that The Organization had gone to great lengths to keep them from talking to one another.

The responses from headquarters to his reports over the past few days had been consistent. And insistent. Find them. Terminate them.

The coroner had determined that Eunice Gale's death had been by asphyxiation, and the police also suspected foul play in the disappearance of Patricia Gale. A full alert had gone out to all law enforcement agencies. Thanks to The Organization's influence, Nathaniel and Peter Cartwright were wanted for questioning. So far, however, there had been no reliable leads.

Raen set down the latest batch of reports and leaned back in his chair. He was in the command center they'd set up at a Marriott near the Minneapolis - St. Paul International Airport. He'd now been in one place for three days. He was bored. He was restless.

And he was frustrated.

He cleared his mind and started from the beginning. He'd originally been tasked with ensuring that Peter Cartwright drop any further attempts to contact Eunice and Patricia Gale or to investigate Apollo 18. Therefore, obviously, there was a connection between the Cartwrights and the Gales. And it had something to do with a tragedy that had occurred while Raen was still in diapers. When the assignment had been given to him, of course, he'd inquired about it. But he was politely informed that it was none of his damn business, and he knew better than to push it. Still, there had to be something there. After a couple of minutes, he stood and crossed the room. One of the operatives attached to his action team was at a computer, scanning police reports. He tapped the man on his shoulder and gestured for him to get up. The man nodded and immediately relinquished his seat.

Raen sat and minimized the program in which his operative had been working. He called up the internet, opened a public search engine and typed in "Apollo 18." There were numerous hits. He selected one at random and opened it. He immediately saw two names that he recognized.

Bob Cartwright and Mason Gale had been two of the three Apollo 18 astronauts. That was interesting. He had no idea what it meant, but it was still interesting. He focused on the name of the third astronaut, Steve Dayton, and stared at it for several seconds. Then he looked up and motioned to the operative whose seat he had taken. The man, who was standing discretely a few feet away, stepped over. Raen tapped the screen.

"I want a full dossier on this man and all living relatives. And I want it yesterday."

He had the report in less than an hour.

Steve Dayton had been an only child. His parents were dead. He had one living uncle on his father's side, Timothy Dayton. He'd married, but his wife had died six years earlier. They'd had one child, Margaret Dayton.

Raen finished scanning the file, then he went back and carefully read through it a second time. He set it aside and thought for a moment, before standing and walking to the door that led to another of the rooms in the suite. Dacoff was seated at a table just inside. He had on a set of headphones, and he was hunched over, making notes. The movement in the doorway caught his attention, and he glanced up, pushing the speaker off one of his ears.

"Find Ozaki," Raen said, "and tell him we leave in ten minutes."

"Oh yeah?" Dacoff asked, with interest. "Where are we going?"

Raen was already on the move, and he tossed the one word answer back over his shoulder.

"Maine."

#

The *Sarah Lynne* lifted and dropped in the gentle swells, and, for a moment, a breeze carried away the stench wafting from the bait tank and, in its place, came a salty ocean redolence. While the bright mid-day sun didn't provide much warmth, it was a pleasant change from the rain and dreariness of the past two days.

Nate closed his eyes and breathed in the salt air. He'd spent most of the previous day poring over the papers that Peter had assembled. He still had a ways to go before he'd be through them, but he'd needed a break, and this, it had turned out, was the perfect change of pace.

Maggie's regular stern man, a fellow named Eddie, had developed a case of adult mumps a few days earlier, leaving Maggie shorthanded for one of the most important stretches in the lobster fishing season. Her Uncle Tim, who had been a lobster man for decades, and whose former license and boat she'd inherited after her mother passed away, suffered from arthritis in his hands and legs, so he was not able to give her a full day's worth of work. The traps, however, needed to be emptied and refreshed, so he'd

107

been doing his best to try to fill in. When Nate learned this, he offered to come along with them the next day and help, and Maggie and Tim had readily taken him up on the suggestion.

They'd started out early that morning, before daybreak. Maggie piloted the *Sarah Lynne* up the coast as the sun was rising, and they began hauling traps. Nate watched Tim for a while and discovered that the procedure was relatively simple. The locations of traps were marked by buoys painted in the unique colors associated with their owners' licenses. The Dayton buoys were blue with an almost fluorescent orange stripe near the top. Maggie steered the boat up to each buoy, and either she or Tim gaffed it using a long hooked pole, then pulled it up into the boat. Maggie attached the line leading off the buoy to a winch called the pot hauler, and a series of traps were pulled up from the bottom of the ocean, one at a time.

As each trap was brought up, it was positioned on the narrow shelf that ran along the starboard gunwale. While Tim emptied the trap, Maggie hauled the next on the line, so that it was ready when Tim finished. Tim opened the trap by releasing a hinged handle, and he retrieved any lobsters that had been lured in by the bait. Only lobsters of a certain size were retained. If they were too small or too large, they were tossed back into the water, the smaller ones to continue growing and the larger ones to serve as breeding stock, thereby, Nate was informed, ensuring the continued viability of the fishing grounds. If there was any question, Tim used a metal device called a lobster gauge that was notched on one side to show the minimum acceptable size and on the other to show the maximum.

The lobsters had immense claws, and the first time Tim reached into a trap with his bare hands to retrieve one of the creatures, Nate cringed. Tim had been doing it for so long, however, it came as second nature to him. He would grip the lobster by its back, lift it out, measure it if its size was in doubt, then either return the lobster to the sea or toss it into a large container in the center of the boat.

One of the lobsters they caught turned out to be a female bearing eggs attached along the underside of her body. Using a crimping tool, Tim made a small notch in the lobster's tail, a defect, he told Nate, that would forever save her from being taken, and he threw her back in the water. When he was done sorting through the catch in each trap, Tim replaced the mesh bag with a fresh set of bait, a foul concoction of fish consisting mostly of herring. Then he re-attached the lid and tossed the trap back into the water. Tim and Maggie developed a rhythm, so that, just as Tim was finishing with one trap, another would slide into place.

After watching Tim handle several traps, Nate felt that he had the hang of it, and he switched places with the older man. Not willing to put his bare hand into the traps, Nate wore a pair of gloves Maggie had given him. Even so, the first lobster he pulled out had been an adventure. In almost no time, however, he found himself confidently reaching in and gripping the squirming crustaceans. Tim had looked on for a while, making pointers. Then he'd thumped Nate on the shoulder and made his way to the back of the boat where he leaned against the transom, pulled out his paperback, and contented himself with reading.

They were now drifting about a mile and a half out. Off their starboard bow was a tiny island, little more than a rock, its entire surface taken up by a forlorn looking miniature lighthouse. The three of them stood around the tank in which the lobsters they'd collected had been tossed, and they were in the process of "banding" the morning's haul, placing a thick rubber band around each claw with a tool that looked like a pair of pliers. Though they'd spent quite a bit of time talking throughout the morning, the three of them had now fallen into a companionable silence.

Nate had gratefully allowed himself to be immersed in the mindless activity, and he was startled when Tim spoke. "What do we have here?"

Nate glanced up, then followed Tim's gaze. Ahead of them, in the distance, just off their port beam, was another boat, closing fast. Maggie stepped over to the left side of the wheelhouse and peered at the approaching vessel. After a moment, she said, "Marine Patrol." She looked back at Nate and Tim with a slightly puzzled expression. "That's odd."

Nate felt a sudden chill. He watched the boat approach for a few seconds, then reached into the waterproof overalls he was wearing on top of his clothes, fished in the pocket of his jacket, and pulled out the two-way communicator Matt had given him. He switched it on, toggled it to speaker mode, and set it down on one of the plastic crates stacked next to the lobster tank. After a moment, Matt's voice came through the small speaker. "Talk to me, Nate."

"Maybe it's nothing," Nate said, trying to keep his voice casual. "But we've got company."

"Tell me where you are and what's happening."

"We're," Nate started to say, then realized he had no idea. He looked at Maggie.

"By Turner's Lighthouse," Maggie said. "About a mile and a half out, opposite the mouth of the Monahauk River."

The other boat was close enough now that Nate could read the words "Maine Marine Patrol" in green lettering on the side of the hull. She was a bit larger than the *Sarah Lynne*, and the deck sat a few feet higher. He could see that there were at least four people on board. As she approached, the patrol boat slowed and turned, her captain guiding her to a spot parallel to the *Sarah Lynne*, facing in the opposite direction, about ten yards away. The wake generated by the larger vessel caught the lobster boat and rocked her from side to side. A man in a khaki uniform and a green baseball cap leaned out of the patrol boat's wheelhouse and hailed them.

"Hello, Maggie. Tim," he shouted.

"Afternoon, Burt," Maggie called back. "What are you doing all the way up here?"

The man didn't answer right away. He tilted his head slightly, and it appeared to Nate as though he was directing a question behind himself. Nate could see that two of the other men in the patrol boat wore uniforms, but the fourth was in civilian clothes. A pair of aviator sunglasses concealed the fourth man's eyes. Nate wasn't sure, but he thought the man might have spoken in response to the question from the uniformed officer.

"Maggie, I'm going to come alongside," the first uniformed man called out. The patrol boat reversed engines, and it began backing away, apparently in preparation for the maneuver that would bring the two boats together.

Matt's voice again came over the speaker. "Do not let them board."

Maggie raised a hand in acknowledgement and stepped over to the starboard side of the wheelhouse. Without warning, she fired the engine and threw the throttle all the way forward. The *Sarah Lynne* bucked, and Nate almost lost his balance. Maggie immediately swung the wheel hard to the right, and the lobster boat began a tight turn taking them around the rocky outcropping on which the lighthouse sat.

The move obviously surprised the patrol boat captain. It took him a moment to halt the rearward movement of his vessel and to start forward. Then, when he did, he had to maneuver around the other side of the lighthouse, taking a longer course than the *Sarah Lynne*. By the time the patrol boat had cleared the outcropping, the lobster boat was a good hundred yards away and moving at a rapid clip.

Nate retrieved the communicator from the deck where it had fallen and joined Maggie and Tim in the wheelhouse. The deck beneath his feet was bouncing, and he had to hang onto a stanchion to avoid falling.

"Nice move, Maggie," Tim shouted above the sound of the engine and the wind passing through the open side windows. "But it's not going to give us more than thirty seconds, and that patrol boat's a lot faster than this old bucket."

Maggie, her eyes focused ahead of them and a resolute look on her face, shook her head. "Thirty seconds can be a lifetime."

Nate realized there was sound coming from the communicator, and he held it up to his ear. "Nate," he heard Matt calling, "tell me what's going on."

"We're making a run for it," he replied, shouting into the device.

"Where are you headed?" Matt asked immediately.

Nate turned to Maggie. "Where are we headed?"

Without taking her eyes off the water in front of them, Maggie shouted, "Up the Monahauk River. Tell him to meet us at the bridge where Highway 1 crosses."

Nate repeated the information into the communicator.

"Maggie, no," Tim was saying, and Nate looked at him in alarm.

"What do you mean, no?" Nate asked.

"Can't be done," the old man replied, a look of panic on his face. "Been tried before. No one's ever made it." He pointed ahead of them. "Too many rocks. Way too shallow."

Nate looked, and, as if to punctuate the man's point, Nate saw the remains of a boat impaled in the crook of a pair of rocks jutting out of the water a couple hundred yards in front of them.

Grimly, Maggie shouted, "Don't have a choice."

Maggie had a set a course to the right of the rocks that dotted the ocean surface, angling slightly away from the opening to the river. They were headed toward a point where the sea met the shore at a massive stone outcropping, its ocean side dropping straight down into the water. Unless they were to turn soon, Nate saw, they would plow directly into the solid rock face.

"Maggie," Tim called out.

Nate glanced back at Maggie. Her expression was set, a look of fierce determination in her eyes.

Something pinged off the top of the wheelhouse. Nate jerked his head around. The patrol boat was behind them and gaining. He saw the man in civilian clothes leaning out the port side of the boat, his hand extended toward them. Nate realized with a start that the man was shooting. Under the circumstances, Nate didn't think it would be possible for anyone to fire a handgun with any accuracy, particularly given the way the boats were bouncing over the waves, but then he heard the sound of another ricochet somewhere near the stern of the lobster boat.

He turned to look forward again and instinctively hunched his shoulders. The sheer cliff was now looming above them.

"Maggie," Tim called out again. "Maybe you should turn now."

Maggie didn't reply.

"Really, Maggie." Tim's voice was plaintive. "Now."

The rock towered over them.

"Maggie. Please."

Suddenly, Maggie pulled back on the throttle, and she threw the wheel hard over to the left. The *Sarah Lynne* wallowed, and it appeared that she would crash into the rock at her starboard beam. Then Maggie again rammed the throttle forward and, just as contact with the face of the cliff seemed inevitable, the lobster boat jumped and began moving away from the stone wall, headed toward a narrow gap between two rocks jutting up out of the water in front of them. It didn't look to Nate as though there was nearly enough space between the rocks to accommodate the boat. He increased his grip on the stanchion and reached forward with his other hand to brace for the impact.

And then, inconceivably, they were through, and Maggie was bringing the wheel hard over to the right. The *Sarah Lynne* swept past yet another large boulder, and suddenly they were in calm water.

For a moment, Nate couldn't move. Then he roused himself and looked back. The patrol boat had veered away and was circling in the ocean just beyond the shoals. The man in civilian clothes stood at the rail. He was no longer firing his weapon. They were obviously out of range.

Nate looked back at his companions. Tim appeared faint, but Maggie's face still bore the same grim determination as before.

He remembered the communicator. "Matt, we made it. We lost them."

After a moment, Matt's voice came back. He was unusually terse and spoke in clipped tones. "Good. We had issues too. On our way."

Ahead of them, the waterway they were on narrowed at the point where it was spanned by a bridge. Maggie reduced the speed, and, as she neared the bridge, she turned the *Sarah Lynne* toward the shore, heading for a spot on the left hand side that appeared to Nate at first to be a sandy beach. When they got closer, however, he realized it was an area from which boats could be launched into the river. A narrow drive led away at a slight incline, apparently connecting with the highway above.

As they approached the landing, Maggie shut down the engine, and the *Sarah Lynne* drifted in, finally making contact with a loud scraping sound.

"Sorry about that Tim," said Maggie.

"Can't be helped," the old man replied. He seemed to have regained some of his regular equanimity.

Nate and Maggie lowered Tim over the side into water that came up to his chest. He waded ashore and Maggie tossed him one of the mooring lines. Then Nate lowered Maggie into the water, and, when she was clear, he jumped in himself. When he emerged, he saw that Tim had tied the boat off on a hooked metal stake that sat to the side of the landing. Without a word, the three of them hurried up the inclined drive.

At the top, there was an open area where vehicles could safely turn off the highway. Nate pointed to a thicket of trees to one side of the opening. Maggie nodded, and they jogged over, slipping into the relative privacy, where they stood, shivering in the cold.

A couple of trucks passed over the bridge, but there was otherwise no traffic on the highway. The communicator crackled, and Matt's voice announced, "We're coming up on you now."

Then the SUV careened into the clearing, coming to a quick stop, kicking up dust and pieces of gravel. As the three of them ran to the vehicle, the doors on the right side flew open. Nate jumped into the front seat, next to Patricia, and Maggie and Tim threw themselves into the rear seat. The SUV was already back on the highway before the doors could be shut.

It took Nate a moment to notice that the front windshield was pockmarked with multiple holes. Not holes, he realized, because the window was still intact, but deep circular impressions that looked for all the world like holes. Not just any kind of holes, either. Bullet holes.

Nate glanced across at Matt, who was gripping the steering wheel tightly. "Looks like you did have issues."

Matt nodded, but he didn't turn. His eyes were focused on the road ahead, though it appeared he was also scanning the areas to either side. "Hold on," he announced, and he suddenly slammed on the brakes. With a loud squealing sound, the SUV slewed to a complete stop. Matt then threw it into reverse and started back down the highway in the direction from which they'd just come. After about thirty yards, Matt yanked the steering wheel hard right, and the vehicle swerved off the road backwards. Nate hadn't even noticed it as they'd passed, but there was a tiny service station sitting by the side of the highway with two gasoline pumps out in front. Matt just missed clipping one of the pumps as he backed the SUV to a spot adjacent to the building, squeezing it in between the huge trunk of an evergreen tree and the side wall of the structure. He pulled the vehicle well back from the front corner of the building and shut off the engine.

There was a sudden silence.

After a few seconds, Nate said, "What are we…" but stopped when Matt held up a hand.

"Wait," Matt said, quietly.

After a moment, Nate heard something new, a thumping noise. It quickly grew louder, until, in a matter of seconds, it reached a crescendo, and, with a massive whoomping sound, a helicopter roared overhead, not more than a hundred feet above the highway, traveling north, as they had been, but at a much greater speed. It was past them and gone before they had much of a chance to register the fact that it was there, the thumping fading into the distance.

"They'll be back soon," Matt said, starting the engine. "With others. We've got to get off this highway, and, more importantly, we need to disappear."

From the back seat, Tim said, "I think I know where we can do that."

Nate turned to look at him. Tim was, in turn, looking at Maggie.

"The cabin," Maggie said.

Tim nodded. "The cabin."

#

Dacoff took one last look at the bloody remains of Ozaki as the medical technician zipped up the body bag. Raen was going to be furious.

They'd had Marek trapped. The Dayton house sat on a high bluff. It was an almost straight drop to the bay below. And, sitting in the bay just off shore had been a pair of marine patrol boats. The only way out was the narrow drive. There was no chance that Marek could outflank them. They'd had their quarry completely outnumbered and just where they wanted him.

Somehow, though, the man had known they were coming. Dacoff had heard stories about Marek's sixth sense. He hadn't believed them. He did now.

As the action team was making its approach, a black SUV with tinted windows had suddenly appeared, flying down the lane, nowhere to go but straight ahead, a suicidal move. Dacoff had been in the lead vehicle, a pickup truck, Ozaki perched behind him in the bed, armed with an assault rifle mounted on a bipod, facing forward. Ozaki waited until they'd closed to a hundred yards before opening fire. He aimed for the SUV's engine block. A single round should have taken it out. But it hadn't.

The SUV had covered half of the hundred yards before anyone realized that the bullets were merely pinging off the front of the vehicle. Ozaki then shifted his aim and put several rounds through the front windshield. Except, inconceivably, those pinged off as well.

At the last possible moment, Dacoff had jumped from the passenger seat. The move saved his life. At approximately eighty miles an hour, the SUV slammed into the pickup, instantly turning it, the driver and Ozaki into a grisly collection of mangled and twisted metal and flesh. The collision barely made a dent in the front end of the SUV.

The driver of their second vehicle, a Suburban, swerved reflexively, the move sending the big automobile over the edge of the bluff into the rocks a hundred feet below. Two of the operatives in that vehicle had been killed outright, and the other two were badly injured.

While it had occurred to Dacoff in advance that Marek might have outfitted his vehicle with armor plating, he'd not even considered the possibility that Marek would have glass that could withstand armor piercing bullets. Dacoff had heard about a new transparent armor made from aluminum oxynitride, but he'd not yet had a chance to study it. Apparently, Marek had gotten his hands on some. That took Dacoff completely by surprise.

Dacoff kicked in frustration at the dusty ground. Yes, Raen was going to be furious.

#

117

The cabin sat on a lake, surrounded by woods. It was about a hundred miles inland from the coast as the crow flew. To get to it, however, they'd driven almost twice that distance.

They turned off the highway less than a mile from the spot where the helicopter had passed overhead, and they began wending their way into the interior of Maine. While the coast had been sparsely populated, compared to where they were now, it seemed to Nate in retrospect positively metropolitan.

On the drive, Maggie and Tim detailed the circumstances that had led to the existence of the cabin. Near the turn of the century, they explained, the fishing boat on which Tim's great grandfather, Benjamin, had been serving was caught several miles off shore in an unexpected northeaster. One of his crewmates was swept overboard, and Benjamin risked his own life to save him. The man, it turned out, was the scion of one of the state's largest landowners. To show his gratitude, he built for Benjamin and his family a vacation cabin at a prime spot in the vast forest owned by the man's family.

There had never been a deed recorded. It was a private arrangement between two families. But the successors of the man whose life had been saved assiduously adhered to the wishes of their predecessor. For generations, whenever anyone from the Dayton family had wanted to get away, the cabin was available. In a drawer in one of the bedrooms was a blue flag with an orange stripe. When the Daytons were in residence, they'd raise the flag on the pole that sat by the lake and could be seen from the homestead of the owners on the far side, and the occupants of the cabin would be left in solitude. Otherwise, the owners kept an eye on the place and made sure it was always ready for a visit.

When Matt heard the explanation, he deemed the cabin an acceptable solution to their need to disappear. As soon as they started making their way inland, they found themselves plunged into a relatively primordial world, leaving behind the majority of civilization, as well as the terrors it had recently visited on them. After evaluating the place following their arrival, Matt, to Nate's profound relief, pronounced it "safe for the moment."

The term "cabin" was a misnomer. Yes, the two-story structure was a bit rough-hewn, but it was quite large and very comfortable. There were six bedrooms, a large kitchen and a spacious
dining and family room. It had electricity, running water and,
Matt and Peter were delighted to discover, wireless internet service, courtesy of the owners who lived across the lake. The pantry
was full of staples, and they even found a decent selection of frozen foods in the large refrigerator.

They'd raised the Dayton flag, secreted the damaged SUV
behind the structure, and gratefully settled in. The first moment
they were alone, Nate told Matt they needed to speak, but Matt
asked for a little time, explaining that he had some things he
needed to do. Reluctantly, Nate agreed.

The following day was unseasonably warm. Nate took Peter's
research down to a spot by the shore of the lake and spread it out
on a large picnic table. With nothing but the sound of warblers,
chickadees and woodpeckers in the background, Nate immersed
himself in the remainder of the documentation.

He'd been at it for a few hours when he was suddenly startled
by the intense sensation of something latching onto his foot -
something alive. He looked below the table in alarm, only to discover, to his immense relief, that Buster had somehow found his
way down from the cabin and was now scrabbling at his ankle, his
stubby tail wagging wildly.

From behind, he heard a laugh. He glanced back just in time
to see Maggie descend the last few steps of the path from the
cabin. In one hand, she held a plate covered by a paper towel, in
the other a tall glass.

"You looked like you were about to come out of your skin,"
she said, an expression of amusement on her face.

Embarrassed, Nate took a deep breath, his heart still pounding.

"Didn't hear you coming," he acknowledged, after a moment.

"I'm sorry about that," she said lightly. She set the plate and
glass down on one of the few spots of the table top not covered in

paper and slid onto the bench opposite him. "I really should have given you some warning."

Chuckling, she added, "But it did look pretty funny."

Unsure what to say in response, Nate took in the plate and the glass. "For me?" he asked.

She nodded. "You've got to keep up your energy."

And, for the first time, it dawned on Nate that he was, in fact, hungry. He lifted the paper towel and saw a sandwich on the plate. "Thanks," he said, reaching for it and taking a bite. Peanut butter and jelly. It tasted remarkably good.

Maggie was studying the piles of paper he'd arranged on the table.

"You were really concentrating hard," she said, looking back up at him.

Nate took a sip of ice tea and shrugged. He gestured to the paperwork with the hand holding the sandwich. "There's definitely something missing. But I haven't figured it out yet. And it's bugging the heck out of me."

She nodded, her gaze not leaving him. For reasons he couldn't identify, Nate felt a little self-conscious.

To cover his discomfiture, he added, "I think if I can just isolate…"

"Stop," she said quietly.

That took him by surprise.

She continued studying him.

Nate opened his mouth to say something, then paused. Her look shook him in an unfamiliar way.

"Don't you ever let up?" she asked finally.

The question was a little confusing. But, though he was loathe to make the acknowledgement, it also struck an uncomfortable chord.

"I…" he started to say, then stopped. Her green eyes bore into him.

She glanced down at the table, then back up at him.

"You're so serious all the time," she said.

A familiar pang of self-criticism stabbed at him. "I'm sorry," he offered.

To his surprise, she laughed. "There you go again." To Nate, her eyes seemed to sparkle with merriment.

"I don't mean it as an insult," she amended quickly. "I think it's endearing."

Nate looked at her closely. She seemed sincere.

"But," she added, "don't you think you ought to cut yourself some slack every now and again?"

Despite himself, Nate chuckled. Impossibly, Maggie's face lit up even further.

"Now that's what I'm talking about," she said.

And for the next half hour or so, while Buster happily splashed in the shallow water along the lake's edge, Nate and Maggie spent the time talking about nothing in particular. When she left, Nate found himself surprisingly refreshed, and he re-applied himself to the research with a renewed vigor.

As he'd reviewed the documents, Nate had organized them into a collection of stacks. Now he moved them from one to the other, shuffling and discarding. He was certain, as he'd explained to Maggie, that there was something lurking just beyond the written pages. But he couldn't quite put a finger on it.

A thought that had been gnawing at him for some time again intruded. He set down the stack of papers he'd been perusing and reached for one of the piles he'd earlier pushed to the side. He rifled through them quickly and found the one he was looking for. It was an innocuous internal memorandum, but for some reason, it was one to which he'd kept coming back. He retrieved another stack of memoranda that he had assembled earlier. He'd done so purely on instinct and without a basis he could identify at the time. There wasn't an immediate connection among them, at least not an obvious one. The subjects were a myriad jumble. The persons to whom they were addressed were all different.

As were the authors.

Or were they?

With a tingle of excitement, Nate pulled a stack of engineering reports he'd slogged through that morning, deadly dry and painful to read. Right there on top was the one he'd just remembered. He flipped to the last page and read the concluding summary. Then he returned to the beginning and carefully read through the entire document. He'd been right. The person who had written the report had not written the conclusion. He knew it for a certainty.

Why not?

More importantly, why had the conclusion been written by the same person who'd anonymously penned the series of memos he'd just reviewed?

Someone, Nate realized, had not only fabricated several documents, but had altered others. The author - could have been a man or a woman, but for reasons Nate couldn't identify, he was convinced it was a man - had a unique and distinctive writing style. Nate picked up the next document in the stack of reports. This one, he saw, had also been written in part by the mystery author. Not just the conclusion, though. Two pages in the middle of the document were in the same unmistakable style.

The writer was clever. In the section he'd inserted, he'd easily picked up the narrative from the preceding page, which had ended not only in the middle of a paragraph, but in the middle of a sentence, and he'd done likewise melding his last partial sentence on the second page he'd written into the one written by the original author that began the next page in the report. Obviously, there had been something in the middle of the report that someone didn't want the world to read. But what?

Having identified the mystery writer's style, Nate doubled back through the documents he'd earlier culled from Peter's materials, isolating the pages that bore the man's distinctive prose.

He now had the key gaps in the story, but he still needed to fill them in. On a legal pad, Nate began organizing the documents containing the replacement pages, using, for lack of a better regimen, a strict chronology. When he was done, he had several pages of notes, but he was still missing the essence of the story.

He sat back, thinking, allowing the old instincts to take over. The one piece of information he did have - and that the mysterious author of the replacement pages wouldn't have known his reader would possess - was Mason Gale. The man was not who he'd been represented to be, or that these documents would have one believe. He'd had some connection with The Organization, that was clear. For all Nate knew, he'd been an operative just as Matt had been. That was the key. Using it as a starting point, Nate returned his attention to what he now viewed as a puzzle with a series of missing pieces.

With a sudden intuition, he jotted down a note next to the entry he'd made on his pad for the report whose conclusion had tipped him off to the unknown author. It was more a question than a note, but no sooner had he written it, than he knew the answer. Two entries below was the memo that had started it all. Nate drew an arrow from that entry to the question he'd just posed to himself. And then he took in a sharp breath.

"Oh, my God," he said quietly to himself.

The dominoes fell quickly after that. The mystery writer had been too clever by half. Nate suspected that someone with as much talent as the man obviously possessed had probably chaffed at the task he was undertaking, and he'd begun to pepper his contributions to the record with little hints. Probably, Nate thought, he hadn't even realized he was doing it. And nobody would have been the wiser had it not been for the disclosure about Gale.

Finally, as the sun was setting, Nate stood, returned the papers to the box where they'd resided since he and Peter had printed them, and walked to the cabin.

Patricia, Peter and Maggie were in the kitchen, preparing a meal. Tim had found a comfortable chair and was reading. When Nate stepped in, Matt appeared at the top of the stairs.

"Anything?" Matt asked.

Nate nodded. Tim set his book aside as Matt descended the stairs. Patricia, Peter and Maggie dropped what they were doing and immediately made their way to the family room. Maggie sat on the edge of an ottoman and looked up at him expectantly. When he had their full attention, Nate took a deep breath.

"You're not going to believe this."

PART TWO

8

"Houston, we are standing by for pitchover."

As he said it, Bob Cartwright unconsciously flexed his gloved right hand and set it on the pistol-grip controller in front of him.

"Roger, *Concord*," came the steady voice of Rick Delahousse. "Looking good from here."

Though it was slightly distorted by the speaker in his helmet, Cartwright could just make out Delahousse's soft Texas drawl, and he found the familiar voice reassuring. He and Delahousse had been friends since the two of them had entered the astronaut program almost seven years earlier. They'd been an unlikely pairing, the affable country boy from the hills outside Austin and the overly-serious hard-charger from the Midwest. But each had found in the other a perfectly balanced counterweight, and they'd thrived in the competitive environment sponsored by NASA. Cartwright had always assumed that, when he finally made the journey into space, it would be at the side of the mild-mannered Texan. Instead, however, through circumstances he still did not fully understand, Rick Delahousse was now 250,000 miles away, in the large mission control room in Houston, serving as the capsule communicator, or Capcom, while Bob Cartwright was minutes from guiding the Apollo 18 lunar module to its landing spot on the moon near the northern edge of the *Mare Crisium*.

"And there's pitchover," said Mason Gale. His voice, like Delahousse's was altered slightly by the speaker. But he, unlike Delahousse, was not hundreds of thousands of miles away. Instead, Gale and Cartwright stood shoulder to shoulder in the cramped space of the small vessel hurtling toward the surface of the moon. Both men were in full spacesuits. Elastic cords extended from hooks at their waists to anchors on the cabin floor so they would not drift away from the controls in zero gravity. Both were concentrating intently.

Arrayed in front of them were a series of switches, knobs and displays filling a broad instrument panel, to either side of which were small triangular windows. As the craft slowly pitched forward, assuming an upright position for the final descent, the bright, jagged surface of the moon rose dramatically into view through the left hand window in front of Cartwright. It was an awe-inspiring moment. And, with a rush of excitement, he immediately recognized familiar features.

"I have the Needle in sight," he announced.

The "Needle" was a tall, narrow rock outcropping that jutted up at the far end of the Sea of Crises. It sat just to the left and downrange of their landing site. During the countless simulations they'd gone through in preparation for the mission, it had been their primary visual cue. If they were on course, the Needle would appear in the center of the window in front of Cartwright when the module pitched over. And, sure enough, there it was. Dead center. God bless the engineers at NASA, Cartwright thought.

"Three thousand," Gale called out, "at seventy-five."

They were now three thousand feet above the lunar surface, descending at the rate of seventy-five feet per second. The module was under the control of the onboard computer, a device officially called the Primary Guidance and Navigation Section, but referred to by the astronauts as "pings." It was, Cartwright knew, a first rate autopilot. However, he was poised to override it if, as they got closer, the landing site did not appear safe.

"Passing through one thousand," Gale intoned. "And we're at forty-five."

Though the reconnaissance photographs the mission planners had used to select their landing site were generally good, the resolution of the photos was simply not sufficient to allow details to be picked out below a certain size. And those as yet undiscovered details could have a dramatic impact on their landing. Of particular concern were boulders. The lunar module required level ground to be set down safely. But it was possible objects as large as sixty feet across would not have shown up in the photos. Even a rock as small as three feet wide could, if they were unlucky enough to come down directly on top of it, overpressure the descent engine bell and cause an explosion. Cartwright peered forward, all senses alert.

"Five hundred at thirty-two," Gale reported.

They would be at "low gate" when they reached two hundred feet, the last point at which the decision could be made to select either automatic or manual control.

"Four hundred at twenty-eight."

In the distance, Cartwright spotted their landing site. To his relief, it appeared to be clear of large rocks.

"Three hundred at twenty two."

Suddenly, Cartwright stiffened. Directly ahead of them, just before the spot where they intended to land, a dark line had appeared. As they approached, the feature came into sharp focus. It was a crack in the lunar surface, commonly referred to as a rille. In the couple of seconds available to him, Cartwright studied it. At its closest point, it appeared to be just a few feet in width, but it quickly widened, and, from this angle, it looked deep. The computer was guiding them straight into it. He made his decision.

"I've got P-66." He increased his grip on the controller in his right hand and clicked it three degrees forward, overriding the P-64 control program that had been guiding them down. He knew he didn't want to go left, as the opening of the fissure trended in that direction, so he nudged the controller to the right. As he made each adjustment, a series of small 100-pound thrust motors mounted in clusters of four on the ascent stage of the module fired in different combinations. With his left hand, he pushed up the thrust/translational controller, increasing the burn in the main engine and slowing their rate of descent.

Off to the right, Cartwright knew, was a field of immense boulders. Not good. The area beyond, however, had appeared in the reconnaissance photos to be clear. Then, again, so had the landing site they'd just overridden. Doing quick calculations, Cartwright decided they would have to take their chances past the boulders. Worst case, he knew, they'd jettison the descent stage, fire the main ascent rocket and abort the landing. There was no way Cartwright wanted that to happen. It would render the mission a complete failure.

The response of the lunar module was sluggish, but familiar. They skimmed across the boulder field. After a short time, the size of the rocks diminished, but the clusters below them were still too big and concentrated to allow a safe landing. He worked the toggle switch to further slow their rate of descent.

"Two hundred," Gale called out. "Now down three, twenty-one forward."

"How's the fuel?" Cartwright asked.

"Seven percent."

Cartwright winced. They were running out of time. To hammer the point home, a light on the instrument panel began to glow. They had ninety seconds of fuel left, and twenty seconds of that had to be saved for an abort. The damn boulder field seemed to go on forever.

"One hundred. Down two, nineteen forward."

They weren't going to make it.

Then, ahead of them, appeared a clearing. Not large. Maybe a hundred feet square, if that. It was, however, the only site that offered any chance of level ground. Cartwright quickly weighed their options. There really weren't any. Putting the module down here would be a little like threading a needle. But it would have to do. He eased back on the controller.

"Coming through eighty," Gale said. "Down two, seventeen forward. Now fifteen." There was a new tension in the man's voice.

He heard Delahousse. His voice also sounded strained. "Thirty seconds."

They had less than half a minute of fuel.

Cartwright fixed his sights on a large, jagged rock that thrust upward beyond the clearing. This would have to be his focal point. To put them in the clearing, he would need to come down perfectly horizontal, and he wouldn't be able to see the landing site as he dropped. As if to emphasize the problem, the area below them was suddenly obscured, the blast from the descent engine stirring up particles of dust on the surface. With no atmosphere to lift it skyward and little gravity to pull it downward, the dust shot out in straight lines in every direction, creating a solid moving blanket and concealing all details on the surface. He kept his concentration on the jagged rock, which now looked like an island in a blurry sea.

"Sixty feet," said Gale. "Down two and a half, three forward. Now two."

Eyes locked on the jagged rock, Cartwright halted their forward progress. The dust being kicked up by their engine had the effect of distorting his sense of motion. He suddenly felt as if they were moving backwards. Shifting his attention to the instruments, he resisted the urge to nudge the controller forward.

"Forty feet," Gale called out. "Down two and half. Down two."

"Fifteen seconds," Delahousse's voice announced with undisguised concern.

It was now too late to abort. Cartwright prayed that the clearing, and not some immense boulder, sat below them.

"Twenty feet. Down one."

Involuntarily, Cartwright braced himself.

"Ten feet. Down one."

A blue light on the console illuminated. It meant that one of the probes dangling a few feet below *Concord's* footpads had crunched into something, the impact completing an electrical circuit.

"Contact," Gale exclaimed.

Hoping it was the surface and not a rock, Cartwright reached out and hit the engine stop button. He experienced a moment of otherworldliness. Then, with a solid thump, the pads of the module made contact with the surface, and they were no longer moving. Thankfully, they were upright and level.

There was a second of stunned silence. Then the men's training kicked in.

While Gale read off the items on the post-landing checklist, the two men quickly set a series of switches and typed numbers into the computer.

Finally, Cartwright keyed his mike and announced, "Houston, *Concord* is safely down in the Sea of Crises."

"Roger, *Concord*, we copy you on the ground. Thank God, and good work."

"Thanks Rick," Cartwright said with real emotion. And he took his first steady breath on the surface of the moon.

He looked over at his crewmate. The man was a good three inches shorter than Cartwright, but stocky and solidly built. Behind the visor of his helmet, the visage that peered back up at him was classic Mason Gale, complete impassivity. Nothing, it seemed, would ever rattle the man. Then, to Cartwright's surprise, a rare grin split Gale's face. Awkwardly, the man reached his right hand across his body and held it out. Cartwright put his gloved hand in Gale's, and they shook.

"Nice job, Commander," Gale said with an odd formality.

#

Though he was tired, sleep eluded Bob Cartwright. He'd been anxious to start their lunar exploration as soon as they landed, but the mission profile called for the two astronauts to rest first. They wouldn't take their initial steps on the moon for another seven hours. In the meantime, they were expected to get some sleep.

Once they'd confirmed the lunar module was secure, he and Gale had climbed out of their bulky space suits, stripping down to their long-johns. The gravity on the moon was only one-sixth that on earth, but it was just enough to enable Cartwright to lie comfortably in the hammock strung in the confined space. After the disorientation of weightlessness that had plagued him over the past few days, he was grateful for the relief it offered. Still, he was too keyed up to nod off.

In the hammock below him, Gale apparently had no such problems. Cartwright could just hear the man's rhythmic breathing over the whir of the cabin recirculation motor.

After all these months, Cartwright still did not know what to make of Mason Gale.

To say the man was an enigma was putting it mildly.

Cartwright remembered the day they met. How could he forget? It was one of the most extraordinary days of his life. It had been Cartwright's thirty-sixth birthday, the first day of April, 1976. Cartwright had landed at Ellington Field in Houston a few minutes earlier after a cross-country flight from Nellis Air Force Base in Nevada, his thoughts dominated by the family gathering to which he was already late. After he descended from the cockpit of the T-38 he'd checked out the day before, a member of the ground crew approached and informed him that he was wanted immediately in the office of Stuart Overholdt, the Director of Flight Crew Operations. Still dressed in his flight suit, and wary, as always, of practical jokes - a residual effect of having been born on April Fool's Day - he arrived a few minutes later at the office of his boss, the man in charge of the astronauts.

At one point in time, the office had been the center of a maelstrom. Much lobbying and intrigue had gone on in and around the place. There had been a tremendous controversy over who might serve as the commander on the first manned mission to the moon. And, though the stakes might have been, on balance, somewhat smaller, there were nevertheless huge consequences, not to mention egos, involved in the selection of the crews who would man the various moon missions that followed.

By 1976, however, the frenzy had died. Overholdt's predecessor had retired. The U.S. space program was in a bit of a hiatus. Skylab had come and gone, and the Space Transportation System, which would become known as the space shuttle, was still in development. While there was a certain amount of jockeying going on for seats on the shuttle missions, all of which were still conceptual, the crown jewel, the Apollo program, had died a painful and premature death, and with it went the ultimate goal: A shot at landing on the moon.

In early 1970, just a month after Cartwright entered the astronaut program, the Apollo 20 mission was cancelled, the victim of budget cuts. Then, in September of that same year, the Apollo 15 and Apollo 19 missions were eliminated. The remaining missions were re-numbered, leaving Apollo 17 in December of 1972 the last hurrah for the U.S. manned lunar program.

In the years subsequent, many of the men, most of whose initial service predated Cartwright, had seen the writing on the wall and packed it in. The effect had been to elevate Cartwright quickly to a senior status among the remaining members of the program.

In the hallway outside Flight Crew Operations, he found Steve Dayton sitting in one of the padded chairs, reading a magazine. Dayton, who had the day off, was in casual clothes. They greeted one another warmly.

Dayton and Cartwright had served together on the second backup crew for the Apollo-Soyuz mission the year before, a joint U.S./Soviet venture that employed some of the unused Apollo program hardware. Cartwright had been the crew commander, and Dayton had served as command module pilot.

Shortly after Cartwright arrived, the door to Overholdt's office opened, and he and Dayton were asked to come in. There were four men already in the room. Overholdt, whom Cartwright had known for years, made the introductions. To Cartwright's surprise, one of the men waiting for them was a United States Senator, Harrison Burton. With him was Adam Huffman, the Deputy Administrator of NASA. Both men Cartwright recognized from photographs. The fourth man he'd never seen before.

"Bob, Steve," Overholdt said, "I'd like you meet Mason Gale. You'll be working closely together."

Cartwright reached out a hand, and Gale practically crushed it with a powerful grip. Stifling a grimace, and still harboring lingering suspicions about practical jokes, Cartwright turned to the director. "And what, may I ask, sir, will we be working on?"

Overholdt smiled broadly. "That, Bob, is the proverbial sixty-four million dollar question, give or take a few million."

It was apparently a private joke, as the senator and deputy administrator chuckled. Gale's expression, Cartwright noticed, did not change.

Overholdt motioned them all to take seats at the long table that took up half of his office. "What you're about to hear is not yet public. I don't need to remind you of your security clearances and your obligations to maintain classified information." With that, he turned matters over to Huffman.

The deputy administrator cleared his throat. "I'm pleased to announce that, thanks in large measure to the considerable assistance of Senator Burton here, additional funding has been put in place to enable the Agency to revive the Apollo program. There will now be at least one additional mission, Apollo 18. And," he paused, fixing Cartwright, Dayton and Gale with level looks, "each of you has been selected to serve together as the primary crew for that mission. Gentlemen, you're going to the moon."

If that, Cartwright thought, was a practical joke, it was the best one anyone had ever played on him.

But it had become quickly clear that it was no joke. Though the mission was not announced to the public until over three months later, the men were immediately plunged into an intense regimen of training. With less than six months to liftoff, the normal schedule that attended preparation for such a mission was dramatically compressed. For Cartwright and Dayton, much of the training was familiar. For Gale, it was all new.

When the opportunity first presented itself, Cartwright privately questioned Overholdt regarding the selection of a man who had previously not been attached to the astronaut program, particularly given the fact that he was taking the seat Cartwright believed should have rightfully gone to his friend, Rick Delahousse.

"Believe me, Bob," Overholdt said, "it wasn't my call. This came down from the administrator's office. Apparently, to sell this additional mission, we've got to show it has an overwhelmingly scientific focus. That means taking a qualified specialist in lunar geology. On the one hand, I know you and Rick have attended the trainings and done the field work, and I have every confidence that you two would do a fine job."

Over the years, Cartwright and Delahousse, like most of the Apollo astronauts before them, had undergone extensive instruction, both in the classroom and in the field, learning how to recognize and describe geological features and how to select the samples that would be brought back to earth with them. Delahousse, in particular, had become something of a standout among the current group of astronauts.

"On the other hand, though," Overholdt continued, "we have to convince a skeptical public that, with all the other demands on the federal budget, this is a worthy expenditure. If the choice is that you go with Mason Gale or you don't go at all, you go with Gale.

"But," he added, "if Gale doesn't cut it in training, then I won't hesitate to ground him, the consequences be damned."

It had been a reasonable arrangement. And, to ameliorate things, Delahousse had been given command of the mission's backup crew. Furthermore, Delahousse would have first shot at Apollo 19 if that mission ever got the green light.

In fairness, Gale gave them no reason to question his selection. The man was certainly competent, and he tackled the training with a vigor. He wasn't the friendliest of crewmates. In fact, he was, on his best days, remarkably brusque and could at times be downright rude. But he'd earned Cartwright's grudging respect, and, as Cartwright now lay in his hammock struggling unsuccessfully to find sleep, he had no doubt that Gale would perform his duties well.

Cartwright's thoughts turned, as they frequently did, to the boys. Once again, he questioned whether it was fair for them that he take the risks associated with what he was doing. What if, God forbid, something did go wrong and he didn't return? It was a possibility he freely accepted. But the boys were given no say in it. And if he didn't come back, they would be all alone.

It would be so much better, he reflected, if Barbara were still around.

For Cartwright, even after seven years, the pain of Barbara's death was fresh. And bitter. The autopsy on the driver of the tractor-trailer had confirmed that the man was hopped up on amphetamines at the time of the accident. According to the trucking company records, he'd been on the road for over twenty hours when he allowed his vehicle to drift across the center lane of the highway, where it slammed headfirst into the little Volkswagen Barbara was driving back from a luncheon at the naval station. The doctors told Cartwright that Barbara had died instantly, and he took some slight comfort in that. The truck driver had not been so lucky. He'd been pinned in the cab by the collision while gas from his ruptured tank had spread around him. The gas ignited about a minute after the crash, but before anyone could get to him. According to onlookers, the man screamed for at least three minutes, first in terror, then in agony. His official cause of death was searing of the lungs, as he breathed in the fire that was in the process of consuming his body.

Despite himself, Cartwright also took some comfort in that.

Fortunately, Cartwright's mother had not hesitated when she'd learned of her daughter-in-law's tragic death. Widowed five years earlier, she immediately uprooted herself from the small Indiana town where she'd lived her entire life, and she moved in with Cartwright and the boys.

Cartwright had realized quickly that the nomadic life of a naval aviator would, without Barbara there to provide stability, be too much to ask his boys to continue to endure. He'd heard there was to be another round of selections for the space program and that priority was being given to qualified pilots. A month after Barbara's death, he applied for a spot in the new group, and two months after that, he was accepted. The five of them were able to settle down in one place, and, over the past seven years, Cartwright had done his best to fill the role of single parent to the boys.

He was very proud of his sons. All three of them were extraordinarily smart, Nate, perhaps, even more so than the twins, which was saying a lot. His eldest was remarkably steady and capable. When Cartwright looked at Nate, he saw himself as a young man, for all that implied, good and bad. He worried, though, that, as serious and hard working as Nate was, he'd burn himself out if he wasn't careful. The one thing Cartwright knew with certainty, and it helped ease his concerns, was that, if anything were to happen to him, Nate would be there for his brothers.

Peter was the sensitive one. He reminded Cartwright so much of Barbara. The boy was at once inquisitive and insightful. He could be serious, but he could also be hilarious. Most importantly, he possessed an inner strength that would serve him well should he have to face life on his own.

And then there was Matt. The wild one. What would become of Matt? There was really no question in Cartwright's mind that the boy would be able to fend for himself. He was as independent as any kid his age could ever be. But there was no getting around the fact that he was impulsive, inclined to leap before thinking. And that, Cartwright feared, could be his undoing. And, if it happened, it would be a terrible shame. Because, he knew, deep inside of Matt, well down below where most of the world could see, was a truly marvelous soul.

Bob Cartwright wasn't a particularly religious man, but, lying there in his hammock, on the floor of the Mare Crisium, a quarter of a million miles from home, he said a silent prayer, asking God that he be allowed to see his boys again.

#

Apparently, Cartwright had finally found sleep, because he was startled to wakefulness by a harsh sound that he didn't immediately recognize. After a moment, he realized that, through the earphone on the cap he wore, the one the astronauts referred to as the "Snoopy cap," Houston was pumping a rousing rendition of *Anchors Aweigh*. It dawned on him after a moment, that it was in his honor. A few seconds later, it abruptly stopped and was replaced by the chipper voice of Rick Delahousse.

"Rise and shine, sleepy heads. Thought you might want to take a walk this morning."

Stifling a chuckle, Cartwright said, "Aw, come on, Mom. Five more minutes?"

"What," Delahousse replied, "and let all the good spots on the moon get taken by everyone else?"

"All right," Cartwright said, pulling himself up by gripping the handle on the overhead docking hatch and swinging his body out of the hammock. "If you insist." Suspended for a moment in the fractional gravity, he twisted his torso, keeping his legs curled, looked down, and identified a clear spot on the module floor. Then he extended his legs, making contact with the deck a couple of seconds later.

Gale, he saw, was already up. The man had stowed his hammock and taken a seat on the ascent engine cover. He was in the process of eating from one of the clear plastic bags in which their meals were stored. He nodded at Cartwright, but said nothing. Knowing there was no point in trying to engage Gale in chit-chat, Cartwright busied himself putting away his own hammock and grabbing a quick bite to eat. Then, the two of them assisted one another putting on their space suits.

When they were ready, they depressurized the cabin and opened the forward hatch, and Cartwright worked his body out onto the short landing that sat above one of the four legs of the module. In part because of their training and in part because of the concentration required to deal with the bulky suit and the small opening, it wasn't until Cartwright was beginning his descent down the ladder that it dawned on him that he was actually outside the craft, truly a man on the moon.

On the last rung of the ladder, Cartwright paused, appreciating the moment. When Neil Armstrong had taken this step, his words had become famous. Subsequent first steps on the moon had been accorded much less significance. Still, it was a moment to remember, and one that Cartwright certainly would never forget. Not wanting to let it pass without some acknowledgement, he'd worked up what he hoped would be a reasonably appropriate statement.

He pushed himself off the ladder and, when his boots made contact with the surface, he said, "With humble respect for those who came before, I'm proud to announce that man has returned to the moon. We come in the name of exploration, science and peace."

A few minutes later, when Gale stepped off the pad, his was a much shorter pronouncement. "I'm down."

Their first order of business was retrieval of the lunar rover from the LRV storage compartment, located in the descent stage of the module, just to the side of the leg that they'd climbed down. Gripping a pair of lanyards, Cartwright and Gale pulled down, and the vehicle slowly lowered, like a drawbridge, unfolding as it did. When they had it on the surface, they removed the pins, cabling and tripods that had held the vehicle in its storage position, and they raised the seats and footrests. After switching on the electronics, Cartwright went through a quick diagnostic check. Everything appeared to be functioning.

Because of the tight quarters in which they'd landed, there was some uncertainty about which direction they would take to get themselves out of the clearing. The two men separated. Taking bounding steps that made Cartwright feel slightly superhuman, but being careful not to allow the weight of his backpack to push him over the balance point and cause him to pratfall, he explored a portion of the area to the north of the module, while Gale investigated another.

"Over here," Gale announced after a couple of minutes. "It looks clear."

Cartwright joined him at the northeast corner of their landing site. There did, indeed, appear to be sufficient clearance for the rover through the boulder field. How far they'd be able to go, however, he couldn't say. Distances in the moonscape, Cartwright was beginning to appreciate, were almost impossible to gauge. But it looked like a reasonable starting place.

They returned to the module and mounted the rover, which had the odd appearance of a dune buggy, and, with Cartwright at the controls, they started out. The rover was capable of moving at speeds of up to seven miles per hour. For the first several minutes of their trek, however, Cartwright maintained more of a walking pace. Gale was quiet, but Cartwright and Delahousse kept up a running dialogue. The field of rocks in which they'd landed was, they discovered, quite vast. Cartwright worked the rover through a serpentine course, endeavoring as best he could to keep them moving in the direction that their first traverse called for. As they picked their way through the broken landscape, it became apparent fairly quickly that Cartwright had, indeed, found the one spot where they could land. Put simply, had he not set them down where he had, they would not have made it onto the surface of the moon.

Finally, the terrain began to clear, but, though they were able to get the rover up to speed, they still found themselves working their way through a landscape dotted with boulders, some quite large. It was not the terrain that Cartwright had been led to believe they'd encounter, and he did his best to describe what he was seeing for the men gathered back at Mission Control, his comments supplementing what they were already seeing through the video camera mounted on the front of the rover.

On the ground ahead of them, a softball-sized rock caught the light of the sun as they approached in such a way as to reflect what appeared to Cartwright to be almost a deep blue, an interesting contrast to the washed out beige of the surrounding environment. Pointing, he said to Gale, "I think we should grab that one."

Gale seemed to hesitate. Then he nodded. Reaching down and using the claws on the end of the aluminum pole in his right hand, he retrieved the sample. When Gale had safely deposited it into one of the bags they were carrying, Cartwright started them up again, and they slowly made their way around a large rock outcropping.

When he saw the object, Cartwright was so startled he actually lost his grip on the steering control. He immediately lunged for the control, pulled back and stopped the forward progress of the rover. He stared, flabbergasted, for a moment. Finally, not knowing what else to say, he blurted, "That shouldn't be here."

9

Krantz heard the door behind him burst open, and, when he glanced back, Adam Huffman stormed in.

"Stand by," Krantz said into his microphone. He flipped the switch on the control box clipped to his belt, muting the line, and turned to face the NASA deputy administrator.

"What's the status?" Huffman asked.

"We've had first contact, and we've effected the switchover."

"So soon," Huffman said.

It was a superfluous comment. Krantz merely nodded.

"What was the contact?" Huffman demanded.

Krantz turned his head and nodded toward one of the large television monitors mounted on brackets hanging from the ceiling. Across the lower half of the screen was a bright lunar surface dotted with rocks and boulders of various sizes. The area above the horizon was pitch black. On the ground in the center of the lunar landscape was an object. With its sharp geometric features, it looked completely out of place.

"Zoom in, again," Krantz commanded.

As the lens of the camera mounted on the front of the lunar rover was refocused, the object grew in size until it practically filled the screen. It appeared to be a square metallic box with a narrow antenna attached. Without any point of reference, however, it was impossible to tell how large the thing was.

"What is it?" Huffman asked.

Krantz shook his head. "We're not sure. Most likely some sort of motion detector."

"This far out?"

Again, Krantz shook his head. "We may be closer than we thought. In any event, it appears they're expecting us."

Suddenly, there was movement on the television screen, and the object was obscured. The man working the remote controls adjusted the focus of the camera, and the image drew back out. As it did, Krantz realized that what he had seen was the back of either Cartwright or Gale moving away from the rover. As he watched, the two astronauts took bounding steps toward the object. When they reached the thing, Krantz was finally able to judge its size. It appeared the base was approximately a foot square, and the antenna extended upward about two feet.

"Did we cut away in time?" Huffman asked.

"Yes," Krantz replied. "Cartwright said something about it just before the switchover, but it never appeared on the screen. And what he said was pretty vague. Could have been referring to just about anything."

"What exactly did he say?"

Krantz turned to one of the men sitting in the row in front of him. "Give me play back on the audio. Start at twenty seconds before switchover." After a moment, the slightly metallic voice of Bob Cartwright filled the room.

"I think we should grab that one." There were several seconds of silence. When Cartwright again spoke, there was an edge to his voice. "That shouldn't be here."

After a moment, Huffman nodded slowly. "Ok. It is what it is. What have you told them?"

"I've stuck to the script," Krantz said. "Said we had a communications glitch and we've switched over to backup."

"What are they saying?"

"Nothing." Krantz consulted the panel on the front wall. "At least nothing we can hear. They've gone to Comm 2." The astronauts had engaged the personal intercom option on their communications system. In that mode, they could talk to one another, and, while they could hear transmissions from ground control, until either of them activated a cable-mounted switch attached to the front of his suit, their voices would not be heard back on Earth.

Of course, even when they did that, nothing would be heard in Mission Control. From the moment Krantz had hit the override switch, the only contact the men on the moon would have with Earth would be with the small cadre of men who had been assembled in this former storage room in the basement of the headquarters building at the Johnson Space Center.

"Ok," Huffman said. "The shit's hitting the fan upstairs. I've got to make an appearance. I'll be back as soon as I can."

Krantz nodded. As Huffman made his way to the door, Krantz returned his attention to the television monitor.

#

Bob Cartwright's mind was a jumble of thoughts as he stood considering the thing. He glanced over at Gale. A distorted image of Cartwright's own helmeted figure stared back at him in the reflection of the man's visor. After a long moment, he looked back down.

The mere fact that a man-made object sat here in a place it had no business being was extraordinary. But, given time, Cartwright could have conjured a series of explanations for it. Off the top of his head, he figured, it could have been a piece of one of the lunar modules that was allowed to crash back onto the surface of the moon after a prior Apollo mission. Of course, it didn't look like any part he recognized. But at least that offered a marginally reasonable explanation.

There was no way, however, he could rationalize the footprints surrounding the thing.

And, as if that weren't sufficiently disconcerting, a small red light on the base glowed, apparently indicating that, whatever it was, it was active.

The two astronauts had switched over to the personal intercom, so he didn't need to worry about the sensibilities of the television audience back home. "What in the hell do you suppose *this* is?" he asked.

Gale didn't immediately respond. After several seconds, he said, simply, "Probably a motion detector."

Given Gale's usual lack of emotion, some dispassion was to be expected. Still, under the circumstances, the man's reaction struck Cartwright as completely out of place. Cartwright's patience, already stretched, was beginning to fray. He again looked at Gale. "Aren't you even mildly surprised at this?"

There was another pause before Gale replied. "I'm surprised to find it this far out."

Cartwright took a long moment to process that. "This far out," he asked, finally, "from *what*?"

The combination suit and backpack units that the astronauts wore - referred to in the acronym-friendly space program as EMU's, or extravehicular mobility units - were too bulky to allow detection of anything other than large movements on the part of the wearer. Even so, Cartwright could have sworn that Gale shrugged.

"We're not alone."

"Oh, really," Cartwright said, unable to keep the sarcasm out of his voice. "What was your first clue?"

Gale didn't respond to that.

A series of choice phrases came to mind, none of which, Cartwright knew, would have played well with the audience back on earth. And, though they weren't currently broadcasting, some vestige of propriety caused him to bite them back. Instead, he took a deep breath and asked, "Is this just your conclusion, or do you know something I don't know?"

Gale turned his body to face him. Each of them had lowered the exterior, "gold," visor on his helmet to cut the sun's glare, so neither of them could see the expression of the other. It was unnerving. Not that Gale was ever particularly demonstrative, but, without even the slightest of facial clues, it was like dealing with an automaton.

"I know something you don't know."

That would have been a perturbing statement had it been offered up on its own. What had just come before blunted some of its impact. Still, it struck a nerve. "Now," Cartwright said, acidly, "would be a good time to share."

#

On the television monitor, the moon's surface rose and fell as the lunar rover bumped its way along the craggy route indicated by the tracks in the regolith. It was, Krantz thought, awfully convenient that the astronauts had been provided a clear trail to follow. Of course, he realized, it could also be a nice way to set up an ambush. In reality, though, there weren't a whole lot of good options. Inevitably, the encounter was going to be on other than their own turf. No reason he could see not to accept the rolled out welcome mat.

And, in any event, he had confidence in Toran's ability to anticipate and react.

"Houston," he heard Bob Cartwright say, "have normal communications been restored yet?"

Krantz spoke into the microphone attached to the stalk extending down from his headset. "Sorry, that's a negative. A major electrical storm moved through the area. Apparently, it fried the primary telemetry and communications server. Not to worry, though. We have multiple backups and full redundancy."

There was a long pause. Then Cartwright's voice came again. "Can you patch in Rick Delahousse for me, please?"

They'd anticipated this.

"No," Krantz replied. "Sorry again. They're down completely."

After a moment, Cartwright asked, "Where are you located?"

Despite himself, Krantz smiled. Bob Cartwright was no fool. He wasn't going to let them just spoon feed this to him. "Alamogordo," he said. It was logical. Alamogordo, New Mexico was home to Holloman Air Force Base, where NASA was in the process of developing a training facility for the upcoming space shuttle program. It was far enough away from Houston that Rick Delahousse wouldn't be expected to just pop in and resume Capcom duties. And, taking no chances, they had confirmed that Cartwright had never been to Holloman, so he would not know whether and to what extent there might be a facility there capable of handling ground control duties.

"Who are you?" Cartwright asked.

Krantz had been ready for this, as well. "My name is Arthur Spelling. I'll be filling in for Colonel Delahousse until they're back up and operational in Houston. Shouldn't take long."

That was apparently a satisfactory answer, because, after a moment, Cartwright asked, "Are you getting the feed from the video camera?"

"Yes," Krantz replied. "It's coming in clear."

"Ok," Cartwright said. "We've got something at our two o'clock. Turning toward it now."

On the television monitor, the front of the rover crested a short rise and began a slow turn. From the far right edge of the screen, a new object slowly emerged. As it slid into view, Krantz realized he was looking at a structure that had the vague appearance of an upside-down water trough. It reminded him of the Quonset huts he'd first seen when he'd gone through basic training. Sitting a short distance away, on squat legs that looked remarkably similar to those on the descent stage of the lunar module, was a craft of some kind. This, however, was taller and had a more rounded and symmetrical shape than that of the *Concord*.

Stenciled in bright red along the fuselage, just below a five-sided star, were the letters "CCCP."

#

Bob Cartwright halted the rover and sat motionless for a long moment. Even though he'd been somewhat prepared for it by Mason Gale, it was still shocking. Twenty minutes ago, he had considered himself to be the thirteenth man to have set foot on the moon. And all others who had come before him had been Americans. That now was clearly not the case.

The competition to be the first nation to put a man on the moon had been a two-horse race for the better part of a decade. Building on the success it had achieved with the launch of Sputnik, the Soviet Union had taken the early lead, becoming the first country to put a man into orbit and the first to have a man walk in space. The United States, however, had rallied quickly, and, by the end of the 1960s, had claimed the grand prize, successfully landing men on the moon and returning them safely to earth. While that was happening, the Soviet Union had endured a string of high profile and embarrassing failures. By the end of the decade, Moscow had abandoned all efforts to reach the moon.

At least that's what the world had thought.

The ostensible focus of the Soviet space program had shifted to the establishment of a permanent manned space station. To that end, a series of platforms under the project name Salyut had been put into orbit around the earth. Salyut 4, Cartwright knew, would soon be entering its third year of deployment, and the Soviets had launched Salyut 5 just three months before Apollo 18 had blasted off. A little over a year ago, he knew, a pair of Russian cosmonauts had set a new space endurance record by spending more than two months aboard Salyut 4.

Apparently, however, the Soviets had been doing more than they'd let on.

Though Gale had been his typically taciturn self, Cartwright had been able to extract some basic information from him to help explain the extraordinary sight that now greeted him.

"Those are Russian footprints," Gale had said as they stood staring down at the object they'd first encountered. "They've been here now for about three months."

After absorbing that bit of information, and not exactly sure what to do with it, Cartwright asked, "Why all the secrecy?"

Gale did not respond to that. Instead, he said, "We received intelligence several months ago indicating the Soviets were moving forward with this. But we didn't get confirmation of the launch until June. That's when our mission got the final green light."

"Who's 'we'?"

Gale did not respond to that, either. After a long, uncomfortable silence, Cartwright asked, "Why am I being told this only now?"

"We didn't want to alarm anyone."

Resisting the urge to inquire again who "we" were, Cartwright asked, "Why would anyone be alarmed?" After a moment, he added, "And who were you trying not to alarm? Me? That doesn't make any sense."

To Cartwright's growing annoyance, Gale again remained silent. Finally, in a tone that suggested he'd given all the explanation he was going to give, the man said, "It wasn't my call, Commander."

That, Cartwright had realized, was probably all he'd get out of Gale. And not for the first time, but with a newfound sense of unease, Cartwright wondered what to make of the man. Obviously, all was not as it appeared. For Cartwright, who liked to be in control, it was exceptionally unnerving.

A movement in the distance caught his attention. To one side of the structure, an opening appeared, and, as he watched, a figure clad in a spacesuit not unlike the one he and Gale were wearing backed out slowly, stood and turned toward them. After a moment, the suited figure raised his right arm and waived it side to side. Then he reached the arm out, turned his palm upwards, and made a clear beckoning gesture.

"Well," Cartwright said, as much to himself as anyone else, "I don't know what the protocol is for this, but I'm taking us in." He eased forward on the controller, and the rover slowly advanced on the structure. At his side, Gale said nothing.

As they approached, Cartwright could make out more of the details of the structure. It looked almost like a large tent, though, instead of canvas, wide strips of a metallic material appeared to be stretched across bowed semi-circular support beams. Based on the size of the suited figure standing next to it, he estimated that the structure was about twenty feet in length and eight feet high along the center line.

When he was no more than ten feet from the thing, Cartwright halted the rover. He undid the strap that held him to his seat and dismounted. Gale did likewise. The figure who had emerged from the structure took a couple of steps to the side and, with a gesture of one gloved hand, indicated that they should enter through the open hatch.

"Alamogordo," Cartwright said, "are you seeing this?"

"Affirmative," came the voice of the man who had taken up Capcom duties after the communications failure in Houston.

"Any suggestions as to how we should proceed?"

There were several seconds of silence before the man responded. "Proceed with caution."

Oh, great, Cartwright thought. Where did they dig this guy up anyway? He turned to face Gale. "Ok," he said, "I'm going in. Wait out here until I give you the word."

"Roger that," Gale replied.

Cartwright stepped over to the Russian. The man's outer visor was up, and Cartwright could see his face inside the bulbous helmet. He was clean-shaven, and he had a surprisingly youthful appearance. There was nothing sinister or menacing about his countenance. In fact, as Cartwright watched, the man gave him a toothy smile. Cartwright raised the exterior visor on his own helmet and made what he hoped, given his general sense of unease, was a friendly nod in return.

Again, the man gestured toward the structure. In the center of the end wall was a hatch with a door that had been swung inward. Bending slightly at the waist, Cartwright eased his helmet and the top of his bulky backpack beneath the upper edge of the entryway and awkwardly peered in. The area beyond the opening extended only about six feet inward, where it met another wall with a similar hatch, this one closed. He was startled by what at first appeared to be another suited figure standing to one side. Upon closer inspection, however, he saw that it was just a space suit, complete with attached helmet, hanging from a hook on one of the support members. What he was looking at, he realized, was an air lock, a transitional chamber between livable quarters and the vacuum that was the surface of the moon.

He cautiously eased one foot over the threshold, then stepped through. He straightened and turned slowly, looking back at the suited figure standing outside the hatchway. He could see the man making the same beckoning gesture as before, inviting Gale to join Cartwright.

After a few seconds, the man apparently concluded that Gale was not going to come. He turned his body toward the opening, and, though his head was not visible, Cartwright could see his hands. The man pointed at the open door to the hatch and made a motion, bringing his palms together. Cartwright realized he was telling him to close the hatch.

"Ok," he said, both to Gale and the men back on earth, "I'm in an air lock, and I'm going to close the outer door."

Cartwright gripped the edge of the hatch covering and swung it shut. Mounted on the inside was a handle similar to those on the lunar module hatches. He rotated it downward and felt it lock into place.

After several seconds, Cartwright detected a new sound over the white noise of the personal life support system mounted on his back. The air lock, he assumed, was being filled with a breathable oxygen mixture. He turned around and saw a panel with a series of dials above the hatch inset in the far wall. He stepped closer and studied them. They were labeled, and, though he did not understand the precise meaning of the Cyrillic words, he guessed that the dial in the middle, a half circle with a single hand mounted on a swivel at the center of the base, showed the status of pressurization in the air lock. As he watched, the hand rotated in a clockwise motion through a succession of marks until it entered the last quarter, dyed a light blue on the face of the dial. After a moment, a blue light illuminated above the panel. He heard a clanking sound, and, a second later, the door below the panel swung open.

He saw a pair of legs in the space just beyond the opening, clad in what looked to be a set of olive green overalls. The figure to which the legs belonged then squatted down. A bearded face appeared in the opening and stared up, considering him.

Finally, the man took a deep breath and said in heavily accented English, "Commander Robert Cartwright. We have been expecting you."

10

A hissing sound from the air lock indicated that the space inside was once again being pressurized. Bob Cartwright glanced over at the hatch. Mounted above it were the same series of dials he'd seen from the interior of the chamber, and the hand on the one in the center was rotating slowly toward the section marked in blue. He returned his attention to the Russian standing across from him in the confined space of the structure.

When he'd been training as a backup for Apollo-Soyuz, Cartwright had been encouraged to study the biographies of the men currently serving in the Soviet space program. He'd even met a couple of them when they'd toured the Johnson Space Center. He did not recognize this man.

The Russian was big, several inches taller than Cartwright, which was something in itself, and he had broad shoulders and a barrel chest. He was standing where he'd been for the past several minutes, his feet planted a few inches apart, arms folded, an unreadable expression on his face. He stared at Cartwright through unblinking eyes set below a pair of bushy eyebrows. He'd said little since Cartwright had entered.

Earlier, while still in the air lock, Cartwright had depressurized his suit and removed his helmet. He'd then allowed the Russian to assist him in shedding his large backpack. Though the cosmonaut, through gestures, had suggested he leave the equipment in the chamber, Cartwright declined to do so. Instead he carried both pieces with him as he followed the man into the interior of the structure. When they cleared the air lock, the Russian latched the door, flipped a switch, and, as the dial above the hatch confirmed, allowed the atmosphere in the chamber to return to a vacuum.

The man then adopted his stance and said simply, "We wait for comrades."

Cartwright nodded and spoke into the microphone mounted to the communications carrier assembly in his cap. "I'm now inside the structure. The atmosphere is safe. There's one other person in here. He seems to expect us all to gather inside."

Gale's voice crackled in his earpiece. "Affirmative. The other is gesturing for me to enter. Actually, he's signaling we should enter together."

"Well," Cartwright said, after a moment, "we came all this way. I guess it would seem rude if we didn't.

"Alamogordo," he added, "do you concur?"

There was the inevitable delay, as the signal was relayed from Cartwright's communicator, through the link on the rover sitting just outside, to the lunar module, perhaps a mile away, then beamed a quarter of a million miles to earth.

After a few seconds, the reply came. "It's your call, Commander."

Once again, Cartwright had to resist the urge to roll his eyes.

The clank of the hatchway door drew his attention. As he watched, it swung slowly inward, and Gale, minus helmet and backpack, stepped into the structure. Then a man wearing coveralls similar to those worn by the other Russian ducked through the opening, straightened and put out a hand. Displaying the same toothy grin he'd given when Cartwright had seen him outside the structure, he said, in surprisingly good English, "Commander, it is great pleasure to meet you."

Cartwright shook the man's hand, again struck by his youthful appearance. Perhaps, it occurred to him, it was because the Russian wore his sandy hair in a style much longer than the military cut of all the other astronauts - and cosmonauts - that Cartwright knew. Some of it fell casually across his forehead. The unlined face and ingenuous expression seemed completely out of place.

As if reading his mind, the man said, "You are wondering what I am doing here, yes?" Then he chuckled, nodded toward his companion, and added. "You are wondering what we are both doing here. Not that you are surprised to find us. You knew exactly where you were going."

Again, he chuckled. "Those arrogant bureaucrats back in Star City. They think they can, what is this expression, pull wool over American eyes? I said they are crazy to think they can keep this secret. And for what reason? We are at peace with United States. We are cooperating. We have Apollo-Soyuz.

"But," he shook his head sadly, "is big problem with Soviet society. Always secrets."

There was a burst of Russian from the other cosmonaut. Though Cartwright had studied the basics of the language, he did not recognize the phrase. The tone, however, he knew well. Shut up and get on with it. He considered the bearded man. Clearly, he was the one in charge.

"Da," the younger man said as Cartwright returned his attention to him. "Allow me to make introductions. I am Alexander Ivanovich Kruchinkin, Cosmonaut-Engineer. My comrade is Colonel Boris Vasiliyevich Petrov."

Petrov. Cartwright knew the name. A celebrated test pilot, Petrov, he recalled, was a veteran of two Soyuz missions. Twice decorated as a Hero of the Soviet Union and a recipient of the Order of Lenin, the man had been one of the most senior members of the Soviet cosmonaut ranks - *had been* being the operative phrase, because, as far as Cartwright knew, Boris Petrov had died a year and a half earlier in a training accident.

He glanced over at the man, trying to keep the confusion and consternation that he was feeling from manifesting itself on his face. He realized he'd likely not succeeded when the older Russian grunted.

"Not dead," the man said, simply.

Cartwright studied him, but could not decipher his expression. After a moment, he again turned to the younger Russian. This man's face he had no trouble reading. The younger cosmonaut seemed to be thoroughly enjoying himself. His grin widened.

"Ah," he said, nodding, "you know about this accident. Is like Mark Twain, yes? 'Rumors of my demise have been greatly exaggerated.'" He said this last statement as if reciting from a text. Then he started to laugh, but it was short lived, as he caught himself and looked sideways at his older colleague.

"I apologize," the younger cosmonaut said. "We have been here now three months. Is long time in small space. And," he added, "is very small space."

He waved a hand around the interior of the structure. "This we have completed only five days ago. While we build, we live in capsule." He gave Cartwright an impish look. "Capsule is very small space."

Petrov cleared his throat loudly.

Adopting a more serious look, the Russian named Kruchinkin continued. "This enclosure is constructed from materials contained in probe that landed before our launch. Landing place of probe is three hundred meters from here." The man waved a hand in a direction that Cartwright realized was the opposite from which he and Gale had come in the rover. "Of course, we bring additional components in vessel you see outside.

"This vessel, we call her *Rodinia*. In English, this means," he paused, apparently searching, then said, "Motherland." He shrugged. "We launched from Salyut space station. You know about Salyut, of course?"

Cartwright nodded.

"*Rodinia* is loaded with cargo and filled with fuel at Salyut space station. Very little fuel is required to send her to moon, because there is almost no gravity to overcome. Three days from now, we return to Salyut, where replacement crew is standing by in Soyuz capsule launched yesterday." He threw a quick glance at his bearded companion that looked almost hopeful.

Petrov said nothing.

Something about the exchange struck Cartwright. Were they not sure about that? If so, why not? He noticed for the first time that neither cosmonaut seemed to be carrying any form of transmitter or receiver. Had the Soviets experienced a communications problem?

"From Salyut," Kruchinkin continued, "we return home, while replacement crew continues work here. This becomes first permanent space station on moon. Is very exciting. Big step in space exploration, do you agree?"

Cartwright wasn't sure what to say. To avoid an awkward silence, he observed, "Your English is very good."

The young man smiled. "Thank you. For two years I lived in America while I earn masters degree in aerospace engineering. At Georgia Tech University." Another puckish grin. "Go Yellow Jackets." Despite the tension, Cartwright found himself liking the man.

"My specialty," the cosmonaut explained, "is materials science." Again, he waved a hand around the enclosure. "Many elements in this structure are result of my work." He looked down, suddenly, and seemed almost embarrassed. "And work of many colleagues, of course."

He paused, while looking down, then pointed to his feet. "This floor you see. Is one piece, constructed much like, what do you call it, balloon, yes?" He looked back up at Cartwright. "But very flat. She is rolled up and stored for transit. When we have exterior of structure in place, we roll her out. We inject special polymer resin under high pressure. This resin remains in liquid form several hours, and floor is leveled by moon's gravity." He stomped a booted foot on the surface. "When dry, she is very solid, will hold much weight."

The floor did look pretty sturdy and level to Cartwright.

"You see," Kruchinkin said, "many times, simple solution is best solution."

The question that had earlier occurred to Cartwright again came to mind. "Why all the secrecy? Why hide this from the world?"

The young cosmonaut shrugged and looked at his companion. Though Cartwright was sure Petrov had understood, he remained silent, continuing to stare with those unblinking eyes. Finally, the senior cosmonaut took a deep breath. "You come. You see. Now, you go."

It wasn't, Cartwright reflected, particularly gracious. He considered his response. He and Gale hadn't exactly been invited, and they had no particular standing. Not sure what the powers-that-be back in Houston might have intended for them to do here, though, he figured that, whatever there was to see, they'd seen it, and he decided there was no point in making an issue of it. He turned around and faced Gale. "I guess that's it."

Gale's usually grim expression was even more ominous than usual. He was looking past Cartwright at the older Russian. The cosmonauts, it occurred to Cartwright, would have no way of knowing that what they were seeing wasn't intended as an affront, but merely standard boorish behavior from Mason Gale. Not wanting the situation to degenerate into an international incident, Cartwright raised a hand. "I mean it. That's it. Let's suit up. We're leaving."

But, instead of turning toward the air lock, Gale took a step in Cartwright's direction and let loose a torrent of Russian. Cartwright was taken aback, and, for a second, he thought Gale might have lost his mind. Then he realized the outburst was directed back over his shoulder at Petrov. In the sudden stunned silence, he considered his crewmate. After a long moment, he said, "What the hell was that?"

Gale's eyes did not leave the senior cosmonaut. "I informed him that we know exactly what's going on."

"*We*," Cartwright said, working hard to keep his voice even, "is a lot of people."

For just a brief instant, Gale took his eyes off Petrov and directed his gaze toward a piece of equipment mounted on a workbench next to Kruchinkin. Returning his eyes to the older Russian, Gale said, "That, Commander, is a weapon."

"No," Kruchinkin said, immediately, glancing down at the device by his side. "Is no weapon. Is navigational equipment. To help guide replacement crews."

Gale shook his head slightly, eye's still locked on Petrov. "That is the control mechanism for a pulse generator. It does have a navigational function, but not the one they want you to think. Its purpose is to disrupt electronics. Basically, disable vessels that come into lunar orbit. Or, to be more precise, disable our vessels. The actual generator was loaded onto Soyuz 22 a week ago."

"No," Kruchinkin repeated, but a tinge of uncertainty had crept into his voice.

Cartwright looked from Kruchinkin to Gale. They were both staring at Petrov. There was a troubled expression on the young cosmonaut's face, but Gale's was as implacable as before. Finally, Cartwright turned around and regarded Petrov himself.

The big man's eyes had gone flat, but his countenance was otherwise unchanged.

From behind him, Gale said, conversationally, "By the way, there was a little problem on the launch pad. Salyut 22 never got off the ground."

"What?" Kruchinkin gasped.

Petrov's eyes narrowed. He began to unfold his arms, and, as he brought his hands out, Cartwright realized that the man had been concealing something under his left armpit, something dark and, in the brief moment he had to consider it, metallic-looking.

Then three things happened at once, or, if not exactly concurrently, within such close proximity they registered in Cartwright's mind at the same instant.

For one, a dark hole appeared in the bushy right eyebrow of the Russian, near the point at which its tip just barely touched the corresponding tip of the other brow. The opening was perfectly symmetrical, perhaps a third of an inch in diameter. And among the flood of simultaneous thoughts that hit Cartwright was the realization that such a hole had absolutely no business being where it was.

For another, Cartwright felt something hot pass by his left cheek, a feeling not so much that it was there, but more that it had been there, gone before he could possibly begin to acknowledge it. If whatever it was made a sound, though, Cartwright would never know, because the third thing that happened overwhelmed everything else.

An extraordinary noise suddenly filled the enclosure, not an explosion, though loud enough to be one. Too sharp for that. More like the immense crack of thunder bursting just overhead in a fierce summer storm, the sound so loud and violent that Cartwright felt it as much as he heard it. There just for an instant, it was replaced immediately by an oddly muffled reverberation.

Petrov, still staring past Cartwright with flat, expressionless eyes, seemed to waver. He'd gotten his large hands out in front of him at shoulder level, but they remained there, suspended just long enough for Cartwright to register the fact that, in the right hand, there was, indeed, a metallic object, a pistol, actually smaller than the fist holding it.

And then the big Russian seemed to fold in on himself, his shoulders slumping, waist bending and knees buckling all at once. He crumpled in a heap, his head lolling back and finally striking the floor with a muted thump, the flat eyes staring upward, unseeing.

Still recoiling from the shock of the noise, it took Cartwright a moment to react. He turned and looked at Gale, whose right arm was extended. Gale also had a weapon in his hand, this one larger than the Russian's pistol and unlike any Cartwright had ever seen before. It had two barrels, one on top of the other, both positioned well above the hand that was wrapped around the grip.

The gun was pointed straight at Kruchinkin.

Cartwright glanced at the young Russian. The cosmonaut was staring at his fallen companion, a stunned expression on his face. There was nothing about him remotely threatening.

"No," Cartwright commanded, his own voice sounding strange and distant.

At the sound of the word, the young man instinctively looked up, and, when he saw the weapon, his already pale features blanched even more.

Gale's eyes did not leave the cosmonaut. "This is not your call, Commander," he said, his voice also muffled. Cartwright realized that the sound of the weapon discharging must have affected his ears.

Without thinking about it, Cartwright took a quick step to the side, putting his body between Gale and the young Russian. "Like hell it's not my call," he said, anger beginning to replace the shock.

The gun in Gale's hand did not waver. "Not a smart move," Gale said.

Cartwright turned and looked back at Kruchinkin, who returned his gaze, his eyes full of fear and confusion. "Do you have a weapon?" Cartwright asked.

The young cosmonaut shook his head quickly.

"Did you know about that one?" Cartwright's eyes flitted toward the pistol that had landed on the floor next to Petrov's body before immediately refocusing on Kruchinkin.

Again, the Russian shook his head.

He looked into the man's eyes for a long moment. Finally, he turned back to Gale. "That's enough. Nobody else is getting shot."

To his surprise, Gale extended the gun toward him. "Sorry, Commander." And then Cartwright's world went black.

#

Spots swam before him, blinking randomly in a vivid multi-colored pastiche. Lights on a Christmas tree, he realized. On the floor, the boys were gleefully tearing into brightly colored wrapping paper, their voices a cacophony of shrieks and exclamations. A warm glow spread through him. He smiled, opening his mouth to speak. But instead of sound came pain. A sharp, intense pain radiating out from his forehead. He felt himself falling backward. The lights were no longer twinkling, but throbbing. And with each throb, came an ache, mild at first, but, with every new pulse, stronger. Soon, the pain was unbearable. Must open your eyes, he heard himself say. Who was he talking to? Himself. And he suddenly knew with an overwhelming certainty that he had to open his eyes.

Cartwright's eyes flew open.

A few inches in front of him he saw metal, a washed out gray cloaked in semi-darkness. He blinked twice before it occurred to him that what he was looking at was the upper bulkhead of the lunar module. He was lying on his back, suspended in his hammock. The vessel was strangely silent, and it took him a moment to realize that he did not hear the normal whirring sounds of the Environmental Control System. He had the sudden thought that he needed to get into his suit, followed immediately by the comprehension that he was already in his suit. But he was not wearing his helmet, nor was he connected to the personal life support system contained in his backpack.

Instinctively, he called out, "ECS failure," and he started to reach up for a handhold to pull himself out of the hammock. His arms would not move.

"Take it easy," he heard another voice say. It sounded strange, almost as if he were hearing it underwater. Gale. And his memory of the events in the Soviet space station came back in a rush.

"Relax," Gale said. "All systems are nominal." His face appeared as he rose to stand next to the hammock. "You're not hearing the usual sounds because our ears have been impaired by the discharge of a weapon in an enclosed space. Hopefully, it's just temporary."

Cartwright took quick stock of his situation. His arms were pinned to his side, a rope or some other restraint having been tied around both him and the hammock at his waist. His legs were similarly immobilized. He felt a hot flush.

"Cut me out of here," he said through clenched teeth. "Now."

Gale raised a hand in a placating gesture. "I will. I just didn't want you to hurt yourself when you came to."

Gale, however, made no effort to undo the bindings. Instead, with his other hand, he held up Cartwright's Snoopy cap. "Before I do, there's someone you need to talk to." He reached forward and slid the cap onto Cartwright's head. Cartwright had to force himself to bite back the expletive that came to mind.

"Houston," Gale said, speaking into the stalk on his own cap, "do you copy?"

Through the earpiece, Cartwright could hear Gale's voice more distinctly. Then the fact that Gale had hailed Houston hit him. The communications problem, he told himself, must have been corrected. At least he had that.

"Roger," came the reply. It sounded like the man who'd been speaking to him from Alamogordo. So he'd had time to get to Houston. Cartwright wondered just how long he'd been out. "Stand by for Deputy Administrator Huffman."

"Hello, Bob," came another voice after a short delay. "This is Adam Huffman. We met in Stu Overholdt's office back in April."

Cartwright recognized the man's voice. He paused before responding. The fact that he was speaking to the second-in-command at NASA while tied into his hammock was disorienting. "Yes, sir. I remember."

"Bob, you've been doing a hell of a job. That landing was particularly impressive."

"Well, thank you, sir, but…"

Huffman had not waited for a reply. "Now I know you have some questions, but I'm not at liberty to discuss them with you over an open channel. Dr. Gale will fill you in to the extent appropriate. Just understand that you have NASA's full support and gratitude. Hell, what am I saying. You have the country's support and gratitude. Listen to what Dr. Gale has to say. And we'll look forward to seeing you back here in a few days."

When he felt confident the man had finished, Cartwright asked, "Sir, am I still in command here?"

There was an odd moment of silence before the deputy administrator replied. "Yes, Bob. Of course."

"Good," Cartwright said, looking directly at Gale. "Now cut me out of this goddamned hammock."

#

They sat awkwardly side by side on the ascent engine cover, each considering the other. After Gale had untied the elastic tethers holding him in place, Cartwright had slung himself off the hammock, unhooked the forward end and angrily threw the thing toward the back of the module. His head throbbing, he'd then retrieved a container of juice from one of the food storage compartments to slake the wicked thirst that had overtaken him.

"Look," Gale now said, evenly. "I didn't want any of that to happen back there. But I didn't have a choice. You saw the weapon in Petrov's hand. If I don't shoot first, he shoots. Probably at you."

"That still doesn't explain why you shot me."

Gale pursed his lips. Finally, he said, "I didn't exactly shoot you. I disabled you. I had to. You were making an already dangerous situation worse." He took a breath. "We incorporated the tranquilizer option in the weapon for a number of contingencies. One of them was the possibility that you might get in the way. I had express authority to use it on you if that happened. Again, it wasn't what I wanted to do."

The suggestion that he was somehow interfering, albeit with something he didn't yet understand, was troubling to Cartwright, and it gave him pause, helping to reign in some of the anger. "All right," Cartwright said after a moment, "let's take it from the beginning. Who the hell are you?"

"I'm Mason Gale. That's my real name."

"Are you a lunar geologist?"

"No."

"Who do you work for?"

"Same as you. The government." Then he added, "Different agency."

Cartwright snorted. "What agency?"

Gale shook his head. "That I can't tell you. But it doesn't matter. You've never heard of it. Let's just say it's one of the intelligence services, and leave it at that. In the scheme of things, it's not important."

Cartwright decided that was probably right and elected not to pursue it. "Why were you sent here?"

"My mission," Gale said, "was to assess the situation, respond to threats, and, if necessary, neutralize them." He put a hand up, apparently recognizing that Cartwright was about to ask what the hell that meant. "For the last several years, we've been closely monitoring the progress of the Soviet space program. Some of it is legitimate. Exploration. Not all of it, though. Publicly, the Soviet Union has committed - same as us - to neutrality in space. Both of our countries have signed a treaty to that effect. But the Soviets have been working hard to do exactly the opposite, under

167

a project code-named Almaz. Salyut 3 was their first success. It was supposed to be for scientific research, but it was really a military space station, armed with a 23 millimeter rapid fire cannon. Salyut 5, which was launched three months ago, is also an Almaz station."

"And the base here is part of that program?" Cartwright asked.

Gale nodded. "Yes, as it turns out. Though we weren't sure. Several months ago, we learned that the Soviets were planning to finally put men on the moon. They'd kept this one really quiet. That, of course, sent up even more warning signals than most of the stuff they do. And," he added with a slight shrug, "we'd had some intelligence setbacks over the past couple of years. Lost some good people, so we were behind the curve. We weren't really sure what they were up to."

"So," Cartwright said, "Apollo 18 was revived. To give us a chance to go take a look."

"Exactly."

"But why not let me in on it? Don't tell me your people thought I'd go blab it to the Russians."

"No, nothing like that. At least I don't think," Gale added, without a hint of sarcasm. Cartwright was once again reminded how humorless Gale could be. "As I said before, it wasn't my call. I can only tell you what I was told. We weren't sure what was going on up here, and we had to play it close to the vest. Simple fact is, you're not a professional operative."

"You mean I'm not a professional liar," Cartwright said dryly.

"That too."

"So now what?" Cartwright asked. "We go public?"

Gale didn't respond right away. There was something ominous about the silence. Finally, Gale said, "We let the higher-ups deal with it. Our job is to sit tight, wait for the launch window, and return to the command capsule. Then we go home. By the time we get there, it'll all be sorted out."

"That's it?"

Gale nodded. "Those are our orders."

It didn't add up, but Cartwright was having trouble putting his finger on the reason. Perhaps, he thought, he was suffering lingering effects from whatever drugs were in the tranquilizer. He closed his eyes and tried to focus. After a moment, he asked, "So what exactly happened back there after you knocked me out?"

Again, Gale hesitated. "Nothing. I got us both suited up, dragged you to the rover, and drove us back here."

That also didn't compute. Concentrate Bob, he told himself. Then something occurred to him. "How was I interfering?"

"You'd put yourself between me and the other Russian," Gale said immediately. "You were giving him an opening. I had to take away his advantage."

Cartwright thought about that. As Gale had noted, Cartwright was not a, what had he called it? A professional operative. Even so, that seemed a bit of a stretch. "Having me unconscious wasn't a distraction?"

"No."

"And nothing else happened?"

"Correct."

The process of getting into their gear was not easy. Putting on the bulky backpack could be done by an astronaut on his own, but it took a long time. For Gale to have accomplished it while ostensibly keeping an eye on someone intent on doing him harm would have been almost impossible. Cartwright looked hard at Gale.

"You're telling me Kruchinkin just stood there watching while you suited us both up?"

"Yes."

Gale didn't blink. He didn't look away. But, then again, Cartwright thought, as between the two of them, Gale was the professional operative. And Cartwright's own words came back to him. Professional liar.

"I don't believe you."

Gale didn't exactly smile, but the corners of his mouth did turn up slightly. It was actually more menacing than his usual dispassionate look.

"I don't care," Gale said.

In the unnatural silence, Cartwright considered the man. Gale almost appeared to be enjoying himself, which was remarkably disconcerting. And then the thing that had been bothering Cartwright, that had been tickling at the edges of his sentience for the past several minutes, frustratingly just out of reach, finally took root. He started to speak, stopped, then, the residual anger taking over, he decided, what the hell.

"Back at the space station," Cartwright began, slowly, "you said the pulse generator was loaded onto a Soyuz a week ago. That was before we even launched." Gale's expression did not change. "We didn't need to come here to determine what the Soviets were up to, did we? We already knew."

He was familiar enough with Gale to know the man wouldn't respond to that, and, sure enough, he didn't. Instead, he continued to regard Cartwright with that ambiguous look.

The seconds stretched into an uncomfortably long period. Gale seemed perfectly at ease in the silence. Cartwright's mind was working overtime, making up for its previous lethargy. Gale, he knew now without a doubt, was a very dangerous man. The two of them were in a confined space. The lyrics of a popular song came to mind. Nowhere to run, nowhere to hide.

Finally, Cartwright asked, "Do you have anything more to say?"

Gale shook his head slowly. If anything, his grim smile deepened. The man, Cartwright realized, really *was* enjoying himself. He was in his element. Sadly, Cartwright was not.

Or was he?

Cartwright kept his own face as neutral as possible, but the gears were turning. "All right," he said after a long moment. "I don't know what's going on, but I can follow orders." He placed his two gloved hands on the engine cover and pushed himself up. As he came to a standing position, one knee buckled slightly, and he fell against the bulkhead to their right. Because of the fractional gravity, the fall was in a slow motion, and he had plenty of time to put out his right hand to break it. As he leaned against the side wall, he held his left hand up to his forehead. Even through his glove he could tell there was a knot in the middle, the result, he guessed, of being shot with the tranquilizer. He shook his head side to side and straightened.

"Wow," he said in a slightly surprised, but groggy voice. "That wasn't a very a smooth move."

Blinking his eyes, he looked back at Gale, still seated on the engine cover. The man stared back, but said nothing.

Reaching for the unattached end of his hammock, Cartwright said, "I'm going to lay down for a little bit, until the dizziness passes." He raised a gloved finger in Gale's direction. "No more tethers."

Gale shook his head slightly, then raised a hand as if giving an oath.

Cartwright hooked the end of the hammock into the eyelet near the front of the module and reached above his head for a grip on the overhead hatch handle to pull himself up into his bunk. Instead of grabbing the main handle, however, his hand closed around the smaller lever for the dump valve on the opposite edge of the hatch, the one that was used to depressurize the cabin when the astronauts were prepared to make an EVA. As he swung himself up into the hammock, Cartwright twisted his wrist, shifting the lever from its standard Auto position to the Open position, allowing air from the cabin to vent out into space.

Normally, the hiss of escaping air would have been detected by both astronauts, but, as Cartwright had suspected, the damage they'd suffered to their eardrums rendered the sound almost inaudible. Cartwright, who was aware the valve had been opened and whose head was now inches away, could barely hear it. If

Gale's audio faculties were as impaired as his, the man would not hear it at all.

Of course, the module was fitted with an alarm that would normally have sounded when the valve was opened, and that sound would have been quite loud and readily heard by both astronauts. But, as Cartwright had fallen against the bulkhead, he'd come in contact with the Environmental Control System mounted aft of the lunar module pilot's station. With his right hand concealed from Gale's view by his body, he'd hit the override switch on the alarm and had shifted the cabin repressurization valve from Auto to Closed. He'd hoped Gale, who, despite the man's intense introduction to the workings of the module over the past several months, was still not nearly as familiar with it as Cartwright, would not notice either of the changed settings. To Cartwright's relief, the man apparently had not.

Timing was going to be critical. What Cartwright intended to do was extraordinarily dangerous, and there was a very good chance he would end up killing the both of them. In his current state of mind, it was a risk he was willing to take.

He knew that, as the air bled from the dump valve, it would take approximately three minutes for the cabin pressure to drop from its normal 5.0 to a mere 0.08 pounds per square inch. When it got near the latter point, Cartwright, assuming he was still conscious, would be able to pull the hatch open against the remaining pressure. Then, all of whatever oxygen was still in the module would rush out through the opening into the vacuum that surrounded them. From that moment, Cartwright would have, at best, maybe ten seconds to do what he needed to do.

Heart beating fast, he counted. Twenty-one Mississippi, twenty-two Mississippi. He was banking on the notion that, as oxygen was sucked out of the module, it would vacate the areas farthest from the source of the leak first. Somewhat counter intuitively, therefore, he hoped the best place to be was where he was now, close up against the spot from which the air was escaping. It was a theory he'd never tested. Or ever imagined he would need to test.

As he passed through a hundred Mississippi, Cartwright felt himself growing faint, the light in the cabin dimming and his field of vision narrowing. He heard, or thought he heard, a grunt from Gale. Then a movement below his feet told him the man had realized there was a problem. Gale had risen and now lurched toward the ECS panel.

To reverse what was happening, Gale would need to diagnose the problem and hit several switches in the right sequence, all while in an already oxygen-deprived state. Cartwright didn't think it was possible. Still, Gale reached for the panel, gloved fingers fumbling for the controls. As he slapped at the panel, he must have toggled the override switch because the alarm suddenly sounded, filling the cabin with an intense noise. A part of Cartwright's mind not only registered the man's actions, but marveled at his strength.

Cartwright knew he couldn't wait any longer. Fighting against the oncoming blackness, his vision and focus entirely on the hatch above him, he planted his feet against the upper bulkhead, gripped the main handle on the hatch with two hands and twisted it. Then he pulled down with all his remaining strength. As he felt the silicone compound seal separate, he expelled what little air remained in his lungs, clamped his lips shut and allowed his legs to drop to the engine cover below him against the sudden rush of the remaining air escaping through the open hatch. The alarm stopped abruptly, and the module was plunged into absolute silence as it was exposed to the vacuum of space.

A common misperception, one promulgated over the years by bad science fiction, was that a human body when subjected to a vacuum, would either explode or instantly freeze. Neither was true. In reality, the body could continue to function in a vacuum for several minutes, skin holding in all the organs, heart still pumping blood to the extremities. The immediate problem for someone cast into the void was lack of oxygen. And it would do no good to hold one's breath. In fact, due to the inevitability of gas expanding in a vacuum, that would be the worst thing one could do, as it would likely lead to a rupture of the lungs.

With mere seconds before unconsciousness, Cartwright levered his feet against the engine cover, pushed up and rammed the hatch closed. With his left hand, he dogged the handle shut, with his right, he rotated the dump valve to Auto. As he dropped to his knees, he gripped the cabin repressurization lever and switched it to the Open position. Then he reached back and flipped over his backpack. He wasn't sure how much oxygen remained in the Personal Life Support System that made up the bulk of the pack, and he wasn't going to take a chance. On top of the PLSS was the small compartment housing the Oxygen Purge System. He grabbed one of the flexible hoses extending from the OPS and shoved the end into one of the oxygen intake valves on the front of his suit. Then he picked up his helmet and lifted it over his head, quickly rotating it and snapping it into place. As the darkness began to descend, he pulled an actuator on the control unit mounted to his chest, heard the whir of the recirculation motor, and, after a couple of seconds, felt the most wonderful breeze he'd ever experienced, as oxygen began to fill his helmet.

He may have blacked out for a time. He wasn't sure. He lay slumped against the rear wall of the cabin for at least a couple of minutes, gathering strength. Finally, he raised himself and awkwardly turned, checking the readout on the ECS panel. Cabin pressure was passing through 3.5 psi. Safe enough. He shut off the emergency oxygen flow from the OPS and removed his helmet. He was going to need to deal with Gale before the man came to. If, indeed, he did actually come to.

There was, of course, every chance Gale's lungs had ruptured or his brain had been deprived of oxygen for too long. A selfish part of Cartwright's mind said neither would be the end of the world. The rest of his mind knew though that he couldn't simply leave the man to die.

And, he thought bitterly, Gale was as strong as an ox.

Gale had landed face down on the deck. With some effort, Cartwright rolled him over and, removing his right glove, checked for a pulse in the man's neck. Steady. The rise and fall of

Gale's chest told Cartwright that his crewmate was still breathing regularly. It figured.

Cartwright patted down the man's body. He found what he was looking for almost immediately. On the right leg of Gale's suit was a large utility pocket. Cartwright had one on his own suit, in which he carried, among other things, the emergency patch kit that he would use if either of them experienced an unexpected suit rupture. Gale's pocket contained none of the usual equipment. Instead, it had been fitted for the handgun that Cartwright had seen at the Soviet base, padding cleverly used to conceal its shape. Cartwright withdrew the weapon and turned the thing over in his hand.

As a boy growing up in rural Indiana, Cartwright had been exposed to guns at an early age. He'd shot his first deer when he was thirteen. It wasn't until he arrived at the Naval Academy, however, that Cartwright had an opportunity to fire a handgun. And, it turned out, he was quite proficient at it. In the summer after his second year at the Academy, he'd shot scores that qualified him for the Marine Corps Expert Marksmanship badge in both pistol and rifle. That, however, had been a long time ago. It had been years since he'd picked up a weapon.

This one, as he'd noticed when he first saw it at the Soviet base, was unlike any he'd seen before. There were two barrels, one on top of the other. And he now understood the reason for that. One of the barrels fired a conventional bullet, while the other was for the tranquilizer dart. He guessed that the latter was the barrel on top, as the gauge was smaller. There was, however, only a single trigger, surrounded by an oversized trigger guard shaped so as to accommodate the bulky fingers of an EVA glove. A lever on the left side of the grip could be slid up and down by a right handed shooter using his thumb, and he guessed that this set the weapon to conventional or tranquilizer mode. At the moment, the lever was down, suggesting that it was ready to fire a regular bullet. He slid the mechanism up. It moved easily, and he felt it lock in place.

One of the most unusual aspects of the weapon was the fact that the rear of each barrel was open ended. He puzzled over that for a moment, then realized why. This gun had been designed to be fired in the vacuum of space. The recoil of a pistol was already bad enough. If a conventional handgun were fired in a vacuum, Cartwright guessed that it might hurl the shooter backwards, or worse. This weapon was designed to fire in both directions at the same time, probably a harmless discharge of gas to the rear, so as not to injure the shooter. It was a practical solution to a unique challenge.

He hoped he wouldn't have to use the thing, but he knew ...

A vice abruptly clamped around his throat, and his head was thrown back. Gale, his face contorted into a feral grimace, had lunged upward with both hands, flung them over the rigid ring collar of Cartwright's suit, and locked them on both sides of his neck. The suddenness and ferocity of the attack took Cartwright completely by surprise, and the gun flew out of his hand, clattering to his left onto the metal deck. Instinctively, Cartwright reached up with both hands, gripping Gale's wrists and pulling at them.

Gale dug his thumbs violently into the flesh at the front of Cartwright's neck, forcing the Adam's apple toward the back of his throat and cutting off his windpipe. Starbursts of light flashed in the back of Cartwright's eyes, and his body began to shake. The harder he pulled on Gale's wrists, the stronger the man seemed to become.

Cartwright let go with his left hand and flung it out to his side, slapping the deck in a desperate attempt to locate the gun. Nothing. His vision began to blur. He slid the gloved hand along the deck surface, searching frantically. Still nothing. He lunged and threw his hand out as far as possible, wildly sliding it back and forth in a wide arc. The tips of his fingers brushed against something hard, knocking it further away. He kicked out with both legs, trying to extend his reach. One of his boots found purchase on the side of the engine cover and, with as much force as he could muster, he pushed against it. The two men tipped sideways toward the front of the module, and Cartwright's outstretched hand fell across a solid object. The pistol.

The agony in his throat was unbearable. His lungs screamed for air, and darkness began to descend. His hand shaking uncontrollably, he rotated the gun on the floor until he could wrap his fingers around the grip. But, when he tried to put his index finger into the trigger guard, it wouldn't fit, and he realized through his panic that, because the gun had been designed for a right-hander, the opening from the left side was not as wide as the right. He felt his energy wane. In desperation, he lifted the weapon and slammed it down on the deck as hard as he could. Thankfully, his finger slid in. With his last bit of strength, he yanked his hand around, pushed the gun up against the side of Gale's head and pulled the trigger.

#

When Cartwright came to, he was lying face down on the deck, his right cheek pressing into cold metal. His throat burned, and his head throbbed. Moving slowly, less by choice than necessity, he slid his left hand under his shoulder, realizing as he did that the pistol was still locked in his grip. With a considerable effort, he pushed himself up.

He had fallen across Gale's body, which lay motionless beneath him. He turned to look at the man, idly wondering as he did whether he'd discover that the gun had blown Gale's head off. But, no, the damned thing appeared to be intact. The man's eyes were closed, and he looked to be sleeping, though not peacefully. A vestige of the animal-like grimace remained and his breathing was ragged. From the side of his cheek, just in front of his right ear, a small orange object protruded. The tail end of a tranquilizer dart.

Awkwardly, Cartwright lifted himself off the unconscious man, using the edge of the engine cover for leverage, and he half threw himself onto the shallow landing, collapsing back against the two EVA backpacks. His own breathing was difficult, and, when he probed gingerly with his fingers, he found his neck raw and sore to the touch. He couldn't say how long he lay there. A few seconds maybe. Perhaps a few minutes.

Eventually, he made himself focus. He was, he knew, damn fortunate to be alive. He considered his options. In reality, he had none. He knew exactly what he had to do. But he was going to need his strength. Just a few more minutes he told himself, and he closed his eyes, trying to will away the pain.

Finally, he took a deep breath, forced himself up, and got to work.

11

Bob Cartwright had pushed the rover to its maximum speed, and, as it hit each bump in the uneven terrain, the vehicle became momentarily airborne, sailing in slow motion over the lunar surface. Then, each time the large steel-woven wheels dug back into the regolith, a fine spray of dust shot out to each side, forming perfect parabolas that remained suspended in the moon's partial gravity until long after the vehicle had passed. Under other circumstances, Cartwright would have marveled at the sight. But he was in a hurry and had too much else on his mind.

After he'd pulled himself together following Gale's attack, Cartwright had set about performing a series of tasks. First, he'd recharged the oxygen and water tanks in the astronauts' two backpacks. Then he'd tackled the difficult process of suiting up the unconscious Gale. When he was done with that, he'd awkwardly climbed into his own backpack. The exercise had taken almost an hour and had served to underscore his unwillingness to believe that the decision to tranquilize him at the Soviet base made any sense. Even given the fact that, in the Soviet enclosure, Gale would have had more room to maneuver the equipment than Cartwright had in the cramped module, it would still have been a major distraction. For that reason alone, he didn't buy Gale's story.

But it begged the question: Why would Gale have shot him and then lied to him? Cartwright thought he knew the answer. The only way to be sure, though, was to return to the Soviet base.

After he'd pressurized both of their suits, Cartwright had again dumped the atmosphere in the module, this time in a more conventional and controlled manner. Then, with difficulty, he maneuvered himself and the unconscious Gale out of the forward hatch and down the ladder to the moon's surface. He had considered leaving Gale in the module, tethered to his hammock. He liked the symmetry the gesture would have represented. But he'd given it some thought and decided not to do it.

He didn't know how long Gale would be out. He figured that the tranquilizer must be fairly long-acting, because, though he couldn't say how long Gale had lingered at the Soviet base or how long it had taken for the drug to wear off after the astronauts had arrived back at the module, he knew there had been at least enough time while he was unconscious for the man named Arthur Spelling to have made it from Alamogordo to Houston. He hoped whatever that amount of time was, it would allow him to make it to and from the Soviet base before Gale came around.

Still, he couldn't be sure Gale wouldn't awaken while he was gone, and, though he felt confident he could tie Gale up sufficiently to keep him immobilized after coming to, in the back of his mind Cartwright couldn't shake the notion that there was something unstoppable about the man. The last thing Cartwright wanted to have to do on his return was stick his head into the module not knowing whether Gale might be standing just inside the hatch with a heavy tool ready to bash in his helmet, bringing a quick and painful death.

So he had decided to truss up Gale outside the module, where the man would be in full sight when Cartwright returned. As further protection, Cartwright had taken the pistol with him. If, by some miracle, Gale did manage to slip his bindings, Cartwright would be aware of it and at least have that advantage.

He used the same tethers Gale had employed, the ones that had held the two astronauts in place when they were manning their crew stations during descent to the moon's surface. He'd tied the restraints around Gale's midsection and ankles, using knots he remembered from his second and first class summer cruises at the Academy, and he'd left the man lying by the forward leg of the lunar module.

Ahead of him now, the sets of tracks he'd been following curved around the side of a gently sloping hillock, and, as he crested the short rise, the Soviet base came into view. At first glance, it looked the same. The exterior door to the air lock was closed, and the vessel that Kruchinkin had called *Rodinia* sat nearby on four stubby legs. When he looked more carefully, however, he noticed something very different. On the side of the capsule, in place of the first "C" in the initials "CCCP," was a jagged hole, about a meter across at its widest point. Then he realized that, below the vessel, there were items that had not previously been there. As he closed the distance, those items revealed themselves to be irregularly shaped pieces of metal that appeared to be embedded in the ground. Cartwright knew immediately what had happened.

Gale had obviously planted an explosive charge in the Soviet space ship. The blast must have been directed mostly downward, through the rocket's engine, destroying the thing. But the explosion had also ripped a hole in the side of the vessel.

Lying on the ground in front of the capsule were the bodies of two suited cosmonauts.

He brought the rover to a stop in front of the enclosure and climbed out. As he bounded over, he realized that what he'd seen weren't bodies at all, but a pair of empty space suits.

Unlike the U.S. version, the Soviet space suit, known as the Krechet, was a one-piece affair with an integrated helmet permanently attached. The suit was entered from a rear hatch, the cover of which contained its life support system. These two suits looked to be intact, but, when Cartwright rolled one over, he saw that the helmet had been crudely caved in with a heavy object. He rotated the second suit and found it similarly damaged. If the fabric had been punctured, there might have been the possibility of patching the tears. But there was no way to repair the helmets. These suits would be of no further use to anyone.

Cartwright straightened and turned toward the enclosure. From this side, he could now see that it, too, had a jagged hole.

Apparently, whatever debris had been blown out the side of the vessel had ripped through the structure at its rear corner. Because of the angle at which the debris had struck, this hole was even larger than the one in the capsule. Knowing what he would find, but needing to see it himself, Cartwright stepped over to the side of the structure and peered in.

Sprawled on the floor below him was the large body of Petrov, lying face up, glassy eyes staring toward the heavens. Cartwright leaned in further and turned toward the front of the enclosure, looking for the body of Kruchinkin that he knew would also be lying on the floor. To his surprise, however, he saw nothing.

That made no sense.

Cartwright stepped back and moved to his right, maneuvering around the damaged corner of the structure to get a better angle. He leaned in again and studied the interior. There was, he confirmed, no second body. He did notice, however, that where he'd expected to see the body was a dark stain on the floor. Could have been blood, though it was hard to tell against the dark background. Then he saw that, whatever it was, it had been smeared across the floor to a point just in front of the closed air lock hatch.

Above the dials at the top of the hatchway, a blue light glowed.

Cartwright took in a sharp breath and stood motionless for several seconds, considering the ramifications of what he was seeing.

With a renewed sense of urgency, Cartwright hurried back to the rover. From the tool kit mounted behind the right seat, he withdrew a small rock pick, which he carried to the air lock hatch. With the blunt end of the tool, he tapped three times on the metal door. Then he knelt down and placed his helmet up against the door, listening intently. Nothing. In the vacuum of space, the tapping had made no sound that Cartwright could hear, but he felt certain that, from within the air lock, if it was indeed pressurized, the sound would have been audible. He wondered, though, whether the sound would be transmitted through his own helmet. He tried again, this time with his helmet still against the door, and he could, indeed, hear the sound of metal striking metal. If he could hear tapping generated from this side, he assumed he'd be able to hear it coming from the other side. There was, however, still nothing but silence.

He repeated the process twice more, each time receiving no reply. As he knelt in front of the hatch straining for a response, it dawned on him that, if anyone could actually see him, he'd probably look a little absurd, knocking in vain on the front door of a dwelling on the moon. Nobody's home, Bob. He shifted his position, the pressure of the suit uncomfortable against his knees. He raised the pick to strike one more time, but, before he could do so, he stiffened. He'd heard a sound.

Three faint taps.

He quickly gave the door another three taps with the pick, and, again, after a few seconds, heard three more in response.

He took a couple of steadying breaths, thinking hard. At the Naval Academy, he'd learned Morse code. As part of survival training, he'd received a series of refresher courses over the years. The code was an international form of communication. That didn't mean the cosmonaut would be familiar with it, but there was nothing to lose. Using the head of the pick for dash and the handle for dot, he slowly tapped out a message. *Do you understand me?*

There was a long delay. Then he heard a series of replying taps. They made no sense.

He tapped again. *Please repeat.*

Another long pause, then more taps. It took him a moment to process what he was hearing. Then it clicked. The Russian had signaled, *I understand.*

With the pick, Cartwright inquired, *Are you injured?*

The reply was short. *Yes.*

183

Afraid of the response, Cartwright tapped, *Do you have a pressure suit?*

Again the reply was short. *No.*

Cartwright's blood went cold. Without a pressure suit, the young cosmonaut couldn't possibly leave the air lock. He was trapped. Assuming he didn't die from his injury, he'd live only as long as the oxygen supply to the tiny enclosure held out. Effectively, he was a dead man, waiting in the bleak, cold chamber for his inevitable end. Cartwright knew it, and, he realized, Kruchinkin had to know it as well.

Cartwright raised the pick to tap out more, but suddenly had no idea what to say. His hand hung suspended in front of the door. After a long moment, he heard more taps from the inside.

This is Commander Cartwright yes?

Slowly, he tapped, *Yes.*

He strained to make out the reply. It came after a long delay and was very faint. *Please find parents. Give them my love.*

Cartwright hesitated, the pick again suspended a few inches from the door. Finally, he signaled slowly, *I will.* Then, he added, *I am sorry.*

Cartwright continued leaning against the door, not because he expected a reply, but more out of an irrational sense that he couldn't simply leave. Logically, he knew there was nothing he could do here. And he knew he needed to get back to the module before Gale came to. But he nevertheless found it hard to let go. Finally he sighed, flexed, and was about pull his head away when he heard one last light series of taps.

Thank you.

He collapsed back against the door. With a heavy heart, he lay a gloved hand against the hatch door. He didn't tap out the message. Instead, he murmured softly, "Goodbye. And Godspeed."

#

As the rover bounded over the surface, Cartwright's head was filled with dark thoughts.

Mason Gale, he knew now, hadn't been sent here to "assess the situation." He'd been sent here to kill the cosmonauts and destroy their vessel. It was murder, pure and simple. And Cartwright had been duped into serving as an accessory. Whoever had planned this hadn't kept him in the dark to maintain secrecy. No, he'd been deceived so he wouldn't question the whole thing sooner. So he wouldn't blow the cover of the assassin. Damn, he castigated himself, why didn't I see through that?

As he had several times after disabling Gale, Cartwright again tried to raise Mission Control on the radio, not sure who he'd get or what he'd say. But, as before, there was nothing but dead air in response. Cartwright wondered whether his calls were being received and just not being responded to. And, if that was the case, he desperately wanted to know who was making that decision. They can't all be in on it, he told himself. Certainly not Rick Delahousse. Which would explain why, he now knew, Delahousse had suddenly disappeared. Somehow, he'd been cut out of the process. Cartwright fervently hoped his friend was ok.

So, he asked himself, who *was* in on the thing? For one, he knew, Deputy Administrator Huffman, which was mind-boggling. He remembered back to the meeting when he'd been introduced to the man. Were the others at that meeting party to this conspiracy? A U.S. Senator? Wasn't he the one who'd supposedly procured the funding for Apollo 18? What about Stu Overholdt? Cartwright had known Overholdt for years. That just didn't seem possible. Same with Steve Dayton.

Dayton.

Given all that had been happening, he'd not focused on his other crewmate, manning the command capsule in orbit above them. With a sudden inspiration, he reached down to the cable-mounted switch attached to the front of his suit, toggling over to Comm 2.

"...*Concord*, come in please."

The sound shattered the silence and made him jump.

"This is *Lexington* calling *Concord*, come in please. Do you read?"

It was the unmistakable voice of Steve Dayton. He sounded as if he were reciting a litany. Cartwright guessed that Dayton had probably been broadcasting the same thing for hours now. An irrational relief flooded through him.

"Steve, it's Bob. Can you hear me?"

"Bob," Dayton replied immediately, clearly startled, "what the hell is going on down there?"

"How long do you have?"

"How long do I..." then he paused, apparently realizing what Cartwright was asking. "About sixty-eight seconds."

It meant that, in a minute, the orbit of the command module would take it below the horizon and they would lose their ability for "line of sight" communication, which was the only way the men were able to speak on Comm 2. Once that happened, Dayton would be on the far side of the moon and out of touch for about an hour.

"Are you able to contact Houston?" Cartwright asked.

"Negative. I've had no contact with anyone since you were a few minutes into your first EVA."

Cartwright thought about Dayton sitting alone in the command capsule for hours on end, cut off from everything and everyone. It had to have been unnerving. "You've tried all emergency bands?" It was really more a statement. He knew Dayton would have done so.

"Affirmative. Nothing's going through. Bob, I think there's something jamming the radio frequencies. And I think," Dayton added in a puzzled tone, "it's originating from your landing site."

"Got it," Cartwright replied. "Listen Steve, I want you to be back on this channel when you emerge from the other side. I'll fill you in more completely when you do. For now, here's the situation: Gale is not who he pretends to be. He was sent here to destroy a Soviet operation, about a mile from our landing spot. He's very dangerous. I've managed to incapacitate him. I'm going to get the two of us off this rock and rendezvous with you as soon as possible. I'll need your help in keeping Gale subdued once I do."

Dayton, Cartwright knew, was level-headed and competent. Before entering the astronaut program, he'd completed a hundred missions in Vietnam, flying the F-4 Phantom II and earning the distinction of being the Air Force's last official ace, having shot down five enemy MIGs in air-to-air combat. He was by far the best pilot Cartwright had ever met, and that was saying a lot.

"Roger that," Dayton said, "I'll be standing by..."

Dayton's voice faded out, replaced by static. Cartwright suddenly felt more alone than ever. He continued listening for a minute until he was certain the command capsule had dropped below the horizon and there would be no further contact. Then he switched the radio back to its normal setting, checked the timer built into his wrist and noted the mission elapsed time. In an hour, he'd attempt to re-establish contact.

Ahead, in the distance, he saw a glint of sunlight on metal, the top of the lunar module. He strained to see their landing site, but a series of rocks in front of him allowed only a peek at the upper half of the ascent stage. He'd reached the point at which the track he was following entered the boulder field on its serpentine course back to the landing site. He slowed the rover and began picking his way through the large stones, alternating his attention between the route and the direction in which the module lay.

As he passed between a pair of boulders, a view of the module opened up on his right. Not enough to see the whole thing, at least not from where he sat in the rover. But it looked as though he might be able to work his way on foot from this point through the few large rocks that sat between him and the clearing. An instinct told him to stop and dismount.

Leaving the rover, he walked over to the boulders and eased himself among them. As he stepped through the final gap, the entire landing site came into view. It was just as he had left it, with two glaring exceptions. For one, the American flag he and Gale had planted shortly after they'd stepped onto the moon's surface was gone. That was a little puzzling, but it paled in comparison to the thing that had caused Cartwright's heart to begin beating at a rapid rate.

At the spot where he'd deposited Gale there was nothing but a pair of tethers lying discarded on the bare ground.

Cartwright swore under his breath. Somehow the man had gotten free.

Unbelievable.

Cartwright had placed the pistol in a utility bag that he'd stored on the rover. He quickly retraced his steps to the vehicle, the silence around him ominous. Not that he was technically in silence. A faint series of whirring and gurgling sounds circulated through his helmet, sounds generated by the Personal Life Support System in his backpack. But, outside his cocoon, he couldn't possibly hear anything, or anyone, approaching him. He felt completely defenseless.

At the rover, he fumbled through the satchel containing the weapon. After several panic-inducing seconds, his hand closed around the grip, and he withdrew the thing. He held the gun out in front of himself, and, involuntarily, he swung around, frantically taking in the harsh terrain surrounding him. Every rock, every shadow seemed to hold danger.

He took a deep breath, forcing himself to relax. Here among the boulders, he knew, he was vulnerable. Gale could sneak up on him and, with a sharp implement, puncture his suit. He had to get into the open, where he would have a chance to see the man coming and where the gun would give him the advantage. He glanced back at the small opening through which he'd just passed. Should he take his chances there or should he re-mount the rover and continue down the path? Gale would be expecting him to return in the rover. Would the man be positioned along the trail, ready to attack from behind a rock? Very possible. He made a decision.

Moving as quickly as his pressurized suit would allow, Cartwright returned to the boulders and again slipped among them, cringing reflexively with each step, pistol held out in front, darting side to side every couple of feet. After what seemed an eternity, but, he realized, was only a few seconds, Cartwright emerged into the clearing. With an exhalation of the breath he'd been holding, he bounded over to the lunar module, braced and did a quick three-sixty. Around him, the bleak landscape was deathly still. He saw no sign of Gale.

Ok, Bob, he told himself, focus. Where would Gale have gone? Logically, he thought, there were two likely places.

One was back into the module itself, where Gale would be poised to strike when Cartwright began to enter, the very scenario that had spooked him previously. If that's where the man was, he might try to wait Cartwright out, let the oxygen supply in Cartwright's Personal Life Support System dwindle down to nothing, while keeping his own suit directly connected to the module's Environmental Control System. The problem with that plan was that, if Cartwright were going to die anyway, he could take Gale with him by simply shooting up the module. The skin on the vessel was thin, to keep weight down. Bullets would easily penetrate it. If the shots didn't strike Gale's body, they'd surely take out critical operating systems. In fact, with a couple of well placed shots into the rear of the module, Cartwright knew he could disable the thing. Gale would know it too. And, it's exactly what Gale would do if their situation were reversed.

No, he told himself, Gale wouldn't risk that.

The other logical place for Gale to be was back along the trail they'd followed in the rover, waiting in ambush to strike as the vehicle passed. It was the reason Cartwright had abandoned the rover.

Cartwright considered starting down the path from this end, trying to sneak up on Gale as the man's attention was focused in the other direction. But that would mean giving up the advantage of the clearing. He didn't want to do that.

They were in a classic stand-off. Somehow, Cartwright thought, he was going to have to try to reason with the man. He wasn't sure he could do it, but he knew Gale wasn't stupid. He didn't think the man would want to die.

Still rotating, keeping an eye about, but focusing more in the direction of the path taken by the rover, Cartwright eased himself around the base of the module to its rear, putting as much distance as possible between himself and the opening through which the rover had been driven. Then he reached up with his left hand and toggled his radio to Comm 2.

"I'm at the module, Gale," he said, hoping the strain in his voice would be filtered out by the electronics. "I don't want to do it, but I won't hesitate to blast off without you. Show yourself, cooperate, and you'll get out of here. Don't, and you'll die."

There was no response. The silence was frightening. Like a slow motion whirling Dervish, Cartwright turned in place, fearing at any moment Gale would come hurtling out of the rocks that sat just a few yards away in each direction, knowing that, if it happened, he would have mere seconds within which to train the weapon and fire.

He'd set the lever on the pistol grip to conventional bullets. He'd thought about trying to tranquilize the man again but didn't feel confident the dart would penetrate the multiple layers that made up Gale's pressure suit. No, he knew that, if he had to shoot, he'd have to use bullets. All he'd really need was one shot to hit home, penetrating Gale's suit. Even if it didn't strike a critical organ, it could still kill him, as the hole would allow the suit to depressurize in a couple of minutes. Unless, of course, Cartwright were to step in with his emergency patch kit. He hoped Gale wouldn't push things to that point.

Though Cartwright's backpack was pumping water through a series of tubes in the liquid-cooled garment he wore beneath his suit, it wasn't sufficient to prevent the sweat that had broken out across his entire body. Perspiration had soaked the garment and pooled uncomfortably in the small of his back. Beads on his brow coalesced into a rivulet that now ran down between his eyes and along one side of his nose. He blew at it, unable to wipe it away. Eyes darting, body in constant motion, he surveyed the bleak landscape surrounding the clearing, harsh in the unfiltered sunlight.

"You're out of your league, Cartwright."

Cartwright jerked to his right, toward the module, the direction from which the voice had come. It took him a second to realize though that, of course, he hadn't heard it come from that direction. He couldn't possibly hear sounds from outside his suit. Instead, Gale's voice had come through the speaker covering his right ear. Damn. Instinct told him he had to turn around, and he whirled as quickly as his heavy suit would allow.

Gale had emerged from the boulders behind the module about fifty feet away and was bounding toward him. In his gloved left hand was an object held out in front of him, something long and metallic, wielded like a sword. Cartwright had maybe five seconds before the thing pierced his suit and he was a dead man. Forcing an artificial calm on himself, he extended the pistol, aiming for Gale's legs, some vestige of decency telling him he needed only to disable the man.

He slowly expelled a breath and depressed the trigger. There was no sound, and the gun made barely a twitch, but the bullet immediately found its mark, opening a hole on the upper right leg of Gale's suit. Gale stumbled, and the sharp tip of the long object dropped down and dug into the ground a couple of feet in front of Cartwright. Gale's body pitched forward, but was brought up short by the other end of the object, hanging balanced for a moment against its resistance. Then Gale tumbled slowly backwards, falling to the lunar surface. The object, which Cartwright now recognized was the missing flag pole, remained embedded in the ground in front of him at a sharp angle.

From the hole in Gale's leg, a fountain of dark liquid erupted, escaping from the suit as it depressurized. It sprayed upwards several feet, where, impossibly, it seemed to form a cloud, the pressure of the geyser from below keeping the initial droplets suspended in the moon's partial gravity. It took Cartwright a moment to comprehend that what he was seeing was blood, and that there was way too much of it to be explained merely by the rapid decompression of Gale's suit. His bullet, he realized suddenly, must have hit the man's femoral artery. As a result, Gale, he knew, had only a couple minutes to live. If the loss of pressure, and the oxygen that went with it, didn't kill him, then the loss of blood would.

Instinctively, Cartwright stepped forward to render assistance. Then he froze. Gale's right arm had been flung outward, and he could see there was something in the man's gloved hand. It took him a moment to recognize it. And with recognition came horror.

The man had used wire he'd obviously pulled from somewhere on the module to bind a small pistol to his glove. With a flash of intuition, Cartwright knew it had to have been the one Petrov had brandished. Cartwright obviously hadn't paid enough attention when he'd been back at the Soviet base to realize the gun was no longer lying by the dead cosmonaut's body.

As Gale began to swing his right arm up, Cartwright saw that the man had rigged the weapon with a scrap of metal so that he could depress the trigger from outside the trigger guard.

Cartwright's knees had already bent as he'd started to kneel. Propelled by the adrenalin suddenly coursing through his body, he straightened, pushing downward with as much force as he could muster, throwing himself away from Gale.

The gun in Gale's hand must have discharged, because Gale's right arm was abruptly hurled back, his elbow slamming into the ground and the arm bending midway between the wrist and elbow at an impossible ninety degree angle, the bones of the lower arm apparently snapping in half.

Cartwright sailed backwards in slow motion, unable to take his eyes off the weapon. A corner of his backpack made contact with something hard and his body twisted while he was still airborne. He landed face down in the lunar dust, scrambled awkwardly to his hands and knees, and crawled forward a few feet before his helmet struck something hard. Then, still on all fours, he rotated to look back in Gale's direction.

Several feet away, the other astronaut lay on his back, blood continuing to spill from the hole in his leg, though the eruption was not as violent as it had been. The initial cloud of blood had settled back to the surface, coating Gale and the dust around him.

Cartwright realized he'd come to rest beneath the lunar module, his backpack having made contact with one of the module's legs while he was in the process of flinging himself away from Gale and his helmet having struck the descent engine bell in his panic to distance himself from the man. He took quick stock of his situation. His suit seemed to be intact, the bullet apparently having missed him. The sounds from within seemed normal, all systems working. He took a deep breath.

He returned his attention to Gale's body. As he watched, the flow from the man's leg ebbed, then stopped entirely. Slowly, keeping his eyes on Gale's prostrate form, he backed his way between the landing pads on the far side of the module before standing. The pistol still clutched in his hand and held out in front of him, he circled back around the module, keeping a healthy distance between himself and the spot where Gale had fallen. He stood watching for several minutes, gun trained on the body, half expecting to see it rise again.

Finally, he was able to get a grip on himself, to quell the irrational impulses. Even then, he continued to stand there for a long time, his mind working furiously.

#

The rover once again crested the slight incline, and the Soviet base came into view. At the enclosure, Cartwright hopped out, the rock pick in hand, and hurried to the closed air lock door. Bending down and placing his helmet against the door's surface, he tapped quickly, then listened. No response.

Over the next two minutes, he tried again several times to no avail.

From the rover, he retrieved the large bundle he'd assembled, and he made his way around to the far corner of the enclosure. He tossed the bundle in, noting with satisfaction as he did that the blue light above the interior hatchway door was still illuminated. Planting a boot on the upper edge of the damaged wall at the point where the jagged hole was closest to the ground and gripping the sides of the hole with both hands, he carefully lifted himself up and over the tear in the structure, being careful not to snag any part of his suit on the sharp edges.

Once inside, he collected his bundle and stepped over to the air lock, where he spent a couple of minutes studying the instrument panel. When he was satisfied, he again knelt and tapped on this door, listening intently with his helmet against it. As before, there was no answering tap.

When he felt he could no longer wait, he straightened, paused and said a silent prayer. It was not for himself, but for the man who lay on the other side of the air lock door, a man, Cartwright realized, who was probably already dead. And, Cartwright knew, if he wasn't dead, what Cartwright was about to do would likely kill him. Still, it represented the only chance that the young man had to live. He had to give it a try.

With a concluding amen, Cartwright reached up and toggled a switch on the air lock instrument panel, opening the dump valve. As the atmosphere in the chamber began venting out into the lunar vacuum, the hand on the center dial started its slow crawl from right to left. Positioning himself to the side of the door, safely away from where it would swing open, Cartwright gripped the main handle. Just as the hand on the center dial passed out of the blue quadrant, Cartwright twisted the handle and quickly let go. With the force of at least four pounds-per-square-inch worth of pent up pressure behind it, the door blew open, swinging around on its hinges and slamming into the wall on the far side.

Cartwright hoped the violent motion and impact had not damaged the door. He would need it to function if his plan were to work.

He reached down, grabbed the bundle at his side with his left hand, paused, then swung it toward the opening. He realized he'd been premature when the still-escaping air from the chamber flung it back. Cartwright simply allowed his arm to swing behind his body and again brought the bundle around, trying to generate as much momentum as possible to push against the residual escaping atmosphere. The bundle fell through the opening and onto the floor just beyond. In a motion he'd practiced several times in his mind, Cartwright then stepped in front of the hatchway with his back turned to the air lock. He reached over, gripped the top of the door and pulled it toward him as he gingerly stepped backwards over the threshold and into the chamber. He grabbed the handle and, with what would have been a mighty bang but for the fact that there was no air pressure to transmit the sound, he silently slammed the hatch door shut, rotating the lever. As he straightened, he reached up, found the switch corresponding to the one he'd used to vent the air lock, and toggled it to re-pressurize the chamber.

As soon as he felt confident the air lock was again filling, he turned slowly and looked down. In the dim light provided by a single fixture in the center of the ceiling, he could see Kruchinkin's body sprawled on its side, head up against the far door. Lying next to him, still clutched in his right hand, was a flashlight. Cartwright realized that it was probably what Kruchinkin had used to tap out his messages earlier. Kneeling awkwardly in his pressurized suit, Cartwright gently rolled the cosmonaut over on his back.

The man's chest was covered with blood. His eyes were shut, so he didn't have the telltale stare of death. But Cartwright had seen enough dead bodies over time, two in the last several hours, to know the young man was gone. He slumped inside his suit, head drooping forward. It had all been for naught.

195

After a few seconds, Cartwright placed a hand on Kruchinkin. He was about to say another prayer for the cosmonaut when he realized with a start that the man's chest had risen slightly. He stared at his own gloved hand. Yes, the chest was, almost imperceptibly, rising and falling. Remarkably, the man was still breathing.

Breathing what?

Cartwright quickly stood, turned and looked at the instrument panel. The hand in the center dial had not yet reached the blue area, and the light above was not glowing. But it was damn close.

He quickly removed his outer EVA gloves and pulled the first aid kit from the bundle he'd previously tossed into the air lock. Returning to kneel by Kruchinkin, he tried gripping the zipper on the man's coveralls. but his interior glove wouldn't allow the necessary dexterity, so he pulled off that glove as well. He yanked down the zipper and pushed aside the flaps of the garment. Beneath the coveralls, the young man wore a gray t-shirt that was now drenched in blood. Arrayed across the front were letters that looked to have at one time been printed in yellow. In the center of the chest, just below the "a" in "Georgia Tech," was an irregular hole.

Using a pair of scissors he'd removed from the first aid kit, Cartwright carefully cut open the t-shirt. He saw that, around his neck, Kruchinkin wore a metal chain. It extended down to a spot in the center of his chest, where the ends seemed to disappear into a bloody hole. Still visible a few millimeters below the level of the skin was a piece of metal. The hole was oozing blood, further evidence that the man's heart was still beating.

Cartwright glanced over at the control panel. The blue light had illuminated. He reached up and adjusted a series of controllers on the breastplate of his suit. Then he twisted and pulled off his helmet. Leaning forward, he put his left hand behind Kruchinkin and carefully lifted the man's upper torso off the floor. With his bare right hand, he pulled down the left top of the Russian's coveralls, exposing the rest of the man's chest and shoulders. He reached around, probing his back for an exit wound. There was nothing, which meant the bullet had not passed through the body. Given the point at which the bullet had struck, though, it should, by all rights, have pierced the man's heart, and Kruchinkin, he knew, should be dead.

As Cartwright brought his hand forward, it slid over something unusual behind the left shoulder. He reached back and fingered the area. Something hard lay just below the surface of the skin. He puzzled over it for a moment, before realizing what it was. And then he knew what had happened.

The bullet fired by Gale must have struck the object that Kruchinkin wore on the chain around his neck. That object, whatever it was, had been driven into Kruchinkin's torso, in the process disrupting the bullet's path and diverting it up and to the right through Kruchinkin's shoulder. Apparently, the combination of the object and whatever the bullet had subsequently encountered had spent its forward momentum, and the bullet had come to rest just below the surface of the skin in the cosmonaut's back.

Cartwright wondered absently whether the ammunition used by Gale had been calibrated so that it would not pass through a body. That would make sense if there was the possibility Gale would be employing the weapon within a pressurized environment. Otherwise, a bullet leaving a victim's body could pierce the shell of the enclosure and have the unintended effect of killing Gale as well. Of course, if Gale were to shoot and miss, he'd still have that problem. That, Cartwright reflected ruefully, was probably not a big concern. He doubted Gale had missed many targets in his life.

He remembered the shot that took down Petrov. Gale had fired it from behind Cartwright, just missing him and drilling the cosmonaut between the eyes. It had been a perfect bull's-eye under challenging circumstances. More to the point, it hadn't led to the discharge of blood and brain matter behind the man that would have accompanied an exit wound. Nor had there been any blood pooling around the dead man's head.

The shot at Kruchinkin had been directed at the man's heart and had also hit its target precisely. It should have killed the young cosmonaut, but it hadn't. That was something of a miracle, attributable to whatever the man wore on the chain around his neck. But, Cartwright mused, as with the bullet that killed Petrov, it had not been delivered with enough force to exit the body.

Cartwright was no doctor, but he'd had training in emergency first aid. He quickly cleaned the wound with alcohol. He knew not to attempt removal of the bullet or the object that had altered the bullet's course. Instead, he stuffed sterile gauze into the entry wound to help stem the flow of blood. Given the man's still regular breathing, he didn't think the bullet had ruptured a lung, but he wasn't going to take a chance. He applied an occlusive dressing over the hole, binding it on three sides and leaving the fourth unbound to act as a potential flutter valve. Then he gave the cosmonaut an injection of antibiotics and a shot of adrenaline.

There was a small metallic thermal blanket in the first aid kit. Cartwright pulled it out, shook it open, and carefully wrapped it around the slight body of the young Russian. He lay the man's head back against a makeshift pillow he'd created with his EVA gloves. Then he finally allowed himself a moment to relax.

They stayed that way for several minutes. Finally, Kruchinkin twitched. A hand flew up involuntarily, then dropped to the floor. A few seconds later, the young man's eyelids fluttered and, after a short beat, suddenly flew open. It took the cosmonaut a moment to focus. When he did, a surprised expression crossed his face, and he opened his mouth to speak, the words faint, barely audible.

"Commander Cartwright, you are dead too?"

12

In the dim light, Cartwright studied the dials above the air lock hatchway. The readout on the large one in the center was holding steady, but two of the others had dropped noticeably from the time he'd last checked an hour earlier, indicating that whatever those dials measured was diminishing. It reaffirmed what his body had already told him. The quality of the atmosphere in the chamber was degrading. They couldn't stay much longer.

He looked back down at the body of Kruchinkin, still wrapped in the thermal blanket. The young man was asleep, though it was a fitful one. A heavy sheen of sweat coated his face, reflecting light from the overhead fixture. As Cartwright watched, the man's lips parted in a slight grimace and a brief moan escaped. Head turning slowly side to side, he seemed to mumble something. Cartwright couldn't make out the words, though it didn't matter. He knew they were in Russian, and he wouldn't understand them.

For the last several hours, Kruchinkin had hovered in a semi-conscious state, alternating between short periods of wakefulness, when the chills tended to overtake him, and longer periods of restless sleep. He was running a high fever, and Cartwright didn't want to have to try to move him unless and until it broke. Cartwright's options, however, were beginning to shrink, and not just because of the pending failure of the air lock environmental system. The launch window for their return to earth would be opening in a few hours. They needed to start back to the lunar module soon.

Cartwright knelt down next to the young cosmonaut, laying the back of a hand on the man's forehead, then on one cheek. Still burning up. He sighed heavily. Can't be helped, he said to himself.

He reached out, gripped the large bundle he'd brought with him and slid it closer. It was bound by the tethers he'd used earlier to tie up Gale. He undid the package and began separating the items. His first order of business was going to be getting Kruchinkin into the A7LB space suit he'd previously removed from Gale's body.

As Cartwright pulled away the blanket surrounding the young cosmonaut, Kruchinkin again swung his head side to side, this time more rapidly. He expelled another string of Russian. Fortunately, he did not open his eyes or regain consciousness. Just as well, Cartwright thought.

He started with the liquid cooled undergarment, essentially a pair of long johns fitted with narrow water tubes. Custom-fit for Gale's body, it hung loosely around the cosmonaut's slight figure. Not perfect, but it would do.

Then came the more rigid, and difficult, torso limb suit assembly.

Cartwright tried to be gentle, but it was simply not possible. The garment was difficult enough to get into under the best of circumstances. Cartwright gritted his teeth and tried to ignore the moans escaping the lips of the injured Russian. When he'd managed to force the young man into the suit, he was relieved to see that, while the thing was also large around the torso, the arms and legs at least fit reasonably well. It, too, would suffice for what they had to do.

Of course, for Gale's suit to function at all, Cartwright would need to patch the hole in the right leg, a task to which he now set himself. There was also a nasty gash to the inside of the right arm, where the shattered ends of Gale's ulna and radius bones had ripped through the undergarment and the first couple layers of material in the outer suit. Fortunately, the bones hadn't pierced the exterior.

When he was done, Cartwright rolled Kruchinkin onto his side and horsed the large backpack into place. Then he returned the man to his back, now propped up against the bulky device, and he began attaching the various water and oxygen hoses to the front panel. After a moment, Cartwright realized that, through barely slitted eyes, Kruchinkin was looking at him.

"How are you feeling?" Cartwright asked.

Kruchinkin opened his mouth as if to speak, but nothing came out. He ran his tongue over cracked lips. Cartwright reached for the tube attached to the drink bag inside the neck ring and brought it to the cosmonaut's mouth. The young man took a long sip and closed his eyes briefly. Then he again fixed Cartwright with a bleak look.

"Why are you doing this?" he asked faintly.

"Well," Cartwright said in a light tone, "I know how much you like it in here, but I figure it's good to get out now and again. Don't you agree?"

Cartwright was pleased to see a faint smile touch the edges of Kruchinkin's lips. But the Russian shook his head slowly.

"I appreciate," the young man said, weakly, "but, is no use."

"Oh, yeah," Cartwright said, "why's that?"

"I am," Kruchinkin paused, taking a couple of labored breaths, "what is expression? A goner, yes?"

"No, you're not." Cartwright gave him a stern look. "You're not."

Kruchinkin looked down, as if studying the unfamiliar suit, almost completely covered in Gale's blood. He looked back up at Cartwright.

"Is no use. I am dead."

"You're not dead until I tell you you're dead, do you understand that, cosmonaut?"

Kruchinkin stared back, pain and uncertainty vying with one another on his face. And something else, Cartwright could see. Hope.

"But I am..."

"You are," Cartwright interrupted, "a ramblin' wreck from Georgia Tech."

The faint smile returned to the young cosmonaut's face. After a long moment, he concluded in a weak voice, "And a hell of an engineer."

"Damn right," Cartwright said, sliding on the overboots. "Now, you'll have to help me. I'm going to get your helmet on and pressurize your suit. Then I'll bleed out the atmosphere in this air lock. When I've got the outer door open, you'll need to stand. I'll assist. The rover is just outside. Are you with me?"

Kruchinkin gave a slight nod.

"Good," Cartwright said, as he positioned the helmet over the Russian's head and snapped it into place.

#

At the landing site, Kruchinkin, obviously in a great deal of pain and extremely weak, nevertheless put forth a heroic effort, climbing the ladder on his own. At no time had he expressed any complaints or balked at doing the things Cartwright asked of him.

Cartwright settled the cosmonaut in a half seated, half reclined position on the ascent engine cover. He removed the man's helmet and backpack, but left the blood-soaked space suit on. He was tempted to keep the suit pressurized, thinking that it might help with the wound, but he opted for comfort. Kruchinkin nodded his thanks, closed his eyes and, it appeared to Cartwright, again slipped into unconsciousness.

Cartwright had still been unable to effect radio contact with Earth. He wondered whether Dayton had been right about the interference originating from their landing site. Could some sort of device have been installed in the module to jam the 48-kilobit signal needed to beam messages back home? If so, could he find the thing and disable it? Possibly, he thought, if it were here in the pressurized crew compartment. The space was tiny and there were limited places it could have been hidden. But he didn't think there was much reason for it to have been stowed here. More likely, it was concealed somewhere in the balance of the module, and it could take hours to find, assuming he even knew what to look for, which, he reflected ruefully, he didn't.

Fortunately, he still had the ability to speak with Steve Dayton in the command module. For whatever reason, the Comm 2 frequency had not been jammed, perhaps because the people pulling the strings had concluded there was no reason to hide short wave communications on the moon. After all, at its peak, there were only five people in the universe who could have tuned in to listen anyway. Now, there were only three, and one of them was unconscious.

Cartwright checked his timer and confirmed that the command module had cleared the horizon.

"*Concord* to *Lexington*," he said, "do you read me Steve?"

"Loud and clear," Dayton replied in his Maine accent. "Are you back at the module?"

"I am," Cartwright said. Then he amended, "We are."

When he'd had the chance to re-connect with Dayton, Cartwright had informed the man about the events that had transpired on the moon's surface. Dayton had been appropriately shocked. Since being briefed, Dayton had completed numerous orbits, and he obviously had a lot of time to think while on the far side of the moon, because each time he'd emerged after the first several passes, he'd cooked up increasingly more fanciful theories regarding the motives and participants behind the whole thing. Finally, the two astronauts had come to the realization that they didn't know what was going on, and they'd concluded that the best they could do was rendezvous and get home. There, to use a phrase Gale had earlier employed, everything would be sorted out.

"Are you ready to go through the checklist?" Cartwright asked.

"Affirmative."

In the absence of a lunar module pilot, the role Gale had filled, Cartwright had asked Dayton to retrieve his copy of the ascent pre-launch protocol, and the two now started through the tedious process of verifying that all systems were ready for the lift off. As Dayton read each item, Cartwright manually verified the applicable readouts and set the appropriate switches.

They were nearing the end of the list, and, thus far, everything had checked out.

"Ascent helium, tank one," Dayton called out.

Cartwright toggled the switch and froze. "Negative," he said, after a moment.

"Did you say 'negative'?"

"I did," Cartwright replied, cycling the switch on and off. "Zero pressure."

There was a long silence. Cartwright guessed Dayton was consulting the manual. Finally, Dayton said, "Ok, check ascent helium, tank two."

Cartwright toggled that switch and got the same result. He took a deep breath. "We have a problem, Steve."

Dayton didn't immediately reply. They both knew the seriousness of this news. The ascent engine on the lunar module was fueled by a hypergolic mixture of propellant and oxidizer, Aerozine 50 and nitrogen tetroxide, respectively. When the two materials were brought into contact, they ignited spontaneously, providing the thrust needed to push the ascent stage of the module off the lunar surface. Earlier in the checklist, Cartwright and Dayton had confirmed that there was plenty of propellant and oxidizer contained in the storage tanks of the module. The problem was, without something to force the two together, the fuel was useless. The transferring agent the module relied on was helium.

And Cartwright had just determined that there was, apparently, no helium onboard.

That wasn't logical. As bizarre as the whole thing with Gale had been, Cartwright couldn't imagine that helium had not been loaded onto the ascent stage of the lunar module and that the two of them had, in effect, been sent on a one-way mission. If that had been the case, he thought, why would Gale have gone to the efforts he did after completing his tasks at the Soviet base? The man had certainly been expecting to live. And, to do so, the ascent engine would have had to function.

No, Cartwright told himself, something else was wrong. Think, Bob.

And, after a long moment, a thought did occur to him. As soon as it did, he wished it hadn't.

"Steve, I may know what the problem is. Or at least the root of the problem." He checked his timer. He was about to lose Dayton anyway. "I've got to go outside again. I'll check back in with you when you re-emerge."

"Ok," Dayton replied. Cartwright could hear the anxiety in the man's voice. It matched his own.

Cartwright once again positioned the helmet on Kruchinkin and repressurized the man's suit. The cosmonaut stirred briefly, then returned to a fitful sleep. When Cartwright had his own suit pressurized, he dumped the cabin atmosphere, eased out the front hatch and clambered back down the stairs. He made his way around the module to the rear, where the pale, broken body of Gale lay in the gray dust, naked but for the soiled fecal containment subsystem around his midsection that looked vaguely like an adult diaper. Cartwright stared at the corpse for several seconds. It looked forlorn and pathetic. He felt no sympathy.

He positioned himself near Gale's body and looked up. It took only a couple of seconds to see it. Just to the side of the aft equipment bay, below a cluster of reaction control thrusters, there was a small hole in one of the panels.

Just great, he thought. Now he knew where the bullet that Gale had intended for him had gone. It had apparently entered a compartment on the side of the module that housed a series of tanks containing oxygen, propellant, oxidizer and, of course, helium.

When Gale had fired the weapon, Cartwright had believed he'd escaped death. Perhaps, he realized now, he had simply postponed it.

To know the extent of the damage, he needed to check inside the compartment the bullet had entered. That compartment, however, sat well above the lunar surface, a good twelve to fifteen feet higher than where he now stood. There was no good way to access it from here. He considered the problem for a minute. Then he returned to the front of the module, stopping at the rover to retrieve a tool kit. He climbed back up into the crew compartment. Kruchinkin, he could see through the clear shield on the man's helmet, was awake, but apparently too exhausted to do anything but follow him with his eyes.

When they'd returned from the Soviet base, Cartwright had stowed the tethers that had most recently served to bind the suit he'd removed from Gale. He now pulled them out again, running them one at a time through his hands, gauging their respective lengths. He selected one he thought would work and clipped an end to the metallic buckle at his waist. Then he threaded the other end of the line through a loop on the tool kit he'd brought from the rover, pulling the kit close to him. He gathered up the balance of the tether and shoved it into the utility pocket at his thigh.

He reached up, unlatched the overhead hatch, and opened it. Planting a foot on the engine cover, he pushed himself up, forcing his way through the narrow opening. This one was smaller than the forward egress hatch, and he experienced a moment of panic when he thought he might get stuck. But he was able to wriggle his way through, and he emerged into the small circular area at the top of the vessel that would, if they were ever able to get back to the command service module, serve as a short tunnel to the command capsule.

Taking a seat on the top of the module, Cartwright withdrew the tether and attached the clip at the other end of the line to a small utility bar inset along the side of the access tunnel. He checked to make sure the line was holding at both ends, then swung his legs up and over the edge, rotating his body so that he was facing the module, and he slowly lowered himself down the side of the structure. He'd had to estimate the length for the tether, but it wound up being just about perfect. At full extension, he was able to reach down and plant his boots on one of the support members at the top of the descent stage. Using the tether to steady himself, he stood upright, facing one of the side panels to the compartment into which the bullet had been fired.

When he had himself situated, he pulled from the tool kit a socket wrench, the end of which he positioned over the nearest of the fasteners holding the panel to the side of the module, and he worked the fastener loose, allowing the small piece to fall free and drop slowly to the lunar surface below. He repeated the process with the other five fasteners, and, when the last of them came away, he also allowed the panel to drift to the ground. Then he worked his way over to the rear of the compartment he'd just exposed.

The bullet Gale had fired had pierced the aft helium tank near its base and had passed clean through. It had just missed a small container of liquid oxygen that sat between the two helium tanks and had embedded itself in the side of the second tank. The first tank, he knew, would have drained immediately. It looked like the second may have taken longer to discharge, but he feared that it too was probably empty. In that case, he and Kruchinkin were dead men. But he had no idea how to determine what was left in the tank or, more importantly, what to do about it.

A sudden movement to his side made his heart jump. Then he realized that Kruchinkin had somehow managed to follow him out of the docking hatch and was in the process of lowering himself down to his side. When the cosmonaut reached him, Cartwright could see the man wincing inside his helmet. After a moment, though, Kruchinkin found a foothold, turned and looked at him.

"Is problem, yes?" he asked, his voice in Cartwright's earpiece still extraordinarily weak.

"Yes," Cartwright said, simply, pointing to the bullet that had flattened itself against the second tank. Kruchinkin squinted, then blinked. After a moment, he raised his head and studied the other contents of the compartment, then returned his attention to the damaged tank. He reached in slowly and ran his hand across a device attached to the top of both helium tanks.

"Pneumatic control assembly," he said softly, apparently by way of explanation. With two fingers, he slightly rotated a threaded piece protruding from the side of the device. Then he pointed to the bullet. "Tank is not yet empty. You have patch for space suit?"

Cartwright nodded. The kit was still in his utility pocket.

"We patch now," Kruchinkin said. "Quickly."

Of course. Cartwright kicked himself for not thinking of it. With a newfound sense of hope, he reached into his pocket and withdrew the small kit. He selected one of the patch sets, tearing open the first half and withdrawing the clean strip of gauze that it contained. He reached in and rubbed the area around which the bullet had come to rest, wiping away the accumulated dust and debris. Then he tore open the second half and withdrew the actual patch, quickly placing the dull adhesive side against the tank and pressing it into place with the heel of his gloved hand. When he pulled his hand back, the patch had sealed over the spot, conforming to the shape of the spent bullet embedded in the side of the tank.

Kruchinkin had continued to study the layout of the compartment. He now turned his head toward Cartwright and said faintly, "Is very little left in tank. Maybe thirty seconds." He winced. "Maybe less." A cough caused him to grimace, and he shut his eyes for a moment before opening them and refocusing on Cartwright.

"Maybe less," he repeated.

Cartwright was doing quick calculations. An ascent burn took seven minutes. The standard profile called for the module to rise straight up from the lunar surface for about twelve seconds, before being taken through a pitch program that would eventually elevate the craft to 50,000 feet, at which point it would enter a coasting transfer orbit in preparation for rendezvous with the command module. The adjustments necessary to bring the module into proper course alignment would normally be performed by the reaction control system, consisting of the various thrusters located in clusters around the vessel.

If all they had was thirty seconds worth of burn, give or take a little, they'd never be able to achieve an orbit. About the best they could do would be to shoot themselves straight up, high enough off the surface to, in theory, allow the command module to drop down and grab them quickly before they lost upward momentum and began the long, deadly descent to the surface. It would take incredible skill to perform such a recovery. But, if there was any pilot who could do it, Cartwright knew, it was Steve Dayton. The big question was could they get high enough if all they had was thirty seconds?

Maybe less.

Pointing to a valve in the line that extended up from the pneumatic control assembly, Kruchinkin said, "We must bypass thrusters. Otherwise, helium is wasted filling line to thruster fuel cells. Must sacrifice control for altitude."

It made sense. Cartwright nodded.

Kruchinkin reached in and rotated the valve shut. Then he looked at Cartwright with a pained expression. "Is best we can do."

#

Steve Dayton floated back to his seat in the command module, scanning, as he did, the readouts from the large instrument panel arrayed before him. He'd spent the last hour inputting data and crunching numbers on his computer. He was as ready as he would ever be.

He knew this craft like the back of his hand, having spent the better part of the last four years learning her abilities. And limitations. She wasn't exactly a jet fighter, and he missed the visceral feedback - and thrill - that came from throwing an F4 Phantom around in the sky while flying on the edge. But he'd come to appreciate what she could do. More importantly, he felt confident that he could maneuver her wherever needed to couple with the lunar module. Just as long as they could get the darn module far enough off the surface.

The limiting altitude on emergency rescue of a lunar module was officially 30,000 feet. Dayton was prepared to go lower if that's what it took to save Bob Cartwright.

He'd known Cartwright for several years, and he liked the man. A lot. He wasn't alone.

Cartwright, Dayton knew, had risen quickly in the astronaut ranks, becoming the youngest by far to command an Apollo mission. His quiet, serious demeanor, while inspiring confidence, could be intimidating for those who hadn't yet gotten to know him. But, when they did, they learned that Cartwright had a keen sense of humor. And, though he didn't wear his emotions on his sleeve, those emotions ran deep and true. He was a born leader, a man who took loyalty to those in his command seriously, and who in turn inspired a profound loyalty from them.

No, Dayton thought, if saving Cartwright meant going below the hard deck, he'd go below.

Well below.

Dayton had used the thrusters located along the side of the command module to drop his orbit down to 50,000 feet. The module was now oriented so that it directly faced the surface of the moon, and Dayton could see the mountains and craters as they passed majestically by the rendezvous window in front of him.

On numerous prior passes over the Sea of Crises, Dayton had tried, unsuccessfully, to spot *Concord's* landing site using the command module's 28-power sextant. He wanted to be able to pick up the lunar module visually as soon as possible as it began its rise from the surface, and he'd hoped to identify landmarks that would assist him in doing so. Of course, on those prior passes, he'd been sixty-nine miles up. This was a whole different perspective.

He checked the timer. Just under three minutes to launch.

Cartwright's voice sounded in his earpiece. "*Concord* to *Lexington*, do you read me Steve?"

"Roger. Loud and clear."

"Ok," Cartwright said, "before I light this candle, I want to go over a couple of things."

"Shoot."

"First, if we don't get the full burn." Cartwright stopped suddenly, as if contemplating the ramifications. Then he continued, "If we don't get the full burn, you will not drop below 30,000. Are we clear on that?"

Dayton hesitated before replying, "Clear."

Dayton did another quick scan of his thruster settings. He'd programmed in a sequence that would take him straight down toward the lunar surface if the module's engine cut out early. All he would need to do is hit the master switch to engage the thrusters in his pre-programmed sequence. His plan, should it become necessary, was to duck down, snatch the vessel, then immediately reverse thrusters to pull himself back into orbit. The move would be not unlike those of the terns and gulls he'd watched growing up on the coast of Maine. Instead of a small fish, though, he would be pulling back up with him a much more precious cargo. And, despite the admonition from Cartwright, he would go as low as necessary to do it. He saw no purpose to be served, though, in making the point, so he kept it to himself.

"Second," Cartwright continued, "if we don't make this rendezvous, you will not hesitate to take the command module out of lunar orbit and get yourself home. When you do, I don't want you telling anyone at NASA you know what happened here on the surface. I don't know who all is involved in this, but I have to assume for now that the entire Administration has been compromised. You tell them you have no idea what happened down here. During the first EVA, you lost all communication, and it was never restored. The module never left the surface. Then you take all of this straight to the Navy brass. Or Air Force," he added, apparently remembering belatedly the arm of the service to which Dayton belonged. "Get this out in the open. Do not let the bastards get away with it."

The notion of returning to Earth without Cartwright was inconceivable to Dayton. How could he possibly do that? But he knew better than to argue with his commander.

"I understand," Dayton said. "But," he added, "we'll do it together."

Cartwright didn't respond immediately. Finally, he said, "Roger that."

They had run the calculations and concluded that a thirty-second burn would be optimal for bringing the module up to Dayton's current altitude before losing momentum. They certainly didn't want to overshoot, so Cartwright would be poised to shut down the rocket when - if - they hit thirty seconds. First, though, they'd have to be able to start the engine. Dayton consulted the elapsed time. Thirty seconds to launch. Showtime.

"All right," said Cartwright, "I'm going to pressurize the line."

Dayton took in a sharp breath. This was the acid test. If there was no pressure in the line, it was all over. The module would never leave the surface of the moon. He held the breath.

"And we have pressure," Cartwright announced, as casually as if it were a routine checklist item.

Dayton expelled the breath. So far, so good. Still, would the engine ignite? And, if it did, how long would it burn?

Again, without a hint there was anything out of the ordinary going on, Cartwright called out, "Standing by to start time on the burn. We will have ignition in three, two, one."

Time seemed to stand still.

"And we have ignition."

Relief flooded Dayton. In fact, he thought he might finally have detected a bit of emotion in Cartwright's voice. Beginning a silent count in his head, Dayton peered forward through the rendezvous window, looking for the first sign of the ascending lunar module. Five seconds. He saw nothing but the scarred lunar surface. Ten seconds. Still nothing.

"There's a slight vibration," Cartwright announced, "but the engine seems to be firing just fine. We're getting elevation fast."

Fifteen seconds. Almost out of the woods.

There. A glint of metal ahead of him and below. The tiny speck that was the lunar module climbing its way up from the surface. A beautiful sight. Dayton knew Cartwright would be looking up through the small window inset above the commander's station, trying to spot the command module.

Twenty seconds. They were going to make it.

And then Dayton noticed something. He blinked, thinking maybe he was just imagining it.

Twenty-five seconds.

"Standing by to cut engine," Cartwright said. Then he immediately amended, "No need. Flame out at," he paused, "twenty-nine point five seconds. How's that for pegging it?"

Dayton said nothing. He was frantically adjusting the settings on the master thruster sequence, inputting a safe trajectory away from the approaching module. He wondered if Cartwright could see what he'd seen.

"Uh, Steve?" There was a new tension in Cartwright's voice. He *had* seen it. "We're coming in way too hot."

Somehow, they had underestimated the thrust. Like a speeding bullet, the lunar module was on a deadly collision course with the command module, and there was no way to slow it down.

"I'm on it," Dayton called out, as he set the master arm switch.

"Fire your thrusters now," Cartwright commanded. "Get out of the way."

"I can do this," Dayton said, eyes locked on the approaching module. With a few deft touches to the controller, Dayton adjusted his course, lining his vessel up so that it was more centered in the path of the lunar module.

"I'm not taking a vote," Cartwright said, his voice firm.

"Seriously..."

"No," Cartwright interrupted. "We'll both break apart. It won't do either of us any good for you to be killed too."

Both astronauts knew full well that if Dayton were to do what Cartwright was saying and pull the command vessel out of the way, allowing the module to blow by, the small craft would quickly escape the moon's gravity. At that point, it would be a runaway train headed for the Milky Way. Of course, it wouldn't get that far. The sun's gravitational pull would eventually slow, then stop, the progress of the wayward module. Somewhere between Earth and Mars, the craft would ease into a solar orbit. By then, though, the men inside would have been dead for a couple of years.

"I can't just let that happen," Dayton said, still working the controller. He could make out the details of the lunar module now, including the little window through which he knew Cartwright was looking back up at him.

"I appreciate it Steve." There was rare emotion in Cartwright's voice. "Please look in on the boys for me." Then the steel returned. "I'm taking the decision out of your hands. This is not a request. This is an order, Major. Fire those thrusters. Now."

Dayton lifted a hand and held it over the switch that would initiate the master sequence he'd plugged in seconds before. He stared out at the approaching vessel, eyes locked on the small window. God help me, he thought. He hesitated for an instant. Then he flipped the switch and fired the thrusters.

SEA OF CRISES

PART THREE

13

When Nate had finished, no one spoke. The large room was quiet, the only sound a soft susurration from the open window as an evening breeze stirred the sheer curtains. In the distance, an owl hooted.

Finally, in a quiet voice Matt asked, "How certain are you of all this? Do you know for sure they weren't able to rendezvous?"

Nate sighed, then nodded. "It's a lot of deduction. I could be wrong about any of it. But," he paused, then added sadly, "I don't think I am."

Matt nodded and looked away.

The others stared at the floor or contemplated spots in the distance. The exception, Nate realized after a few seconds, was Patricia Gale. She was looking up at Nate, a stricken expression across her face. She opened her mouth to speak, then froze, her lower lip trembling slightly. "I…" she managed in a weak voice. "I…"

It seemed to rouse the others. As they turned to look at her, she blurted, "I am so sorry."

Nate started to respond, but before he could speak, she gasped, "My brother killed your father. Oh my god." Tears welled in her eyes.

"He wasn't alone," Peter said immediately. "He had a lot of help. And it's not your fault, Patricia."

"But still," Patricia said, plaintively.

"It's not your fault," Peter repeated.

She looked from Peter to Nate. Nate nodded. "He's right."

"But," she protested, the tears now working their way down her pale cheeks, "if I had said something."

"Stop," Nate said firmly. "*They* kept you from saying something. It's *their* fault. Not yours."

Nate turned to look at Matt. "And you know who they are."

#

At the dinner table, there was little conversation. It seemed to Nate as though they were all still processing what they'd learned. He noticed, though, that, at various times, surreptitiously, each seemed to be looking to him. For what, he wasn't sure. Maggie in particular appeared anxious to speak, her emerald eyes searching, questioning. But, she, like the others, kept her thoughts to herself.

Nate's feelings were a confusing jumble. Of course he was mad. His father's death had not been the accident he'd always believed. There were people who were responsible for that. And he had no intention of letting them get away with it.

But, for the moment, his thoughts were less on revenge and more on his father's unfair fate.

Over the past few days, Nate hadn't been quite as ready as Peter to accept the notion that the capsule that had splashed down thirty-five years ago with three burned bodies was not Apollo 18. He'd questioned whether there might have been a last minute switch of the capsules before launch. That would have explained the anomaly Peter had discovered. But the NASA documents Nate had reviewed today had convinced him that the command module that lifted off from Cape Canaveral had not been the one retrieved from the Pacific Ocean. And, if that weren't enough, the body count made no sense. If only Steve Dayton had made the return journey, there would have been but one corpse in the capsule, not three.

Nate wasn't sure how to deal with the knowledge that his father had not died in the inferno of his capsule, as he had always believed. Could the death that had finally taken him as the lunar module drifted in the cold vacuum of space been a better way to go? Would he have preferred knowing the end was nearing? And, would a slow suffocation have been better than a quick but agonizing death by immolation?

Nate asked himself what he would have done in his father's situation. Would he have waited until the oxygen was depleted, drawing things out as long as possible? Or would he have just opened the hatch and allowed himself to die in the relatively shorter period of time it would have taken for the atmosphere to drain from the module?

The thought of the excruciating dilemma his father had faced was disturbing, and, as the others did, he spent the meal picking desultorily at the food on his plate, not even really focused on what it was. When everyone seemed to run out of the energy to do even that, Patricia rose quietly and began removing plates. Peter and Tim did likewise.

From across the table, Matt cleared his throat, gave Nate a direct look and said, "You and I need to take a drive in a little bit."

Surprised, Nate nodded.

"I've got a couple things I need to do right now," Matt said, and he stood. "We'll leave in an hour."

As his brother strode from the room, Nate followed him with his eyes until they abruptly and unexpectedly locked on Maggie's. She was staring at him from the end of the table with an intense expression. After a moment, she leaned forward and said softly, "Can we talk?"

"Of course."

"In the other room?"

"All right," Nate said. He stood and followed her toward the living room. As soon as they'd rounded the corner, though, she suddenly halted and turned to face him. Taken by surprise, he almost ran her over, managing to stop just inches away. He looked down, and she stared back up at him, her eyes still imploring. He realized once again how incredible those eyes were. And, with the proximity, he detected a faint but pleasant scent. Perfume. Or maybe just the shampoo in her hair. Despite all the other things that were happening, his heart began beating faster, and he felt a pleasant sensation wash over him.

When she spoke, her words helped cut through the distraction.

"I'm so sorry about your Dad," she said.

Nate took a steadying breath and gave a slight nod of appreciation. He was about to say something in response, but she continued urgently.

"Do you think my father is alive?"

The question caught Nate up short. It wasn't one he'd really focused on, but, of course, it was a fair one. He considered it now.

By all accounts, the command service module had left lunar orbit as scheduled and had returned to Earth. There were details Nate had culled from his review of the documents that could only have made it into those documents if the capsule had come down in a condition sufficient to enable them to have been retrieved. Wouldn't that suggest Dayton had survived? Nate did the quick math. If Dayton had lived, how old would he be now? Sixty-nine, seventy? No reason why he couldn't still be alive. But, if he was, where was he? What happened to him?

He focused again on Maggie. Her extraordinary eyes bore into his, and in them he could see so many things, anxiety, confusion, hope. And, he realized with a start, he wanted to know everything else.

He blinked, forcing himself to concentrate.

"I guess," he said, slowly, "it's possible."

As her eyes got wider, he added quickly, "But after all this time…" He didn't know how to finish, and his voice trailed off.

"But it's still possible," she insisted.

After a moment, he nodded.

"Will you help me find him?"

She had such a look of desperation and need that Nate had the sudden impulse to reach out for her. He held back though. The two of them didn't really know each other, and he was loathe to appear too forward or familiar.

Instead, he gave her a direct look and said softly, "I will."

She continued staring up at him with those unbelievably expressive eyes. Then she abruptly stood on her toes, reached her face up and planted a soft kiss on his cheek. It caught him completely off guard.

"Thank you," she said, stepping back and suddenly glancing down, perhaps, he thought, embarrassed. After a brief moment, she looked back up. Her eyes were as brilliant as ever, and there was something new in them, something that made his already rapidly beating heart start pounding furiously.

She pointed vaguely with one hand and said, "I better go help the others." And, with that, she stepped past him and walked to the kitchen.

Nate unconsciously put a hand up to the cheek where she'd kissed him. The feeling of it still lingered. He didn't mind.

#

As he slid into the passenger seat of the SUV and closed the door, Nate noticed again the pockmarked windshield.

"I'm not sure where we're going, but I bet we'll stick out like a sore thumb."

Matt chuckled softly as he cranked the engine. "That's one of the reasons we're taking this little excursion."

Matt backed out the SUV and turned it up the narrow lane that connected the cabin to the small two lane highway they'd last been on a day and a half earlier. The moon had yet to rise, and,

223

with the exception of the pool of illumination cast by the head-lights, the darkness around them was complete.

"I also promised you we'd talk," Matt added.

It was what Nate had been thinking as well, and he wasted no time.

"Who is the man in Patricia's picture? Don't tell me it's Raen."

Matt shook his head. "He's not old enough to have been around back then. No, the man who visited Patricia and her mother, the one who called himself Arthur Spelling, is named Krantz. He's the director of The Organization."

"He was your boss?"

"No," Matt said. "Well, technically, I guess, he was for a short time. He took over after my boss died. But it was right when I was retiring, so I never really reported to him. When I started, though, he was working in the field. Pretty senior by then. I was assigned to a couple of action teams he headed. He knew his craft, but I never really cared for him personally." He glanced over briefly. "I'll tell you this: The Organization was his life. Still is, as far as I know."

"Well, he was part of the operation that killed our father," Nate pointed out. "And he knows who else was involved."

"Yep," Matt said. "He's the key."

"So, can we get to him?"

Matt grunted. "That's going to be tricky."

They reached the end of the lane and Matt turned the SUV onto the public road.

"We've got three problems," Matt said. "First, this guy has resources that," he paused, thinking. Finally, he said, "Let's just say they're unlimited. And that's no exaggeration."

Matt waved a hand indicating the dark nothingness around them. "If they wanted to land a 747 out here in the middle of no-where, they could. They'd find a way. They have, essentially, an unrestricted budget. You can't imagine what can be done when money is no object."

"Ok," Nate said. "So we just need to be a little more cost-effective, that's all."

Matt seemed to crack a brief smile. But his expression quickly became serious. "Second, we're talking about a guy who knows more secrets than God. There's no way they just let someone like that be exposed. He's got a whole organization around him that knows the thousand ways you might try to get to someone like him. And it knows a thousand and one ways to prevent it." After a second, he added, "They've been doing this for a long time."

"Are you saying we can't get to him?"

Matt shook his head. "I'm not saying that. I'm saying it's not going to be easy."

He fell silent, eyes focused on the winding road in front of them.

After a minute, Nate prompted, "You said there were three problems."

Matt took a deep breath. "Yeah." He glanced over briefly. "The third is the fact that this guy was in the field for a long time. He knows all the tricks. All the dodges. Hell, he came up with a lot of them. Even if we're able to isolate him, he'll be very dangerous. We're going to need something new. Something different."

"You got any ideas?"

Matt seemed to hesitate. Then he said, "Maybe." There was a new reluctance in his voice. "I'm still working it through."

"You'll share it with me at some point?"

Another quick smile. "Of course."

They drove in silence, the highway snaking through a dense forest, trees packed in on them from both sides. There was no other traffic. It was as if they were the only people on the planet, their world having been shrunk to the cabin of the SUV and the splash of light that preceded them in the darkness.

Nate wasn't sure how to broach the next subject. He'd spent time trying to come up with a way to ease into it, to blunt the impact. He'd not succeeded. But he knew it couldn't wait any longer.

"We need to talk about Peter," he said abruptly. "And you."

In the dim light, Nate saw Matt's look tighten. His mouth turned down in a contemplative frown, and small creases appeared along his temple as he squinted his eyes.

"There's nothing to talk about," Matt said after a moment.

"Like hell there isn't."

Matt didn't respond.

"Look," Nate said, reasonably, "I know it bothers you that Peter's gay. But, the fact is, he's…"

"No," Matt interjected. "It doesn't."

Surprised, Nate sat back. "What…"

Matt raised a hand slightly, and Nate stopped. Matt returned his hand to the wheel, took a deep breath and let it out slowly. A long minute passed before he spoke.

"Not any more," he said quietly. "At one point, sure. Thing is, I don't have the first clue why. It was a long time ago. I was eighteen, for God's sake. I'd like to think I've grown a little since then. But," he added ruefully, "I realize there's some basis for questioning that."

"All right," Nate said slowly, "so what's the problem now?"

Matt laughed, but it was without humor. "Where do I start?"

"Excuse me?"

"Literally," Matt said, "where do I start?"

The question was confusing. Nate opened his mouth to speak, but stopped, considering what his brother had said. Still uncertain, he asked tentatively, "Are you saying you don't know where to start explaining the problem? Or you don't know the first step to fix the problem?"

Matt shifted uncomfortably. "Both, I guess."

Unable to hide the anger that suddenly flared, Nate said, "Are you kidding me? Seriously? You ran out on..." Nate paused, taking a breath. "Hell, you ran out on all of us. But mostly you ran out on Peter. He needed you, and what did you do? You gave him the finger. 'Sorry, pal. You're on your own.' Right?"

Matt started to say something, but Nate was too busy getting worked up.

"Did you ever stop to think how the news of your death affected Peter? You know him as well as I do. Don't you think he might have considered himself at least partly responsible? Let me answer that for you. Yeah, he did. He carried that guilt around with him for years. It didn't matter what I said, or what anyone else said. He figured it would never have happened if he hadn't come out of the closet. How do you think that played out while he was trying to deal with everything else?"

Again, Matt began to speak, and again Nate cut him off.

"And then, to top it all off, you suddenly reappear, and what's the first thing you say? 'I'm not going to have anything to do with Peter.' Just perfect. You hadn't crapped on him enough, huh? One more zinger, right between the eyes. Doesn't that pretty much cover it?"

Nate hadn't realized how loud his voice had become, and the awkward silence that suddenly filled the vehicle was startling in contrast. He turned to peer out the windshield, watching idly as the underbrush on his side of the road rushed by in the harsh illumination of the headlights.

"Well," Matt said finally, "I've got to say that was a pretty good job of describing the problem."

Nate looked back at his brother. Matt's eyes were on the road. Nate couldn't read the expression on his face.

"Yeah?" Nate asked quietly. "So what are you going to do about it?"

Matt shook his head slowly. "I don't know. Honestly. Look, I understand what I did was wrong. I'm becoming an expert at that.

But how do you undo things when they're," he paused, then concluded softly, "really bad?"

"You don't."

Matt looked over at him, brow furrowed.

"You don't," Nate repeated. "You can't just *undo* things. But what you *can* do is start making up for them. What's the expression? Every journey begins with a first step. You owe Peter an apology. I'd start with that."

"An apology's not going to cut it."

"Maybe not," Nate said harshly, "but not apologizing is going to cut it even less."

Matt was silent for a long time. Then, to Nate's surprise, he laughed, and this time there was humor in it. It helped ease the tension.

"You know who you just sounded like?" Matt asked.

Nate shook his head. "Who?"

"Dad."

The incongruity made Nate laugh as well. "Sorry," he said after a moment.

Matt turned and looked at him, his face again serious. "I don't mind." He returned his attention to the road. "Really."

A stop sign appeared ahead. At the intersection, Matt turned left onto another two-lane highway. After a short distance, he turned left again off the highway and onto another road that seemed to wind back in the direction they'd already traveled. Nate had no idea where they were. Matt, however, seemed to know exactly where he was going.

They crested a short rise, and, as they started down a relatively straight stretch, Nate noticed another vehicle pulled off on the opposite side of the road. As they passed, he saw that it was a large tractor-trailer rig painted in the ubiquitous colors of a popular moving and storage company. An odd place for a moving van, he thought. Matt slowed and, about thirty yards beyond the truck, pulled the SUV onto the left shoulder, facing in the wrong direction.

"This is it," he said, shutting off the engine. He opened the door quickly and stepped out. Nate noticed that he left the key in the ignition. Nate climbed out as well.

A three-quarter moon had risen, so Nate was able to make out the truck clearly as he and Matt walked toward it, their feet crunching in the gravel.

"The man we're about to meet is named Carson," Matt said quietly. "We're all friends. Do him a favor, though, and keep your hands where he can see them."

"Ok," Nate said, hoping his voice didn't betray his surprise. "Is Carson his first name or last?"

"Just Carson."

They reached the rear of the truck and stopped. Nate looked around but saw no one. Then, from behind, he heard a soft voice.

"Hello Marek."

Nate turned and saw a man dressed in a pair of jeans and a work shirt with a name tag embroidered above one of the breast pockets. In the moonlight, Nate couldn't make out the name on the tag. The man was slight, not quite six feet tall, and he had graying hair that was just a little too long to be fashionable, excess strands pushed behind each ear.

"Good to see you Carson," Matt said, reaching out and shaking hands with the man. "Thanks for this."

"Any time." The man glanced over at Nate, a neutral look, but said nothing. Matt made no effort to make introductions, so Nate simply returned the look, his hands held self-consciously by his side, fully visible. From behind him, there was a sudden muffled clanking sound, and, when Nate turned reflexively to look, he saw that the back end of the truck was rising like a garage door on well-oiled hinges. From the darkness of the trailer, a small platform at floor level slid toward them, cantilevered out, then tilted down and made contact with the ground, forming a ramp. With the moon in front of the truck, Nate could not see into the black of the interior.

"It's all there," the man said.

"Thanks," Matt replied.

"You know," the man said, "Yesterday morning I had a visit from a couple of our old amigos." He hawked and spat. "Just checking in, they said. I suppose they must be part of some new retirement committee. Making sure there's no problem with pension benefits and all."

"Oh, yeah?" Matt said it casually, but Nate could hear a slight tension in his brother's voice. "They have anything interesting to say?"

The man shook his head. "No. They dropped a few names. Yours was in there, believe it or not. Just wondering if we kept in touch. Told them I hadn't heard from you in years."

"Any chance they…"

"None."

Matt nodded. "Good."

Nate looked from his brother to the stranger. They seemed completely comfortable with one another, standing here on a dark, deserted roadway in the middle of nowhere. It was a little surreal.

"Listen," the man said, "I know a few of the guys would be happy to…"

"Not yet," Matt said, "wouldn't be the right move. They'd tumble to it fast. They're already scrambling."

The man lifted his head slightly and tilted it to the side in an acknowledging gesture. He was quiet for a moment. Finally, he said, "Well *I* can certainly help."

Matt was shaking his head. "You already have. Now you've got to get back and be very conspicuous doing nothing."

After a short pause, the man nodded, though it seemed to be with some reluctance. "I've gotten pretty good at that, I guess. It's just," he added quietly, "I hate to see you try to do this alone."

In the faint light, Nate could see a slight smile flit across his brother's face. Matt glanced at Nate briefly before returning his attention to the stranger. "I'm not. Don't worry. I've got it covered."

The man chuckled softly. "I hear that." He tipped his head at the truck and then back toward the SUV. "Let's do it."

He put a hand out and he and Matt shook. He glanced at Nate and gave a quick nod. Then, without another word, he turned and began walking in the direction of the SUV.

Matt tapped Nate on the shoulder and said, "Let's get our stuff." He turned toward the truck and stepped quickly up the ramp. Nate followed.

At the top, Nate's eyes adjusted to the darkness, and he realized that inside the trailer were two vehicles. The one closest to the rear was a light-colored Ford Explorer, maybe four or five years old. Matt had opened the rear hatch and was apparently checking some contents. Then Matt closed the hatch, stepped around the rear corner of the vehicle and, turning sideways, made his way forward. At the driver's side door, he paused and looked back at Nate.

"You take the other and follow me."

Nate nodded, and, when Matt had slipped into the Explorer, he continued up the side of the trailer. Parked immediately in front of the Explorer, its bumper touching that of the Ford, was a compact sedan. A Honda Civic, he realized. He opened the door and eased his body inside. It was an automatic, he was relieved to see. He hadn't driven a stick shift in years. The car wasn't new. In fact, it looked to be at least ten years old. But, from what he could tell sitting in the dark interior, it seemed to be in decent condition.

From behind him, Nate heard the Ford's engine start, and, through the rear view mirror, he saw the vehicle back up and out

231

of the trailer. There were keys in the Honda's ignition. He reached forward and cranked the starter. The engine turned over immediately, with more of a punch than he'd expected. Then it quickly settled into a soft purr. Nate put the transmission into reverse, looked behind himself to ensure the Explorer wasn't in the way, and backed out, the underside of the front bumper scraping just slightly against the rear of the ramp as the wheels found the shoulder of the road.

Matt, he could see, had guided the Explorer out onto the road, parallel to the truck, his headlights now illuminated. Nate turned on his own lights, put the car into drive and, as Matt started forward, pulled out behind him. In tandem, they began retracing the route they'd taken earlier.

As he drove, Nate considered the meeting he'd just witnessed, parsing the comments and looking for hidden meanings. He couldn't shake the notion that there was more to Matt's story than he'd let on. It was all so mysterious, shadowy. Hell, Nate thought, what about the fact that he was now sitting behind the wheel of a car he'd never even seen before. He wondered idly to whom the thing was registered. And where. He hadn't noticed license plates before he'd gotten in. In light of everything that was happening, he realized he'd better start paying more attention to details around him. In the illumination provided by his headlights, he could see the plate on the Explorer in front of him was white with blue lettering. He wasn't sure, but he thought it might say Pennsylvania across the top.

The road they were on dead-ended, and Matt turned right onto the narrow highway. After a short drive, they came to an intersection, and Matt again turned right. Nate did his best to try to spot landmarks, but it was difficult in the dark.

After several minutes, they rounded a sharp curve, and Nate thought he might recognize where they were. A short distance ahead, if he was right, would be the point at which they would leave the highway and start back down the lane to the cabin. Sure enough, the glow of the Explorer's brake lights indicated that Matt was preparing to turn. Nate began to slow the Honda. Suddenly, however, the brake lights ahead went out, and Matt gradually accelerated. Surprised, Nate followed suit.

They passed the turn off, and Nate thought perhaps both he and Matt had been mistaken. After a couple minutes, they came to a long narrow bridge, and, as they crossed, Nate could see to either side reflections of moonlight off water, most likely, he realized, the lake on which the cabin sat. They had not, Nate was sure, crossed a bridge on their drive earlier this evening, nor, to his recollection, during their initial drive to the cabin. A feeling of unease began to tug at him.

Near the end of the bridge, the Explorer's brake lights again glowed. Just after they had traversed the span, Matt eased his vehicle to the side. Nate pulled up behind him. Matt jumped out and came jogging back. Nate rolled down the window and Matt leaned in. His grim words sent ice through Nate's veins.

"They're here."

14

The instant the flash-bangs ignited, Raen was on the move. He sensed, rather than saw, the others in his team as they descended on the dwelling, each moving in perfect synchrony.

Less than three seconds after the initial shock, he cleared the front door, turning right and moving parallel to the front of the cabin, the .45 in his left hand held out at the ready. As he did, he noticed bodies down on the floor of the large main room, covered at gunpoint by the men who had entered from the lake side. He counted three, which meant there were still three targets to go.

Ahead of him to his left, a door opened, and an older woman with closely cropped grey hair staggered out. He grabbed a handful of her hair and violently yanked her to the floor, stepping past quickly and leaving her for the team member behind him.

At the end of the hall was an empty bathroom. To the left was another door, this one closed. He paused briefly, leaning back against the opposite wall for leverage. Then he threw a booted heel against the door, crashing it inward. He waited a beat to see if there was return fire, then, at a crouch, he entered, sweeping the room with the barrel of his pistol. A lamp in the far corner illuminated the small space, and he saw that it was empty. He put two rounds into the closet before throwing open the doors to confirm that none of their quarry was hiding inside.

"Clear," he called out, stepping back into the hallway.

"Clear," one of his men echoed as he exited the adjacent bedroom.

Shots sounded from above where his men were conducting a sweep of the second floor. Gun still at the ready, Raen returned to the main room. Four bodies now lay face down on the floor. Their hands were bound behind them with plastic restraints, and their ankles were similarly fettered. Two were women, and he immediately dismissed them. One of the men was older, his thin silver hair matted with blood from a nasty gash. The fourth, Raen saw, was Peter Cartwright. He had his head raised awkwardly, looking about the room with a frantic expression. He did not, however, appear to be injured.

From the space beyond the balcony above, Raen heard several shouts of "Clear" as his men checked each room. A moment later, Dacoff appeared at the head of the stairs. "All clear up here. No targets."

"Shit," Raen muttered under his breath. Where the hell was Marek?

One of the men assigned to his action team, an older agent, entered the room from the kitchen area, a 10 mm Auto Glock in his right hand. He'd taken a couple of steps in Raen's direction, clearly about to say something, when his eyes went wide. He raised the weapon and pointed it toward the center of the room. Instinctively, Raen reached out with his gun hand and slapped down hard on the agent's weapon just as it discharged. He glanced quickly back at the prisoners lying on the floor. The bullet from the Glock had left a gouge in the floorboards just a couple feet short of Peter Cartwright's head.

The agent tried to raise his weapon again, but Raen's outstretched arm prevented it from coming up. "What are you doing?" the man exclaimed. "That's Marek."

"No, it's not," Raen replied quickly. "That's Peter Cartwright. Stand down."

The agent looked at him sharply, then glanced back at the figure lying on the floor, alarm and doubt playing across his face.

Raen had given strict orders. They would kill only in self-defense. Otherwise, he wanted as many of the targets taken alive as possible in case he needed hostages to trade for Marek. The exception, of course, was Marek himself, whom they were authorized to shoot and kill on contact. Unfortunately, most of the operatives, like Raen, had never met Marek, so they wouldn't necessarily know when they'd encountered him. They didn't even have pictures of the man. They'd all been provided surveillance photos of Peter Cartwright and had been told that Marek was his twin. Raen, though, had not fully appreciated how alike the two brothers apparently were. There was no doubt in his mind that the figure on the floor was Peter Cartwright. But here was an experienced officer who'd obviously known Marek, and he had been - still was, as near as Raen could tell - convinced to the contrary.

Raen refocused his attention on the figure lying a few feet away. He stepped toward him and, as he did, he heard the older agent behind take in a quick breath. Oh, for God's sake, Raen thought. The prisoner was bound hand and foot. Even if it *was* Marek, what could he do? Raen, of course, had heard all the stories. He didn't believe half of them.

He knelt down by the prostrate figure. The man looked up at him. Raen could see that he was afraid, but there was still defiance in his eyes.

"Where are your brothers?"

The man blinked a couple of times, then said, "I don't know."

Raen roughly jammed the barrel of his .45 against the prisoner's forehead and repeated slowly, "Where are your brothers?"

Cringing, both eyes shut tightly, the man said, "I don't know. They took the car and left."

"When?"

"I don't know."

Raen pushed the barrel hard against the man, driving his head back and up in an unnatural position.

"It was about an hour ago," the man said quickly.

"Where?"

"They didn't say."

Raen resisted a strong urge to pull the trigger. Instead, he shoved even harder, generating what had to be excruciating pain in the man's neck and forehead.

"Honestly," the prisoner exclaimed. "They never told us where they were going."

Raen believed the man. Still, he kept the pressure on for a few more seconds before finally pulling back and standing.

"Set up a perimeter," he commanded. He turned to Dacoff, who had descended the stairs. "Do a full sweep."

Dacoff nodded. He'd already pulled out one of his electronic detection devices. Pointing to one of the other agents, he said, "You take the upstairs."

While one of Raen's men remained in the large family room, his M-16 trained on the prisoners, the others quickly dispersed, taking up defensive positions around the cabin.

Again, Raen cursed quietly. His best opportunity to get Marek had come up double-zero. Now, he was going to have to hunker down and wait for the man. And, he'd have to do it with less than a full action team. The six men he'd lost in the assault outside Bar Harbor had yet to be replaced. A pair of operatives from the Boston office had been scrambled, including the older agent who'd almost killed Peter Cartwright just now, and he'd been promised replacements within the next two to three hours. But Raen had opted for speed, and now he'd have to make do with what he had.

And Marek was out there.

His thoughts were interrupted by Dacoff. "Ah, hah," Raen heard the man say from the dining room, "what do we have here?"

He turned to look just as Dacoff reached a hand up over the decorative woodwork lining the top of a china cabinet. There was a sudden loud bang, and Dacoff jerked his arm back. Only half of it came, however, and he stood there, dumbfounded, looking down at the point where his arm now ended in a jagged stump near the elbow. Blood began pooling at the man's feet.

An explosion ripped through the second floor, and a moment later, the agent Dacoff had ordered upstairs appeared, staggering toward the head of the stairway, face bloodied, a gaping hole in his chest. His body struck the newel post, spun and came tumbling down the stairs, landing in a disorderly heap near the bottom, lifeless eyes staring out of a head that now lolled back at an unnatural angle.

"Out of the house," Raen yelled. "Now."

He pointed to the prisoners. "Bring that one," he said, indicating Peter Cartwright and looking at the agent who'd been standing guard. The man nodded, slung his weapon and reached down. He put a hand under one of Peter Cartwright's armpits and began dragging him toward the front door. Raen selected one of the women, a redhead, and did the same, following the other operative out the door.

He deposited the woman in the dirt next to Cartwright and turned just as Dacoff stumbled out and collapsed on the stoop.

The older agent from Boston materialized out of the darkness surrounding the cabin. He punched a finger toward a stand of trees near the rear of the structure, then at Dacoff. Another agent emerged from the shadows and hurried over to the fallen figure, crouching down over him. The older agent turned to Raen with a questioning look.

"The bastard's got the place rigged," Raen said through gritted teeth. "He's controlling the damn things remotely."

Another explosion shattered the evening silence, and there was a cry of pain from the darkness.

Jesus Christ, Raen thought. We're on his turf here. We need a better defensive position. He made a snap decision. He pulled the communicator from his pocket and keyed the microphone. "Hammer One to team," he said, using the code word for the mission. "Back to the vehicles."

Raen holstered his pistol, then pointed to the M-16 in the hands of the agent guarding the two prisoners sprawled in the dirt. The agent wordlessly handed the weapon to him. Both of the prisoners were straining to look up at him, eyes wide with panic. His hands on the barrel and upper grip, Raen raised the rifle and slammed the butt of the stock into the back of Cartwright's head. The man's eyes rolled up and his face slumped in the dirt.

He pointed a finger at the terrified woman. "Give me any trouble, and I'll do the same to you." He handed the rifle back to his agent, unsheathed his knife and cut the bindings on Cartwright's ankles and wrists. Then he leaned down and lifted up the unconscious body, slinging him over his shoulder in a fireman's carry.

"Move," he ordered, and he began running toward the vehicles they'd concealed in the underbrush about a quarter of a mile up the private lane.

They had come in two Suburbans. By the time Raen reached the spot, his men had cleared away the camouflaging brush and had pulled both vehicles out into the lane, facing in the direction of the highway, engines running, but lights still off. The rear door on the trailing Suburban was open, and he threw Cartwright's body into the back.

"Assemble at Rally Point Bravo," Raen called out, stepping to his right and looking forward. One of his men standing by the side of the first Suburban raised a hand in acknowledgement. Then he opened the passenger's side door and slipped into the vehicle, pulling the door shut. The driver put the first car in gear and started forward. Raen had a sudden thought, and he'd just opened his mouth in what he realized belatedly was a futile gesture to warn when the vehicle was suddenly engulfed in a brilliant fireball, the blast from the explosion catching Raen flush against the front of his body and hurling him backwards.

When he hit the ground, he instinctively rolled to the side. As he did, a gunshot rang out, and he sensed a bullet thudding into the earth at the very spot he'd landed. He heard the faint whine of the spent projectile as it ricocheted over him. He continued rolling until he encountered brush and dropped down slightly into a shallow furrow by the side of the lane. He pulled out his .45 and, staying low to the ground, backed his way further into the foliage until he was confident he could not be seen. Then he raised himself into a crouch and, staying low, began working in the direction of the cabin, eyes focused on the lane and the woods beyond.

From the darkness the figure of the agent carrying the still-bound female prisoner over one shoulder emerged into the glow cast by the burning Suburban. There was the crack of another shot, and the man's legs buckled. He pitched forward and the woman's body was thrown clear. As he tumbled to the ground, the man gripped the M-16 slung on his shoulder and in one motion brought it around and up in a firing position, a smooth and well-practiced maneuver. It did him no good, however, as the back of his head exploded at the sound of the next shot, and his body crumpled to the ground.

Suddenly, there were shots from the direction of the cabin, and Raen realized that the remaining members of his team were returning fire. Good. He took quick stock of the situation. In addition to the man who'd just been shot, there had been at least two agents plus Dacoff behind him. And, he thought, there should have been at least one man in the undamaged Suburban. He glanced back and saw that, indeed, one of his men had crawled out the passenger side of the car and was hunkered down next to it, using the vehicle as a shield, gun at the ready.

As he watched, though, there was a quick three shot burst from the other side of the lane and the man crouching by the Suburban jerked, his body twisting awkwardly. Then the man fell to the ground, writhing in apparent pain. Another shot, and the man abruptly stopped moving, obviously taken out by fire directed under the vehicle.

More shots from the woods across the lane told Raen that his men were advancing on the shooter, laying down disciplined fire in that direction. At least one of the men, he knew, would be executing an enveloping movement. The shooter would have to withdraw toward the public highway unless, of course, he tried to cross the lane. If he did, Raen was ready to take him down from his position. And the shooter would know it.

No, he knew, Marek would have to reposition down the lane. In fact, if he hadn't started by now, it might be too late. Out of an abundance of caution, Raen stayed where he was for another minute, alert for movement in the lane, listening as the shots from his men in the woods across from him advanced past his position. They were hewing closely to protocol. When he was confident they had the shooter on the run, he darted from the brush. The woman his operative had been carrying was lying face down in the roadway. She had long hair tied in a pony tail. He reached out, grabbed her hair, and roughly dragged her back into the brush, where he dropped her and resumed an alert stance.

The sound of gunshots stopped and was replaced by a silence that was profound in contrast. He again retrieved the communicator.

"Hammer One. Report."

After a long pause, he heard, softly, "Hammer Five. Found the shooter's nest. He's flown."

"Hammer Seven," came a second voice. "He didn't come east."

It meant that, as Raen had suspected, Marek had withdrawn toward the highway.

"What about Hammer Two?" Raen asked, referring to Dacoff.

"Here," the man's voice replied weakly, "with Five."

Good man, Raen thought. He'd had half an arm blown off and was still functioning tactically. "Anyone else?"

From the speaker of the communicator came nothing but silence. They were down to four men and one of them was badly injured. Shit. Raen toggled the frequency on his communicator. "Hammer One to Tool Box."

"Tool Box, go ahead," came the immediate reply.

"I have eight, repeat, eight men down. I need reinforcements immediately."

There was a long pause. Raen could only imagine the impact this report had on those at the other end. There would be hell to pay later. Well, he thought, what do you expect? It's Marek, goddamn it.

Finally, the reply came. "Thunderbird is on the way with six assets. ETA twenty-five minutes. More to come. Please confirm rally point."

"Rally Point Alpha," Raen said quickly. The helicopter would be setting the additional men down at the cabin. They'd have to rappel from the hovering craft. Not optimal, but necessary.

"I'll need further backup at Rally Points Bravo and Delta," Raen continued. "I am without vehicles." Raen knew he couldn't use the remaining Suburban. He was certain Marek had also planted a charge in that car. The only reason it hadn't been detonated to this point was because the unconscious Peter Cartwright was lying in the rear of the thing.

"Roger Hammer One. That's going to take a bit longer. Will advise. Out."

Raen stared at the silent communicator for a moment. Yeah, ok, he said to himself finally. He'd have probably had the same reaction. This operation was not going well. Goddamn you, Marek.

He switched frequencies. "Hammer One to team. Draw back to Rally Point Alpha. Pick up the prisoner from the back of the Suburban."

A series of clicks sounded as his men keyed their microphones in acknowledgement.

He looked down at the bound figure of the woman lying beside him. She was on her back. In the darkness, he couldn't really make out her expression, but the terror he'd seen earlier seemed to have dissipated. All right, he said to himself. We'll do this the hard way.

He leaned down. "Remember what I told you," he said softly, reaching for the KA-BAR knife he kept in a sheath strapped to his lower leg. He withdrew the weapon, bringing it slowly around and passing it near her face, where he knew she'd be able to see it in the diffuse moonlight. He set the blade against the plastic restraint between her ankles and severed it with a quick slice.

"Keep your mouth shut, do what I tell you, and you might live. And," he added with emphasis, "you just might be able to avoid having your face cut to shreds. I haven't made my final decision on that yet."

He was gratified to see some of the fear return to her eyes. He gripped one of her arms and, in a quick motion, roughly yanked her up off the ground and deposited her on her feet. She stumbled slightly but managed to catch herself and remain upright. He re-sheathed the knife, shoved his right hand under her left arm and began pushing her toward the roadway.

#

Heart pounding, Nate slowly crawled forward. He could see the lights of the nearby cabin through the underbrush in front of him. He didn't know where their assailants might be, however, and he feared that, at any moment, he'd come up on one of them. In his right hand, he clutched the pistol Matt had given him, finger on the trigger and thumb on the safety, ready to flip it forward into firing mode as Matt had shown him. He'd never fired a pistol before. He hoped he wouldn't have to tonight. But he was grimly prepared to do so if necessary.

He eased himself up to the spot Matt had described and expelled a relieved breath. From where he lay now, he could see clearly the door of the cabin, which hung ajar. He also had a good view of the dirt-covered clearing in front the structure. Soft light spilling from the door and a few windows combined with the moon overhead to illuminate the space. He couldn't see or hear anyone else.

Earlier, he'd worked his way through the darkened woods in the direction Matt had laid out for him, his mind full of horrible images, while gunshots and explosions ripped through the night. Matt had warned him about that and had admonished him not to worry. Of course, that was easier said than done. The shooting, thank God, had finally stopped, and silence had descended.

Nate was desperately afraid for the others. His brothers. Patricia and Tim. Maggie. And, now that he was no longer moving, his instincts told him he needed to be doing something. What, though, he had no idea. And Matt had told him to wait.

A rustle in the nearby brush startled him. Then something pounced. An animal, he realized in panic. He was about to jump up when the creature began licking his face furiously. Buster. With his free hand, Nate reached out and pulled the little dog to him, cradling him in his arm and holding him close to his side. The poor creature was shaking uncontrollably. Rubbing a thumb against the loose skin behind one of Buster's ears, Nate made a gentle shushing sound. Slowly, the dog's shaking subsided. Eventually, Buster lay his head across Nate's forearm and began to pant softly.

Nate thought he saw movement in the lane, and, then, out of the darkness, two figures appeared. His breath caught. Maggie, her hands apparently tied behind her back, staggered forward, being pushed by a man who looked vaguely familiar, though Nate couldn't immediately say why. Then he realized where he'd seen him. He'd been on the patrol boat that had chased them the day before.

Nate peered down the barrel of the pistol, wondering if he could hit the man from here. More likely, he realized, he'd hit Maggie. He kept the safety on.

As the two neared the cabin, the man yanked Maggie to a stop, reached into a pocket and withdrew something that he held up near his head.

"Hammer One," he heard the man say. "Go ahead."

A second voice, metallic and faint, but still audible in the quiet, said, "There's no prisoner here."

The head of the man holding Maggie jerked up, and he whipped around just as another large explosion tore through the night.

"Shit," he heard the man exclaim. "Shit."

The man looked around quickly, then pushed Maggie toward a stand of trees near the rear of the cabin. She almost fell, but the hand on her arm kept her upright. When they reached the trees, they melded into the darkness.

Though he couldn't see them, Nate could hear the man apparently speaking urgently into the communications device. "Hammer One to team. Report." Nate did not hear a reply. "Hammer Five, check in." Still nothing. "Hammer Seven, report." After a few more seconds, Nate heard the man swear once more. Then the night was again still.

Eyes trained on the spot where Maggie and the man had gone, Nate sensed movement to his left. His initial thought was that Buster was stirring, and he had the sudden panicked concern that the little dog would give him away. He turned and was shocked to find himself staring at the face of Matt. There was an incomprehensibly serene and relaxed expression on his brother's face.

"How the hell do you do that?" Nate whispered.

Matt shrugged slightly and said in a return whisper, "What have we got?"

Nate tipped his head in the direction of the stand of trees and pointed with the barrel of his pistol. "One of them has Maggie. I heard him trying to talk to the others on his radio. It didn't sound like he was getting anyone."

Matt gave a slight grin. "He won't."

Nate felt a little better. But he was still on edge. "Now what?"

Still grinning, Matt said, "Watch this."

Matt put both hands up to his mouth, cupping them, and turned his head to face down the lane, away from the cabin. Nate could see him take a deep breath. Then, from the spot where Matt seemed to be looking, Nate heard a faint voice. "You and me, Raen. And I know you're in that stand of trees by the back of the cabin."

Startled, Nate whispered, "Who's that?"

Matt turned back and cocked an eyebrow. "Me."

Nate was about to say something when movement caught his attention. Maggie came stumbling out of the trees and staggered awkwardly to the center of the clearing, where she stood looking about in a slightly bewildered fashion, hands still bound behind her back. There was what looked to be a canvas bag at her chest, hanging by a strap around her neck.

Then a man's voice came from where Maggie stood, loud, but somewhat distorted. "I've still got you outnumbered, Marek." The object hanging from Maggie's neck, Nate realized, contained a communications device. The voice from the device's speaker continued. "Here's the deal. I'll let your brothers live. I'll even let this woman live. You have my word on it. But you'll have to give yourself up. You do the math."

Matt leaned toward Nate and said quietly, "He's bluffing."

"He's bluffing," Maggie called out. With a surprised look, Matt returned his attention to the clearing. Maggie was staring down the lane in the direction from which Matt's voice had seemed to come a moment ago. "But he has reinforcements coming," she shouted. "They said twenty-five minutes. That was about ten minutes ago."

Matt tapped Nate's arm and nodded toward Maggie. "I like her."

Nate wasn't sure why or how the next words out of his mouth came to be. He'd given them no thought. They just popped out, unbidden. "She's taken," he blurted.

Matt looked back at him with another grin. "Ok," he said equably.

Feeling his face flush, Nate said, "I've got to go for her." He started to gather himself.

"Easy there," Matt said softly, his face now serious. "You'd probably be dead before you even got close. Though," he added, looking thoughtful, "he might not shoot. He might just wait until you were near and blow that C4 charge in the satchel around her neck."

Nate felt like a dagger had been driven into his heart. He stared out at the forlorn figure of Maggie, standing alone in the dimly lit clearing.

"He probably wouldn't ignite it though," Matt continued. "Better to shoot you and save the hostage to get to me. In fact," he mused, "he'd probably only take out your legs. Make the bait even better. That's what I would do."

"Will you knock it off," Nate hissed. "What are we going to do?"

Matt took a deep breath. "I'm going to go finish this."

"What do I do?"

"You stay here. If I need you, I'll call you."

Nate started to object, then realized it was foolish. Matt knew what he was doing. A hell of a lot more than Nate did. He nodded.

With his own nod of acknowledgement, Matt rose slightly and, in a series of graceful movements, backed away. Then, without a sound, he was gone.

The silence was again complete. Nate watched Maggie. She stood stock still, the tension that gripped her body evident even from this distance in poor light. He wondered if she knew there were explosives hanging around her neck and realized she'd probably been told. He desperately wished he could do something to comfort her.

Buster stirred in his arm, but then settled back, apparently content, oblivious to what was happening.

Minutes passed. Nate strained to hear sounds. The breeze from earlier in the evening had died down, so even the trees were still.

Suddenly, the calm was again shattered by the sounds of gunfire. It came from the direction of the lake, on the opposite side of the cabin from where Nate was lying. He listened intently. There were definitely two different weapons being discharged. His instincts told him to move, and he was up and running without having given it further thought.

Maggie had turned in the direction of the shots. But she obviously heard the pounding of his feet, and she lurched around as he approached.

"Nate," she cried out.

He reached out with his left hand, gripped the satchel at the point where it connected with one end of the strap and yanked upwards, allowing his momentum to carry him a couple steps beyond Maggie. The satchel and strap came up over Maggie's head, and, as soon as it was clear, Nate planted his right foot and slung the bag away with a sidearm motion. It flew out of his hand, sailing in a lazy arc. The thing had traveled maybe twenty yards and was just starting its downward track when it suddenly disappeared in a blinding white blast.

The concussion caused Nate to stumble backwards, striking Maggie, and they both sprawled in the dirt.

Shaking his head to clear it, Nate turned to look at Maggie, but his attention was suddenly arrested by the sight of a figure rounding the far corner of the cabin. It was the man he'd seen earlier. Raen, he now knew. The man's right arm was thrown across his chest, hand gripping his left shoulder and blood oozing between his fingers. In his left hand, which hung limply at his side, was a large pistol.

A venomous look crossed the man's face. He released the grip on his shoulder and brought his right hand down to retrieve the gun from his apparently useless left hand.

Nate realized he still had the pistol Matt had given him in his own hand. He rose to one knee, lifted the weapon and pointed it, trying to keep it steady against the shakes that suddenly engulfed him. The other man's mouth curled up in a grotesque smile.

"You don't have the balls, Cartwright," he said, taking his own gun from the hand hanging at his side and bringing it around. Nate thumbed the safety and pulled the trigger.

He hadn't really aimed, and he'd been shaking badly, so he feared he'd missed. But a crimson stain suddenly appeared at the man's crotch. The man looked down and almost absently said, "Well, that's ironic."

Then he refocused on Nate. Time seemed to slow. The man grimaced, apparently in pain, and he moved his gun hand slightly, lining up on Nate. There was motion at the man's feet, and he suddenly jerked his leg. His left foot came up, along with Buster. The little dog had his jaws clamped around the man's ankle. Nate, his gun pointed at the man's chest, again pulled the trigger, and, at that moment, the sound of multiple weapons discharging shattered the night.

Nate was sure his bullet struck the man in the upper torso. But, incomprehensibly, the man's forehead exploded, a mist spraying out in front of him. The man toppled forward, his knees striking the ground first, and he landed face down in the dirt, a few feet from Nate and Maggie. Behind the spot where the man had been standing, Nate could see the figure of Matt, poised at the corner of the cabin, a pistol held out in front of him in a two-handed grip.

Nate took frantic stock of his own body. He didn't feel like he'd been hit, but he was suddenly unsure whether he might be in too much shock to know it. Then he realized his hip and elbow hurt from where they'd struck after falling to the ground. That had to be a good sign, he decided. His heart, which had been on emergency overdrive began to settle, and he found his breath again.

He looked quickly at Maggie. She was lying on her side, hands behind her back, staring up at him. There were no apparent wounds. He searched her face and saw no pain, only concern.

"Are you hurt?" he asked.

"No," she said, immediately. "You?"

He shook his head.

"Oh, Nate," she said. He reached for her and pulled her up to him. She lay her head against his chest. "Oh, Nate," she repeated.

Matt appeared behind Maggie and knelt down, moonlight flashing off the knife in his hand. "Let me help," he said in an almost playful voice. A moment later, the bindings around her wrist having been cut, Maggie threw her own arms around Nate. They clung to one another, and Nate's heart once again shifted into overdrive. This time, he didn't mind.

"Peter," Nate heard Matt say, "we could use that car now." After a moment, he heard the sound of a vehicle approaching, and the Explorer pulled into the clearing. Nate reluctantly relaxed his grip on Maggie, shifted his weight, and, as he stood, helped her to her feet. She again fell against him and he happily wrapped his arms around her. The driver's side door to the Explorer opened, and Peter climbed out.

"Yeah, I see how it is," Peter said. "While I sit in the dark with a splitting headache, everyone else is having a good time." He stopped when he saw the body of the man Nate and Matt had shot lying in the dirt. "Well maybe not everyone." He was about to say more when he suddenly stopped and cocked his head.

Nate heard it too. A distant slapping sound.

Matt slammed shut the rear door to the Explorer and stepped back, something long and slender balanced on his shoulder. He looked at Nate. "Back into the woods."

Alarmed, Nate pulled his arms from around Maggie. He could hear the thing clearly now. A helicopter, and it seemed to be headed in their direction.

Matt pointed to the spot where he and Nate had been previously. Nate took hold of Maggie's hand and led her to the edge of the clearing, stepping into the cover of the trees. Peter and Matt followed.

Matt turned to face the clearing, and, from one of his pockets, he retrieved a small object that he inserted into the device he was carrying. The thump of the approaching helicopter quickly became louder, and then it was directly above them. Nate couldn't see it in the darkness, but the downdraft of its rotors stirred the branches overhead.

Matt stepped quickly from the cover of the trees, putting his eye up against the rear of the sighting mechanism that jutted out at an angle from the front portion of the tube-like device on his shoulder. He pointed the front end up toward the helicopter, the longer end extending back and down almost straight to the ground. With a sudden whoosh of gas discharging behind Matt, an object jumped from the tube and rose quickly, a slight glow revealing its path.

There was a loud explosion, followed almost immediately by an even louder one, and suddenly they were all bathed in a harsh light as the helicopter above them was engulfed in flames. For an instant, Nate could see the thing, hovering about a hundred feet off the ground. Then it tipped forward and slipped away over the top of the cabin with an intense whining sound that abruptly stopped with a loud smack as it apparently struck the surface of the lake, and there was yet another explosion. The cabin was outlined for a moment by an intense backlit glow, which quickly dissipated, then disappeared altogether. With it went the sound, and the silence of the evening once again enveloped them, eerie in its sudden contrast.

Matt tossed the tube aside and looked back at them. "We need to get Patricia and Tim and leave before they realize we've completely rained on their parade."

#

Krantz sat back and dropped the report on his desk. He reached up and gently massaged his temples with both hands.

Marek.

The man had just cost The Organization, what? He did the quick math. A few minutes earlier, one of the men injured in the Bar Harbor assault had died in the hospital in Portland. So the total body count was now up to - for God's sake - twenty-five? Are you kidding me?

He took a deep breath. He'd never intended to open up this Pandora's box. In fact, he still had a hard time understanding how it had happened. Marek had taken himself out. He was gone. Good riddance. And then? How stupid was that? He let out his breath.

He'd have to deal with it. Quickly. Certainly before the idiots in Washington got hold of it. What a nightmare.

His laptop pinged.

That was unusual.

He stared at the device lying on the desk, cover down. There were only three people in the world who could send him a message that would trigger the signal. One of them was in a coma, and the other two were not likely to attempt a communication at this time. He reached out and slowly lifted the top, revealing the screen. The familiar prompt greeted him. He put a finger over the "enter" button, then paused, a sudden, irrational sense of unease overtaking him. Then, with the certainty he'd always possessed, he pushed down on the button.

A brief message appeared, with no return or identifying information.

"I'm coming for you."

15

Nate tapped lightly, and, after a short pause, Patricia opened the motel room door. She gave him a broad smile.

"Well, good morning Nate," she said with an exaggerated cheeriness. "Are you here to call on Maggie?"

Hoping the flush that came to his cheeks didn't show, Nate said, "I'm here to let *both* of you know that we're pulling out in three minutes."

At the rear of the motel room, Maggie stepped from behind the wall separating the bathroom from the rest of the small space, drawing Nate's attention. She had an expectant look, and there was a radiant glow about her. At least that's the way it appeared to Nate. After a moment, he reluctantly refocused on Patricia, who was chuckling.

"We'll be out in two minutes," Patricia said. Then, with a knowing look, she slowly closed the door.

Nate took a steadying breath, turned and almost ran into Matt, who had once again somehow managed to sidle up next to him without making a sound. Matt's arms were held at his side, weighed down by a gym bag in one hand and a large duffle in the other. He had a smile on his face.

"What?" Nate blurted.

"Have you asked her to the prom yet?"

Nate raised a finger. "Don't start with me."

Matt shrugged. "I'm just asking," he said innocently.

"You're just asking for trouble is what you're asking for."

His brother's smile widened. "Ok," he said, "have it your way." He stepped past Nate with a studied nonchalance and walked to the Honda, which was backed into a nearby parking space. He set the bags down and opened the trunk.

Nate could see that Tim was already in the back seat of the sedan, his head swaddled in the bandage Matt had fashioned for him.

They'd arrived at the small motel well after midnight, following a long, winding drive through the back roads of Maine and New Hampshire. When they'd gratefully pulled themselves from the cars, Matt, to Nate's surprise, had produced keys to the three rooms.

"Contingency," he'd explained when Nate had given him an inquiring look.

Matt, who'd quickly field dressed Tim's wound before they left the cabin, had stitched the gash after they arrived and stayed in the same room with the older man. Nate had bunked with Peter, keeping a wary eye on his brother, concerned that he might have a concussion after his encounter with the butt of the M-16. Fortunately, Peter looked to be none the worse for wear.

And then there were Patricia and Maggie. The two women, it seemed to Nate, had formed a bond, leaning on one another for support, and, though they'd been thoroughly terrified the night before, each had subsequently, it appeared, adopted a philosophical attitude and, with the help of the other, was coping with the circumstances.

Obviously, Matt's demonstrated ability to anticipate and fend off those who were set to do them harm had given the group confidence. Nate, however, wasn't buying the notion that they were out of the woods. He could see that Matt, despite his outward appearance of relaxed joviality, was still very much on edge.

From behind him, Peter asked, "Are we ready?"

Nate nodded. "Just waiting on the ladies."

"You know," Matt called out, giving Nate a sly look, his hand on the open trunk lid, "I think you and Maggie should have the Explorer today."

Because the Ford was packed with so much gear, it had room for only two people. On the drive the night before, Patricia had ridden with Matt, while Nate had followed in the Honda with the other three. Now Matt was suggesting that Nate and Maggie travel together.

Just the two of them.

It was a tempting proposition, but Nate pushed it down. He'd already made a decision that, unfortunately, conflicted with his brother's matchmaking. He gave Matt a direct look and said, "No, I'll stay with the Honda. I think Peter should ride shotgun with you."

Matt's expression became serious, but, after a moment, he nodded and turned his attention to fitting the bags into the trunk.

Nate glanced back at Peter who glared at him with a look that clearly said, What are you doing? Nate merely shrugged.

The door on which Nate had earlier knocked opened, and Maggie and Patricia stepped out. Patricia held up both hands, her two index fingers extended and, in a questioning gesture, crossed them, pointing at the Explorer and the Civic.

"You're both with me in the Honda," Nate said. That, he noticed, seemed to please Maggie.

"I'll sit in the back with Tim," Patricia announced immediately, and she walked briskly to the sedan.

Nate and Maggie stood staring at one another, Nate uncertain what to say and Maggie apparently having a similar problem.

"Let's go kids," Matt said airily as he passed them, headed for the Explorer.

Peter had walked over with an excited Buster straining at the end of his leash. He wordlessly handed the leash to Nate. Then, with one last thunderous look, he turned and climbed into the Explorer.

#

They worked their way south, Matt choosing a more inland route and avoiding the major metropolitan areas along the east coast. Outside Albany, they stopped for gas and a quick bite to eat. Peter, Nate noticed, was unusually reserved, saying little as they sat around the table at the small roadside diner. When they were finished, though, Peter climbed back into the Explorer without hesitation. Nate chose to take that as a good sign.

While Tim had predictably buried his nose in a paperback shortly after they'd started out, Patricia had tapped into a side of her personality that Nate hadn't previously seen, and she was quite talkative on the drive, keeping up an impressive running commentary on the scenery, the towns they passed, the weather and myriad other subjects of which Nate soon lost count. It seemed to Nate that she might be making an intentional effort to keep from thinking about the people who were chasing them. He didn't mind. In fact he appreciated her garrulousness.

For the first time since, well, he wasn't sure, but maybe since high school, he found himself at a complete loss for words. He was so aware of Maggie sitting next to him that it was palpable. And the cat that he thought he'd long ago outwitted had once again gotten his tongue. He was beginning to wonder if Maggie might think there was something wrong with him.

After they merged back onto the interstate, Nate rested his right arm on the center console, and, to his surprise, his fingers brushed lightly against Maggie's. She had set her hand by the gear shift and was looking out the passenger side window. The contact sent a jolt through Nate, and he involuntarily jerked his hand away, keeping his eyes fixed on the highway in front of them. A few seconds later, though, he casually put his hand back where it had been. With an unusual mixture of relief and excitement, he found that Maggie had not withdrawn hers. Again, he felt the soft touch of skin on skin. Cautiously, he relaxed, delighting in the feeling.

After a moment, he felt Maggie move one of her fingers, a careless gesture. Maybe. Afraid to overreact, he waited a few intense heartbeats, then slightly moved his own small finger. With a silent thrill, he felt an immediate corresponding movement.

"Oh, for heaven's sake, Nate," Patricia called from the back seat, "just take her hand."

Nate felt himself flinch. For a moment, he was at a loss. Then, despite himself, he laughed. He glanced over at Maggie. She had turned and was looking at him with those incredibly green eyes. And she laughed.

He lifted his hand, moved it over Maggie's and set it down. She immediately brought her other hand over and placed it on top.

"There we go," Patricia said. "That's so much better."

And Nate had to agree with that.

They stopped again near Harrisburg as the sun was setting. When they'd finished eating, Matt pulled out a map and showed Nate their destination, a spot in rural Northern Virginia outside the town of Leesburg.

"Is it safe?" Nate asked.

Matt nodded. "It's off the grid."

"I take it that's a good thing."

"It is."

#

Matt's "off the grid" destination turned out to be a small farmhouse tucked up against the base of Catoctin Mountain at the eastern edge of the Blue Ridge. It was accessed off a rural road down a long straight drive that passed between two lines of rugged split-rail fences.

Though it was too dark to tell when they arrived, Nate would see in the morning that small herds of dairy cows grazed the fields on both sides of the fences. As they drove down the lane now in the darkness, their headlights illuminated a series of signs that had been erected along the side in a haphazard fashion. "Private Property, No Trespassing." "No Solicitations." "Beware of Dog." And, Nate's favorite, the outline of a handgun with the words "Beware of Owner." Given their recent experiences, it made him chuckle.

At the end of the lane, they came to a gate, which Matt quickly unlocked. They passed through and pulled around behind the house. After they climbed out of the cars, Matt led them not to the rear door, but rather to a squat wooden structure attached to the back wall, on top of which was a weather-beaten trap door secured by a rusty padlock. Matt pulled a key from his pocket and, after springing the lock, lifted the door, propping it open with a hinged slat. Following Matt, they descended a set of wooden steps to a basement below the house, their way lit by an overhead bulb that Matt illuminated by yanking on a chain near the entrance.

"Peter," Matt said, looking back up from the basement floor, "will you please close the door behind you?"

Peter, who was bringing up the rear, nodded, reached up, freed the slat holding the door open, and allowed the trap to lower and close.

The small basement was lined with old brick walls and appeared empty, save for a couple of dust-covered steamer trunks stacked in one corner and a hot water heater in another.

Matt walked over to one of the walls and paused. It appeared to Nate that he might be counting. After a moment, Matt reached out and placed a hand against one of the bricks. It moved, and the hand partially disappeared into the cavity left behind. Suddenly an entire section of the wall separated and swung away.

The area beyond was dark. Then a series of lights came on, and Nate could see a furnished room on the other side of the old wall. Matt looked back and grinned.

"It's not the Ritz," he said, "but it'll do for now."

The location, Matt explained, was one he'd used in his previous career. He did not further elaborate. There were two bedrooms. Maggie and Patricia claimed one. Matt and, to Nate's surprise, Peter, the other. That left Nate and Tim to sleep on the two sofas in the communal room. It didn't matter to Nate. He was exhausted.

In the morning, Nate arose early while everyone else was apparently still asleep. He was anxious to follow up on something he'd been mulling on the drive south. He found some instant coffee, made himself a cup, then carried it to the desk in a corner of the room, where he turned on the laptop Matt had produced the evening before, after Nate had lamented the fact that he didn't have one. Nate had once again been struck by the resources Matt had at his disposal.

Once he was on line, Nate pulled up a series of data bases to which he had access. He found what he was looking for after only a few minutes.

Matt emerged from the bedroom and took the seat next to him.

"Any luck?" he asked, keeping his voice low, apparently not wanting to disturb the still-sleeping Tim.

Nate nodded. In an equally quiet voice, he explained to Matt what he'd found. After a moment, his brother nodded as well.

"Worth a shot, I guess," Matt said. "Of course, there's always the possibility…" His voice trailed off. He didn't have to finish.

Matt was right, Nate knew. With everything else he'd come to learn in the past few days, anything was possible.

Still, he shook his head. "I don't think so. And I'm willing to take the risk."

Matt gave him a long look. Finally, he said, "Ok. But I go with you."

"No," Nate said immediately. "The others need you. And I need you to be with them."

Matt frowned. He was about to say more, but Nate interrupted.

"It's not open to discussion."

Matt looked away for a moment, but then he nodded.

Changing the subject, Nate asked, "Have you figured out how to get to Krantz?"

Matt returned his attention to Nate. "I've got a working plan."

"Really?"

A slight smile played on Matt's face. "You want to see?" He stood before Nate could answer. "Wait here."

Matt walked into the bedroom. He returned a moment later, a small object in his hand. He sat back down and held the thing out for Nate's inspection.

"Do you see it?" he asked.

Nate studied the device. It looked vaguely like a remote control, though he was no electronics expert.

"May I?" Nate asked.

"Of course."

Nate took the thing and held it in the palm of his hand. It was light. There were a pair of unmarked buttons on one side. Otherwise, the plastic casing was smooth. He turned it around, looking for inscriptions or other writing. Nothing.

Puzzled, he looked at his brother, who stared back impassively.

"I don't get it."

"Look more carefully."

Nate held the thing closer, peering at it from every angle he could. Finally, he shrugged and glanced up. "I don't know," he said, before looking back down at the device. "What is it?"

"Hell if I know."

Startled, Nate jerked his head up and realized he was staring at Peter's grinning face. Matt stepped out of the bedroom behind him. He was in a t-shirt, and it dawned on Nate that the sweater Matt had been wearing a minute earlier was now on Peter. Matt was grinning as well.

"I figure," Matt said, "if we can fool you, we can fool anybody."

Nate gave Matt a dubious look. "That's your plan? He's you?"

"I said it was a working plan."

Nate turned to Peter. "And you're ok with this?"

"Why not?"

Nate stared at his brothers, both grinning like a couple of school children who'd just pulled off a prank in home room. Despite himself, he chuckled. After a moment, the chuckle became a laugh. Then Peter was laughing. And Matt. Suddenly, all three brothers were howling uproariously, tears running down their faces.

The door to the other bedroom opened and Maggie stepped out, a blanket draped over her shoulders, the edges clutched at her chest. She gawked at them for a moment. Then she started giggling. Patricia appeared behind her with a look of alarm that quickly morphed into amusement. And she began to chuckle.

Buster, his stubby tail jerking back and forth, ran from one person to the next, adding an occasional "hmmph."

From across the room, Tim propped himself up on one elbow, a bemused expression on his face, and asked, "Why are we laughing?"

Nate paused and looked at his brothers. They stopped and looked back at him. Then all three burst out again. Nate held his hands up and shrugged. How could he possibly explain? Would the others understand if he told them a mighty wind had suddenly blown through their lives, sweeping away years of accumulated cobwebs and fog, leaving behind the three brothers as they had been before. So long ago? How could they?

But he knew it. And his brothers knew it. And it felt wonderful.

After a moment, though, Nate took a deep breath. Wiping his eyes, he gave Matt a level look. "You better know what you're doing."

Matt returned the look. "Yep."

#

The house was located in the affluent area of Montgomery County, Maryland known as Potomac. It was not as large as some of the other nearby estates, but it was still a comfortable-looking dwelling. It sat a good thirty yards back from the road, the space in front sparsely landscaped, but well-tended, dominated by a large sprawling elm tree to which a few remaining leaves still clung in the late autumn chill. The ground below the tree was littered with a sprinkling of leaves that had recently succumbed to the inevitability of time and gravity.

Nate, carrying a small leather folio, walked up the driveway and turned onto the brick path leading to the front door. He pressed the doorbell and heard a soft chime from within. A few seconds later, the door opened, revealing a trim man with short-cropped gray hair. The man, Nate knew, was in his early seventies, having retired twelve years ago, but he had the fit, energetic appearance of someone who could have been ten, maybe even fifteen years younger. He regarded Nate with a mildly curious expression.

"General Delahousse?" Nate asked.

The man nodded.

"My name is Nate Cartwright. You knew my father, Bob Cartwright."

At the mention of his father's name, the man's expression instantly changed. He broke into a smile and his eyes became animated.

"Of course," he said. "I can see that. My god, you're the spitting image." He opened the door wider. "Please, come in."

They exchanged pleasantries, and Delahousse led Nate to the kitchen. Nate took a seat at the small table in the breakfast nook while the man busied himself making coffee for the two of them.

"My wife," Delahousse said, his attention on the coffee maker, "is out running errands, but she should be back soon. I know she'd want to see you. She always had a soft spot for your dad."

He turned and considered Nate again. "I guess the last time we saw you was at the memorial service." His face took on a mixture of sadness and embarrassment. "I should have kept in touch. I'm sorry."

"No reason to apologize, sir."

The man poured coffee into a pair of mugs and carried them to the table, setting one down in front of Nate. "Do you take cream or sugar?"

Nate shook his head. "Just black."

"Like your father." He set the other mug on the table across from Nate and sat down. "So, how are your brothers?" Though the man had been away from Texas for a long time, Nate could still hear the slight drawl.

Nate hesitated, then said, "They're as well as can be expected under the circumstances."

Delahousse studied him for a moment, then said, "This isn't just a casual call, is it? You're here for a reason."

Nate nodded slowly. "Yes sir."

The man smiled slightly. "You are very much like your father. He was a no nonsense kind of guy too. What can I do for you?"

Nate tipped his head toward the leather folio he'd set on the table. "I'd like to tell you a story. I think you'll find it very interesting."

The man looked intrigued. He nodded.

Nate tried to be as concise and direct as possible. He knew the general was used to being briefed and would appreciate it. But he punctuated parts of the story with reference to certain of the documents he'd brought with him, and Delahousse asked to see a number of them. When he was done, the general set the papers aside and sat motionless, staring for a long time out the bay window overlooking the backyard.

265

Finally, he returned his attention to Nate. "Is there more?"

"There is." Nate took a deep breath. "Sir, the people who were responsible for this thought they had covered it up. Now they know at least part of it is out. They seem determined to put the genie back in the bottle. My brothers and I have been on the run for the past several days. These are very bad people, and they'll stop at nothing." He hesitated, then continued, "It's possible I've put you in jeopardy by coming here."

The man raised a hand slightly and shook his head. Then he seemed to realize something, and he gave Nate a shrewd look.

"Did you consider the possibility that I was in on it?"

Nate did not hesitate. "I did, sir. And I rejected it."

Delahousse nodded. "Thank you, Nate." He absently drummed his fingers on the table. "The question is, Who was?"

"To pull something like this off," Nate ventured, "a big part of the administration must have been compromised."

The general shook his head. "I have a hard time buying that." After a moment, though, he said, "There *was* that weasel Huffman." He looked at Nate, and by way of explanation, said, "Deputy administrator at the time of Apollo 18. I could believe pretty much anything about that guy."

"Is he still around?"

Again, the general shook his head. "He died almost immediately after the mission. Heart attack. Surprising, too, because he wasn't that old."

Nate arched his eyebrows.

Delahousse started to say something, then stopped. He dropped his eyes to the table, obviously thinking. After several seconds, he looked up, staring at the ceiling with a distracted look. Finally, he again focused on Nate.

"When Apollo 18 was revived, Bob learned about it at a meeting in Stu Overholdt's office." His look sharpened. "There's no way Stu was involved in anything like this." He glanced away for a moment. "And, in any event, Stu died a few years ago. Pancreatic cancer.

"But," he said after a few seconds, and there was a new expression on his face, "at that meeting, there was someone else."

Nate felt his heart quicken. "Do you remember who it was?"

The general nodded slowly. "I do," he said, almost reluctantly.

Nate waited patiently. It seemed as though the general was having a difficult time processing what he'd remembered. Finally, the fire returned to the man's eyes.

"This wasn't just anybody," he said.

Nate hesitated. Then he said, "Who was it?"

#

Senator Harrison Burton leaned forward, his face flush, the perpetual scowl deeper than Krantz remembered it.

"How is that even possible? One man?"

Krantz chose his words carefully. "This man is… different."

"Bullshit," the Senator growled. "That's just an excuse. You have an entire organization. Unlimited resources. There's no way one guy trumps that." He gave Krantz a penetrating look. "He's got to be working with others."

Krantz shook his head. "He works alone. For the most part. In almost twenty years, he only had contact with two other operatives, the members of his tactical team. They're both retired. We've got them under surveillance, and we know exactly where they are at this moment. One's in Eastern Ohio, the other's in South Florida. They haven't moved in the last twenty-four hours."

"But you have no idea where this Marek fellow is."

"That's not true."

Burton cocked his head.

"He was moving south," Krantz said. "We got a positive identification from two nights ago. He and the others stopped at a restaurant in Pennsylvania, just outside Harrisburg."

"Two nights ago," Burton snorted. "He could be anywhere now."

Krantz nodded slightly. "We think he's here."

"Here? Where's *here*?"

"Here in the D.C. area."

Krantz was amused to see the Senator glance involuntarily around his own office. After a brief moment, the man seemed to realize the absurdity of it, and he again fixed Krantz with a black look.

"I'm losing my patience," he said, a menacing softness to his voice.

Krantz resisted the urge to point out that Burton wouldn't know patience if it bit him in the ass. And, not for the first time, Krantz considered how easy it would be to kill the Senator. There were a dozen ways he could do it at this very moment. A quick blow to the windpipe would bring on a slow and painful death, which, under the circumstances, had a certain appeal. Of course, the man would probably flail and make noise. That wouldn't do. Better to just yank him out of that stuffed chair, whip him around and snap his neck. A nice, quiet, instant death. Krantz could then set him back down in the chair, call for medical assistance, and, by the time anyone realized the man had been internally decapitated, Krantz would have quietly slipped away.

But, as tempting as it was, Krantz knew he wouldn't do it. The Organization, and his ambitions for The Organization, depended on the political cover the Senator provided. Theirs was a truly symbiotic relationship. As long as Burton controlled the oversight, Krantz could do what he wanted. Provided he arranged the occasional dirty work for the Senator. The wet work.

Of course, over the past few years, Krantz had been preparing for Burton's succession. The man couldn't live forever. He'd already cheated death for an impressive length of time, too attached to his power to let go. Too damn mean to die.

The practical problem Krantz had was that the next ranking Republican on the Armed Services Committee was that boy scout from Nebraska. No way he'd play ball. And forget the Democrats. No, Krantz' future was tied to the other two senior Republicans in line for the Committee chairmanship, both reasonably malleable and both possessing some nice ugly skeletons in their closets. If the boy scout hadn't retired by the appropriate time, he'd meet with a tragic accident. It would be so much easier, Krantz reflected, when he would be able to function without having to kowtow to his political overseer. To be able to call all the shots, rather than have some called for him by a worthless bureaucratic hack.

"I want them all terminated," Burton was saying, and Krantz refocused.

"We're working on it."

"You're not understanding me," the Senator said quietly.

"You mean Marek's former team members?"

"I mean everyone."

Krantz took a deep breath. Taking down Carson and Kemp would be ugly. And, there would be repercussions. The rest of it, no big deal. But those two former operatives were well-regarded. There'd be dissention in the ranks. And, it wasn't as if he hadn't already pissed off Marek enough …

He considered the Senator. The man scowled back at him.

Finally, keeping his face impassive, Krantz said, "All right."

#

The elevator doors opened, and Krantz stepped into the hallway.

"I want those orders coded Juliet Charlie Actual," he said into the cell phone. "And no exceptions. The target is to be destroyed, no matter the circumstances."

He turned and headed toward the exit. With Marek on the prowl, he felt vulnerable, and his senses were on high alert. He was traveling with a larger security detail than usual. They were waiting for him just around the block, and they'd meet him outside the main entrance as soon as he gave the word. Because of the strict scanning provided by the Capitol Police, no one could enter the senate office building with weapons, so he felt reasonably safe inside. Still, he was taking no chances, and he was very much aware of everything and everyone around him.

"Now, as for Carson and Kemp," he said, entering the rotunda. His steps slowed. Then he came to a halt. "Stand by," he said abruptly, and he terminated the connection.

Somewhat incomprehensibly, not thirty feet away, bathed in the light of the midday sun pouring through the overhead oculus, was Marek. The cocky son of a bitch was just standing there, looking at him. He had his hands in plain view, not that it mattered. Even Marek wouldn't have been able to smuggle in a weapon.

Of course, it was possible the man was playing the decoy, distracting him so an accomplice might sneak up and take him from behind. But Krantz knew there was only one man alive who'd be able to perform that kind of maneuver against him with success. And that man was standing right in front of him.

Krantz sighed. "You can't run forever."

"I'm not running," Marek replied calmly.

"What do you want?"

"I want to know who ordered it. Who's calling the shots."

Krantz shook his head slowly. "You're here. That means you already know." His own words suddenly gave him pause.

Marek said nothing. His eyes, unblinking, studied Krantz.

A warning sounded deep in Krantz' consciousness. But the realization that, instead of Marek, it was the man's twin he was looking at didn't strike him until the moment the hands from behind came gracefully across his chest and up under his chin, clamping themselves in place, quickly and effectively immobilizing his upper body. A part of him couldn't avoid a professional nod to the technique. And the setup.

It was an awesome kill.

The last thought that went through Krantz' mind was the idle question whether he'd actually hear the snap of his neck before the spinal cord was severed. He didn't.

#

From the far side of the rotunda, Nate watched as Matt lowered the limp body of the man known as Krantz to the marble floor. The whole thing had happened so quickly, if he'd blinked, he'd have missed it.

"I need help here," Matt was saying loudly. "Someone call 911."

A woman cried out and pointed in Matt's direction, but whatever she said was drowned out by the sudden cacophony that filled the large area. People began crowding around the prostrate figure, talking at once, their voices echoing off of the domed ceiling. Matt allowed the onlookers to push past him, casually backing away. No one seemed to be paying him any attention. Peter, who had turned as soon as Matt had put his arms around Krantz, had calmly strolled to the main entrance. As Nate glanced his way, he stepped out and was gone.

A pair of Capitol Police officers pushed their way through the throng and began urging people back.

"I'm a doctor," a man in a tweed jacket called out, and he was allowed through.

Matt had eased his way to the rear of the crowd. He now pivoted and, without hurry, walked to the entrance. Nobody tried to stop him. He pushed open the door, and he was gone as well.

Nate took an involuntary step toward the people gathered in the center of the room. Through the crowd, he saw the doctor kneeling by the body. After a moment, the man looked up and spoke to one of the police officers. Nate couldn't hear him, but he could read his lips clearly. "He's dead." The police officer asked him a question, and the doctor merely shrugged, as if to say, I don't know.

There was another commotion near the entrance. Two men in uniform, arms held down at their sides, laden with equipment, had been halted by Capitol Police officers just beyond the metal detectors. After a moment, they were allowed to pass, and Nate saw that they were emergency medical technicians. Behind them, a similarly uniformed man appeared wheeling a portable gurney.

Nate felt a tap on his shoulder. He turned quickly and found himself staring into a face he realized with a start he'd seen before. The man's gray hair had been died blond and trimmed, so it was no longer pushed back behind his ears. And, instead of a work shirt, he was wearing a sport coat and tie. But there was no mistaking who it was. Though it had been dark, with only a three-quarter moon for light, Nate knew he had met this man a few days earlier while standing behind a moving van on a deserted country road in Maine.

"We've done everything that needs to be done here," the man said quietly. "Time to go."

Then he stepped past Nate and walked nonchalantly to the entrance. With one last quick glance back at the pandemonium in the center of the rotunda, Nate turned and followed.

16

Under a brilliant blue sky, Nate ascended the steps to the United States Capitol Building. General Rick Delahousse waited for him at the top with two others. The general, like Nate, wore a business suit, but the men with him were in military uniforms. When Nate reached them, the general made the introductions.

"Nate, I'd like you to meet General Bryce McConnell, Vice Chairman of the Joint Chiefs. In a prior life, the general and I served together in the office of the Air Force Chief of Staff. Of course, that was a few years ago."

"More years than any of us would like to remember," General McConnell said with a slight smile, reaching out and shaking Nate's hand.

"Thank you for agreeing to this meeting, sir," Nate said.

"And this is Admiral Logan Vance, Chairman of the Joint Chiefs of Staff."

The admiral also smiled and proffered a hand. "Nate," the admiral said, "I had the privilege of meeting your father. I was an ensign, fresh out of the Naval Academy, on my first cruise. Your father was the executive officer in one of the strike squadrons assigned to the USS *Midway*. There was no particular reason why he'd give me the time of day. But he sought me out the first week, showed me around. Made sure I was squared away. He was a good man."

"Thank you, sir."

"He didn't," the admiral added, grimly, "deserve what happened to him."

Nate nodded, not sure what to say in response. He was still processing the fact that he had just shaken hands with the two highest ranking officers in the United States military. When Nate had met with Delahousse three days before, the general had told Nate he'd "pull some strings." Delahousse had, indeed, delivered on that promise.

"We have a few people waiting for us inside," Admiral Vance said, "so we should get going. Will either of your brothers be joining us Nate?"

Nate had talked this over with Matt and Peter, and they had agreed with Nate's suggestion.

"Sir, we thought it best that I come to this meeting alone."

The admiral nodded. He seemed to understand.

Their entry into the building was expedited by a cadre of uniformed Capitol Police officers who had obviously been standing by waiting for them. Two of the officers accompanied them to a room on the second floor near the Senate Chamber. When they entered, Nate discovered that a handful of others had already gathered around a large oval table. Nate instantly recognized the man at the head of the table.

Anthony Strickland had recently been confirmed by the Senate as the new Attorney General, the nation's top lawyer. He stood when they entered the room, and Admiral Vance introduced Nate.

"Please have a seat," Strickland said, and Nate took the adjacent chair indicated by the Attorney General. Admiral Vance and Generals McConnell and Delahousse sat to Nate's left. Across the table were two men approximately Nate's age. They had not been introduced, and they had said nothing from the time Nate had entered. There was something about their watchful manner that struck a familiar chord. Nate was pretty sure he knew what it was.

Between the two men was an elderly woman. Nate knew exactly who she was. Matt had described her to a tee. She nodded to him, not unpleasantly, but she also said nothing.

Strickland looked at Vance and said, "Admiral, if you don't mind." The other man nodded.

"Mr. Cartwright," Strickland began, "I've just been briefed by these gentlemen." He indicated the two men sitting across the table. "You don't know them, but I believe you are somewhat familiar with their organization."

Nate considered the two men. They returned his look without expression.

After a moment, Nate nodded and said slowly, "I think so."

"Yes, well," Strickland said, dryly, "I can understand your less than enthusiastic reaction." He gave Nate a direct look. "Believe me when I tell you that, until yesterday, I was not aware this organization existed. Nor, for that matter, was my boss."

That caught Nate by surprise. Strickland's "boss" was none other than the President of the United States.

To his side, he heard Vance clear his throat.

Strickland looked at Vance and gave him a tight smile. "I've also received a briefing from the Joint Chiefs. I understand the dynamic at work here."

He returned his attention to Nate. "We walk a fine line at times with our intelligence services. The need for such assets is a difficult but necessary thing in a less-than-perfect world. But, as a nation, we still have certain values we consider important, and we endeavor to guard against encroachment on those values. In an effort to maintain discipline, we've put procedures in place. Checks and balances, if you will. Most of the time, they work. Occasionally, they don't. In this case, our procedures failed miserably."

Strickland looked down at a legal pad in front of him on which he'd scratched several notes. "After considering the relevant facts, I've concluded that we did not provide adequately for the appropriate oversight here. That's a collective failing."

He glanced up and took in the entire room.

"However," he continued, "this could not have happened - would not have happened - without some extraordinary misconduct. And that, I believe, falls at the feet of one man."

There was a sudden commotion in the hallway outside, and the door banged open. Speaking loudly to someone behind him, the hunched figure of Senator Harrison Burton entered. He'd taken a number of steps into the room before he realized it was already occupied. That brought him up short. Behind him, a number of others spilled in, gathering around the older man and looking with curiosity at the collection of people sitting at the table. In addition to Burton, Nate recognized several other senators.

"What in the hell are you doing in my conference room?" Burton snarled. The man's eyes were fierce, and the look on his face was withering. His reputation, Nate could see, was well-deserved.

Burton seemed to notice Admiral Vance and General McConnell for the first time, and Nate saw just a flicker of uncertainty in the old man's eyes. Then the fury returned and Burton focused it on Strickland.

Pointing a slightly bent finger at the Attorney General, he roared, "Clear this room."

"Strategic Security Force," Strickland said calmly.

That caught Burton by surprise, and the man's face froze in mid-sneer. The uncertainty Nate had seen a moment before flashed, but, again, the man recovered quickly. He drew himself up and, impossibly, the scowl on his face deepened. In a commanding voice, the senator said, "This is an outrage. I'll be goddamned if I'm going to let the president's lap dog come sniffing around on my turf without so much as a courtesy call. This is my jurisdiction. Not yours."

Strickland's expression didn't change. "Under other circumstances, I might take issue with the lap dog comment, but there are too many more important things we need to deal with at the moment. Suffice it to say this is very much my jurisdiction. I'm here on official Department of Justice business. With," he added, "the full concurrence of my colleague, the United States Attorney for the District of Columbia."

The Senator, Nate could see, was practically apoplectic. Cheeks flushed, breathing hard, the man opened his mouth to say something, and Strickland interrupted.

"You are familiar with a man named Krantz?" Though he posed it as a question, Strickland didn't wait for an answer.

"Of course you are. In the past twelve years, you met with the man," Strickland consulted a page from the top of the stack of notes in front of him, "forty-seven times. The reason I know that, by the way, is because I have the transcripts from each of those meetings."

The Senator hadn't moved. Though his face was still twisted in anger, his mouth hung open and there was a new look in his eyes. It wasn't exactly fear or panic, though Nate couldn't completely rule out either. In any event, it certainly lacked the imperiousness of a moment before.

"I take it you weren't aware your conversations were being recorded. Well, they were," Strickland said, as though he were having a casual conversation.

"And not only do I have the transcripts, I have the original source tapes. We went to the trouble of verifying the voice signatures. I didn't want there to be any mistake. Of course, there's a sticky issue regarding the recordation of conversations without notice. That would normally put Mr. Krantz in some hot water. But there's not much point in belaboring it now, since he's dead."

The Senator, Nate saw, actually flinched at that.

"Ah, I see the report of his death is news to you. Yes, a few minutes after leaving your office two days ago, the man you know as Krantz experienced a medical emergency in the rotunda of the Russell Senate Office Building. You may have heard from your staff that there was a bit of excitement that morning."

Strickland leaned forward and clasped his hands in front of him.

"Senator, I'm placing you under arrest on multiple federal counts of first degree murder. I have a warrant to that effect signed by the presiding judge of the District Court. These charges will likely be supplemented by several other lesser offenses, including the misuse of your office, but I don't want the tail to wag the dog. Here's the bottom line: Just preliminarily, we're looking at over thirty capital cases. Even if you avoid the death penalty, you're still facing several life sentences. Perhaps, with some luck, you might be able to work a plea bargain that will make you eligible for parole some time in, oh, I'd say, the twenty-third century. Maybe."

The other senators, Nate noticed, had moved away from Burton, putting distance between themselves and the man.

Strickland nodded to the two uniformed Capitol Police officers who'd escorted Nate and the others to the conference room and had remained just inside the door. "Please take Mr. Burton into custody and read him his rights. In light of the seriousness of the charges, I think it would be appropriate to cuff him."

Burton seemed to dig deep, summoning reserves. His well-known scowl returned. "You're making a big mistake."

"No," Strickland said, immediately. "I'm correcting one."

The two police officers stepped over to Burton. They towered over him, and Nate guessed that it was not a coincidence. Strickland, he thought, had probably arranged to have two of the largest men assigned the duty. Burton looked suddenly diminished between them. They quickly and efficiently put the man in handcuffs. Though Burton, Nate could tell, was trying to keep up a facade of defiance, it was crumbling quickly. One of the officers pulled a card from his back pocket and read Burton his rights. Then his colleague turned the man toward the door, and, as the crowd parted, marched him out of the room.

There were murmurs from the other senators. Finally, one of them, a woman Nate recognized as one of the two senators from California, turned to face Strickland. "Tony, what's this about?"

278

"The organization known as the Strategic Security Force," Strickland said. "Are you familiar with it?"

The woman's brow furrowed. She turned and looked questioningly at a couple of her colleagues, who both shook their heads. Finally, she returned her attention to the Attorney General. "I don't think so. Should I be?"

"That, Senator," Strickland said, with some irony, "is a complicated question. The organization falls under your committee's oversight responsibility. But, I'm not surprised you haven't heard of it. Your soon-to-be-former colleague apparently became quite adept at keeping it hidden."

Strickland indicated the people sitting around the table. "I need to finish up here. I apologize for taking your committee's room. But I think, under the circumstances, it would be best if you and I and Senator Greeley," he nodded toward another of the gathered senators, the one Nate knew was the senior senator from Nebraska, "discuss this privately. Perhaps I can come to your office this afternoon?"

The woman hesitated. Nate could see that she was thinking, making, he thought, somewhat uncharitably, political calculations. Finally, she nodded.

"Call my administrative assistant," she said. "We'll talk this afternoon."

Then she turned and nodded toward the door. The collection of legislators began filtering out of the room, exchanging quiet comments. When they'd all gone and the door had again closed, Strickland turned to Nate.

"The suggestion," he said with a slight smile, "that we consult Ms. Branson turned out to be a good one."

Nate glanced involuntarily at the woman across the table from him. At Strickland's mention of her name, she had looked over at the Attorney General, but, after a moment, she returned her attention to Nate, considering him directly. There was no hostility in her expression. Just simple curiosity.

It had been at Matt's insistence that Nate requested her involvement through General Delahousse. Matt had explained to Nate that, if there was anyone in The Organization who might know where all the bodies were buried, it was Ruth Branson. She had been there forever, Matt explained, having seen several directors come and go. She, Matt suggested, had been the ultimate fly on the wall. Nate now studied her.

"Ms. Branson," Strickland said, "provided us the transcripts and tapes from the meetings with Senator Burton. And, while we appreciate that," Strickland added, with a bit more emphasis, "we're still working through everything else."

The man to the woman's left said quietly, "Ask your questions."

Nate was struck by the man's self-possession. Though it was an innocuous statement, the man had, in effect, just told the United States Attorney General to stop screwing around. Nate was impressed.

Strickland seemed to take it in stride. Nate realized he was in the company of some extraordinary people. It was, despite everything else, fascinating.

"There is," Strickland said, looking at Nate, "a lingering question about what happened to the man named Krantz."

Nate had been prepared for this. "And what is that?" he asked innocently.

A brief smile flitted across Strickland's face. Then he became serious. "As I mentioned a moment ago, the man died in the senate office building. There was a lot of confusion at the scene, and I have a number of conflicting reports about the cause and nature of the death. At least three witnesses saw someone approach the man and wrap his arms around him while he was still standing. This person was apparently the one who called for medical assistance."

Nate held his tongue, waiting for the man to continue.

"What I find particularly fascinating," Strickland said, "is that two of the witnesses swore this person looked identical to another man who was talking to Krantz just before he died. Does that seem odd to you?"

Nate shrugged. "It's very common for people to become confused in stressful situations."

"Yes," Strickland said. "But here's the thing: I've been told that you have a pair of identical twin brothers. Though," he added, raising a hand palm up and adopting a mildly perplexed expression, "I find no record of that. As near as I can tell, you only have one brother." He looked keenly at Nate.

Keeping his face as impassive as possible, Nate returned the look. There was a long silence.

Finally, Strickland nodded. "Well, the whole thing is apparently somewhat moot, as the body seems to have been misplaced."

That came as a surprise to Nate.

"Shortly after the man was pronounced dead," Strickland continued, consulting another piece of paper in the stack before him, "by a doctor whose legitimacy I have confirmed, emergency medical technicians arrived at the scene. It was an impressively quick response. Unfortunately, they never made it to the emergency room at the George Washington Medical Center. A few minutes later, another ambulance arrived. From the medical center."

He set down the piece of paper and considered Nate. "That's very strange, don't you think?"

Nate wasn't sure what to think. *All* of this was news to him.

Strickland turned to the man on his right. "Do you have any idea how that might have happened?"

The man didn't reply immediately. After a few seconds, he said, quietly, "No." Then he looked at Nate. Strickland also turned to Nate.

"Do you know anything about this?" the Attorney General asked.

"No," Nate said immediately.

Strickland nodded slowly. "What makes it even more interesting is that the security tapes from the rotunda for that morning seem to have disappeared. The Capitol Police are at a loss to explain how that happened. As is," he said, turning again to the man across the table from Nate, "your organization. Correct?"

"That is correct," the man said, again looking at Nate. The man's expression did not change, but Nate could swear there was a new look in his eyes. For lack of a better term, it seemed almost respectful.

Nate gave the Attorney General a direct look. "Sir, I assure you I do not have an explanation for these things."

Strickland glanced down for a moment. Then he returned Nate's look. "No reason why you should. I understand you've been a victim here. We have much to unravel, due in large measure to the actions of this man Krantz over the last several years. In light of that, I'm not inclined to make what happened to him my top priority."

He tipped his head in the direction of the people sitting across the table from Nate. "I've received assurances from these gentlemen that you, and the others with you, are in no further peril. I'd like to extend an apology on behalf of the federal government for the difficulties you've experienced, and I give you my word that I will make certain we redress the wrongs that were visited on you."

He gave Nate a look that seemed genuine. "I can't set everything right. Some things," he paused, then continued, "can't be undone. But I'll do my best."

The Attorney General's words stirred a renewed melancholy. After a moment, Nate nodded. "Thank you," he said simply.

Strickland looked around the room. "I'd like to thank all of you for coming…"

"One moment, please," Nate interjected. With a curious expression Strickland looked at him. "I'd like to ask a question," Nate said.

The Attorney General hesitated, then nodded.

Nate looked across the table. "I'd like to know what happened to the Apollo 18 capsule. I have reason to believe that Steve Dayton made it back to Earth safely."

The two men on the other side glanced at one another. Then, the one who was to Strickland's immediate right said, "We don't know anything about that."

The man gave Nate a direct look. "Sorry," he added.

Nate, however, was not looking at the two men. Instead, his focus was on the woman sitting between them. When he'd started to ask his question, she'd nodded slightly, and Nate had taken heart. But then a look of mild surprise had come over her, and Nate's spirits sank. Still, he pressed forward. "I'd like to ask if Ms. Branson knows anything about it."

Everyone in the room turned to consider the elderly woman. Obviously uncomfortable, she looked at the man on her left. After a moment, he nodded slightly. She licked her lips and returned her attention to Nate. Hesitantly, she said, "I do."

Nate's pulse quickened.

The woman's eyes shifted between Nate and the Attorney General. In a quiet voice, she said, "They told me I couldn't reveal any secrets. National security. I'm not supposed to question anything. I've seen what happens to people..." Her voice trailed off. Then she took a quick breath. "Every year, I have to sign a renewal of my confidentiality covenant." A pained look crossed her face. "I've wanted to..."

She became quiet, her gaze still darting between Strickland and Nate.

Strickland looked hard at the man to his right, who again nodded. The man turned to the woman and said, "This is something you can talk about."

The woman took a deep breath. "Oh," she said haltingly, "ok." She glanced at the table, then back up at Nate. "I do know what happened to Major Dayton. And," she paused, her face clouded, "your father."

Nate nodded, and said softly, "Yes, I know what happened to my father."

The woman's brow knit. "If you know that, then, why?"

A residual anger welled in Nate. Working to keep his voice calm, he said, "I promised Major Dayton's daughter I would follow up on her father's fate. It takes nothing away from what happened to my father. He was a great man. I see no reason to trample on his grave."

The woman nodded slowly. "I meant no disrespect," she said, and it sounded sincere to Nate. "And, believe me, I wouldn't do it if I could. But, even if I wanted to, I couldn't possibly trample on your father's grave. I couldn't do it for a very simple reason."

She looked at him with a new intensity.

"Your father's not dead."

#

When Bob Cartwright opened his eyes, he was greeted by a splash of early morning light on the concrete wall beside his cot. Just a narrow horizontal line, it would soon thin to nothing as the sun's arc carried it up and out of view from the slit in the east wall of the bunker. In a few minutes, the enclosure would return to semi-darkness, until late in the day, when sunlight would once again peek through the corresponding opening in the west-facing wall. He glanced over at the other two cots. Empty.

Then he remembered what day it was. He threw back the thin blanket and slid his legs over the side of the bunk. On the bare floor were his flip-flops, actually a pair of old boots from which he'd cut away everything above the soles except for a narrow strip of leather still attached to either side and permanently laced together on top. He slid his feet in, stood and shuffled to the doorway, where he had to duck in order to pass through. Once outside, he straightened and looked up.

It was a cloudless day, with no wind. Perfect. Over the past several days they'd been inundated with rain. October was drawing to a close, and the next six months would bring more of the same. But for Drop Day, they couldn't have asked for better weather.

Instinctively, he looked around. From the spot here on the top of the Rock, there was nothing but the brilliant blue of the water, stretching out in every direction as far as he could see, merging at the distant horizon with the cerulean sky.

With not even a mild breeze to contend with, he could use the more convenient west side to urinate. He took the few steps to the familiar spot, pushed aside a leg of his shorts, and sent a stream of piss down the shear face of the rock wall to the ocean eighty feet below. When he was finished, he turned and followed the well-worn path leading down to the Parade Ground.

Dayton, he saw, had taken a seat on the Bench, which was really just a worn cleft of rock near the bottom of the path providing a view to the east out across a small flat area. As usual, Dayton had the triangular piece of cloth he wore on sunny days draped over his head and tied in the back to protect his bald pate from burning. He, like Cartwright, was dressed only in shorts, consisting of a pair of coveralls cut off at the waist and mid-thigh and held up with a belt fashioned from parachute lines. Except for those rare winter days when the temperature dropped below seventy degrees, it was the only garment each of the men ever wore.

Dayton obviously heard Cartwright's footsteps. He turned briefly, then slid to one side, offering space on the Bench. Cartwright took a seat.

"When do you think?" Cartwright asked.

Dayton squinted at the sun, now a few degrees above the horizon. "Soon."

Of course, "soon" could mean five minutes or it could mean fifty minutes. Time, as the men had come to learn, had little meaning here on the Rock. With the exception of Drop Day, there was really nothing to mark. Still, Dayton religiously kept the log, so they knew the day, the month and the year. Were it not for Drop Day, though, they'd probably have long since let it go.

Cartwright looked around. "Sasha?"

Dayton tipped his head. "Doing his morning constitutional."

Cartwright nodded, and the two men sat in companionable silence. After a couple of minutes, Kruchinkin's head appeared at the far end of the Parade Ground, gray tousled hair hanging to his shoulders. He came walking up the steps they'd carved into the far side of the island, a roll of toilet paper in one hand. He also wore shorts and was shirtless. Around his neck, a silver chain extended down to a spot in the middle of the chest where it disappeared into scar tissue that had grown over the bullet wound from all those years before. From a distance, it almost looked like the scar dangled from the chain like a pendant.

When the Russian got closer, he smiled his familiar toothy grin. "Drop Day," he said, unnecessarily. Cartwright and Dayton both nodded. Dayton slid further to his right, and Cartwright did the same. Kruchinkin took a seat. All three men turned their attention to the eastern horizon.

Dayton heard it first, of course. Both Cartwright and Kruchinkin still suffered residual hearing loss from the gunshots in the small enclosure of the Soviet space station. When the man stiffened, Cartwright glanced over. "Coming?"

Dayton nodded.

All three men reflexively leaned forward.

After a minute, Cartwright heard it too. Faint, but growing louder. Then the thing materialized on the horizon. Just a speck at first, but it, like the sound, grew quickly, until, in a moment, Cartwright could make out the shape of her wings extending out from the rounded front of her fuselage.

The throaty growl of the C-130's four turboprop engines became more distinct. Cartwright felt the familiar excitement. The ground began to vibrate. At the last moment, the air seemed to shimmer. And then the massive thing was roaring over them, no more than three hundred feet off the surface of the water, an even shorter distance from the spot where the men sat.

From the open rear, a dark object appeared, trailing white cloth which quickly morphed into a small canopy as it filled with air. The object dangled beneath it momentarily, suspended above the Rock for no more than five seconds before gently settling onto the small flat area the men had dubbed the Parade Ground. A perfect drop.

The sound of the large aircraft faded quickly as it receded to the west, until, in a moment, the quiet returned, and the plane was just a memory.

Cartwright had to give some grudging credit to the men who, every twelve weeks like clockwork, performed the duty they'd just witnessed. In thirty-five years, they'd only missed the Rock twice, once overshooting and, on the other occasion, missing wide in a stiff cross wind.

He looked at the other two. "Shall we?"

Kruchinkin nodded. "Let's do it," said Dayton.

They rose and walked the short distance to the spot where the bundle had landed. There was no hurry. They had nothing but time. And this was more about anticipation than anything else. The likelihood that they'd find other than the normal fare was extraordinarily remote.

As usual, the bundle was bound in a mesh netting. Cartwright pulled from his pocket the blade he'd fashioned by honing the edge of a dinner knife to a sharp point, and he cut the top of the bundle, releasing its contents. There were several five gallon bags of water which they removed and set aside. They carefully sifted through the rest and found that it was, as usual, almost exclusively food, boxed in the flimsy cardboard containers that, when emptied, were mostly useless for anything other than lighting fires. There were several rolls of toilet paper this time, and a canvas bag containing a few bars of soap and some disposable razors. Unconsciously Cartwright put his hand up to his face and rubbed his jaw. He hadn't shaved in a week, not that it mattered.

They'd had no reasonable expectation there would be more. Still, it was a let down. None of them said anything, though. No point. Instead, they went about the task of organizing the supplies.

It was in the early 1980's they'd first hit pay dirt. After opening the re-supply bundle, they'd found a sports page from a Honolulu newspaper wedged between two of the water bags. Two years later, an advertising brochure from an electronics store had somehow made its way into the bundle. The real gem, however, had come in late 1999. A tattered copy of Newsweek, the decade in review, covering the 1990's. The men had devoured it, practically memorizing every word. Unfortunately, over the past dozen years, there had been nothing more.

The world, they knew, still apparently functioned, because their supplies kept coming. Beyond that, however, they had no clue what was happening.

Perhaps it was because it was Drop Day, and they'd just been shut out once again, but, as he trudged up the path carrying two of the water bags, Cartwright found himself sliding into what had become, of late, a familiar funk, wracked by the insidious questions that had recently bedeviled him. Chief among them was whether, had he known they'd still be here thirty-six years later, would he have just packed it in from the get go? Spared himself the long, quiet agony? Despite himself, he thought he might.

And, if so, why keep going now?

Of course, the fact that he and Kruchinkin had even made it back to Earth was a miracle. By all rights, they should have died a long time ago, drifting in the void of space.

But Dayton, God bless him, had set his thrusters perfectly. Instead of a course out of the way of the approaching lunar module, he'd plugged in a sequence that would draw the command vessel straight up from the moon's surface, and he did it in such perfect synch with the module that, after several thousand feet, he was able to bring the smaller ship into a flawless rendezvous.

Cartwright doubted that there were many, if any, other pilots alive who would have been able to pull off such a maneuver.

What, though, had Dayton's heroics bought them?

After a silent transit back from the moon, they'd managed to re-establish contact with Mission Control. Just before separation of the capsule from the service module in preparation for re-entry, the same man who'd been handling Capcom duties from Alamogordo had given them instructions for a supplemental burn to adjust their re-entry point, explaining that the original landing site was subject to high winds and dangerous swells. The three of them had debated whether or not to follow the instructions. Cartwright had demanded that he speak with Rick Delahousse, but was told in no uncertain terms that Delahousse could not be put on because he'd experienced a family emergency. Stu Overholdt was likewise unavailable. All of Cartwright's instincts told him he couldn't trust the instructions he was receiving. But, when all was said and done, his training and his military discipline overrode his gut feelings. It was, he feared to this day, a tragic mistake on his part.

He knew there was something amiss just after splashdown. They hadn't even had the chance to reach for the hatch when it popped on its own, obviously accessed from outside. From the narrow opening, two objects had been hurled into the capsule. The last thing he remembered before blackness overtook him was the mist of fog that suddenly filled the small enclosure.

He'd awakened to discover that his world had suddenly shrunk to a couple acres of land, perched high on a craggy piece of rock jutting up out of the ocean, nothing around but water as far as the eye could see. By taking celestial bearings, he'd been able to fix their location as somewhere in the Pacific, likely well to the northwest of Hawaii. Many years before, Cartwright had stopped for refueling at the Naval Air Station on Midway Island. At the time, he'd considered that place a lonely and forlorn outpost. Ironically, it now most likely represented the nearest civilization.

Their home, which they'd dubbed the Rock, had been, as far as they could tell, a military installation at one time, probably dating back to the second world war. Whether it was built by the Americans or the Japanese, however, was anyone's guess. Whoever had claimed the pitiful piece of land had blasted the tip off and constructed a small bunker with wide slits on each of the four sides at about eye level. They provided fine views of the absolute nothingness that surrounded them. At one time, perhaps, this particular patch of earth might have been considered strategic, but that had long ago ceased to be the case.

For years, the three men had diligently monitored the ocean in all directions, hoping to spot a passing ship they could signal, but they'd long since given up any hope that would happen. Occasionally, aircraft would fly over, but much too high to be signaled. Other than the C-130 that dropped their supplies every three months, they'd had absolutely no contact with the outside world.

Though he wasn't a man normally given to despair, there were limits to everything, and Cartwright had experienced his fair share of struggles with the demons. Before his most recent bout of questioning, the worst had come shortly after they'd found themselves deposited here, abandoned in the middle of nowhere like so much detritus. When it had become apparent that their circumstance wasn't temporary, all three of them had battled serious depression.

Ironically, it had been Kruchinkin who'd rallied them. The young man - Cartwright smiled inwardly at that - though still weak and recovering from his gunshot wound, had pointed out that, even if escape from their predicament did not seem imminent, eventually an opportunity would present itself, and they would feel foolish if they weren't prepared to seize it. Of course, that had been a long time ago. A very long time.

Still, it had helped keep them from just giving in. They'd adopted a regular exercise routine and adhered to it religiously. The food that came in the aerial drops was fairly bland, but it was reasonably nutritious. In the early days, Dayton had rigged a net, crude compared to the one they now used, but still effective enough to enable them to catch fish from the schools that teemed in the water surrounding them. To his own surprise, Cartwright had discovered a hidden talent for cooking, and he had become quite adept at devising recipes combining elements of the food provided them by their captors with the different varieties of fish they managed to catch.

As a result, the men were fit, more so, Cartwright guessed, than most men their age. More importantly, and against the odds, they had managed to avoid serious illness and injury. The lone exception had occurred three years earlier, when Dayton had come down with some kind of malady that they couldn't identify. They had plied him with the few antibiotics on hand and had experienced a fretful two weeks before the man's fever broke.

Naturally, they'd spent quite a bit of time trying to devise a scheme to escape their captivity. At the outset, they'd begun collecting the bags in which their water came with the intent of fashioning a raft. To their dismay, however, they discovered that the material was biodegradable, and it broke down after a few months, quicker if exposed to salt water. Other than those containers, they had no access to anything that would float. With the exception of a few hardy lichens that clung to the leeward side of the island, there was no vegetation on the Rock. And, though they kept their eyes out for flotsam, they'd never spotted anything of value. They didn't even have a beach on which it could wash up.

They'd tried signals to the men who flew the resupply missions. "Help us," they'd spelled out with parachute canvas on the small Parade Ground. If the aircrew had noticed, however, they'd not responded. After a while, they'd given that up.

At the top of the path, Cartwright deposited the water bags near the entrance to the bunker. He took a deep breath, turned, and started back down. Dayton, he saw, had stopped halfway up and set the bundle of food he was carrying in the mesh container on the ground beside him. He had his head cocked slightly.

"What is it?" Cartwright asked.

"Do you hear that?"

Cartwright gave him a look.

"Oh, yeah," Dayton said. Then he raised a finger and turned to the northeast.

After a few seconds, Cartwright detected a new sound. The resupply plane coming back around, perhaps?

Kruchinkin reached them and set down his load. "What is that?"

Cartwright was just beginning to shake his head when two aircraft suddenly materialized, as if from nowhere, and screamed over the Rock, accompanied by a huge clap of sound that shook the ground beneath them. It took Cartwright a second to realize that the clap was a pair of sonic booms.

"Jesus," Dayton exclaimed. "What the hell was that?"

In the instant he'd had to observe, Cartwright had seen that they were twin engine jets, with U.S. Air Force markings. But he'd never seen this type of aircraft before. From below, the fuselage and wings on each seemed to have almost a diamond shape.

"Wow," was all he could say.

Though Cartwright could no longer hear the things, apparently Dayton could, as he moved his head, obviously following them. From where Dayton was looking, Cartwright guessed they might be circling back. His heart began beating faster.

"You think they saw us?" Kruchinkin asked.

"Maybe," Dayton said.

Excitement flashed through Cartwright. "Back to the Parade Ground. Sasha, you light the signal fire. Steve, you and I work the flag."

The men scrambled down the path. At the bottom, Kruchinkin turned left and headed for the edge of the clearing, where a mound of material lay beneath a line they'd strung between two rock outcroppings. They'd draped over it a parachute canvas tarp in pup tent fashion. Cartwright prayed that the tinder was still dry after all the rain they'd had recently. He and Dayton made for the spot where they kept the flag anchored by four large rocks. They kicked the rocks aside, bent down and each grabbed two corners.

The flag was composed of several pieces of parachute cloth that they'd sewn together using needles fashioned from the tines of dinner forks. It was about four feet by eight feet, and they had used dye extracted from octopi they'd netted to spell out "SOS" in large letters on the thing.

Cartwright and Dayton took up positions in the center of the Parade Ground, holding the flag between them. Cartwright looked anxiously back to the spot where Kruchinkin had pulled aside the tarp and was hunched over the signal fire, working the two rocks they used to generate sparks. He returned his attention to Dayton, who had his head up, moving it side to side.

"Where are they?" Cartwright asked.

Dayton squinted his eyes. "I think they split up. Maybe," he hesitated, then nodded in the direction over Cartwright's shoulder, "there." They rotated quickly, aligning the flag and holding it up to face in the indicated direction. Cartwright looked back again and saw that Kruchinkin had gotten the fire to light. A small wisp of smoke began to rise from the bottom of the pile as the cardboard caught. When it was hot enough, it would light the strips of parachute cloth, and that, in turn, would begin melting the plastic webbing material, giving off a putrid, but nevertheless visible line of smoke.

Kruchinkin rose and joined them in the middle of the clearing, holding the tarp, ready to wave it.

"Here it comes," announced Dayton.

Cartwright looked in the same direction, and he could, again, hear the whine of the jet engines. This time a single aircraft came streaking over them at a much higher altitude.

They knew they couldn't be heard, but each of the men instinctively called out. Cartwright and Dayton shook the sides of the flag in large motions, hoping to draw the attention of the pilot. Next to them, Kruchinkin jumped up and down, frantically waving the parachute cloth.

A tremendous explosion shook the Rock and a huge geyser of water appeared along the north face of the island, rising a good hundred feet above them. The concussion threw each of the men to the ground, and Cartwright lay still for a moment, stunned, as sea water crashed down around him. He glanced over at Dayton, who returned his look with a shocked one of his own.

"Holy shit," Dayton managed after a second.

"They're dropping bombs," Cartwright exclaimed. He looked at Kruchinkin who had pulled himself up onto his hands and knees and had a bewildered expression on his face.

Cartwright's instincts took hold. "To the bunker," he yelled, pushing himself up and grabbing Kruchinkin's arm to help him.

The three of them began running toward the path. Before they'd reached it, Cartwright heard Dayton call out from behind. His blood went cold.

"Oh, shit," Dayton blurted, "here they come again."

17

Lieutenant Colonel Willis "Bud" Budnarsky banked his F-22 Raptor slightly as he approached the small island. Then, having seen what he needed, he leveled his wings and raised his nose. He eased forward on the throttles, and the two Pratt & Whitney F119-PW-100 jet engines rocketed him skyward as he scanned the heads up display in front of him, looking for threats. There were none.

"I concur," he announced. To himself, he asked, What the hell?

Seconds before, his wingman, Lieutenant Scott Timmons, had made what Budnarsky had thought at the moment was a pre-posterous statement: "There are people down there." It had come shortly after Timmons had pulled away from his targeting run, his bomb falling short of the tiny rock, an extraordinarily unchar-acteristic miss, both for the weapons system and Timmons. Now Budnarsky understood why.

The two pilots were on a live-fire training mission out of El-mendorf Air Force Base in Alaska. Three days before, they'd re-ceived orders to target this tiny chunk of land and essentially blow it out of the water, a simple proposition for the 1,000 pound bombs he and Timmons carried in their respective weapons bays. In fact, though each had two of the devices, a strike by just one would be enough to pulverize the little rock.

Their bombs were fitted with the Joint Direct Attack Muni-tion, a guidance kit converting "dumb bombs," into all-weather "smart" munitions capable of being guided to their targets. As a result, their assignment could easily have been carried out from high altitude. For that matter, it could have been done at any time over the prior three days, notwithstanding the terrible weather that had been pounding this part of the Pacific Ocean. Budnarsky, however, had decided to turn this into a close attack exercise and give Timmons, one of his younger pilots, an opportunity to practice precise delivery of the weapon. He'd held off until this morning, wanting to conduct the practice in clear weather and observe Timmons.

The plan had been to guide the pickle into the north face of the rock. Timmons, however, had, at the last moment, redirected the bomb away from the tiny island when he'd seen the figures below. Whoever the people down there were, they owed their survival to the keen eyesight and quick reactions of the junior officer.

But, it begged the question: Who the hell were they? And who in the world would be inhabiting a rock out here in the middle of nowhere?

They were at the outer edge, but still within, an area known informally as the Pacific Range, a desolate patch of ocean northwest of Hawaii in which the U.S. military from time to time conducted training exercises using live munitions. Though the vast majority of the Range was technically within international waters, and, therefore, foreign nationals couldn't be excluded from sailing or flying through it, there was no particular reason why anyone would want to, and most nautical charts and aviation maps clearly delineated the area as one to be avoided.

The figures he'd seen a moment before - there looked to be three of them - must have arrived by boat, though he'd seen no sign of a vessel. They were playing a dangerous game. If Timmons hadn't reacted as quickly as he had, or if Budnarsky had elected, as originally proposed, to have the bomb launched from altitude, those people would be dead now, and no one would be the wiser.

"Tangier Leader to Top Hat," Budnarsky called, "we are on station at the primary target."

"Roger Tangier Leader," came the reply from the combat air control center. "Has the target been destroyed?"

"That's a negative," Budnarsky replied. "There are unknown persons occupying the target."

"Stand by."

There was a minute of silence from the other end, and Budnarsky assumed his report was being routed up the chain of command. Finally, the controller came back on.

"Orders are to destroy the target."

That surprised Budnarsky. Something had to have been lost in the translation.

"I repeat," Budnarsky said, "there are people down there."

"That is understood. The orders are to destroy the target. No exceptions. Colonel, these orders are flagged Juliet Charlie. And that's 'Actual.'"

Jesus, thought Budnarsky. These orders came directly from the Joint Chiefs of Staff? He'd never heard of such a thing.

Off to his right, Timmons eased his Raptor into formation. They were at 10,000 feet, flying a wide circuit around the tiny islet. Budnarsky checked his radar display. No contacts. Old instincts being what they were, however, he glanced around. They were alone in this remote patch of the sky. He took slow, deep breaths.

Budnarsky had never disobeyed an order. Never considered disobeying an order.

"What are we going to do, skipper?" Timmons asked.

Budnarsky didn't answer right away. He absently tapped a gloved finger on the side-stick controller. His eyes flicked across the cockpit display, noting their fuel status. All systems were functioning properly.

He was, he knew, stalling. Finally, he made a decision.

"I'll tell you what we're not going to do," he said firmly. "We're not going to drop our bombs on that rock. My gut tells me there's something wrong with that order."

A new voice sounded in his earphones.

"Your instincts have always been good, Bud."

Startled, Budnarsky demanded, "Who's this on my frequency?"

The voice came back immediately. "This is General Bryce McConnell, and I'll bet that bucket of bolts you're sitting in right now is called the King of Clubs. And, for the record, I'm still not buying that inside draw."

The words came as a surprise. And, despite the tense circumstances, Budnarsky had to laugh out loud. After a moment, he said, "Still can't get over that, huh, General?"

"Nope," came McConnell's reply, "never will."

As a young second lieutenant, fresh out of advanced fighter school, Budnarsky had been roped into a game of five card draw late one night with several of the senior officers in his squadron. Playing conservatively, mainly because he couldn't afford to lose the kind of money being thrown around by the other pilots, he'd managed to pretty much break even throughout the evening. Then, on the last hand, something extraordinary happened.

He was dealt the ten, jack, queen and ace of clubs, along with the three of hearts. The initial round of bets hadn't been too bad, and Budnarsky had decided, what the hell, he'd stay in and see if he could catch lighting in a bottle. Putting the three face down on the table, he'd called for a single card, which drew hoots from the other players. He was hoping, of course, to fill the straight or complete the flush, but he was ready to settle for a decent pair.

What he got was the king of clubs, giving him a royal flush. An unbeatable hand.

One of the other players, his squadron commander, then-Lieutenant Colonel Bryce McConnell, had the misfortune of being dealt three sevens and then drawing the fourth. It gave the colonel a hand that wasn't as good as Budnarsky's, but one that had to have seemed unbeatable to the senior officer.

McConnell and Budnarsky raised each other so many times Budnarsky lost count. At first convinced the junior pilot was trying to bluff him, it took the squadron commander far too long to finally realize his opponent had to have a pretty damn good hand. By the time he called, the pot had swelled to an amount in excess of two months' pay for the young lieutenant. When McConnell learned that Budnarsky had won by filling the royal flush with an inside draw, he was beside himself.

Ever since, Budnarsky had christened each of the planes he'd been assigned to fly the "King of Clubs." That included the stealth fighter he was flying today. And, whenever he'd encountered his former squadron commander, now the highest ranking officer in the Air Force, Budnarsky had taken good-natured grief. Happily.

"If it's any consolation, General," said Budnarsky, "my wife still wears the ring I bought with your money."

McConnell laughed. "In that case, I feel better."

"General," Budnarsky said after a moment, "what do you know about this order?"

"I just learned about it myself," McConnell said, "monitoring your transmissions. I think I know how it was generated, though. We've recently dealt with an issue I can't go into here. This was obviously something that got out before we corrected the situation. You were right to question the order. And I'm hereby countermanding it."

As Budnarsky took a relieved breath, he noticed that, on his cockpit readout, a blip had appeared to the east. It was unidentified, but coded friendly. "Sir, don't tell me that's you in the slow moving aircraft at the far east edge of my radar."

"Well," McConnell replied, "I'm not sure I like the 'slow moving' part, but, yep, that's me."

"What are you flying today, General?"

"I'm not in the driver's seat, Bud. I'm catching a ride out of Pearl in a Sea Stallion."

Budnarsky whistled softly to himself. The unidentified blip to his east was a Sikorsky CH-53 helicopter. It had a range of about 540 nautical miles. "Sir, you're a long way from nowhere out here. What's your fuel situation?"

"We just topped off."

Budnarsky whistled again. They'd done at least one mid-air refueling. Of course that would be the only way for a land-based helicopter to be this far out. But this wasn't just any helicopter. It happened to contain the Vice Chairman of the Joint Chiefs of Staff. Something extraordinary was going on.

"If I may ask, sir," Budnarsky said, "where are you headed?"

"We are inbound your position," McConnell replied. "ETA fifteen minutes."

"Why in the world would you be coming out here?"

McConnell's answer was surprising.

"We're coming to collect the men on that rock."

#

"Can you see them?" Cartwright asked.

He and Kruchinkin were hunched down just inside the entry to the bunker. Dayton stood outside, head up, eyes and ears alert. Cartwright felt a little foolish hiding in the enclosure, but there was no way he'd be able to hear either aircraft before it was on them. They'd decided Dayton would perform the reconnaissance just outside, ready to dive in if the planes returned.

"No," Dayton said, "but I can still hear them. Near as I can tell, they're circling."

Kruchinkin looked at Cartwright. "Maybe this is a good thing, yes?"

Cartwright was overwhelmed with an irrational fear that he'd get his hopes up only to have them dashed horribly. Still, he couldn't completely tamp down the excitement. He shrugged. "Maybe."

Kruchinkin's eyes shone. "Yes, I am certain it is."

Dayton spun around suddenly. There was a new tension in his body language.

"What is it?" Cartwright asked.

"I think," Dayton said slowly, "it might be..." He was silent for a long moment. Suddenly he turned and looked intently at Cartwright and Kruchinkin.

"A helicopter."

Cartwright's heart missed at least two beats, but it didn't matter, as adrenaline surged through him. "I'm coming out."

He stepped out of the bunker, Kruchinkin behind him. He looked around, but saw nothing but the sea and sky. He strained to hear something, anything. But the only thing registering was the muffled beat of his own heart as it pounded blood to his head.

Dayton had taken a few steps down the path leading to the Parade Ground. He was looking east, in the same direction from which the re-supply plane had come. Cartwright focused his attention in that direction. And then he heard it. Faint. Distant. But unmistakable.

"I'll be damned."

Dayton looked back at him with a questioning expression.

Cartwright shrugged. "We're either rescued or we're dead. Either way," he waved a hand in the direction of the Parade Ground, "we might as well."

Quickly, the three hurried down the path. At the bottom, they stopped and stood, side by side, squinting to the east, Cartwright's heart doing a fair impression of a jack hammer.

"There," Kruchinkin exclaimed, pointing.

Low on the distant horizon was a small black spot. Cartwright could now clearly hear the rhythmic slapping sound of helicopter rotors. The spot grew, not as quickly as the re-supply plane had, but still steadily until Cartwright could make out a blunt nose with a long horizontal line above it, extending far out to either side. He dared not move or blink for fear of it suddenly vanishing.

As the aircraft approached the island, the sound became overwhelming. And then the massive thing loomed above them, the downward draft of its rotors washing off the bare surface of the Parade Ground and over and around the three men. From beneath the fuselage, small landing gear appeared, and the pilot slowly eased the large ungainly-looking craft down, settling onto the ground with a slight bounce, her nose pointed at the men huddled together a few feet away. There was an abrupt change in noise as the roar of the engines faded away, leaving a residual high pitched sound that, in turn, began to fade slowly.

On the right hand side of the fuselage, just behind the cockpit, the lower half of a door swung downward, forming a set of steps. A trim man in a blue windbreaker stepped out and began walking toward them. Something about the man seemed familiar to Cartwright. And then it hit him.

Oh my god, he thought. Damned if the son of a gun hadn't gone and gotten old. Cartwright took a couple of awkward steps in the man's direction. A huge smile split the man's face and he opened his arms. Cartwright reached out and, when he was near, pulled Rick Delahousse to him, wrapping his arms around the man. Emotion overwhelmed Cartwright, his knees buckled slightly, and he had to hold on to his old friend to avoid falling. He wanted to speak, but his throat was suddenly constricted, and he realized with some embarrassment that there were tears running down his face.

Delahousse planted his feet and clung to Cartwright. They stayed that way for a long time.

Finally, still leaning against Delahousse, Cartwright reached up with his left hand and wiped his eyes. Then he relaxed his grip, took a deep breath and stepped back. Delahousse, he saw, had tears on his own face.

"Rick," he managed to croak, "what..." He didn't even know how to ask.

Delahousse shook his head. He seemed at a loss for words himself.

Cartwright suddenly remembered his companions. He glanced back. Dayton had come up behind him. Delahousse took a step toward the man, and they embraced. When they let go, Dayton looked as unsteady as Cartwright felt, and he, too, seemed unsure what to say.

Kruchinkin, who had held back, now stepped forward. "I do not know who you are," said the Russian, his voice trembling, "but I love you." And he grabbed Delahousse and enfolded him in a huge bear hug. It caught the Texan by surprise. After a couple of seconds, his startled look gave way to a laugh. It seemed to break the spell, and suddenly all four men were laughing.

Stepping back from Kruchinkin, Delahousse used both hands to brush the tears from his face, then he gave Cartwright a direct look. "Sorry it took us so long, Bob. Honestly, we thought you were dead all these years. We only just figured it out.

"We wouldn't have," he added, "if not for your sons."

The weakness returned to Cartwright's legs. "My sons," he said faintly.

Behind Delahousse, another man had emerged from the helicopter. Cartwright looked at him and experienced a moment of lightheaded disorientation. It was as if, for the first time in thirty-six years, he was looking in a mirror, his own dark countenance peering intently back at him at eye level, a look of concern mingled with excitement.

Cartwright's breath came rattling out of him along with a single word. "Nate."

"Dad," his son said quietly. And then they were in each others' arms, and again Cartwright's throat wouldn't allow him to say anything for a long moment. Still clinging to Nate, he was finally able to get out, "Peter and Matt?"

"We're here, Dad."

Cartwright glanced up and saw Peter, brows furrowed. From behind him, Matt emerged. He had a smile on his face. My god, Cartwright thought, his boys had become men.

He reached out his left arm, and the twins stepped into the embrace. For how long Cartwright couldn't say - but a wonderfully long time - the four of them remained there, no one saying anything. Finally Cartwright straightened and looked at each of his sons in turn. "How did you..." He was again at a loss for words.

"It was Peter," Nate said quickly. "He started looking into Apollo 18. If he hadn't..."

"It was Matt," Peter interrupted. "He did the hard stuff."

"No," Matt said firmly. "The fact is, we wouldn't be here, we wouldn't be together, if not for Nate."

Peter nodded.

Cartwright looked at Nate, who shrugged. "It was kind of a joint effort. We'll tell you all about it. But first, we're going to take you home."

Cartwright smiled. "Back to the world?"

Nate nodded. "Back to the world," he agreed.

Cartwright turned excitedly to Dayton and was about to say something when he saw the anguish on his friend's face. "Steve?"

Dayton gave him a bleak look, tears brimming. "Jean," he said simply.

Delahousse, who had an arm draped protectively over Dayton's shoulder, glanced at Cartwright and said softly, "She passed away a few years ago. Cancer."

Cartwright felt an intense weight press on his chest. "Oh, god, Steve. I'm so sorry."

From behind him, Cartwright heard Nate say, "Major Dayton?"

Cartwright looked back and saw a striking young woman with vivid red hair standing next to his oldest son. Nate had one of her hands in his and was looking intently at Dayton.

"Sir, I have someone I'd like you to meet." Nate let go and gently put his hand on the woman's back, urging her forward. She took a couple of tentative steps. Her eyes, Cartwright noticed, were a startling green. And, he realized, she looked like someone he knew. Or used to know, he amended ruefully.

Then he realized who it had to be.

"Maggie?" Dayton exclaimed. The young woman nodded solemnly. Dayton stepped toward her on wobbly legs. She immediately rushed forward and threw her arms around him.

Cartwright looked at Nate, and, after a moment, his son returned the look. Cartwright tipped his head. Nate returned the gesture.

"Commander Cartwright?" another voice said. Cartwright turned to see a man dressed in camouflaged fatigues with matching cap. Above the left breast was the notation "U.S. Air Force," and over the right, the name "McConnell." Four stars were arrayed along both collars and across the front of the cap.

"I'm General Bryce McConnell, and it's an honor to meet you, sir." He reached out a hand, and Cartwright took it. "I can't begin to tell you how sorry I am for what you've had to go through. You're owed a full explanation, and I'll make sure you get it. For the moment, I'll tell you that you were the victim of some very unscrupulous people who took advantage of the system. We owe a debt to your sons for bringing it to our attention."

Cartwright again glanced at his boys.

"And," the general continued, "we owe a debt to you. One that we'll never be able to fully repay. For what it's worth, however, I can tell you I've spoken with both the Navy and Air Force personnel offices. Since neither you nor Major Dayton were ever mustered out, you each have a little over thirty-six years' worth of back pay accumulated. Supplemented by hazardous duty pay. Not to mentioned your unused housing and food allowance."

He gave Cartwright a grim smile. "It can't make up for everything, but I'm happy to say that each of you has a few million dollars coming."

Cartwright was stunned. But then he thought of something. He turned and looked back at Kruchinkin. "Sasha."

"Ah, yes," McConnell said, quickly, "Doctor Kruchinkin."

The Russian smiled self-consciously. "Thank you. But I am not a doctor."

"That's not completely true, sir," McConnell said. "Before you left on your mission, you had completed all your class work and submitted your thesis. You never had a chance to defend it, but there were some extenuating circumstances."

Kruchinkin shrugged. "A few things did happen."

"Indeed," McConnell continued. "Over the past few days there have been some awkward and delicate discussions taking place between our respective governments. Not all the details have yet been worked out, but I can tell you that your degree has been awarded by the Lomonosov Moscow State University retroactive to 1976. And an appropriate stipend has been set aside to compensate you for the services you've rendered in assisting our two officers."

Kruchinkin looked between McConnell and Cartwright. Then, he smiled his toothy grin. "Yes," he said, "this is good."

"One other thing, Doctor," McConnell said. "Earlier this morning, I was on the phone with our embassy in Moscow. Our military attaché had just met with your parents. They are retired and live in an apartment in Reútov. They're looking forward to seeing you."

Kruchinkin appeared as though he might faint. Cartwright stepped over quickly and put an arm around him. Dayton, he saw, had placed two hands gently on the sides of the young woman's face, and he kissed her lightly on the forehead. Then he turned and walked over to them, putting his arms out, and the three old friends embraced.

#

The mid-morning sun glistened off the tops of the waves in Frenchman Bay, and the sound of gulls drifted across the small peninsula. In the distance, a sailboat turned, her pilot tacking in the soft breeze, and, as Nate idly watched, her sail filled with air, and she began a leisurely east to west transit. Nate reached up, closed the lid on his laptop and set it on the small table next to him. The day was just too glorious to spend working.

Laughter from the far end of the long veranda interrupted his reverie, and he glanced over. His dad, a smile on his face, was in the process of gathering playing cards scattered on the portable table around which the three men sat, and he began shuffling them while his two companions kept up an animated conversation that Nate couldn't quite hear.

His father had filled out nicely over the past eight months. Gone was the sallow, gaunt look he'd had when they'd found him on that pathetic rock in the middle of the Pacific Ocean. The doctors had pronounced him to be in marvelous shape, and he looked particularly tanned and rested this morning.

Dayton and Kruchinkin had likewise recovered well from their ordeal. The staff at Tripler Army Medical Center had been frankly amazed at the health of the three men. For a couple of weeks after their rescue, they'd been housed in a series of bungalows at the facility, located on the slopes of the Moanalua Ridge overlooking Honolulu, while undergoing a battery of physical and psychological tests. The first couple of nights, the men had insisted on sleeping in the same room, which the psychiatrists said was a perfectly normal reaction. Eventually, they'd become comfortable in their own rooms, but, during the day, they'd spent much of their time together.

The men had possessed a seemingly unlimited thirst for information. They'd scrutinized every magazine, book and newspaper they could put their hands on. Everything was new and wonderful. Then Peter introduced them to the internet, and that was it. Each man had spent hours a day surfing the web. Nate had taken his dad to see a movie at the nearby cineplex, and the man had been awestruck, insisting he return the next day with Dayton and Kruchinkin.

After two weeks, the doctors had cleared the men for travel, and Kruchinkin had flown home to Moscow for a reunion with his parents. Sadly, his mother passed away three months later, but he reported that she had been overjoyed in her last weeks having her son with her. Kruchinkin's father had eventually returned with him and was now living in the large condominium Kruchinkin had purchased in downtown Atlanta. The Russian had made the trip north for the gathering in Bar Harbor, but he would be returning soon to resume caring for his father, and, in a few weeks, he would begin his first semester teaching at Georgia Tech University.

Dayton had been delighted when his two former colleagues had arrived a week earlier. Theirs was a bond Nate could only imagine, and the three men had spent days reminiscing and - because they now could - laughing about things only they could possibly understand.

The rear door to the house opened and Maggie stepped out. She glanced over at the three men huddled around the card table, smiled and turned to Nate.

"Your brother's here," she said. "He's out front talking to Tim."

Nate was surprised. Peter and Matt weren't due to arrive for another day.

"Which one?"

Maggie suddenly looked sheepish. Despite himself, Nate laughed.

"Don't worry. You'll eventually get it," he said.

She gave him a rueful look. "I don't know about that."

Nate reached a hand out. "Just give it time."

She stepped toward him, took his hand, and allowed him to pull her close. Then she leaned down and softly placed her head against his. "I'll give it all the time in the world."

Nate brought his other hand over and lay it against her cheek. They stayed that way for a long moment.

Finally, Nate took a deep breath and said, "I better go see what's up."

In the parlor, he found Matt crouched by the front door, an animated Buster licking his face.

"Didn't expect you until tomorrow," Nate said. "And I thought you and Peter were traveling together."

Matt stood, held his arms out, and the two brothers embraced.

"Peter's taking a flight in the morning from New York," Matt said. "He had to meet with his editor."

That was no surprise. Peter's book detailing the true story behind Apollo 18 was due to be released shortly, and it had generated a lot of pre-publication buzz. Nate had read an advance copy and had been thoroughly impressed. In addition to things they'd learned from their father, Peter had somehow managed to uncover an extraordinary amount of previously undisclosed information, including the answer to something that had vexed Nate for months: Where did that capsule with the burned bodies come from? According to Peter, on the day of their father's re-entry, shortly after the real Apollo 18 had initiated a supplemental burn altering its entry point, the command module intended for use on the cancelled Apollo 19 mission, staged with three cadavers spirited away from the Houston morgue, had been dropped from a B-52 flying at high altitude a few miles north of the awaiting navy task force.

Nate wasn't sure where Peter was getting his information, but he had a suspicion. Peter had moved from San Francisco to Northern Virginia, and he and Matt - once again, two peas in a pod - had taken up residence at the site of the old farmhouse out-side Leesburg. They'd apparently knocked the thing down and constructed a new, larger structure. Nate didn't know whether that included the secret apartment accessed through the base-ment. He also wasn't sure he wanted to know.

"So what brings you up early?" Nate asked.

Matt affected a bewildered look. "What? I need an excuse to see my big brother? And spend time with him before he straps on the old ball and chain?"

Nate put on his own show of surprise. "Are you saying you have a problem with my marrying Maggie?"

Matt looked suddenly serious. "No, not at all. As a matter of fact, if you'd waited any longer, you and I were going to have a serious discussion." He grinned. "I'm really happy for you."

His face, again however, became sober. "But you and I need to talk."

"That sounds ominous."

Matt nodded toward the front door. "Let's take a walk."

With Buster pulling on his leash, the two brothers casually sauntered down the narrow lane connecting the Dayton home to the highway. Neither spoke for a couple of minutes.

Finally, Matt said, "I had a meeting the other day with Tony Strickland."

Nate glanced over. Recalling his conversation months ago with the Attorney General, he said, "Last I heard, he didn't even know you were alive."

Matt shrugged. "I guess he was briefed. He knew all about me." Then he added, "So did his boss."

Surprised, Nate asked, "Was he at the meeting?"

Matt nodded.

Nate contemplated his own feet as they strolled along the weathered blacktop. After a moment, he asked, "So, what was the purpose of this meeting?"

With a grim smile, Matt said, "Apparently, the unexpected departure of Krantz left The Organization in a bit of turmoil. At first, it didn't matter, because they were planning to shut it down. Until they started looking into it. That's when they realized they had something a little too valuable to just get rid of."

Matt gave him a frank look. "It really is a powerful weapon. Provided," he amended, "it's used right."

"And where do you fit in?"

"They need someone to come in and clean it up," Matt said.

Nate stopped. After a couple more steps, Matt did likewise and turned to face him.

"Don't tell me," Nate said. "You're not thinking about going back to work for those guys, are you?"

"No," Matt said immediately. "They're going to work for me. I'm going to report directly to the President."

"But," Nate said, trying to process the information, "after all you went through?"

Matt looked out at the bay for a long moment, then returned his attention to Nate. "Yes. Especially after all that." He gave Nate a level gaze. "I owe this to a lot of people, including myself. You're the one who said it. Every journey begins with a first step. This is mine."

Nate rubbed a hand over his chin. Buster, who had apparently tired of exploring the scrub next to the roadway, pawed at Nate's leg. Nate reached down and picked up the little dog, who gave him an affectionate lick on his neck and settled comfortably in the crook of his arm. Nate glanced back at the house, then returned his attention to Matt.

"You're sure about this?"

Matt nodded.

Nate could see the resolve on Matt's face. And the purpose to his look. Finally, Nate took a deep breath. "Ok."

Matt gave him a grin. "Ok," he repeated.

311

Then the two brothers laughed. After a long moment, they turned and, shoulder to shoulder under the brilliant blue of the summer day, slowly made their way back to the house.

A Note from the Author

Ok, bear with me. Instead of making things up, I'm going to be honest for a moment.

For years, I dreamed of writing a novel, one that I would feel comfortable putting "out there." But I didn't. Instead, I hemmed. I hawed. And I let an embarrassingly long amount of time go by. Then, one day, I asked myself, What am I waiting for?

It was a damn good question.

And, as is the case with a lot of damn good questions, it answered itself.

So, I finally did it. And, it feels good.

However, I'd be less than honest if I suggested that this book could possibly have happened without help. A lot of help.

Where do I start?

Well, first of all, with my wife, Martha. I've dedicated this book to her. But that's completely inadequate, and I know it. Truth be told, I wrote this story for her. As with just about everything I do in my life, I wanted to impress her. Once I finished each chapter and massaged it until I thought it was just right, I printed it and gave it to her for the initial read. Then I waited anxiously for her judgment. And, God bless her, she loved each one. (For that, and for so much more, I love her.)

But I knew I needed more objective feedback. So, I turned to my beta readers: Damon Jespersen, Cathryn Cormier, Geri Hunter, Lisa Siegel, Hal Light, Brad Neel and Paul Lusby. Each read a fairly raw version of the manuscript, and, through feedback, contributed greatly to the final version of the story. To all of them, I extend my profound thanks.

I would be remiss not to acknowledge the assistance of two industry professionals for their advice and editorial assistance: Kathryn Johnson and Hillel Black. Their guidance was invaluable, and this novel is so much more than it would have been without their help.

Finally, my thanks to Ben Lizardi, who designed a fabulous book cover and who, more importantly, has been a terrific friend for many years.

It's humbling looking back and realizing just how important others have been in one's "personal" endeavors. But it's also uplifting.

Of course, all of the foregoing being said, the final product is mine. And all criticisms of this book, good and - yikes - bad, fall on me. That's as it should be. I hope you enjoy it. If you do, tell others. If you don't, purge it from your memory.

After all, life is about the good stuff.

CPSIA information can be obtained at www.ICGtesting.com
Printed in the USA
LVOW06s1730280813

350044LV00004B/677/P